ALSO BY ANNE BISHOP

THE BLACK JEWELS SERIES

Daughter of the Blood
Heir to the Shadows
Queen of the Darkness
The Invisible Ring
Dreams Made Flesh

THE TIR ALAINN TRILOGY

The Pillars of the World
Shadows and Light
The House of Gaian

THE EPHEMERA SERIES

Sebastian
Belladonna

Praise for
Sebastian

"Bishop's talents lie both in her ability to craft a story filled with intriguing characters and in her flair for smoldering sensuality that recommends her to fans of Tanith Lee, Storm Constantine, and Anne Rice. Highly recommended."   —*Library Journal* (starred review)

"[Anne Bishop's] worlds are so fully realized and three-dimensional, they jump right off the pages. . . . Exotic, original, sensual, there's nothing here I didn't love. I can't recommend this author and her newest novel highly enough."   —Fresh Fiction

"[A] page-turner . . . [an] impressively unclichéd battle between light and dark . . . pure originality and lyrical prose . . . will delight fantasy readers."
                         —*Publishers Weekly* (starred review)

"I enjoyed every page of the book from beginning to end and absolutely love the characters that inhabit it."
                                   —Romance Reviews Today

"Highly recommended. . . . Glorianna is a fantastic presence, a nascent goddess."   —SFRevu

"A wonderful book to get lost in." —Romance Junkies

"A fantastic book. Bishop has built a compelling world that is filled with fascinating and complex characters."
                            —*Romantic Times* (top pick, 4½ stars)

continued . . .

ANNE BISHOP

Sebastian

A ROC BOOK

ROC
Published by New American Library, a division of
Penguin Group (USA) Inc., 375 Hudson Street,
New York, New York 10014, USA
Penguin Group (Canada), 90 Eglinton Avenue East, Suite 700, Toronto,
Ontario M4P 2Y3, Canada (a division of Pearson Penguin Canada Inc.)
Penguin Books Ltd., 80 Strand, London WC2R 0RL, England
Penguin Ireland, 25 St. Stephen's Green, Dublin 2,
Ireland (a division of Penguin Books Ltd.)
Penguin Group (Australia), 250 Camberwell Road, Camberwell, Victoria 3124,
Australia (a division of Pearson Australia Group Pty. Ltd.)
Penguin Books India Pvt. Ltd., 11 Community Centre, Panchsheel Park,
New Delhi – 110 017, India
Penguin Group (NZ), 67 Apollo Drive, Rosedale, North Shore 0632,
New Zealand (a division of Pearson New Zealand Ltd.)
Penguin Books (South Africa) (Pty.) Ltd., 24 Sturdee Avenue,
Rosebank, Johannesburg 2196, South Africa

Penguin Books Ltd., Registered Offices:
80 Strand, London WC2R 0RL, England

Published by Roc, an imprint of New American Library, a division of Penguin
Group (USA) Inc. Previously published in a Roc hardcover edition.

First Roc Mass Market Printing, March 2007
10 9 8 7

Copyright © Anne Bishop, 2006
Excerpt from *Belladonna* copyright © Anne Bishop, 2007
All rights reserved

ROC REGISTERED TRADEMARK—MARCA REGISTRADA

Printed in the United States of America

*For
Pat York
who crossed over to other landscapes.*

I'm glad you were part of my life.

ACKNOWLEDGMENTS

My thanks to Blair Boone for continuing to be my first reader, to Debra Dixon for being second reader, to Kandra and Doranna for maintaining the Web site, and to Pat and Bill Feidner for all the things that make them special.

Long ago, in a time that has faded from memory,
a mother's tears forged the bridge that, ever after,
connected the power of the living, ever-changing
world to the human heart.
—Myth

Chapter One

Present

Standing at the kitchen counter, Sebastian closed his eyes and inhaled slowly and deeply to savor the smell of freshly ground koffea beans. Better than a woman. At least, a more sensual experience than the last two he'd been with.

When an incubus found sex boring, it was time to take a break—or think about another line of work.

Pushing that thought into the mental trunk where he'd shoved so many unpleasant memories, he followed the rest of the instructions for brewing the koffea beans.

What would it be like to rise in the first wisps of dawn and come out to the kitchen to grind the beans while someone who truly mattered was snuggled in his bed, waiting to be awakened with a nuzzle and a kiss—and a cup of freshly brewed koffee? What would it be like to stand outside, cup in hand, and watch the day come alive?

Sebastian shook his head. Why was he rubbing salt into emotional wounds, thinking about things that couldn't be? He lived in the Den of Iniquity, which consisted of a few blocks of crowded buildings and cobblestone streets—a place that, most likely, had been an unsavory part of some large city, nothing but a dark smudge in a daylight landscape. Then a Landscaper had altered the world, turning those streets into a separate landscape, and that had changed the feel of living on those streets, had changed the taverns, gambling houses, and brothels into a carnal carnival.

But it was more than a place where human vices were openly enjoyed, more than a place where humans who didn't fit into the daylight landscapes and demons like the incubi and succubi could live. The Den was at the center of a cluster of dark landscapes some of Ephemera's demon races claimed as their own. It was a place where those demons could purchase supplies or buy a drink in a tavern without being hated or driven away because they weren't human.

It was also a place that had its roots in the darker side of the human heart, a place where the sun never rose.

He'd been a bitter fifteen-year-old boy when he'd stumbled into the Den. Having escaped his father's control two years before, he'd disappeared into the landscapes and struggled to survive. The dark human landscapes were too desperate and frightening even for a boy whose demon nature eclipsed whatever human blood might flow through his veins, but the people in the daylight landscapes didn't want something like him living among them, and he'd been driven out of village after village as soon as the people realized he was an incubus—and that hunger for the emotions that were produced by sex was something that couldn't be hidden or denied for long.

So when he found the Den and felt the dark, edgy, carnival tone of the place, he'd embraced it with all his heart because he'd finally found a place where being an incubus didn't make him an outcast, a place where the never-ending night suited who and what he was—a place where he could belong.

And he still belonged here. The Den was his home. But now, as a man who had recently turned thirty . . .

I'm so tired of the night.

A sudden yearning for *something* washed through him, making his heart ache, filling him with a need and a longing so powerful it staggered him. He braced his hands on the counter and waited for the feeling to pass. It always did.

But the yearning had never been this powerful before, had never swept through him like this. Didn't matter. Those feelings came and went—and nothing changed.

Disgusted with himself for not being content with what he had, he plucked a mug off the wooden stand—and almost dropped it when someone knocked on the cottage's front door. He never brought anyone to his home, never invited anyone to visit. The only two people who ignored that demand for privacy were his human cousins, Glorianna and Lee, and neither of them would sound so hesitant about applying knuckles to wood.

He'd just ignore it; that's what he'd do. He'd ignore it, and whoever—whatever—was on the other side of the door would go away.

The door creaked open. Sebastian's heart pumped against his chest as he set the mug on the counter, careful to make no sound. Just as silently, he eased the biggest knife he had out of the wood block. Maybe he wouldn't win, but he'd go down fighting.

"Sebastian?" a voice called. "Sebastian? You here?"

He knew that voice, but he still hesitated. Then he swore silently and slipped the knife back into its slot. There were very few things in the Den that couldn't be bought, but trust was one of them.

Moving to the doorway that separated the kitchen from the main living area, he peered into the room and studied his visitor.

The other incubus stood on the threshold, almost bouncing with nerves. Yet his eyes were bright with curiosity as he looked at the simple furniture and the framed sketches on the walls.

"What do you want, Teaser?" Sebastian asked.

If Teaser noticed the harsh note in Sebastian's voice, he ignored it and bounded into the main room. Then he stopped, spun around, and closed the outer door before moving toward Sebastian with the cocky swagger that was at odds with his boyish good looks.

Women were often deceived into believing he acted the way he looked. With Teaser, sometimes that was a serious mistake.

As youths, they had trolled the Den's streets together—blond-haired, blue-eyed Teaser projecting an image of a boy out for a bit of naughty fun, while Sebastian was the handsome piece of danger with his sable hair and sharp green eyes. They'd played their games of seduction, providing physical sex to women who crossed over to the Den from the daylight landscapes or using the power of the incubi to connect with another mind through the twilight of waking dreams, feeding on the emotions they created by being fantasy lovers. Unhappy wives. Foolish girls who wanted the romance of a mysterious admirer. Lonely women who craved the warmth of a lover, even if that lover came to them only in dreams. They were all prey to the incubi.

For five years, he and Teaser had rented adjoining rooms at an expensive bordello and trolled the Den. Then, when he turned twenty, Sebastian could no longer ignore a growing need for something beyond the Den and the sexual games, so he walked away from the colored lights and the dark buildings. He found a dirt lane that began a few steps away from where the Den's main street ended—a lane he was certain hadn't been there before. He followed it, not sure if he was just taking a walk or really leaving the one place he'd felt at home.

That was how he found the two-story cottage. It didn't look like it belonged in a landscape like the Den, but it wouldn't have been there if it hadn't belonged. That was the way things worked in Ephemera.

He went inside, wary of being caught by whoever laid claim to the place. But it wasn't inhabited. Half the rooms were empty, but there was enough furniture left haphazardly in the other rooms to set up a comfortable bedroom, living area, and kitchen. He found linens and towels, as well as everything he needed in the kitchen to prepare and eat a simple meal. He prowled the rooms for an hour—and realized something inside him had relaxed, as if he'd taken his first full breath in months.

Finding cleaning supplies in a cupboard in the kitchen, he dusted, polished, swept, and scrubbed until the cottage was clean and the furniture arranged to his liking. Then he went back to the Den, removed most of his possessions from the room he rented in the bordello, and moved into the cottage. A week later, when he returned from trolling the Den's streets, he discovered someone had planted a moonflower beside the cottage's back door.

That was when he realized this place had been waiting for him to find it, to want it. *She* would have known the moment something in him had changed enough to match the cottage, and the moonflower was her way of saying, "Welcome."

In Ephemera, there were few secrets of the heart. And nothing could be hidden from Glorianna Belladonna.

He had lived in the cottage for the past ten years, still a part of the Den and yet apart from it.

"Didn't see you around yesterday," Teaser said, pulling Sebastian back to the present. "Just thought I'd stop by and . . . see."

He'd spent yesterday sketching—and had burned all the sketches when he realized he'd been trying to capture daylight memories of Aurora, his aunt Nadia's home village. Things he'd seen as a child during the times he lived with her. Then his father, Koltak, would show up again and take him away, dumping him on some woman in the poor section of the city where Koltak lived—a woman who was paid to tolerate his presence and provide him with food and a place to sleep. Half the time he lived on the streets, running wild with other abandoned children and remembering all over again how barren and miserable his life was supposed to be. Then Nadia would arrive and take him back to her home.

Nadia's and Koltak's battle of wills, and the cycle of loving acceptance and coldhearted misery, finally ended when he'd gotten away from his father the last time Koltak arrived at Nadia's house to take him back to the hated city.

"I was occupied," Sebastian said, pushing aside the memories.

Teaser grinned wickedly. "Still offering comfort to aging spinsters and lonely widows? You need to look for something a bit more lively. Someone with a bit more kick. Can't imagine any of them are much fun when you cross over to give them a ride in the flesh instead of just romantic dreams." Then he sniffed the air. His eyes widened. "Is that koffee?"

Sebastian sighed. He'd ground enough beans for two cups. Looked like he was going to share. "Come on, then."

When he walked back to the counter, Teaser was right behind him.

After eyeing the bag of koffea beans, the grinder, and the perk-pot, Teaser whistled. "Got the whole setup. Maybe giving spinsters and widows sweet dreams and hot nights is more lucrative than I thought." He paused. "But you don't usually buy from the black market."

Sebastian took another mug from the wooden stand and filled it with koffee. "I didn't get this from the black market. This was a gift from my cousins." As he turned to hand the mug to Teaser, he caught the flash of fear in the other incubus's eyes, noted the slight tremble in the hands that accepted the mug.

The prissy prig humans in other landscapes called the incubi and succubi vile demons, although enough of those humans craved the kind of sex that could be had only with an incubus or succubus partner to provide the Den's residents with a good living. But there were more dangerous demons that roamed their world, and the incubi and succubi could end up being prey as easily as any human. It had taken him a few years to realize the reason other demons who came to the Den were wary of him wasn't because *he* was a badass demon; it was because of his human connection. They didn't fear Lee, who was a Bridge with a rare ability to impose one landscape over another, but Glorianna ...

No demon wanted to incur her wrath—because Glorianna Belladonna was the Landscaper who had created the Den of Iniquity.

Filling his own mug, Sebastian leaned against the counter, sipped his koffee, and said nothing.

After a few minutes, Teaser said, "This place. It's ... nice." He looked at the small table tucked against the wall, where Sebastian ate his meals, then at the larger table in the dining area. "It looks ... nice."

It looks human, Sebastian thought, feeling as if he'd been caught doing something lewd. In public. In a human landscape, since doing something lewd in the Den was commonplace. Embarrassed that anyone had seen evidence of his need to stay connected with whatever humanity he might claim, he felt the old bitterness well up inside him.

Nadia wasn't blood kin. She'd been married to his father's brother and had no reason to fight with Koltak over the well-being of a half-demon boy. But she had fought—and had won often enough that there were islands of time throughout his childhood when he'd known what it was like to be loved and accepted. Everything good that he had experienced in the human landscapes had come to him because of her.

That was why the cottage had tugged at him. That was why it looked like a human home instead of an incubus's lair. He had the room at the bordello for seduction. This place reminded him of how he had felt when he lived with Nadia and Glorianna and Lee. When he'd still had some connection with the Light.

But if the other incubi and succubi found out he lived like a human, the malicious teasing would never end—and he'd end up being an outcast again.

He swallowed the last of his koffee to choke the bitterness back down. "Why are you here, Teaser?" he asked roughly.

Teaser drained his own mug, started to set it aside, then hesitated, crossed the kitchen, and carefully placed the mug in the sink, as if keeping the cottage tidy were of the utmost importance. When he turned back to face Sebastian, his expression was bleak. "We found another one."

Currents of power dance through Ephemera, this living, ever-changing world. Some of those currents are Light, and some are Dark. Two halves of a whole. Nothing has one without some measure of the other. That is the way of things.

And there is no vessel for focusing the Light and the Dark that can compare to the human heart.

How do we tell people, who are still shaken by the horrors the Eater of the World set free in Ephemera, that this thing they fear cannot be destroyed completely because It was manifested from the darkest desires of their own hearts? How can we tell them *they* planted the seeds of this war that shattered the world? How can we tell them it was their own despair during this fearsome time that changed rich farmland into deserts? How can we tell them that, even with our guidance and intervention, the link between Ephemera and the human heart is unbreakable, and the world around them is nothing more or less than a reflection of themselves?

We can't tell them—because, despite the dangers that exist within it, the human heart is our only hope of restoring Ephemera someday. Nor can we let people completely deny the part they play in the constant shaping and reshaping of this world.

So we will teach them this warning: Let your heart travel lightly. Because what you bring with you becomes part of the landscape.

—The Lost Archives

Chapter Two

Three weeks earlier

Lukene gathered the frayed threads of her patience as she pulled out a chair at the study table and sat down next to the sulking girl. She'd been kind and understanding the first time this complaint had been voiced. And the second time. And the third. But no matter how many times she explained it, the girl refused to acknowledge the truth.

"You're not going to promote me to Level One Landscaper, are you?" the girl asked, her tone one part desperation and two parts hostility.

Lukene sighed. "No, Nigelle, we're not. The Instructors considered your abilities very carefully before making the decision, but it is our conclusion that you haven't, as yet, achieved the skills necessary to advance. Until you have fulfilled all the requirements, you will not be granted a Landscaper's Badge."

Nigelle pressed her fists against the top of the table. "I've been studying for *four years.* You have to achieve Level Two or better in five years in order to remain and continue studying for the higher levels. How am I supposed to fulfill the requirements for two levels in a year's time if you won't promote me to even the first level?"

You can't, Lukene thought. *And that is a blessing for us all.* "What is the Heart's Blessing?"

The girl's eyes darkened with anger. "Is this another test, Instructor Lukene? Although I don't see the point in asking a question every child knows the answer to."

Guardians and Guides, let me finally explain this in a way she'll understand. "Then it should be a simple question to answer," Lukene replied. "Heart's Blessing."

Nigelle sneered. "Travel lightly."

Lukene nodded. "Travel lightly. Because what you bring with you becomes part of the landscape. That is true for every person who lives in this world. It is especially true for Landscapers, because we are the sieve through which Ephemera manifests what is reflected in all those hearts. The resonance of *our* hearts provides the bedrock through which the currents of Dark and Light flow, keeping people safe from the turmoil of their own feelings while still allowing the true desires of the heart to become real. We are the bedrock, Nigelle. Other people, and Ephemera itself, depend on us to find a balance between the Light and Dark aspects of ourselves in order to filter the Light and Dark currents that are this world's wonderful and terrible power."

"I know all that," Nigelle snapped.

"Up here." Lukene tapped a finger against her own temple. Then she tapped the finger against her chest. "But not here. You carry too much baggage, Nigelle. You show up for the lessons, but you make only token attempts to practice those lessons. You're angry and envious whenever other students fulfill a requirement and go on to the next stage, but you won't do the work they did to achieve the goal. And yet you still expect us to grant you power over our world. We can't. Open your eyes, Nigelle. *Look* at what you manifest in your garden. Until that changes, until *you* change, we *cannot* allow you to have control of places other people will have to live in."

The girl's sulkiness shifted, changing into something sly and ugly. "I know the real reason you won't advance me."

Lukene sighed. Why did the "real" reason never have anything to do with the student's skills?

"You're afraid of me," Nigelle said. "You know I'm better than you. Better than all of you. I'm like Belladonna, and you can't stand the thought of there being another Landscaper who can do things you can't even dream of."

Unable to hide the shiver of fear that went through her, Lukene said nothing. Instructors never engaged in discussion once a student mentioned *that* name.

After the silence stretched out, Nigelle let out a nasty little laugh and stood up. "You better keep that in mind the next time you evaluate my work."

Lukene waited until Nigelle left the room before whispering, "We'll keep it in mind. Oh, we'll definitely keep it in mind."

She braced her hands on the table to help her shaking legs support her as she stood up. She wasn't forty yet, but right now she felt ancient.

"I know they're necessary," a male voice said from the doorway, "but these thrice-yearly evaluations take more out of the Instructors than the students."

Tears stung Lukene's eyes as she looked at the solid man filling the doorway. "Gregor."

He hurried across the room to reach her. His warm, strong hand rested on her shoulder.

She turned into that strength, that warmth, wrapping her arms around him as his arms closed around her.

"Difficult day?" Gregor asked, resting his cheek against her hair.

"Not so bad . . . until this last student."

"What did she do?"

"Spoke the name every Instructor in the school fears."

Gregor tensed. "Belladonna."

Lukene nodded. "I broke, Gregor. I showed fear."

"With good reason if this was more than schoolgirl romanticism of a rogue Landscaper."

"More like another manipulative ploy to push the In-

structors into granting her a status she hasn't earned."
She eased back enough to look at the man who was the
Head Instructor of Bridges—and her lover. "And how
was your day?"

"Better than yours. Teaching the young men who
have the gift to provide a connection between landscapes isn't nearly as unnerving as teaching the young
women who will control those landscapes." He studied
her, his dark eyes full of concern. "Why don't you go to
Sanctuary for a day or two?"

"Maybe I will. But I think I should be here right
now, in case the other Instructors . . . " She couldn't
finish, couldn't say the words.

"In case the other Instructors feel this girl is too dangerous and needs to be walled in," Gregor said grimly.
When Lukene nodded, he asked, "*Is* she that dangerous? *Could* she be another Belladonna?"

Lukene thought for a moment, then shook her head.
"She has enough anger and . . . soul muck . . . to resonate
with dark landscapes, but she'll never be like Belladonna. She doesn't have the power—or the heart."

Nigelle glowered at every student she passed as she hurried down the wide flagstone paths that would eventually lead to her walled garden. She should have known
from the moment she'd seen how far away her training
ground was from the school's central buildings that the
Instructors would be against her. *Other* students had
training grounds that were no more than a five-minute
walk from the classrooms. Granted, there weren't many
students who were given a space among the walled gardens reserved for the Instructors, but there were some,
and *she* should have been one of them.

"Cold, heart-rotted bitches," she muttered. Abruptly,
she turned down another path that headed back toward
the school. A path that, while as well tended as all the
others, always had a dusty, little-used feel to it. A path

students were forbidden to follow to the end unless an Instructor was with them. Maybe that was why it intrigued her enough to risk sneaking down that path several times a year to ponder the mystery at its end.

The path ended in an archway that was the only break in a high stone wall. In the center of this garden was another high-walled garden that had a locked wrought-iron gate. The only things that grew on the land between the inner and outer garden walls were large, bloated mushrooms and thorn trees that produced a fruit the color of a putrid wound.

Students whispered that the Dark Guides sneaked into the school during the dark of the moon, harvested those mushrooms and fruits, and cooked them with the hearts of people they had lured into the dark landscapes.

She liked that story. She spent a lot of nights imagining that one of the Dark Guides had come to the school and snatched all those snippy-bitch Instructors who *said* they were trying to help her learn how to use the power inside her but were really doing everything they could to ensure that she failed.

She'd like to see someone like Lukene face a Dark Guide. Snippy-bitch Lukene would wet herself if she came face-to-face with anything *truly* dark. But *she* wouldn't be afraid.

Yes, something whispered inside her. *You have nothing to fear from the Dark. There is power in the Dark, waiting for you to embrace it.*

Maybe that was the other reason she so often ended up standing in the archway, looking into this place that caused every Instructor to pale whenever it was mentioned.

Late at night, the older students would whisper stories about that garden, saying that forbidden landscapes were contained within it—landscapes so terrible they had been taken out of the world to protect people from the things that lived in those places.

But as she stood in the archway, all she could see beyond the wrought-iron gate was a low stone wall in the middle of barren, hard-packed earth. What was so frightening about that? Oh, there was a dark resonance in the garden. You could feel it as soon as you stepped beneath the archway. But if there was something *really* bad, why not tell the students what it was instead of making a secret out of it?

The Instructors were always making secrets out of things. Yes, this school was good at keeping things away from people who could make use of them.

Anger swelled inside her until there was nothing else.

Looking at the ground around her, Nigelle spotted a fist-sized stone. She picked it up, cocked her arm, and threw the stone at the lock on the wrought-iron gate. She didn't expect anything to happen; she just wanted to vent her anger at being held back *again*.

But the metal, fragile with age, crumbled where the stone struck. The gate, and whatever secrets were contained within that inner garden, was now open to her.

Licking dry lips, Nigelle stepped through the archway. The place smelled slightly of rotted meat, but that could have been the mushrooms or the fruit covering the ground around the thorn trees.

She hurried across the ground that separated the inner and outer garden, then wrapped her hands around two of the gate's bars and pulled as hard as she could. Frozen, rusty hinges screamed in protest, but the gate opened far enough for her to squeeze through.

Nigelle waited, her hands still wrapped around the bars, certain someone would come running to find out what had made that noise. But the air felt heavy and still, muffling sound.

She counted to one hundred, ready to run to avoid being caught in a forbidden place. When no one came to investigate, she relaxed enough to study the barren ground on the other side of the gate.

They say even Belladonna was afraid of this place, that she wouldn't come near it. But I'm not afraid. I'm going to see what's enclosed within these walls.

That didn't mean she wouldn't be careful. She retreated to the nearest thorn tree. Plenty of deadfall, but nothing suitable, so she went from tree to tree, checking the ground until she found a branch that was the right size and length to prod at anything of interest without having to get too close to the thing itself.

Excited now, she hurried back to the gate, slipped inside, and approached the low stone wall.

Just an old, waist-high wall barely two man-lengths long. Mortar filled all the spaces between the uneven stones, which meant someone had built it with care.

She looked around. There was nothing else within the inner garden. Nothing at all. Which meant the wall itself was the thing being guarded. Why guard a wall?

Maybe the wall was an access point to a landscape the Instructors wanted to keep hidden—a landscape that was the source of the dark resonance that permeated the walled garden.

She walked the length of the wall, studying it. Old stones. Old, crumbling mortar. She poked at the wall here and there, but her excitement at being in the forbidden garden waned, and she'd almost convinced herself that an old wall couldn't really be the access point to an interesting landscape. Then a poke with the narrow end of the branch loosened a piece of mortar, revealing a space between the stones as big as the circle she could make with thumb and forefinger.

A hole big enough to look through if she could clear it out to the other side.

She rammed the branch into the hole over and over, scraping out the crumbled mortar to clear the space. Finally, when her hands were raw and her muscles ached, she punched through to the other side. Tossing the branch away, she dropped to her knees and peered through the opening.

A narrow stretch of rust-colored sand that led to dark, still water.

Several minutes later, Nigelle sat back on her heels. This was it? Sand and water? *This* was the scary, forbidden landscape that made the Instructors shrill whenever a student asked about it?

Disgusted, Nigelle stood up and brushed the dirt off her trousers. "Should have known this was just an excuse for the Instructors to penalize anyone whose landscapes weren't sugarcoated nice-nice."

Slipping through the gate, she hurried back to the archway. Then she paused to check the position of the sun.

Too late to go to her own garden. If she didn't show up on time for the evening meal, it would be another mark against her. So she'd make the effort to be on time and come to class and be nice for all the Instructors— even if it killed her.

Although she'd prefer it if the effort killed *them*.

Lured by the resonance of a dark heart, It rose to the surface, barely making a ripple in the deep, dark water. Nothing in the water around It, so It stretched out a tentacle and delicately touched the place where sand met water—a border between two of Its landscapes. But the resonance in the sand was enough warning that It was near the hated stones that had shaped Its cage for so long.

And yet . . .

Its tentacles moved across the sand, rapidly changing their color from the dark gray that matched the caves deep beneath the water to the sand's rust color, making them invisible while they flowed toward the stone wall.

Before the first tentacle touched stone, It knew something was different. Something had changed. There was a different feel in the air, a trace of the dark heart's resonance right . . . there.

Tentacles elongated, thinned to slender cords of flesh that flowed through the small opening between the stones. Bit by bit, the large, fluid body moved across the sand and through the opening until the tip of the last tentacle brushed the other side of the old wall.

Free.

It had not understood Its Enemy's power, had not known It and the landscapes It had shaped could be locked away. But not completely. Never completely. It had not been able to reach the physical world beyond Its own landscapes, but It had always been able to whisper to the truly dark hearts, sending Its resonance through the twilight of waking dreams. And the Dark Ones, who had brought It into being so long ago, had found a way to send humans into Its landscapes often enough to keep It amused—and to keep It and Its creatures fed. But now It was free of the magic in the stone wall that had kept It caged; now It could bring Its landscapes back into the world. Now It could find the Dark Ones, who would help It alter the world into what *It* wanted the world to be. Now . . .

The vibration of footsteps. Coming closer.

Tentacles condensed and changed into eight legs. The body's shape altered to fit the legs. It climbed up and over the wall of the inner garden, then raced across the ground to the archway, Its belly brushing the tops of bloated mushrooms. It climbed the wall beside the archway. Within moments, Its large body blended perfectly with the stones, even mimicking the shadows cast by the thorn trees.

There It waited, savoring the anticipation of hunting again.

With her arms wrapped around herself, Lukene stared at the sealed, barred gate. A wooden door on the other side of the gate kept anyone from seeing what was held within the stone walls.

"Belladonna," Lukene whispered.

A mistake made fifteen years ago and impossible to rectify. But there were still times when she thought she could have done something, *should* have done something, to stop what had happened.

She'd been twenty-four and a new Instructor the year fifteen-year-old Glorianna came to the Landscapers' School. A bright girl, eager to learn. And so gifted.

They hadn't understood how gifted until halfway through the first year, when the Instructor Lukene was assisting assigned the students the task of making an access point for "a home." Since students that age had, at best, fledgling control over the power that lived within them, the access point would become the connection to the landscape that was *their* home. That was what the Instructor expected; that was what the lesson was meant to do.

But Glorianna had done something no other Landscaper could have done. Somehow she had *altered* Ephemera, rearranging pieces of the world to create an entirely new landscape, a place called the Den of Iniquity. The Instructors who judged the student efforts were horrified when they crossed over and got their first look at the Den—and were even more horrified when they saw the "residents" of that landscape.

When they returned to the walled garden that was Glorianna's training ground and demanded an explanation, the girl had smiled and told them even demons needed a home.

No one had asked Glorianna why she would create a place for demons that would surely also attract the darker elements of the human heart. No one contacted her family to make any inquiries—at least, not while it would have mattered.

Instead of asking the questions that should have been asked, the Head Instructor gave Glorianna a false smile and told the girl she was being given one of the advanced tests. For a fortnight, she was to stay within her walled garden and anchor her foundation landscapes—that is, the landscapes that resonated for her and were her "personal world."

She was given a basket of food, her clothes and books, water, and blankets.

She stood on one side of the gate and smiled while

she watched the Head Instructor put a stout padlock on the barred gate to keep anyone from going in.

And she had waved cheerfully at Lukene when the Instructors walked away.

The last morning before it was too late, Lukene stole the padlock key and entered Glorianna's garden. What the girl had done in a fortnight had left her awed and breathless—and terrified. The Den of Iniquity hadn't been a fluke. The girl truly had the power to change the world and needed to be nurtured very carefully.

She'd run back to the Head Instructor, stammering in her desperate attempt to make herself understood. But the Head Instructor shouted her into silence, telling her the decision was made; the wizards had arrived to seal the gate. Glorianna and her unnatural power would be walled in to keep the landscapes safe.

By the time she ran back to that walled garden, the wizards were gone, the seal was in place, and no one would enter that ground ever again—or leave it. Whatever Glorianna could coax Ephemera into manifesting within that garden was all the world the girl would know.

But a month later, she was walking with a few of her students and noticed a black-haired girl standing in front of that sealed gate.

"What are you doing there?" Lukene asked. "You know students aren't supposed to . . ." The words died when the girl turned and looked at her.

"So this is why none of you have come to see my work," Glorianna said.

"Perhaps," Lukene said carefully, aware that her students were shifting about uneasily, "now that you've found your way back—"

Glorianna shook her head. "No. There's nothing I want from you anymore. You chose to close me in. Now I choose to shut you out."

"I didn't choose to close you in!"

The girl smiled sadly. "No, you didn't. Good-bye, Lukene. Travel lightly."

As Glorianna walked away, one of Lukene's students said, "Who are you?"

She stopped, looked back, and said, "I'm Belladonna." Then she walked away—and was never seen at the school again.

Lukene wiped the tears off her face and started walking, paying no attention to where she was going, just needing the movement.

There was nothing she could have done, not then, not now. But the mistake they'd all made fifteen years ago still ate at her sometimes until she felt the cut of it right down to the bone.

There were seven levels of Landscapers, seven levels of skill in using the power that kept people, and the world, safe from the manifestation of every heart's desires. And then there was Glorianna Belladonna. If only . . .

A feeling of dread swept through Lukene, making her stop and look around.

What had drawn her to *this* path? Why did everything feel out of balance? The dark resonance, usually suppressed by the presence of so many Landscapers, felt as if it were leaking out of the forbidden garden, seeping into the ground and spreading out to contaminate the rest of the school. And it was strong now. Terribly strong.

Which was impossible. Unthinkable. She was overreacting to something that was always there in the background of the school. This was probably nothing more than a reaction to her confrontation with Nigelle and her thoughts about Glorianna.

But she hurried along the little-used path, and when she reached the archway and saw the open wrought-iron gate, she froze for a moment. Then she spun around, intending to run back to the school buildings and warn everyone that the unthinkable had happened.

Has the unthinkable happened?

A whispered thought. Calm, soothing, coaxing.

Lukene hesitated, turned back to look through the archway.

If she went running back now, what could she tell the Head Instructor? That someone had opened the old gate? That would cause an uproar among the Instructors in both the Landscapers' and Bridges' schools, but it wouldn't tell them anything. And she didn't actually *know* someone had opened the gate.

You don't want to make another mistake, the voice whispered.

Lukene shook her head. No, she didn't want to make another mistake.

She stepped through the archway—and gagged on the smell of rotting meat.

No more mistakes, the voice whispered. *They eat at you. Eat you right to the bone.*

Mushrooms burst as Lukene kicked them in her rush to the gate. Just a quick look to confirm nothing had changed inside, she thought as she squeezed through the opening. Then she would report to the Head Instructor, who would assign workers to replace the gate. Nothing to worry about. Nothing to fear.

The small hole in the old stone wall throbbed inside her like a bad tooth.

"No," she whispered. "Oh, no."

Back through the gate. Racing across the short distance to the archway. Distracted by a movement on the wall, she stumbled as she glanced up and . . .

. . . she ran across endless, rust-colored sand beneath a sky the color of ripe bruises. Her heart pounded, her arms and legs pumped for speed, but the creatures behind her kept getting closer, closer.

Guardians and Guides, how had she gotten here? One moment she was running for the archway. Then a movement, a stumble, and . . .

She ran, gulping air that felt too hot, too dry. Feet pounded the endless sand.

Travel lightly. All she needed was a few moments to calm her mind, find her balance, and resonate with the access point of one of her landscapes. That would bring her back to her garden at the school. Then she'd be safe. Then she could warn the others that—

One foot slid over something just under the surface, breaking her stride. She flung her arms out to keep her balance, but that brief hesitation cost her. She felt the slashing bite on her left calf, felt blood flowing down her leg as fear gave her speed.

The calf muscles in her left leg seized up. She lost her balance. Fell on her hands and one knee. Up again in a heartbeat, but it was still enough time for another one to reach her, to slash at the back of her right thigh.

Running again. Running and running, trying to ignore the wounds, the blood, the muscles that were getting too stiff to obey the mind's frantic commands.

Then she caught a glimpse of white and veered toward the mounds, not wondering what they were or why she hadn't noticed them before. If she could reach the top of one, maybe she could keep the creatures away long enough to get back to her garden at the school.

But as she got closer, fighting for every stride, she saw black, chitinous, segmented bodies pouring out of the top of the mounds, running toward her.

She tried to veer again, but the calf muscles in her left leg stopped working. She staggered. Barely kept herself from falling. In a scream of terror and defiance, she turned and grabbed the creature that was almost on top of her, lifting it up in both hands.

For a second she looked at the head, the jaws, the legs. Her mind supplied a word: ant. But this thing was as long as her arm from elbow to fingers. Screaming, she hurled it at the others rushing toward her.

She tried to run, but her legs didn't work anymore. She fell full-length on the sand.

And they were on her, the ones that had chased her, the ones from the mounds. She screamed as their jaws ripped out pieces of flesh, as her blood drenched the sand. She kept bucking, trying to throw them off, but there were so many now, her movements produced no more than another ripple under the mound of glistening black bodies.

Then she stopped moving. Stopped screaming.

When they finally left, the workers returning to the mounds, the scouts returning to the endless landscape, all that was left was a darker patch of wet sand, scraps of cloth, and clean bones.

Chapter Three

Present

Clutching the penny, Lynnea crept toward the wish well. There was no one around at this time of night. No one would see her here and mention it to Mam, who said tossing coins into the wish well was a waste of good money. And Mam would be very angry if she even suspected Lynnea wished for something beyond what Mam thought she deserved to have—food, serviceable clothes, and a place to sleep.

Besides, if Mam found out she'd gone to the wish well, she'd have to explain where she'd gotten the coin, since she wasn't allowed to have money. And since Mam searched her tiny, barren room several times a week to make sure she wasn't hiding anything she was forbidden to have, she wouldn't keep the penny for long.

So she *had* to come tonight, had to sneak out of the farmhouse after Mam, Pa, and Ewan had fallen asleep. You *needed* a coin in order to make a wish at the well, and there was no telling how long it might be before Mam bobbled the egg-money jar again, spilling a few coins on the kitchen floor. Mam's sharp eyes hadn't noticed the penny next to a leg of the kitchen table. But Lynnea had seen it—and had convinced herself that the sunlight coming through the windows at just that moment, casting the shadow that had hidden the coin, meant she was supposed to have the penny in order to have this one chance to make a wish.

Holding her hand over the wish well, Lynnea whispered, "I wish . . . " But there were so many wishes crowding up inside her, she didn't know which one to choose. And all she had was a penny. Maybe you could get only a small wish granted if you dropped a penny in the well. But a small wish wasn't what she wanted. What she really wanted . . .

I wish I lived in a different place. I wish I could have friends. I wish I could do things right instead of always doing the wrong thing, no matter how hard I try. I wish I could find someone special to love. I wish someone loved me.

Something strange and powerful washed through her, startling her so much her hand snapped open.

The penny dropped into the well, and the feeling faded.

Lynnea stepped away from the well, wiping her hands on her much-mended skirt. Then she glanced at the sky and felt fear—such a familiar sensation—ripple through her. The farmhouse was beyond the other side of the village. If she didn't hurry, she wouldn't get back before the others got up and discovered she'd been out.

Wondering if anything good would come from the risk she'd taken tonight, Lynnea lifted her skirt above her knees and ran back to the farmhouse.

Sebastian stood at the end of the alley. The colored pole-lights that gave the Den's main street a festively decadent appearance barely touched the entrance, as if even created light didn't want to enter that dark space.

He was a demon. This was his landscape. But he didn't want to walk into that dark, didn't want to see whatever was at the other end of the alley.

Didn't matter what he wanted. The crowd that had

huddled at the edge of the alley, waiting for Teaser to fetch him, simply watched him now. Humans and demons alike, they watched him.

Beside him, Teaser extended a hand and took the torch someone passed to him.

"I'll go with you," Teaser said, looking pale and sick.

"I too," a voice growled. "Go with you."

The crowd parted for the bull demon. Big, mean, and not too bright, they came to the Den to drink in the taverns and bellow at the dancing girls. The wickedly curved horns could gore a man, and despite the bovine cast to their features, it was said they ate raw meat ... of any kind.

This one held a thick wooden club that ended in a ball filled with metal spikes.

Walking into a confined space with a bull demon that was carrying a vicious-looking weapon wasn't something any sane person would do, so feeling relief at the offer told Sebastian better than anything else could how deeply he feared what had been found in the alley.

"Thank you," Sebastian said. He closed his eyes for a moment, gathered his courage ... and walked into the alley.

Something wrong here. The ground felt soft, fluid ... as if it might ripple under his feet at any moment.

No. Hard-packed ground didn't shift, didn't ripple. He just felt sick, a little dizzy. Which was understandable considering what he expected to find.

As they walked forward, the torchlight finally unveiled the other end of the alley.

The three of them froze. The bull demon's breathing suddenly changed, sounding harsh and wet.

The body of the succubus they'd found a week earlier had been bad. This one was worse. Much worse.

Female. So mutilated he couldn't say if he'd ever seen her in the Den before, could barely say with any certainty that the thing spilled over the alley *was* female.

"Human," Teaser whispered.

Sebastian jerked, breaking the awful hold the corpse

had on him that had kept him staring at it. He looked at Teaser. "You recognize her?"

Teaser shuddered. "The bracelet. She always wears that wide gold bracelet. Has a rich husband. She's a mean bitch who likes to play rough games in bed. Husband likes meat-and-potato sex, so she comes here to roll in the muck and do it naughty."

She's not going to do anything anymore, Sebastian thought, worried about the way Teaser talked as if the woman were going to sit up at any moment and laugh at them for being taken in by her hideous joke.

"Let's—" Fear suddenly clamped icy hands around his spine. "Did you hear that?"

The bull demon waggled his ears and snorted. Sebastian had no idea if that meant yes or no.

The ground felt soft again, fluid again. And he would have sworn on everything he held dear that he heard a whisper of sly, wicked laughter coming from nearby.

He knew the Den. Knew these alleys as well as he knew the main streets. Something wasn't right here.

"Let's go," he said, backing away from the corpse. Was there something moving up there on the walls? Something just beyond the torchlight? "Teaser, let's go."

The alley wasn't long, but he felt as if he labored for hours to gain each step.

Halfway back to the street and the crowd. He turned and focused on Philo and Mr. Finch, two humans who had found their way to the Den and had settled in to stay.

Then he heard it. A faint scratching as something shifted on the wall.

He didn't think. There wasn't room inside him to think, not when he was certain that if he didn't get out of that alley *now*, he'd end up like that woman. Or worse.

He sprinted for the mouth of the alley. Between one step and the next, the alley stretched like warm taffy, and the people waiting for him receded as the hard ground turned to sand that pulled at his feet, slowing him down. In another moment the alley would disappear and there would be nothing but sand, nothing but—

No! He was in the Den, in an alley. A *short* alley. Hard ground beneath him. Stone walls on either side of him. Teaser and the bull demon running just behind him. Familiar people waiting for him a few steps away. Just a few steps away. Just—

They burst out of the alley and were caught by the crowd.

His heart pounding, Sebastian spun around, deaf to the cries and questions of the humans and demons around him.

He'd almost slipped into another landscape. The alley had almost changed into another landscape. A terrible place ... from which he would never return.

The certainty that something terrible had existed in that other landscape made his legs weak.

"I need a drink." Now as desperate to get away from the crowd as he'd been to reach them, Sebastian shoved his way through the bodies and headed for Philo's place.

Standing at the back of the alley, It watched the crowd follow the incubus like a herd of trembling sheep. On another night, It would have walked among them, looking like a well-to-do, middle-aged gentleman who had come to the Den for a little gambling, a little whoring. On another night, they would have looked at It and seen potential prey. The succubus It had killed a few days ago had certainly seen It that way. The human female stinking up the alley had been less convinced that another "human" could give her the same sensual thrill as an incubus. It had shown her It wasn't human—and then It had shown her other things. Not that she'd been able to see most of them, since her eyes were one of the first pieces of forfeit.

Her fear had spilled out with the rest of her, a delicious feast of emotions, spiced at times with the hope that someone would see her, help her. Killing the succubus, a creature so diluted from the purebloods of her kind, had produced the first shivers of fear in the hearts of the people who lived in this place. But the human female's terror, coaxed and nurtured in the few minutes It had taken to kill her, had seeped into the ground, changing the alley's resonance into something It could use as a connection to one of Its own landscapes. Then It wouldn't have to move through landscapes held by Its enemies in order to reach this hunting ground.

But something had fought Its attempt to shift the three males into the bonelovers' landscape. They had almost crossed over, had felt the sand beneath their feet for a moment. But something—or someone—had been strong-willed enough to hold on to the alley and keep them in this place. Anything that strong was a rival to be eliminated.

But even a strong rival could be beaten if fear was molded into a sharp enough weapon.

It resonated, imposing Its will on the ground around It—forcing Ephemera to yield to Its desire.

Between the alley's stone walls, the ground changed into rust-colored sand around the corpse.

It shifted form, Its large body changing color to match the stone while Its eight legs climbed the wall. Then It waited.

A few minutes later, the first bonelover appeared. Not long after that, the sand was hidden under a mass of glistening black bodies.

A little girl's fear of ants had been the seed It had nurtured long ago, feeding that fear until the girl had been glutted with it, then hollowed out by it. Her terror, day after day, had pulsed through the land, giving It the power to reshape something small and natural into a nightmare come alive—a nightmare people called bonelovers because that was all that had been left of the little girl who had been their first prey.

Sighing like a sated lover, It watched the last bonelover disappear. Being simpleminded creatures, they couldn't cross over into the alley. For them, the alley didn't exist. But anyone on this side of that fluid border who could be lured or driven onto that sand would disappear into the bonelovers' landscape—and never return.

It climbed down the wall, Its body changing as It touched the sand. As a bonelover, It raced across the sand to the access point It had created that would take It back to the enemies' lair—the place they called the Landscapers' School. It had found a safe place there, a dark place where It could hide while It anchored Its landscapes within other landscapes—and searched for the landscape where the Dark Ones now lived.

As for the humans and other creatures who lived in this hunting ground . . . When they came back for the female's body, they would find sand instead of hard ground, an elegant dress that was now tattered rags, a wide gold bracelet . . . and clean bones.

Sinking into a chair, Sebastian braced his arms on one of the tables scattered around the courtyard of Philo's place. His body shook, as if it comprehended something his mind couldn't bring into focus.

Teaser, collapsing into a chair opposite his, looked just as sick, just as frightened.

What had happened in that alley? Glorianna had told him once that a person couldn't cross over into a landscape if the heart wasn't open to what it held, just like you couldn't always get back to a landscape you'd known if something had changed inside you so that your heart no longer resonated with that place. When you crossed a resonating bridge, the borders and boundaries that defined the landscapes could become as fluid as a dream. The only constant in Ephemera was that it was ever-changing.

So what did it mean that he, Teaser, and the bull demon had almost stumbled into another landscape without crossing any kind of bridge? How could two landscapes meld so that you saw one fade as the other became dominant?

Nothing like that had happened in the Den before.

Philo, a short, round, balding man who served the best food in the Den, hurried up to them and clattered two whiskey glasses on the table. Sweat beaded his forehead, but his hands were steady as he poured drinks and pushed the glasses toward Sebastian and Teaser.

Teaser gulped down the whiskey. Sebastian, afraid to haze the edges of his mind and slip into nightmare, took a cautious sip.

The crowd gathered in the street just beyond the courtyard, but there were a few precious minutes of silence before Philo shifted from one foot to the other, drawing Sebastian's attention.

"This is the second one in two weeks," Philo said. "There is no demon race that kills like that. Nothing in the Den kills like that. That's why, when we found this one, we asked Teaser to fetch you."

Sebastian frowned. "I don't understand."

Philo and Teaser wouldn't look at him. When he glanced at the crowd, none of them would look at him.

Finally Teaser asked softly, "Are we being punished, Sebastian?"

"How should I . . ." But he did know. Looking at the naked fear in Teaser's eyes, he did know. He shook his head. "She wouldn't do this. Belladonna wouldn't bring something like this into a landscape."

At the edge of the crowd, Mr. Finch made distressed chirpy noises.

Philo wrung his hands. "If we have done something to anger the Landscaper—"

"She wouldn't do this!" Sebastian snapped.

Silence. Then Philo said, "Someone did."

Keeping his eyes focused on the table, Sebastian sipped his whiskey, feeling the tug of conflicting loyalties. The Den was his home. He'd spent the past fifteen years living among these people. But every good thing that had happened in his childhood had come from Glorianna, Lee, and their mother, Nadia. Every happy memory from the years before he escaped his father for the last time had a connection to at least one of them.

And the year the wizards, those self-righteous pillars of law and justice, had tried to destroy the Den . . .

Six years after the Den was created, the wizards came with a Level Seven Landscaper whom they had convinced somehow to take over control of the Den and "balance" the landscape.

Sebastian stood on one side of the main street with Philo, Teaser, and Mr. Finch, watching the Landscaper take a position between the line of wizards and the line of residents, her hands slightly lifted, her head tilted back, her eyes closed. Then he stared at the wizards, at one in particular who finally met his bitter stare with eyes filled with hatred.

Demons were a blight on the world. Demons were a threat to humans. Demons had no place in Ephemera, and creating a haven for such vileness . . . The wizards hadn't been able to prevent the Den's creation, but now they were determined to put an end to it.

They could have done it anywhere. They could have picked a quiet place on the outskirts of the Den, wouldn't have needed to go more than a few steps beyond the bridge they'd used to cross over into the landscape. It would have made no difference in terms of what the Landscaper could do. Instead, they marched into the Den's main street, taunting the humans and demons who had gathered with the knowledge that their place in the world was going to be splintered beyond recognition. The changes were already in motion, and not even killing the Landscaper would have stopped what was to come.

Finally, when he felt something swirl around his heart and knew the Landscaper was tapping into the heart's core of every creature that made a home in the Den, he looked away from the wizards and the woman and focused on the colored lights and the buildings and the small islands of dwarf trees and night flowers that could gather sustenance from the cold light of the moon instead of the sun's warm glow. He wanted to remember the Den as it was in this moment—because when the wizards and Landscaper were finished, there was no telling what he and the others might be able to salvage.

The swirl faded. Everyone was silent.

Then the Landscaper, one of the most powerful of her kind, rubbed her arms as if chilled and took a hesitant step away from the wizards as she looked around. As they all looked around.

Nothing had changed.

"This landscape already has a signature resonance," the Landscaper whispered. "A very powerful signature resonance. I'm . . . not welcome here anymore."

"Stupid bitch," Teaser whispered. "Did she really think she was welcome before?"

Sebastian just watched the woman, who looked more and more uneasy with each passing moment.

"Who controls this landscape?" the Landscaper asked.

The wizards didn't answer her, so he did. "The Den belongs to Belladonna."

She whirled around to face the wizards. "You didn't tell me that."

"It wasn't significant," one of the wizards replied.

"Are you mad?" she screamed. "No one touches one of Belladonna's landscapes. No one!" Her voice broke on a sob.

Pity stirred in Sebastian. The Landscaper looked like a terrified child who suddenly realized all the bad things she feared were lurking in the dark spaces truly existed.

The wizards shifted uncomfortably. "Since there is nothing more to be done here, we will go," one of them said.

"Where am I supposed to go?" she wailed. "There's no safe place to go."

The wizards stared at her in disgust. Then they walked away—and never looked back.

The Landscaper crumpled in the street.

Philo lifted his hands in a helpless gesture. "Perhaps—"

"Daylight," *Teaser muttered, looking up the street.*

Looking in the same direction, Sebastian felt his heart jump.

She stood beneath one of the pole-lights, staring at the Landscaper. He walked forward to meet her, once again startled by the fact that this slim, lovely woman with green eyes so like his own and a river of silky black hair could do things to their world that terrified even the fiercest demons.

"Glorianna," *he said softly when he stood before her.*

"Sebastian." *Her voice still held a hint of the country lilt that had enchanted him the first time he'd met her.*

"I don't think the Landscaper truly meant us harm." *He studied her eyes, looking for the fiery compassion he knew burned within her—and found only ice.* "Judge her with your heart."

"It is not my heart that will judge her, Sebastian," *Glorianna replied.* "It is her own." *She swung around him and walked toward the Landscaper.*

He caught up to her, walking close enough to make it clear he was with her, whatever she chose to do, and still keeping enough distance so that she knew he wouldn't interfere.

They stopped a few paces away from the Landscaper, who made no move to get to her feet and face them as an equal. She just looked up at them, knowing no plea she made would change anything.

No one around them spoke. No one so much as shifted a foot while Glorianna and the Landscaper stared at each other.

Finally, Glorianna said, "Go back to your landscapes."

The Landscaper scrambled to her feet, wobbled as she took a few steps away from them, then turned and ran in the same direction the wizards had taken.

Sebastian looked at Glorianna. The sadness in her eyes was so unexpected it made him ache. He knew she'd been cast out of the school, had been declared a rogue Landscaper. Lee had told him that much, but not why. Never why.

He sidestepped, bringing him close enough to nudge her with his elbow. "Come on. I'll treat you to Philo's specialties—Stuffed Tits and Phallic Delights."

No sadness now. Just shock swiftly changing to the suspicious look she used to give him and Lee when they'd try to convince her that something preposterous could really be true. Of course, they'd all been young enough then not to understand that nothing was preposterous in Ephemera. Especially for Glorianna.

"Stuffed Tits and Phallic Delights," she said. "And what might those be?"

He gave her a wicked grin. "Come with me and see for yourself."

So they went to Philo's, and when the plates were set before her, her laughter rang through the courtyard—and for a few hours, while they drank wine and ate the various offerings Philo placed before them, he saw her as the bright-eyed girl he remembered and not whatever being an outcast and a rogue was shaping her into.

Sebastian raised his glass, discovered it was empty, and reached for the whiskey bottle.

No one dared touch one of Belladonna's landscapes. That was the lesson wizards, Landscapers, and demons alike had learned nine years ago. Which meant a Bridge had linked two landscapes recently, enabling a killer to cross over to the Den, or another Landscaper *had* managed to add something to the landscape—or Philo and Teaser were right and Glorianna herself had brought something into the Den.

Which he didn't believe. *Couldn't* believe. But if it wasn't Glorianna . . .

"Could be a human," Sebastian said.

Philo stiffened. Teaser looked at him, shocked.

"It could be a human," he repeated. "A sick mind, or an evil one, that's come to hunt in the Den because it's a dark landscape."

"Well, daylight! What are we supposed to do about that?" Teaser said.

The words lodged in Sebastian's throat like sharp stones, while the whiskey churned in his stomach along with heart-deep revulsion. "We have to inform the wizards."

"Guardians and Guides, Sebastian," Philo sputtered. "You'd give *those* creatures a reason to come back here?"

"What choice is there? A human died here."

"Humans have died around here before," Teaser muttered. "They cross over, see a pretty horse that acts tame enough to give them a ride, and they're in the lake and drowning before they understand a waterhorse has ensnared them. Or they follow marsh lights instead of keeping to the path that leads them home and end up the guest of honor at a Merry Makers feast. Or they figure a bull demon isn't smart enough to notice if they cheat while playing cards."

"It's not the same thing," Sebastian said. "Anyone who wanders through the dark landscapes that surround the Den is taking a chance of never getting home again. And anyone stupid enough to cheat a bull demon is asking to be gored. This is different. Besides, you said this woman had a rich husband, which means she probably has some status in her own landscape. Someone's going to start looking for her when she doesn't come back."

"Maybe," Teaser replied. "But she gave me a different name every time I saw her, and she never said which landscape she came from."

"Which brings us back to informing the wizards," Sebastian said, suddenly weary.

Philo said hesitantly, "Perhaps we should wait and ask the Landscaper?"

"No one knows how to find her," Sebastian replied. Which wasn't quite true. Aunt Nadia probably knew how to get a message to Glorianna, but he didn't want to tell his aunt what was happening in the Den and see a horrible truth in her eyes: that Belladonna *had* sent that evil to walk among them.

"So that leaves the wizards, since we *do* know how to find those bastards. Besides, the *Justice Makers* are supposed to take care of this kind of . . . problem." He looked at Philo and Teaser . . . and accepted that there really was no choice. "I'll go."

Teaser pushed back from the table. "I'll try to convince a demon cycle to give us a ride."

"Us?" Sebastian asked, surprised. "You're coming with me?"

Teaser moved his shoulders in what was probably meant as a shrug but looked like an uneasy twitch. "As far as the bridge, anyway."

Which was farther than he'd thought the other incubus would go. "I've got to go back to the cottage and pack a bag." Even if the journey didn't take more than one rising and setting of the moon, he'd still need a fresh shirt to wear when he presented himself to the bastards who lived behind their walls and rituals.

He borrowed Philo's bicycle and rode back to the cottage as fast as he could. By the time he packed some toiletries and clothing, changed into the leather pants and jacket that would probably outrage the wizards but made him feel less like a supplicant, and walked out of the cottage, Teaser was waiting for him, straddling a demon cycle.

Like the motored carriages that had been invented in one of the big-city landscapes, the motored cycles had been unknown in the Den until a dozen men had crossed over a few years ago to cause some trouble and have a spree. They'd thought they were bad. They'd thought they were mean. They'd thought they were powerful—until they'd clashed with demons who were badder, meaner, and much more powerful.

The wheels were gone. So was the motor and whatever else had originally powered the cycle. The demons who had taken up residence in the cycles didn't need those things.

The demon who inhabited this one stared at him with red eyes. Its pushed-in face and tufted ears made it look comical—if a person could ignore all the razored teeth, the powerful torso, the thick arms, and the fingers that ended with curved talons.

Satisfied that the other passenger was the person promised and not a potential meal, the demon flowed back into the hollow belly of the cycle until only its head stuck out of the hole that had once held a light.

Adjusting the straps of his pack so it settled comfortably against his back, Sebastian mounted the cycle behind Teaser.

Since the demons had the ability to float the cycles above the ground, they didn't need roads, but this one followed the lane from the cottage back to the main street of the Den, then beyond the crowded buildings to the open countryside.

About a mile outside the Den, they stopped at a wooden bridge that crossed a stream.

There were two kinds of bridges. The stationary bridges linked one or more specific landscapes and were usually a reliable way of crossing over from one landscape to another. Resonating bridges allowed a person to cross over to any landscape that resonated with that person's heart. Most of the time, focusing the will was sufficient to reach a particular destination. But there were other times when a resonating bridge ignored the will and listened only to the heart—and a person ended up in a landscape that wasn't remotely close to where he intended to go. Which made traveling in Ephemera a gambler's adventure.

And this was a resonating bridge.

Teaser looked over his shoulder. "Will this do?"

Sebastian took a deep breath, then let it out slowly. "This will do." It wasn't as if he had a choice. There weren't any stationary bridges that linked any of Belladonna's landscapes to the landscape that held Wizard City.

He got off the demon cycle and walked to the edge of the bridge. He tried to clear his mind of everything but the need to reach Wizard City.

"Sebastian?"

He looked back.

Teaser shifted his shoulders, looking embarrassed. "Travel lightly."

Heart's Blessing. It warmed him to hear someone say it. "I'll be back soon." He hoped.

Wizard City. Wizard City. Other images tried to intrude—the feel of sand beneath his feet—but he chanted the words "Wizard City" under his breath as he crossed the bridge.

The land didn't look any different, but the sky was now a predawn gray or the fading light of dusk. And when he looked back across the stream, there was no sign of Teaser or the demon cycle.

So. He'd crossed over. Now all he could do was hope he'd crossed over to the right landscape.

A rough cart path led away from the bridge. Settling the straps of his pack more comfortably on his shoulders, he followed the path to wherever it would take him.

Glorianna walked into the alley, then stopped and opened the lantern's shutter to illuminate the ground as much as possible. One cautious step, then another. Always studying the ground, the walls, the shadows. When the light found the bones and the rust-colored sand, she stopped. Crouching, she touched a fingertip to the ground, then studied the grains of sand clinging to her skin. There were a few landscapes that had that color sand, but combined with clean bones . . . only one.

So this was the source of the dissonance she had felt when she'd walked through her private garden to check on her landscapes. She'd felt a ripple of uneasiness a few days ago and had intended to visit the Den and talk to Sebastian, but there had been stronger ripples of dissonance in two other landscapes. She'd crossed over to check on the disturbances in those landscapes but had found nothing unusual, so she'd decided a wizard must have been passing through those places, since their presence always created a dissonance in her landscapes. By the time she'd returned home, the ripple that had disturbed the Den had disappeared.

Until now.

She rubbed thumb against finger until she was absolutely certain she was clean of every grain of sand. Then she rose and carefully backed away.

Glorianna, these past few nights I've had dreams full of disturbing images, and a . . . sense . . . that something old, something evil is swimming beneath the surface of the world.

I know, Mother. I've had the same dreams.

She went back to the mouth of the alley, opened the pack she'd left there, and took out a jagged piece of stone. Then she walked back into the alley and carefully studied the ground, looking for the grain of sand farthest away from the bones. Setting the stone on top of the last grain of sand, she called to the world.

Ephemera, hear me.

The currents of Dark and Light power that flowed through the Den mingled with the currents of Light and Dark inside her while the world waited to manifest her will.

Take the sand before me and send it deep into the place of stones. Let the sand have the bones. They belong to that landscape now. Let nothing remain here that does not come from my heart.

She felt the currents of Dark power flow into the alley, along with a thread of Light. She watched the sand and bones disappear, along with the jagged piece of stone that would act as the anchor point connecting the place of stones to the bonelovers' landscape.

She watched Ephemera manifest her will, responding to her in ways it responded to no other Landscaper.

Her resonance filled the alley once more. But there

was still a tingle of fear where the blood had seeped into the ground, and that fear would linger, smearing the heart of every person who passed the alley.

She felt a playful tug from the currents of Light. Before she could respond and impose her will, shoots pushed up from the hard-packed ground, rapidly growing into lush, dark green leaves. Within a minute, the blood-soaked ground was covered in living green.

It was an awkward place for plants to grow, to say the least.

There's no light here. Even moonlight won't reach the plants. They can't survive here.

The Light would give them what they needed. And seeing them would make the hearts happy. Wouldn't it make the hearts happy?

Ephemera was alive, but it didn't have an intelligence of its own. At least, it didn't think in a way that people would consider intelligent. But long ago, Ephemera had harnessed itself to the human heart, and it constantly made and remade itself in response to those hearts. Since it responded to her heart over any other in her landscapes, the plants must have been Ephemera's response to her desire to somehow soften the violence that had filled the alley.

She sighed, but she also smiled—and wondered what the Den's residents would say when they discovered the greenery.

Stepping out of the alley, she picked up her pack and looked around. She could spare an hour or two. Might as well take a stroll along the main street and listen to the hearts of the Den's residents before she went searching for Sebastian.

Lynnea slipped into the dark kitchen. But as she breathed a sigh of relief, she heard the scuff of a slipper, felt the stir of air before the heavy leather strap hit her across the back.

She cried out, but softly, knowing the punishment would be worse if she made any noise that was loud enough to wake up Pa or Ewan.

One of Mam's strong hands grabbed her hair, yanking her head down to hold her in place, while the other hand worked the strap with brutal efficiency up and down her back, buttocks, and thighs.

"Trollop," Mam hissed. "Slut. Whore. You think I don't know what you're up to?"

"I didn't do anything bad. I just went for a walk."

"I know what kind of walk girls take when they slip out of the house at night. I didn't take you in and raise you up so you could run off and keep house for some man. As if something like you deserved to have a husband and children. You're nothing but trash abandoned by the side of the road. Just trash I took in out of the goodness of my heart, hoping I could raise you up to be a decent girl. But you were born trash, and you'll always be trash. Should have left you to die. That's what I should have done."

"I just went for a walk!"

The protest made no difference. The words and the blows continued until Mam had said what she wanted to say. Until Lynnea's back ached unbearably from the strap and her heart felt scoured by the words.

Then a creak of a floorboard upstairs had Mam giving Lynnea's hair a final yank before she stepped back.

"The man's up. Get out to the henhouse and fetch the eggs."

Lynnea shuffled over to the wooden counter next to the kitchen sink. Her hands shook so badly, she spilled the matches all over the counter when she opened the matchbox to light the lantern.

Cursing quietly, Mam grabbed the box and lit the lantern's candle. "Useless. That's all you are. A waste of time and money. Git out there now. Git."

Taking the lantern, Lynnea moaned as she bent down to pick up the egg basket.

"And don't you be whining and moaning," Mam said. "You got less than you deserve, and you know it, missy."

Another floorboard creaked.

Lynnea left the kitchen as fast as she could. If Pa came down and realized something was wrong, things would get worse. Much, much worse.

But when she got to the henhouse and hung the lantern on the peg by the door, she just stood there, staring at the sleepy hens.

This was her life. Nothing but this.

She couldn't remember her life before the farm. Didn't have her own memory of how she'd come to live with Mam and Pa and Ewan, just Mam's story about finding a little girl abandoned by the side of the road.

I found you by the side of the road, and I can put you out again just as easily, and don't you forget it, missy. You earn your keep or you go back to the road with nothing more than the clothes you're wearing—just like I found you.

There had never been any kindness in Mam. She seemed to love Ewan and Pa in a cold sort of way, but she'd never shown even that cold kind of love to the little girl she'd taken in. Maybe she'd longed for a daughter of her own and that was the reason she'd stopped that day to pick up an abandoned child.

Why didn't matter anymore. Every mistake—and a child could make so many—had been followed by the threat of being taken down the road and abandoned again. She'd never felt safe, had lived in fear that this would be the day she would make the mistake that would end with her being tossed out like a used-up rag.

And yet, when she tried to remember that day on her own, she remembered it differently. She could feel herself as that little girl, happy and full of anticipated pleasure as she roamed the edges of a clearing and then followed a path in the woods, picking flowers for her mama. When she came out of the woods, she was standing on the edge of a road, holding a double fistful of flowers. And her mama had gotten lost.

Then the lady, Mam, came by with the horse and little wagon. She stared at Lynnea, who was trying to be brave and not cry because her mama was lost.

You're the answer to a wish, Mam said as she got down from the wagon. What's your name, child?

Lynnea. I picked flowers for Mama, but she's lost.

I'm going to be your mama now.

Mam picked her up and put her in the wagon. Not on the seat, but on the floor. Then Mam climbed into the wagon and slapped at the horse to make it run very fast.

Lynnea used her sleeve to wipe away the tears. She didn't know if that was a true memory or just wishful thinking that changed Mam's story so it didn't hurt so much. Just as she didn't know if she really remembered a man and woman calling her name, over and over, as if they were searching for her.

Didn't matter now which story was true. It had all happened a long time ago. Sixteen years, in fact. She knew that because not long after she'd come to live with Mam, Ewan had his sixth birthday and Mam had baked a cake as a special treat. That evening, when she was getting ready for bed, she'd told Mam her birthday so Mam, who was her new mama now, would know what day to bake the cake.

But she didn't get a cake for her birthday. Not that year, not any year. Because cakes took time and money to make. Cakes were for real children, not someone like her.

She no longer remembered when her birthday was. Didn't want to remember. And she couldn't remember how old she had been the day Mam found her by the road. But she knew it had been sixteen years ago because Ewan had turned twenty-two last week—and Mam had baked him a cake.

I wish I lived in a different place. I wish someone could love me.

Foolish wishes. Just like every other wish she'd ever made.

Wiping her eyes one last time, Lynnea began collecting the eggs.

Muttering to herself, Glorianna tromped down the lane toward Sebastian's cottage. She'd seen him and Teaser zipping down the main street on a demon cycle, heading for the other end of the Den, but there hadn't been time to call out. Sebastian had a pack, so he must be planning to cross over to another landscape for a visit.

Opportunities and choices. She'd missed the chance to talk to Sebastian, so another pattern of events would take shape. That was the way of the world. That was the way of life.

She had known from the moment she'd looked into the green eyes of a wary boy and felt his heart's strong desire to belong in the nice house with the kind woman and the children who weren't being cruel that her connection with Sebastian was different from her connection with Nadia and Lee. She had known, in a child's instinctive way, that she and Sebastian would have a powerful influence on each other's lives. She hadn't known then that loving her cousin and wanting to help him would break the pattern of her life so completely, but . . .

Opportunities and choices. She had made the choice because of Sebastian, but it had been *her* choice. And even though she'd never been able to put the pattern of her own life back together in a way that made it whole, she didn't regret her choice. Had never regretted her choice. Because it had saved him.

"Sebastian," she said—and smiled.

A swell in the currents of power washed through her, leaving her breathless. She stopped walking, just stood in the middle of the lane while she absorbed the feeling that had touched her.

Heart wish. A powerful one. The kind that would send ripples through the currents of the world.

"Sebastian?" she whispered—and felt the heart wish wash through her again.

So. The heart wish *had* come from him. Maybe that was the reason for his urge to visit another landscape.

Despite what she'd seen in the alley—and her suspicions of how *that* particular landscape had been inserted into her own—she felt her heart lift. There had been so much possibility of Light in Sebastian's heart wish. He'd had opportunities to leave the Den and cross over to another landscape, but he'd been blind to them because, despite wanting a change, he hadn't been ready to change his life. Maybe this time he would follow his heart.

The Den wouldn't be the same if he left, but the Den, too, had been changing over these last few years, so this might be the time for the man and the landscape to go their separate ways. A bad time, to be sure, but a Landscaper had no right to interfere with a person's life journey, no matter the cost.

She started walking again, anxious to reach the cottage. Sebastian wouldn't mind her bedding down on his couch for a few hours. She needed some time to rest. She needed the peace of solitude so she could think.

But when she got close to the cottage, another swell in the currents of power washed through her. This one was fainter, as if it were a ripple of something that had begun a long way away, but no less powerful.

Another heart wish. And something more.

Glorianna reached under her hair and rubbed the back of her neck to get rid of the prickly feeling.

For good or ill, a catalyst was moving toward the Den—a person whose resonance would bring change. And that change seemed to center on the cottage.

She went inside and hoped Sebastian hadn't rearranged the furniture since her last visit. Feeling her way in the dark, she reached the couch without tripping over anything, dropped her pack beside it, then slumped in one corner, knowing that if she stretched out she would never make the effort to get up and rummage for something to eat.

Nothing to be done about the heart wishes or the catalyst. Things were in motion, but a hundred possibilities could change the pattern that might bring those heart wishes and the catalyst together. Right now she needed to think about the alley and a landscape that had been taken out of the world long ago and shouldn't be able to touch the rest of Ephemera. And she needed to think about a possibility she didn't want to consider.

Sighing, Glorianna rubbed her hands over her face.

Only one way to find out. After she got some rest, she would go to the Landscapers' School and look at the forbidden garden, just to reassure herself that the Eater of the World was still contained behind a stone wall.

Chapter Four

"Hoo-whee! You lucky I came along," William Farmer said.

"Yeah," Sebastian muttered. "Lucky."

"Don't usually pick up strangers this close to a bridge. Can't never tell what might be crossing over from another place. But you look like a regular fella."

The farmer spent a minute making various noises at the two horses pulling the wagon, which didn't seem to have any effect on the animals. It certainly didn't increase their speed.

Travel lightly. Sebastian closed his eyes and tried to feel grateful that the farmer had offered him a ride. Even if he'd followed the cart path that had led from the bridge, he could have spent days trying to reach Wizard City, getting detained one way or another over and over again. His reluctance to get anywhere near the wizards was at odds with the knowledge that it was what he needed to do. But Ephemera responded to the heart, not the head, so the landscape would have provided obstacles to keep him from reaching the city, turning the journey into a battle of wills—his against Ephemera. He still would have reached the city eventually, but the people he'd left behind in the Den didn't have time for eventually.

So when he'd reached the spot where the cart path joined the main road at the same moment the wagon was passing by, he'd accepted William Farmer's offer of a ride for what it was—a sign that the journey would go smoothly if he didn't turn away from the gifts that were offered.

No one ever said gifts like this came without a price.

But, he thought with a sour glance at the farmer, if he had to listen to the man *hoo-whee* all the way to Wizard City, the price of this particular gift was a bit steep.

"You really going up to Wizard City to talk to a wizard?" William asked.

"I am."

"Hoo-whee! Don't know as I'd want to do that. They's not like regular folks. Don't matter that they's the Justice Makers. Got that magic in them that makes them different. Wouldn't want to be jawing with the likes of them."

Sebastian looked sideways at William. "Have you ever seen a wizard?"

"Seen 'em, sure. They prowl the marketplaces in the city from time to time just like everybody else. But never talked to one—and hope I never do."

Something—a change in inflection, a shift in the way William held himself—made Sebastian look at the man more closely.

"Why do you do that?" he asked, curious.

"Do what?"

"Talk like that. You're not a hayseed."

"What makes you think I'm not?" William sounded indignant.

Sebastian smiled, but it wasn't a friendly smile. "You try too hard. The hayseeds I've run across always give themselves away, but they try to talk better than they do at home. You roll in the words like a . . ." He couldn't think of anything to compare it to that wouldn't be an insult.

"Like a pig in muck," William said.

Sebastian tipped his head. "All right." He paused,

then added, "You may be a farmer, but you're not a hay-seed."

William was silent for the first time since he'd picked up Sebastian. Finally he said, "Are you going to rob me?"

"I'm not a thief," Sebastian snapped. "Besides, robbing you after you gave me a ride"—*Wouldn't be a kindness*—"would be wrong." He studied the farmer in the dusky light. The clothes were sufficiently worn-out to be a practical choice if a man was going to spend a day traveling along muddy or dusty roads—or they could have been the best clothes the man owned. As soon as he'd heard William speak, he'd assumed the latter. And any would-be thief, after listening to William for a minute, would figure there was nothing easy to steal and either endure the chatter for the length of the journey or escape at the first crossroads that offered an excuse to leave.

All in all, it provided a camouflage against potential predators that didn't change the resonance of the man's nature, like a rabbit whose fur changed from brown to white to better match the land when summer turned to winter.

Sebastian looked over his shoulder at the baskets of fruits and vegetables that filled the back of the wagon. "Isn't there a market closer to your home? You said it's a day's journey to the city."

William nodded. "And today it was a long day's journey. I usually reach the city well before sunset. Guess those delays were meant for a reason." He shrugged. "I sell half of what I harvest at the market in my town. The other half I bring up to the city."

"Why?"

"It's a kindness." William hesitated. "Someone told me that what you give to the world comes back to you. I guess there's truth in that."

Sebastian looked away. The waning daylight was enough to travel by, but not enough, he hoped, for the farmer to see his face clearly.

He remembered Glorianna, with those clear green eyes focused on him, telling him the same thing. *What you give comes back to you, Sebastian. It's not tit for tat—life isn't that simple—but what you give always comes back to you.*

His heart ached. He missed his cousins. Especially Glorianna. There was a bond between them, something more than he felt with Nadia or Lee. Nothing . . . carnal. Never that, despite his nature. But her words had always sunk deep into his heart, had been the reason he'd learned to consider human needs as well as his own when he hunted as an incubus. Hearing her words coming from a stranger . . .

No matter what landscapes she might be walking now, no matter what she might be doing as a rogue Landscaper, Glorianna Belladonna wouldn't bring terrifying death into a landscape. Guardians and Guides, the world held enough of its own terrors without unleashing more.

"It's like this," William said. "A few years ago, things were bad. The farm is good land, and I worked hard, but I could never make things what they could be. Crops were poor, and I couldn't get a decent price at the market. I turned to drink, and I turned mean. Stone-hearted, I guess you could say. Blamed my neighbors, blamed the merchants, blamed the land. Blamed everyone and felt sorry for myself.

"So one day I packed the wagon and came up to Wizard City. The merchants laughed at the country farmer, and the price offered for what I had in the wagon . . . Might as well throw it in the street as take what they were offering.

"It was close to sunset, and I was on my way home, since I couldn't afford to spend the night in the city. I picked up this girl walking along the road. Was going to drive by, but she lifted a hand and asked if she could have a ride to the next bridge. Said it would be a kindness."

William shook his head. "Don't know why I stopped.

I wasn't feeling kindly toward anyone. But I gave her a ride. She asked about the produce in the wagon, and I spoke my mind, poured it out like I was draining a festering wound.

"When I was done, she said, 'There are people in the city who could use the food in this wagon. The poor in the outer circle. The children who are outcast for one reason or another, who feed on despair and never know the sweet taste of hope. A stone heart can only harvest stones. What you give to the world will come back to you.' "

"And I said, 'Who says so?' and she said, 'I do.' "

" 'And who are you?' And she said—"

"Belladonna," Sebastian whispered.

William nodded. "Didn't know what that name meant. Not then. But after I let her off near the next bridge—almost the same place where I met up with you, as a matter of fact—I turned the wagon back to the city. Went to a poor section in the outer circle and sold off my produce for pennies.

"Some of the youngsters couldn't even scrape up a penny between them for a handful of fruit and a few vegetables."

Sebastian swallowed hard. There had been times when he'd been one of those children—running wild in the streets, as cunning and dangerous as animals. Then Nadia would arrive and take him back to her home for a few weeks or months—until Koltak showed up and the cycle started again. The children in Aurora, Nadia's home village, knew what he was, and their name-calling and taunts revealed a nature more vicious and cruel than any creature he'd met in the Den, but being with Nadia meant being with Lee and Glorianna. Their love and acceptance couldn't erase the cruelty, but without that tempering, he would have become the kind of incubus that was feared—the kind that thought of humans as nothing more than prey.

"So I told them they could have the food in exchange for doing a kindness for someone else," William continued.

When the farmer didn't say anything more, Sebastian prodded. "What happened?"

"Things changed," William said quietly. "Not all at once. It doesn't happen that way. But I brought up a wagon of produce each week once the land started to ripen and sold it in that section of the city. And things started to change. The children who paid for the food I gave them by doing a kindness for someone else helped old shopkeepers by sweeping the sidewalk or cleaning the shops. Some began to learn the merchant trade and were given cots in the back rooms and food as pay.

"Things changed for me, too. The land became richer. What I brought to the home market got a better price, and I began to prosper. One day at the market, I met a fine woman who wasn't too proud to be a country farmer's wife. We've got two children now, and that's a wonder to me." He paused and cleared his throat, as if emotions and memories had choked him for a moment.

"It's still a poor part of the city, but it's different now. Troublemakers aren't comfortable there and don't stay long. Folks look beyond their own doors these days and give their neighbors a helping hand. And I still bring a wagon of produce each week once the land ripens."

"Did you ever see her again?" Sebastian asked.

William nodded. "Couple years ago. I was selling my last bushel of apples, and this woman held out a penny and smiled at me. By then I knew who she was, what she was, how *dangerous* she was. But I tell you, I don't care what other folks say about her. She gave me a chance to change things the day I gave her a ride, and nothing but good has come from it." He raised a hand and pointed. "There's the city's south gate. I'll be turning off once we get past it. Will you be able to get on all right after that?"

"I know the way to the Wizards' Hall," Sebastian replied.

The land around them wasn't flat, but the hill upon which Wizard City had been built dominated the countryside, as if some massive creature swimming beneath the surface had suddenly arched its back. No, more like a giant dog stretching its back and front legs in an invitation to play and pushing the earth up with its movement. The hill sloped gradually on this side, giving people enough of a foothold to build houses and spiraling roads that led to the plateau where the Wizards' Hall and Tower looked down on the rest of the city. The other side of the hill was too steep for anything but pasturing sheep and goats.

They drove through the south gate in the high stone wall that circled the hill. William stopped his horses long enough for Sebastian to climb down.

"Travel lightly," William said.

Sebastian nodded. "Thank you for the kindness." He watched the wagon until it disappeared around a curve. Then he strode in the opposite direction toward a courtyard that was as old as the city.

In the beginning, the courtyard had been a place for meditation, for quieting one's heart and thoughts before climbing the Thousand Stairs to Justice. Now it was flanked by barracks for the hard-eyed guards who kept order in the lower levels of the city, and he doubted if anyone who lingered in that tired place, with its dying trees and weed-choked flower beds, found any peace there.

He didn't know if there had been a thousand stairs when they had been created or if someone had called them that because it sounded impressive. There wouldn't be a thousand now, since the roads that were built afterward eliminated some of them, but it was still a climb that tested the strength of a man's legs—and his determination to reach the top.

And it was still the fastest way up to the plateau where the wizards, the Justice Makers, reigned.

He heard the bell chime nine times as he stepped into the courtyard. Guards who had been lounging against the buildings straightened when they saw him. Ignoring them, he settled one strap of his pack over his shoulder and strode to the back of the courtyard as if he had every right to be there.

And he did. Anyone could petition the wizards for help. Of course, asking for help wasn't the same as getting any.

The moment his foot touched the first stair, the guards lost interest in him. Wizards' magic supposedly had built the stairs and still resided in them. It was said that the audience was merely a formality, that the wizards knew all that was needed about the petitioner by the time the person climbed the last stair.

He didn't believe that was true. Even so, as he climbed he tried to empty his mind of everything but moving from one stair to the next. He didn't want to remember the other times he'd been in this city—or the one and only time he'd seen the Wizards' Hall.

But his muscles tightened, his heart pounded, and the despair and bitter anger that had colored so much of his childhood was a heavy rock strapped to his back with chains forged by cruel words.

He'd climbed these stairs once before.

How old had he been? Five? Maybe six? Just lingering at the edge of the street where he lived, as much to get away from the latest woman who was looking after him as to watch three girls playing catch with a bright-colored ball. He watched them, drinking in their laughter and happiness, unaware of his own nature or why their emotions made him feel as if he were gulping down cool water after being thirsty for so long.

A girl missed the catch, and the ball rolled right to him. He picked it up, and as he looked at the girls, he felt their happiness change to wariness. He knew what other boys would have done—kept the ball, since it was the kind of pretty toy rarely seen in this part of the city, or thrown the ball hard at one of the girls to scare her or hit her so she'd cry. But he wanted to hear the girls laugh again, so he tossed the ball gently to one of them. They studied him a moment, then went back to their game. But when the ball came around to the one who had missed it before, she motioned him forward and tossed the ball to him. And the triangle of girls became a square of four children playing catch and having fun.

Then the woman stomped out of the building and dragged him inside to the cramped, smelly rooms he called home.

She screamed at him about the demon inside him and the depraved nature she'd been told to watch for. Then she hit him, her heavy hand cracking across his face hard enough to send him to the floor.

But he'd scrambled to his feet, dodged past her . . . and ran until he reached the courtyard and the Thousand Stairs to Justice.

Some of the other women who had looked after him had been a little kinder. They'd told him his father was an important man, a wizard. But children weren't allowed to live in the Wizards' Hall, so he had to stay with them. He'd accepted that, had never questioned their explanation.

He raced up the stairs, his young legs fueled by anger. He hadn't seen his father often, and the feelings that flowed out of the man made him uneasy, but that didn't matter now. His father was an important man. His father was a wizard. And his father, after learning how mean the woman had been, would take him someplace else to live.

Yes, that's what would happen. He would go live in a nice house with a *kind* woman who didn't yell at him all the time or say bad things about him or hit him. And maybe there would be children to play with. Children who liked him, who wouldn't call him names.

The need for that kind woman and those children swelled inside him, blotting out the anger. Hope filled him as he raced up the stairs.

When he finally reached the top of the stairs and ran along the path that led to the street and the high stone walls beyond, a vine of doubt curled around the hope and tried to smother it.

How was he supposed to get inside and find his father? What if he went inside the Petitioners' Hall and asked for Koltak and the other wizards just sent him away? He *had* to get inside!

Then luck, or fate, or the nature of Ephemera gave him the opportunity. A man walked out of the wrought-iron gate next to the Petitioners' Hall and gave it a negligent shove to close it. The gate stopped a hand-width away from locking.

He ran across the street and pulled the gate open just enough to slip inside. A different world, with more trees and greenery than he'd ever seen. He wandered along the paths, his father momentarily forgotten. It was so *clean* here. No smell of garbage or sour bodies.

Then, hearing laughter, he turned and made the discovery that changed his life.

Boys, not much older than him, running along another path toward the buildings at the other end of the courtyard garden. Boys. Living at the Wizards' Hall.

He could have lived here, in this clean place—if his father had wanted him.

He stepped off the path and sat down next to a bush, curling up as much as he could to keep from being noticed. He cried silently while all the cruel words that had been said to him over the years took root deep in his heart.

Hearing footsteps on the path, he curled up tighter. But the footsteps stopped suddenly, the person stepped off the path and came around the bush—and he looked up at a woman with dark hair and dark, angry eyes. He flinched at the anger pouring off her, but when she crouched down, her voice was gentle.

"Who hit you?" she asked.

"The woman," he muttered.

"Your mother?"

He shook his head. "The woman I lives with. She . . . keeps me."

"Are you an orphan?"

Another head shake. "Don't know my mother. My father . . . he doesn't want me because I'm an incubastard." He wasn't sure what that was, but he knew now it was the reason he would never live in a clean place with kind people.

"What's your name?"

"Sebastian."

"I'm Nadia." She hesitated, studying his face, staring deep into his green eyes. "Are you Koltak's son?"

He nodded.

"Well, then. I guess that makes me your auntie." She stood up and held out her hand. "Would you like to come live with me, Sebastian?"

The anger inside her had faded to sadness, but the warmth and kindness beneath the sadness, at the core of her, dazzled his young heart.

Getting to his feet, he took the offered hand—and the two of them walked away from the Wizards' Hall.

Opportunities and choices. That was how Aunt Nadia explained how the currents of power worked. When a person made a heart wish, that wish resonated through the currents and things would happen to give the person an opportunity to make that wish come true. Like a gate not closing all the way. Like a woman, distressed and angry over the disappearance of her husband, hurrying down a path and stopping suddenly at the exact spot where a boy, who had the same green eyes as her own children, was hiding. Like a hand offered—and accepted.

Sebastian shook his head as he continued to climb.

Travel lightly. Think of something besides the past. Think of sitting in Philo's courtyard on a summer night, drinking wine and watching the ebb and flow of people looking for a taste of the dark side. Think of sitting in Nadia's kitchen, a room that felt bright and warm on even the dreariest day. Think of Nadia's birds, those bright, playful little chatterheads. Travel lightly—or this place will swallow you whole.

His legs burned by the time he climbed the last stair. His heart burned, too, but not from exertion.

A cobblestone path cut between the stone walls that protected the houses of the wealthy who now shared the plateau with the wizards, leading to the street. Directly across the street was the Petitioners' Hall—the only entrance common folk had to the part of the hill the wizards considered their exclusive domain.

As he crossed the street, he glanced at the structure that dominated the right-hand side of the wizards' estate.

The Tower was the oldest structure in the city, and even now, centuries after it had been built, wizards still walked sentry duty, still kept watch.

For what? What had they once feared that they had built on the highest piece of land in this landscape? What did they still fear that they continued to keep watch?

He shook his head and banished those thoughts. Wizards claimed they feared nothing. He knew that wasn't true—at least, not for the last fifteen years. Which was the only reason he risked entering this city.

The Petitioners' Hall was connected to the wall surrounding the wizards' private domain, separated from the buildings that made up the Wizards' Hall by the expansive courtyard and garden he'd wandered through so many years ago. It still looked open and friendly with all its trees and greenery—if you didn't consider the fact that only one gate next to the Petitioners' Hall provided a way back into the rest of the city.

He opened the door of the Petitioners' Hall and stepped into a long room. Stone floor, stone walls, and unadorned wooden benches that were, no doubt, uncomfortable if anyone had to sit on one for very long. The room was lit by oil lamps suspended from the ceiling, which had to burn all the time, since there were no windows to let in light. The place felt cold and hard as the stone it was built from.

He left the door open, more to give himself a way to escape than to indicate discourtesy, and strode to the desk at the back of the room.

Here there was some luxury. The big wooden desk gleamed in the lamplight. Beneath it was a pool of thick carpet that would keep the cold damp of stone from seeping into the feet of whoever was on duty.

Tonight it was a surly young man who closed the book he'd been reading and folded his hands over it. The badge he wore on his robe declared him a second-level wizard to anyone who knew what the symbols stood for.

"I need to see Wizard Koltak," Sebastian said.

"It's late," the young wizard snapped. "Wizard Koltak isn't on duty this evening to see petitioners. Take a seat and I'll see who—"

"Nevertheless, Koltak will see me."

The wizard looked outraged. "And who are you?"

"Sebastian. From the Den of Iniquity."

The surly look gave way to fascinated revulsion. So. This one had heard the stories that had been whispered in the student quarters—and perhaps still were. A lesson for the lusty and foolish.

The wizard grabbed a small piece of parchment from the stack on the corner of his desk. Snatching up the quill and dipping it into the inkwell, he didn't notice that he dribbled ink on the desk's gleaming wood. Hurried scribbles. The ink barely had time to dry before the wizard folded the parchment and shouted, "Boy!"

A boy dozing on a bench close to the desk scrambled to answer the summons. The folded parchment was handed off, and the boy dashed out the door in the back of the room.

Your pen dribbles. A simple phrase that held a wealth of meanings when an incubus said it. It was tempting to see if this young wizard would find the call of an incubus more alluring than that of a succubus, but he already had enough enemies among the wizards.

So he just gave the wizard a lazy smile that suggested traveling to reach this place wasn't the reason he looked disheveled.

A few minutes later, the boy dashed back into the room, breathless, and handed a folded piece of parchment to the wizard. The man looked startled as he read the command, but he said, "The boy will lead you."

Giving the wizard an insolent salute, Sebastian fol-

lowed the boy out the back door and across the courtyard. Instead of going through the door of the main
building, the boy turned to the right and led him to another door.

The hair on the back of Sebastian's neck rose as he
noticed that the windows on either side of the door had
a queer sparkle in places where the light from the courtyard lamps touched the glass. Wooden shutters were
folded back on the outside of the windows.

The boy pushed the door open and entered the dark
space.

Sebastian heard the clink of glass against metal, then
the scrape of a match. Staying in the doorway, he
watched the boy light the candle and replace the globe
over the metal candleholder.

When the boy turned to leave, Sebastian stepped into
the room to let him pass. But when the boy reached for
the handle to pull the door closed, some instinct made
Sebastian grab the wood and growl, "Leave it open."

The boy bolted into the night.

Not sure why he'd responded that way, Sebastian
looked at the door—and felt a shiver run down his
spine.

No handle on this side. No way for a person inside
this room to open the door.

Slipping his pack from his shoulder, he set it against
the door and went over to one of the windows, alert for
any sound in the courtyard.

Thick glass that extended into the stone. A mesh of
wire embedded in the glass. Even if someone managed
to break the glass, he still wouldn't be able to escape
through a window.

Turning, Sebastian studied the room. A table, two
chairs, and the globed candleholder. No other visible
means of exiting the room, although there probably was
a hidden door or other kind of opening.

What it all meant was that once the door was closed,
the only way a person could leave this room was if
someone on the outside opened the door.

His hands trembled as he went back to the door and picked up his pack. After settling it over his shoulder, he shifted so his back wasn't completely exposed to the courtyard. At least he'd have some warning if someone tried to rush him and shove him into the room.

A scrape of boot on stone. Sebastian scanned the courtyard. The place *looked* so open, but the lamplight played with the surroundings in such a way that there were patches of deep shadow that could hide anything.

"Why are you here?" a harsh voice said behind him.

Sebastian whipped his head around to look into the room and felt a muscle in his neck twinge in protest. He swore silently as he realized he'd been caught by a sleight of hand. There was no one in the courtyard, but that magical distraction had allowed Koltak to slip into the room without revealing the location of the hidden door.

"Did you hear that I was finally being considered for a seat on the Wizards' Council and decided to remind everyone of why I've been passed over all these years?" Koltak kept his voice low, but that didn't diminish the venomous tone.

I don't give a damn about you or your ambitions. "I came here to report an incident to the Justice Makers," Sebastian said, keeping his voice just as low. "I asked for you because I thought you would prefer it rather than have me talk to another wizard."

"The Justice Makers have no interest in the Den of Iniquity or what goes on there," Koltak said.

"Even when a human is murdered?"

Koltak hesitated, then made a sharp, angry gesture with his hand. "Come in then. You may think nothing of making your affairs public, but things are done differently here."

"I'll stay where I am."

Spots of color blazed on Koltak's cheeks. "What do you think I'll do? Lock you in this room and deny you were here?"

"If you could get away with it, you'd do it in a heartbeat," Sebastian snapped.

"As if anyone would care if you disappeared."

"One person would."

The unspoken name—and the threat—hung between them.

Belladonna.

"We think the woman who was killed came from a wealthy family. She always wore a wide gold bracelet."

"Every wife of a prosperous man wears a gold bracelet," Koltak growled. "What did she look like?"

"I don't know! There wasn't enough left of her face to describe it!"

Koltak paled, but Sebastian couldn't tell if it was because of what he'd said or because he'd raised his voice.

"Listen to me, Koltak. Something came into the Den that is brutal and vicious. It killed a succubus a few days ago. Now it's killed a human woman."

"Maybe it will wipe the Den clean and stop all you demons from luring decent humans into doing things that will ruin their lives."

"It's not just demons who live in the Den. And I'm half-human, remember?"

Koltak's lips pulled back in a rabid snarl. "There's *nothing* human about you!"

Sebastian looked away. Apparently those heart-wounds hadn't scarred over enough after all. Then he forced himself to look Koltak in the eyes. "You're right. How could there be anything human in me with a succubus for a mother and you for a father?"

"Get out!"

He took one step back, which left him standing on the threshold. "There's something out there, Koltak. The Den may not be its only hunting ground. I did what I was supposed to do. I reported this to the Justice Makers. If you do nothing because I was the one who came here, then the blood of the next person who dies will be on your hands, not mine."

He stepped out of the room, unwilling to turn his back on the man whose seed had helped create him— the man who hated him for existing.

When the door swung shut, hiding him from Koltak's view, he pivoted and moved across the courtyard as fast as he could without running. He had to get off this hill, get out of this city. Wizards ruled here, commanded the guards. He could be detained, locked away.

It felt like forever before he reached the wrought-iron gate next to the Petitioners' Hall. When the gate resisted his efforts to open it, his chest tightened until he struggled to breathe.

Trapped. Was Koltak watching, exerting his will and wizard's magic to keep the gate closed until . . . ? Until guards showed up and decided a man who couldn't get out of the courtyard must be dangerous and should be detained for questioning. Or, worse, Koltak would appear and tell the guards to take him back to that room for questioning. Latch the shutters and close the door— and no one but Koltak would know he was trapped in that room. Oh, the guards would know, but they wouldn't care what happened to an incubus who had dared enter the city.

Detain him. Contain him. Kill him.

He had to get out of here!

Travel lightly, travel lightly, travel lightly.

Sebastian took a step back from the gate and closed his eyes.

A simple gate designed to open only from inside of the courtyard. A simple latch that might be a bit rusty. That was all. A simple gate that would open easily at his touch. Then he would leave this courtyard, leave this city . . . and go home.

Sebastian opened his eyes and reached for the gate. A gentle tug. A click as the lock slid back.

The gate swung open.

His heart pounded, but he walked through the gate and headed for the Thousand Stairs, keeping his pace easy, as if he were strolling the main street of the Den.

As he reached the stone path that led to the stairs, he glanced back—and saw guards hurrying toward the Petitioners' Hall.

They have no interest in me, nor I in them, beyond simple curiosity, Sebastian thought. His stride lengthened, despite his efforts to appear unconcerned that the guards might notice him. *My business in the city is done. I'm going home to enjoy a meal and a pleasant evening with friends. I'm going home. To the Den.*

No hue and cry sounded behind him, and by the time he reached the stairs, he was trembling with relief. He paused at the edge of the stairs to give himself time to regain his composure—or as much as he could while he was still within the city walls. No point getting away from the Wizards' Hall if he took a spill down the stairs and ended up with broken bones that would leave him helpless.

He took a deep breath and let it out slowly. Then he put his foot on the first stair for the descent that would begin his journey home.

Koltak watched the guards mill around the courtyard gate. No point slipping a suggestion beneath their surface thoughts a second time. There was no longer anything tangible for them to deal with to confirm the "instinct" or "intuition" that had compelled them to check on the gate beside the Petitioners' Hall. Even if he gave them another nudge, Sebastian had too much of a lead now and could elude any guards long enough to get out of the city.

Stepping back into the room, he closed the door, then snuffed out the candle. He walked to the back wall and, with the experience of the years he'd lived within the Wizards' Hall, touched the concealed latch for the hidden door.

As soon as the door swung open, Koltak slipped out of the room, then paused long enough to make sure the door was securely locked before hurrying along the corridors that were used mostly by the servants.

He gave silent thanks to whatever Guide was watching over him that he made it back to his suite of rooms without running into anyone who might wonder why he'd been coming back from the direction of the Petitioners' Hall—and the detention rooms.

Not that the other wizards would wonder for long. By morning, they'd *all* know who had asked to see him. It would have been different if he could have contained the problem, but . . .

Koltak stared out his sitting room window. It didn't face the right direction, but he stared anyway, as if that alone would somehow locate Sebastian before he got out of the city. Again.

For thirty years he'd been punished for that indiscretion, that weak hungering for the kind of sexual gratification that made human women little better than a container for a man's seed. Plenty of wizards had indulged themselves with succubi. *Plenty.* But their liaisons hadn't threatened to topple the power structure that gave wizards a place in the world, that made them the Justice Makers.

How could there be anything human in me with a succubus for a mother and you for a father?

Just words flung out in anger. Sebastian didn't know the truth. *Couldn't* know what his existence meant.

Secrets tightly held within the Wizards' Hall were flaunted daily because that whelp had been born. Oh, most of the citizens wouldn't realize what it meant that a mating between a wizard and a succubus had borne fruit, but the wizards knew it branded them for what they were.

Something not quite human. Beings whose ability to influence minds sprang from the same roots as the seductive power the incubi and succubi unfurled to attract their prey.

We've paid for our secrets. We pay every day by keeping order, by standing for justice. We've paid.

But tonight, the thing he'd personally feared the most had finally displayed itself.

Sebastian was not only an incubus; he also had some

measure of the wizards' kind of power. He couldn't have opened that gate otherwise, couldn't have shrugged aside Koltak's mental persuasion so quickly that there wasn't time for the guards to arrive.

If the other wizards realized Sebastian controlled the same magic as the Justice Makers, everything he, Koltak, had done for the past thirty years to make up for his lustful mistake and prove himself worthy of the kind of authority he'd always craved would have been for nothing. So there really was only one thing to do.

Somehow, some way, Sebastian had to be eliminated once and for all.

Sebastian was a stone's throw beyond the city's southern gate when he heard the bell ring twelve times. Midnight. The city gates were locked at midnight, and no one could enter or leave until the following dawn.

A shiver of relief went through him. Turning east, he struck off across the open land. Not that it would make any difference if Koltak ordered guards to come after him on horseback or on foot, but being off the road made him feel like he had a better chance of getting away from this landscape before his father—he let out a quiet, bitter laugh—found a way to force him to remain.

Besides, if he went back along the road, there wasn't a closer bridge than the one he'd crossed to get to this boil on the world's backside. Out here, there were bound to be other bridges. They might not take him back to the Den, but they would get him away from here, and that was the most important thing right now. Except . . .

If he was delayed in getting back home, who else might die in the time he was away?

He *had* to get back to the Den!

He'd put a fair distance between himself and the city when a veil of clouds covered the moon. He froze, unwilling to shift his feet. The land suddenly felt soft and strange, as if it were strewn with hidden traps. Which was foolish. He'd spent the past fifteen years in a landscape that never saw the sun rise. He was used to traveling at night.

But that was different. He knew the dangers that lived in and around the dark landscape he called home. Out here . . . There was something *wrong* out here.

A chill went through him. His skin felt clammy, as if he'd brushed against something that had smeared some kind of illness inside him.

Trying to shake off the sensation, he listened for any movement or sound that would confirm the wrongness. All he heard was the burble of water. He forced himself to move, and, following the sound, he found the creek. It was narrow enough that a man could scramble down the bank and jump across the water, but there were two rough planks stretched from one bank to the other. Since the planks didn't look sturdy enough or wide enough to support the smallest cart, there was only one reason for them to be there.

A Bridge had put those planks across the creek, using that particular magic to create a link between landscapes.

Sebastian studied the planks. Had to be a resonating bridge. Those were the ones that tended to be in places that were found more by chance than design. Which meant he could end up anywhere the moment he stepped off the other side of the bridge.

Just cross over, Sebastian thought as he hooked both arms through the straps of his pack and settled it comfortably on his back. *You can't end up in any place that doesn't live in your heart. Isn't that what every child is taught? That a person is where he deserves to be? Isn't that what Koltak always said when he dragged you back to that thrice-cursed city? But Nadia always said life was a journey, and the landscapes reflected the journey. That even when bad things happened, the journey eventually would lead a person where his heart needed to be.*

He looked back toward Wizard City. He hadn't deserved to be caged inside those walls simply because he'd been born and the succubus who had birthed him handed him over to his father instead of leaving him somewhere to die. He hadn't needed the cruelty or pain that had shaped his childhood.

But if he hadn't been shaped by those things, would he have known Nadia or Lee or Glorianna? Would he have ended up in the Den, a place where he belonged?

Sebastian shook his head. Pointless thoughts. An exercise in self-indulgence.

Then the feeling of sickness shuddered through him again. The memory of feeling sand beneath his feet instead of the hard ground of the alley made him shiver. And with every second that passed, the conviction grew stronger that if he didn't cross the bridge *now,* he might never again see a landscape he recognized.

"Guardians of the Light and Guides of the Heart, please listen to me," he whispered as he set one foot on the planks. "I need to get back to the Den. I *need* to get back to the Den."

He hurried over the bridge.

Night. Open land. Nothing significantly different enough to tell him where he was—or even to indicate that he *had* crossed over to another landscape.

Get away from the bridge.

His body was in motion before he could decide on a direction. Maybe because there was only one direction that mattered—*away.*

✳

In this flat, undulating form, It flowed beneath the surface of the land as easily as It flowed through water, moving swiftly toward the mound of earth. It had found the Dark Ones—the ones who had opened up the darkness in human hearts and had forced the world to bring It into being.

Then It slowed, circled, headed back to that finger of

water that was too insignificant to hold any of the creatures It controlled.

For a moment, as It had passed the water, It had brushed against something . . . familiar.

Nothing there now. And yet . . .

It reshaped a piece of Itself. A tentacle broke through the soil, rising up like some strange, malignant weed. The tip explored, found the planks that still resonated with the heart that had recently crossed over to a different place. More of the tentacle emerged from the soil, elongating as the tip moved across the planks.

Yes, It recognized the resonance of this heart. One of the ones who had eluded Its attempt to alter the alley in that dark hunting ground called the Den.

The tip reached the other side, pressed into the dirt to feel the resonance of this other landscape.

Ah! It recognized this place. It had hunted in this dark landscape recently. The creatures who lived there had been a delicious feast, although not as savory as human prey.

Nothing was as savory as human prey.

Its power flowed through the tentacle. Pulsed in the tip that pushed into the ground.

The world struggled to resist Its dark resonance, which surprised It. It probed a little more, trying to tap into the Dark currents that flowed through this landscape. Then It withdrew, wary now. Almost afraid.

A powerful resonance flowed through the Dark currents. Something much stronger than anything It had found in the lair made by the enemies who had caged It long ago.

Unwilling to yield completely, It tried again, pushing the tentacle back into the ground near the wooden planks.

Just a small bit of darkness, It wheedled. *A change that won't even be noticed in a dark landscape. Something that will protect this place from dangerous hearts.*

Ephemera hesitated. Then the world surrendered a

small circle of ground near the bridge—a piece now malleable to Its will.

Perhaps that was for the best. A small anchor would be hard to detect by whatever heart flowed through this landscape, but that anchor would be enough to give It access to this place.

Careful to conceal Its glee in having tricked Ephemera into giving up a piece of itself, no matter how small, It reshaped the ground to provide an access point into one of Its own landscapes.

The tentacle tip withdrew from the soil. The ground in front of It lifted slightly, revealing sod covering a latticework of sticks that formed a trapdoor big enough to fit a full-grown man. Two large legs emerged from the trapdoor, testing the ground around the burrow.

Satisfied that It had a way into this landscape, It drew Its tentacle back across the plank and reshaped it to match the rest of Its current form.

Then It turned and headed for the mound and the minds that resonated so closely with Its own. It was time to slip into that twilight place between wakefulness and dreams. Once the Dark Ones knew It had returned, It would be that much closer to regaining what rightfully belonged to It.

The world.

Tired and thirsty, Sebastian trudged up another low rise. He still didn't know where he was, had seen nothing but open countryside since he crossed over at the bridge. At least the trees he'd passed didn't look alien, even in the moonlight, so there was hope that he'd crossed over to a landscape that had some connection to the Den.

As he headed down the other side of the rise, a black horse pricked its ears and ambled over to meet him—and he knew where he was.

It was a beautiful creature, but its looks didn't make it any less a demon. Seeing the waterhorse confirmed he was in a dark landscape that bordered the Den. Unfortunately, it also confirmed he still had a long walk ahead of him before he got back to the Den itself.

Sebastian kept walking, aware that he could be ensnared by the demon's magic as easily as any human. But the waterhorse suddenly lunged, blocking his path. Its nostrils quivered, as if it wanted to get a good whiff of his scent but was afraid to get within reach. Which was queer behavior for one of these demons. They usually wanted to entice humans into taking a fatal ride.

Moving slowly, Sebastian held out his hand. The waterhorse stretched its neck, bringing its muzzle close enough to snuffle him. Then it stepped back, tossed its head, and headed toward a glint of water.

When Sebastian didn't follow, the waterhorse returned.

Sebastian shook his head. "I know what you are. I'm not going near water with the likes of you."

The waterhorse tossed its head. Stamped a foot.

"No," Sebastian said.

A whicker that sounded sad. Almost a plea.

Not knowing what to make of the demon's behavior, he looked toward the glint of water—and felt a sick certainty that he already knew what the waterhorse wanted him to see.

He moved blindly toward the water, not even realizing his hand now rested on the waterhorse's neck. They stopped close to the remains of something dark and bloated that rested on the bank of the large pond. He tried to move closer but couldn't do it. The waterhorse had used its particular magic to bind his hand to its neck, preventing him from getting too close to the edge of the pond.

Not that he really wanted to get closer. Guardians and Guides, this was a *pond,* probably fed by small streams. The waterhorses were the creatures to be feared in this landscape. But something had not only killed a waterhorse; it had ripped out great chunks of flesh. Feeding.

The waterhorse's body quivered as it backed away from the pond, pulling him with it.

No humans would regret the death of a waterhorse. After all, those demons drowned any humans foolish enough to ride them.

But the way that body was ripped up . . .

How many predators had found their way into the dark landscapes? And where had they come from?

"I . . ." Sebastian cleared his throat. "I have to get back to the Den. I have to tell the others about this." He tried to step away from the waterhorse, but his hand was still ensnared in its magic.

It turned its head and studied him. Then it released its hold on his hand. But when Sebastian started walking away from the pond, it blocked his path.

"What do you want?" He was tired, hungry, frustrated, and scared. Oh, yes. He was scared. He didn't need another demon playing games with him.

The waterhorse tossed its head, then lifted each foot in turn.

Four feet that weren't tired. Four legs that could run faster than his own.

"You're offering me a ride?" Sebastian asked.

The waterhorse bobbed its head.

"No tricks? No gallops into deep water to drown me?"

Head shake.

"Why?" He knew the answer before the waterhorse turned its head to look at the pond. *They're scared, too.*

He wasn't used to riding horses, and he mounted with little skill and no grace. The waterhorse didn't seem to care, and as he felt the tingle of magic ensnare his legs, he acknowledged one advantage to riding this particular mount—unless a waterhorse chose to release its prey, a person *couldn't* fall off.

So they raced over the land and splashed through streams until Sebastian saw a cairn. As they passed it, he felt the tingle that meant they'd passed through a border and were now in another landscape.

Borders and boundaries, Glorianna called them. Boundaries separated one kind of landscape from another—or the landscapes controlled by one Landscaper from those controlled by another Landscaper—and could be crossed only by using a bridge. Borders marked the places where similar landscapes belonging to a Landscaper were connected, despite how much physical distance existed between them.

That was the way things worked in Ephemera. A man might not be able to cross a bridge to reach a neighboring village if he didn't resonate with that particular landscape, but he could cross a border and walk through a village in an entirely different part of the world.

A few minutes later, they were racing along the edge of a cliff Sebastian recognized—just as he recognized the lake. He felt the waterhorse hesitate, no doubt tempted by the combination of deep water and a rider. But it kept to the land instead of looking for a way to scramble down the cliff. Shortly after that, the waterhorse slowed to an ambling walk and stopped at the door of Sebastian's cottage.

They could still hear the lake performing a slow dance with the sand and stone on the beach.

The waterhorse sighed—and released him.

Sebastian slid off its back, grateful for its help and wary of its nature. "Thank you," he said, moving around the other demon until he had his hand closed around the handle of the cottage's front door.

It watched him for a moment, then turned and trotted back the way it had come.

He'd intended to drop his pack and head out for the Den, but a lingering scent of woman made him check the other rooms in the cottage.

He found Glorianna's note next to the bag of koffea beans.

Sebastian,
There's something I need to see in another landscape. Then I'll be back. We need to talk. Be careful.

No signature. She never signed her notes. Not even with an initial. Since he saw her so infrequently anymore, the unsigned notes made her seem less . . . real.

Considering what the wizards and other Landscapers thought of her, maybe that was her intention.

But—daylight!—the note meant she'd been close by. If he'd waited a few hours before riding out to Wizard City, he could have talked to *her* instead of facing Koltak.

A shiver went through him. He rubbed the back of his hand over his forehead. Was he ill? He certainly didn't feel well. But that could be nothing more than a sick feeling in his gut caused by seeing Wizard City again—and remembering things he tried hard to forget.

He rode Philo's bicycle back to the Den. As he coasted up to the courtyard, he wondered how long he'd been gone. Were the daylight landscapes now passing into another evening or just beginning to see the sunrise?

Since the Den never saw sunrise or sunset, what did it matter?

Admit it. You were disappointed that you hadn't seen daylight. That's one of the reasons you were willing to go to that city. To see the world in daylight. To feel the sun on your face. Didn't happen, though. Hasn't happened in years. After all, an incubus is the kind of lover women only want to meet in the dark.

Feeling unsettled, and trying to ignore the craving for the hunt growing inside him—a craving that was sharper than anything he'd felt in weeks—Sebastian walked the bicycle to the storage shed at the back of the courtyard. Teaser sat at a nearby table. Since there were plenty of tables available, the other incubus must have chosen to avoid the flirtatious games that usually took place at the tables closer to the street.

Which wasn't like Teaser at all.

"Why aren't you out trolling?" Sebastian asked as he pulled out a chair and sat down.

Teaser gave him a pale imitation of his usual cocky

grin. "Wasn't in the mood for it." He raised his half-empty mug of ale, then pointed a finger at Sebastian.

A few minutes later, Philo came to the table with a full tray. He set down two mugs of ale, a bowl of melted cheese, and a basket of Phallic Delights.

"He's been swilling ale for hours now," Philo muttered, not looking at either incubus. "Get him to eat something before he's so drunk he can't even manage a blundering grope."

Teaser snorted. "Like I'm interested in playing slap and tickle."

Sebastian, reaching for his mug, froze for a moment. Teaser wasn't interested? *Teaser?*

"What's wrong?" Sebastian looked from Teaser to Philo and back again. "Has something else happened?"

Philo wiped his hands on his apron and kept his eyes focused on the table. "You didn't tell him?"

"He just got here, didn't he?" Teaser snapped. "Hasn't even had time to swallow some ale and wash the taste of Wizard City out of his mouth."

"What's wrong?" Sebastian asked again.

Someone at another table called to Philo. He hurried away.

Teaser picked up a penis-shaped roll, swirled it in the melted cheese, and took a bite. Chew, swallow, swirl the next piece of the roll.

Sebastian plucked a Phallic Delight from the basket and swirled it in the cheese. The first bite was a sharp reminder that he hadn't eaten anything while he'd been away from the Den. Since Teaser didn't seem anxious to tell him what had happened—or find out what had taken place in Wizard City—he gave his attention to the simple meal.

Then Teaser glanced toward the front of the courtyard and muttered, "Could have done without seeing *her.*"

Glorianna? Sebastian looked in the same direction, his heart suddenly pounding. Then he looked away as quickly as Teaser had, hoping the succubus eyeing the other customers was too preoccupied with her own games to notice them.

"Can't say I'd feel sorry if that one disappeared," Teaser said, tearing off a piece of the Phallic Delight before dipping it in the cheese.

"You don't mean that," Sebastian said sharply.

Teaser flinched. "No, I don't. It's just . . . well . . . *that* one. You know the bitch will ooze over here and make snide comments about incubi eating cocks."

Sebastian huffed. "It's bread and cheese. We don't get a vote on what shape Philo chooses to make the rolls."

"Tell *her* that."

I'd rather not get that close. Since they usually weren't competing for the same prey, the incubi and succubi who lived in the Den tended to get along fairly well— and sometimes even played with one another for a night of mind-blowing sex. But that particular succubus . . . She didn't live in the Den, but she visited often enough, and every time he encountered her he felt . . . uneasy. She was sharper, darker, more predatory than the Den's residents, and there was a maliciousness to the way she played with her prey that made it clear to those who also played the game that she deliberately stripped all the fun out of sex and turned her prey's need into desperation and addiction. And she was just as malicious when she tried to lure an incubus into playing her particular game.

They sighed with relief when the succubus turned away from the courtyard.

Breaking the last roll in half, Sebastian scraped the remaining cheese out of the bowl. He handed one piece to Teaser and ate the other. Full, and yet still hungry for something food couldn't ease, he leaned back in his chair. "You ready to tell me what happened?"

Teaser lifted his mug, then set it down again without drinking. "The alley changed."

"What does that mean?"

"It's been altered," Teaser said, his voice sharpened

by uneasiness. He paused, clearly struggling with some strong emotions. "We figured we should move the ... remains. Couldn't just leave them there to attract other kinds of predators, could we? But the body was gone. In its place there are green plants growing in the middle of the alley right where the body had been."

Teaser stared at him. Sebastian looked away.

"Belladonna was here," he said reluctantly.

"So she did—"

"*No.* She wouldn't bring a killer into the Den. She had to be the one who altered things after we left the alley, but that's *all* she did. Although why she'd put plants in a dark alley is anyone's guess."

"Covering her tracks?"

Sebastian swore. "How many times do I have to say it, Teaser? I *know* her."

"You know the girl she was," Teaser replied. "Do you really know the Landscaper she's become?"

No. But he wouldn't admit that. Not to anyone. Because he had to believe Glorianna wasn't so different from the girl he'd known.

Teaser hesitated. "Maybe you should stay at the bordello tonight instead of going back to the cottage."

He almost snapped that an incubus couldn't afford to be afraid of the dark. Then it occurred to him that Teaser *was* afraid—afraid to be alone right now and afraid that anyone he invited to his room might give him more than he'd bargained for.

"I'm going back to the cottage," Sebastian said. "There's only one bed, but the couch is comfortable enough."

"You asking me to stay?"

Sebastian shrugged. He wasn't willing to play scaredy-boy, but he also wasn't going to insult his friend by indicating he knew which of them really needed company. Besides, Glorianna had said she would be back, and he wanted to be where she could find him easily.

"A couch," Teaser grumbled. "Course, you've also got

koffee, so I guess that's an even trade. All right, I'll keep you company. You settle with Philo, and I'll see if I can snag another ride with a demon cycle."

Sebastian remained at the table, knowing Philo would come to clear the dishes.

"Well?" Philo said, keeping his voice low even though there was no one at the nearby tables. "What happened in Wizard City? Did you get an audience?"

"We'll get no help from the Justice Makers. They don't care what happens in the Den."

Philo sighed. "We're on our own then."

Belladonna will help. He didn't think anyone else in the Den would find that thought comforting, so he said, "Yes, we're on our own."

🦂

It stretched out beneath the place where the Dark Ones dwelled. In the land above It, dogs howled a warning, only to be hushed or ignored; flocks and herds of animals stirred, alert and edgy, their simple minds aware that a hunter had come among them. But the best prey ignored their instincts, believing themselves powerful and superior.

It unfurled a thousand mental tentacles, sending them into that twilight place between wakefulness and dreams—that place that revealed the heart's hopes and fears. The wakeful mind denied or caged so many desires. The dreaming mind cloaked fears in symbols. But here, in the twilight, the heart couldn't hide or be denied. Here, in the twilight, was the true feast upon which It fed.

She's acting strange. My business depends on her family's wealth. Has she discovered I have a mistress?

I put those coins in the money box. I did! But they'll think I'm a thief and will send me to a different landscape. Maybe even a dark landscape.

It fed, and fed on, the fears, glutting Itself as It hadn't been able to do since that long-ago time when It lost the battle to control the world.

Yes, It whispered through the tentacles. *You are right to fear that. It will happen, has already happened.*

Sated, It withdrew the mental tentacles. It had found the Dark Ones. But something tickled old memories, nudging them into a different pattern. So It turned away, intending to leave the city, pleased that It knew where to find the Dark Ones but they didn't know how to find It.

Then a mind, rising up into the twilight from uneasy sleep, caught Its attention. Seduced by the powerful emotions, It extended a tentacle, slipped into that mind.

Yes, It whispered eagerly. *Yes, you have reason to fear, reason to hate. Yes.*

But the mind was rising to wakefulness too fast. There was strength there . . . and power that would recognize an intrusion.

It left the city, looking like a rippling shadow as It moved under the landscape. The last mind It had touched puzzled It. So much fear, so much rage, so much loathing. But It didn't understand the word that was the source of all those delicious feelings.

Sebastian.

Feeling awkward, Sebastian dropped a blanket and pillow on one end of the couch.

Foolish to feel that way. Lee had bunked on the couch any number of times when he'd come to visit.

But Lee was human. Teaser was not.

"Need anything else?" he asked.

"Nope," Teaser replied, pulling off his boots.

"Sleep well." Sebastian walked to his bedroom doorway. Before he stepped into the other room, Teaser said quietly, "Pleasant dreams."

He turned to face the other incubus, who watched him with too much understanding.

"There's a . . . feel . . . about you when you've abstained from hunting for too many days," Teaser said. "I know you need to feed the hunger, but . . . Just be careful, all right?"

Not knowing what to say, Sebastian nodded, walked into the bedroom, and closed the door.

Was it apparent to everyone? Or was it that Teaser, being an incubus, could spot the signs of a craving that had taken on the sharp edge of need?

He undressed, tossing his clothes on to a chair to deal with them later. Then he slipped into bed, extinguished the oil lamp on the bedside table, and pulled the sheet up to his waist.

In the dark, he felt the steady beating of his heart as he unfurled the power that made the incubi what they were. He let his mind drift as he sought a female mind yearning for a dream lover. This time he wouldn't try to shape the scenario. She could set the stage for this interlude. And in the twilight of waking dreams, he would provide a face and voice to her imaginary lover, would provide the sensation of touch, would create the stimulation that would arouse her until she came.

And he would feed on that arousal, on that orgasm, until it eased the hunger inside him. It wouldn't hurt her. He never hunted to cause harm. But the feelings he stimulated in the female were as necessary to his well-being as food and water and air.

Please.

He narrowed his focus to that female thought that resonated with something inside him and tried to strengthen the link between their minds.

I didn't want him to feel that way. I didn't encourage him to want . . . lustful things . . . from me. I didn't!

Ssh, Sebastian whispered soothingly. *It's all right.*

Why can't someone love me?

I can. I will.

The Landscapers will send me to a bad place. I just want—

What? What do you want?

I want to be safe. I want to be loved. I want to be someplace where I'm not afraid all the time.

He hesitated. This wasn't a female yearning for pleasure. Daylight! Why had his power pulled him toward her when she wasn't going to do anything to ease his hunger?

Please.

Something warm and sweet flowed through the link between them. Something that lived inside her, waiting to bloom. Something elusive and so seductive it took his breath away.

Come to me, he demanded. *Come to me.*

I—

The link between them snapped.

Sweating and frustrated, Sebastian furled his power.

What had just happened? And why? He had no sense of who she was or where she was. Nothing that would help him retrace his path and find her again.

And why would he want to find an obviously troubled female?

Something warm and sweet inside her and so, so seductive. Something that made him feel as if he'd just gotten the tiniest taste of something he'd been searching for—and craving—all his life.

Sitting up, he rubbed his hands over his face. He was past tired, but he wasn't going to fall sleep anytime soon.

Come to me, he thought, feeling his heart ache with wanting. *Come to me. Because I don't know how to find you.*

We have saved the world with stones and mortar.

And we have made our own prison.

We cannot leave this place undefended. The Dark Guides, the ones who used the malevolent side of the human heart to create the Eater of the World, have disappeared in the shattered landscapes of Ephemera. We cannot take the chance of them finding this place and releasing this evil. We cannot take the chance of anyone breaking that wall.

There are too few of us left. We came from lands all across Ephemera to fight the Eater of the World, but now that the world has become a confusion of shuffled, broken pieces, we can no longer find the places we called home. We have no hope of going back to our lives and the loved ones we left behind.

So we will stay and guard this place. We will protect the people by restraining Ephemera as much as we can. And we will nurture the hope of someday restoring our world by protecting Ephemera from the human heart.

—The Lost Archives

Chapter Five

I t swam beneath the sand, but only those with magic running in their veins would notice the rippling dark shadow that soured the land as It passed—and left behind a seductive lure to give in to the dark feelings the heart usually kept well hidden. All creatures responded to the Dark and the Light, but humans, with their agile minds, had always been the best prey—because It had been made to be their predator.

Which was what brought It back to the part of the bonelovers' landscape It had anchored to the place called the Den. Full of darkness, yes, but at the core there was Light that made It greedy to devour—and made It shiver. The Den was filled with the same powerful resonance that had given Ephemera the strength to resist reshaping more than a small anchor point in that other dark, demon landscape.

That would change. The incubi and succubi had become feeble creatures, contaminated by the human prey. But the purebloods that had been caged in Its landscapes were still powerful, still belonged to the Dark. They would be *real* hunters—and once they reached the Den, their presence would change the Den's resonance, would dim the Light.

As It rose to the surface, Its massive form shrank, shifted. A moment later a handsome, elegantly dressed man stood on the rust-colored sand.

A moment after that, Its scream of rage made even the bonelovers scurry away from feelings so dark and primal.

Where an alley should have been, there was nothing but stone. Huge tumbled boulders blocked Its path. Even if It made the effort to scramble over them, It knew It would find nothing but stones.

As It beat Its fists on the stones, It felt that same powerful resonance at the core of this strange landscape.

Panting, It braced scraped, bloodied hands against the stones as It tried to crush the fear taking root inside It.

The creatures called Landscapers were so diminished they were no longer a threat, were no more than feeble barriers standing in the way of Its desire to turn all of Ephemera into dark landscapes full of terrors shaped from the heart's deepest fears.

But the one who had touched this place . . .

A True Enemy was still out there. Somewhere.

Changing back to Its natural form, It swam beneath the sand until It reached the pile of bones that were Its anchor to the lair of the Landscapers and Bridges.

Its form shrank, shifted, grew eight legs. Its front legs lifted the bones It had turned into a trapdoor that led down to the tunnel that would take It back to the school.

Fifteen years had passed since she'd walked down this path at the school, but she remembered the feel of it— the sly rage, the envy and jealousy, the bitter despair that seemed to seep up from the ground beneath the flagstones. Feelings none of the other students, or even the Instructors, had been aware of.

It felt different now, muted, as if those feelings, once so concentrated under this path that led to the oldest garden at the school, were spread out in a thin skin. But just as potent.

And she remembered her mother's warning as she took another step toward the forbidden.

Being at the school . . . It's an exciting time in your life, Glorianna. You'll be with so many young women who have a power like yours, the same life's work. And there will be the young men who are training to be Bridges. They provide a different kind of excitement. But despite the power you and the others will learn to wield for the good of Ephemera, you are all, in many ways, still children. And children are not always wise, because they want to be strong and brave and adult—and, therefore, they do not always want to believe that the things adults are afraid of are things that truly should be feared, that should be left alone. That was true when I attended the school. I doubt your classmates will be any different.

So you must heed this warning, Glorianna.

"You there!"

She walked toward the archway. Each step took a moment, took a lifetime.

The Instructors will take you to an archway and show you the walled garden with the wrought-iron gate. Inside that old garden is a simple stone wall. They will tell all of you that you must never step through that archway, must never approach that sealed gate.

But children will always want to prove their daring and bravery in front of their peers. So some of them will sneak out at night and go to the archway. They'll taunt one another into proving their courage by crossing that poisonous ground of thorn trees and bloated mushrooms—and then they will touch the gate to prove they aren't afraid of what was sealed behind that stone wall.

"You there! Stop!"

They'll tease you, call you names, say that you're afraid. But, daughter, you must not step through that archway. You must not touch that gate. You are not . . . quite . . . like the rest of the students. We come from an old lineage, a secret held by the women of our house. It must remain a secret for the sake of our world.

Those children, your classmates . . . They won't be-

lieve what the Instructors tell them—that what is contained will become aware of their presence once they cross the archway and step on ground It defiles with Its existence. They won't believe something locked away from the world can truly sense them—or harm them.

But sometimes It does sense them, Glorianna, and It can harm them. Those who approach without the respect due a powerful enemy . . . Well, things . . . happen. People get swallowed by the world, lost in the landscapes instead of making their life journey. Even Bridges. Even Landscapers.

"You there!"

What is contained within that garden, Mother?

The—

The flagstone shifted under her foot, just enough to banish memories and make her see her surroundings with painful clarity.

She looked down, then carefully lifted her foot and took a step back. Instead of hard earth, the space between that flagstone and the others was filled with rust-colored sand.

Boots slapped the flagstones on the path behind her.

She looked at the land near the archway—and shuddered.

A hand clamped on her upper arm and yanked her around to face a stern, middle-aged man who wore a Bridges badge on his tunic.

Not stern, Glorianna decided as she studied his face. Grim. Worried. Afraid.

"What are you doing here?" he demanded. "This part of the school is forbidden to everyone. You should know that, Landscaper."

Of course he knew she was a Landscaper. He'd be able to sense that power in her, just as she would have known he was a Bridge even without the badge.

"The wall has been breached," she said. "*It* is out here in the world, Bridge, and the landscapes that were sealed by that wall are no longer contained. *It* is no longer contained."

"Nonsense. That wall has stood for centuries."

"The wall has been breached." She stabbed a finger in the direction of the archway. "Look at the ground. If everything was as it should be, *that* shouldn't be possible."

He looked where she pointed—and she felt him tremble.

To the right of the path, growing in the shadow of the wall, the ground was speckled with young mushrooms. To the left, dark seedlings rose up from the rotted fruit of the thorn trees.

He shook his head. "The magics—"

"Aren't strong enough anymore to hold back the things It shaped." She jerked free of his hold on her arm. "You have to warn the Landscapers to guard the places in their keeping and hold those places in the Light, regardless of how strongly the people there may resonate the darker feelings of the heart. You have to tell the Bridges to break the bridges they've created and isolate the landscapes. It's the only chance to find—"

"Find what?" he snapped. "You want to spread a rumor that a myth—"

"That wall wasn't created to contain *a myth*, Bridge," she snapped back.

He seemed thoughtful, willing to bend to the idea that the horror that had caused the first Landscapers to break the world into pieces was once more free to unfurl Its full power and turn Ephemera into a nightmarish hunting ground. Then he shook his head, and his face firmed into stubborn lines. "There's enough uneasiness because of the incidents without—"

"What incidents? When did they start?"

"Three weeks ago, right after Lukene disappeared."

Glorianna stared at him. "Lukene disappeared three weeks ago and no one checked the wall?"

But he was staring back at her, as if finally seeing her. "Where's your badge, Landscaper? You're supposed to wear your badge when you visit the school."

A stab of shame, the scrape of old memories, must have shown in her eyes.

"You're—"

She raised her hand in a sharp move to silence him. It wasn't safe to have anyone speak her name. Not here. Not now. "It doesn't matter who I am. Warn the Landscapers, Bridge, before it's too late."

"And tell them what?"

"That the Eater of the World is hunting in Ephemera."

Something rippled under the land. Something dark and predatory.

Did It have a lair at the school? It wouldn't want to keep Its pieces of the world in that old garden. Too much possibility that the Landscapers might be able to reestablish the boundaries, repair the wall, and trap It again. But because of Ephemera's nature, this was the only place that would give It access to all of the landscapes.

At least, all of the landscapes that were anchored in the gardens at the school.

The man facing her looked feverish. Ill. Ugly emotions swam in his eyes—and weren't quite banished by his true nature.

"Get away from this path, away from that garden," she said, her voice low and urgent. "Warn the Landscapers."

Another dark ripple. Closer this time.

She had to get away from here. *Now!*

Turning, she strode away from the archway, ignoring the shouts of the Bridge, who, for his own reasons, didn't follow her.

At least, she hoped they were still his own reasons.

Guardians and Guides, let the Bridge turn away from that garden and give the Landscapers her warning. Not that they'd believe a warning that came from Belladonna. She was a rogue, a "threat" to maintaining the landscapes that made up Ephemera.

She wouldn't be surprised if they decided *she* was the cause of the "incidents." After all, an embittered Landscaper who had, somehow, escaped the wizards' justice would want to cause mischief and harm to those who could achieve what she had not—status among her own kind and an acknowledged place in the world.

They had condemned her because she had made a patchwork out of some of the dark places in the world and shaped them around the Den of Iniquity.

Did any of them realize she had also made a patchwork of the most powerful places of Light? Did any of them know she was the Landscaper whose power resonated through Sanctuary?

She came to the circle of sand-colored bricks and walked toward the sundial at the center of the circle.

The Landscapers and wizards had wondered all these years how she had escaped from a magically sealed garden. This was part of the answer.

Students were taught that their walled gardens were their anchor points to the school. Every connection they established with one of Ephemera's landscapes was anchored within their individual gardens, so they could return to the school from any of those places without needing a bridge to cross over.

The walled gardens were the Landscapers' anchors to the school. Students never questioned that teaching. Neither did the Instructors, since all of them had been students here as well.

Having another anchor point between her garden and the classrooms had seemed a practical way to give herself a little more time to work without having to run all the way back to the school building to be on time for her classes. She'd chosen the sundial as the second anchor point simply because she liked the look of it, the warmth of its stone. And because it was a daily reminder that Dark and Light were together in an eternal dance, and where there was one, the other also dwelled.

That day, fifteen years ago, when she'd discovered a solid stone wall where her garden's gate should have been, she'd assumed it was another part of the "test." She might have spent weeks without realizing the meaning of that solid wall if the Instructors had given her all of her books when they'd closed her in for the "test." So she'd crossed the boundary between here and there, stepping from her garden to the sundial in the space of a heartbeat.

But she hadn't gone back to her room at the student lodgings. Instead she'd walked back to her garden to look at the gate from the outside in order to figure out why it had become solid stone so she could change it back and pass that part of her "test."

That was when she'd found the wizards' seal on the wrought-iron gate and realized the solid stone existed only for someone inside the garden. That was when her trust in those who were supposed to be wise enough to make decisions about other people's lives turned to ash swept away by the sharp winds of anger and hurt . . . and fear.

She lost her innocence that day, and in losing it, began the next stage of the life journey that would make her as dangerous as the wizards and Instructors had feared.

Glorianna shook her head. This wasn't the time or place for dark memories, especially if the Eater of the World was hiding somewhere in the gardens. It would be drawn to the resonance dark memories produced in the heart, and she wasn't ready to fight It. Didn't know if she *could* fight It.

She brushed her fingers over the sundial as she walked past it, keeping her mind focused on where she needed to be. In that moment, between one step and the next, the ground beneath her changed from sand-colored bricks to an overgrown path in the abandoned garden.

A pang of sorrow pierced her, making her stop and look around.

The garden should have been lovely, should have been tended and nurtured. It should have been hers.

You've no time for this. Get what you came for and be gone.

Clenching her hands to resist the temptation to free

some of the flowers that were still struggling to grow despite the smothering tangle of weeds, she walked to the center where the small fountain, the garden's focal point, still burbled, spilling fresh water over the stones into the surrounding pool.

She'd run home the day she'd discovered the seal. Had rushed back to this garden just long enough to cross over to the landscape that was her mother's domain—a place where she safely could weep out the hurt and bitterness.

"You must find another place to anchor your landscapes, daughter. You must build another garden in a place that can't be reached by your enemies."

"There isn't such a place!"

"There is. If you want it to exist, there will be such a place. Break your ties to the school, and I will teach you all that I can."

"I'm a rogue now, Mother. If you help me . . ."

She looked into her mother's eyes, stunned by the anger she saw in them.

"You're going to break your ties to your garden at the school. Aren't you?" she said.

"Sending you to the school was a necessary risk, just as your grandmother took that risk when it was my time to go for the formal training. Now there's another risk, one too great for me to take chances. So, yes, I will break my ties to that garden. But I promise you, Glorianna, I will not lose anything I do not choose to release."

"But . . . Mother—"

"There are things I must tell you about our family, but not now. Not yet. Just shift your landscapes' anchors to some other place, and do it swiftly."

"What about Lee?"

Nadia hesitated. *"When the time comes, he'll have to go to the school to train as a Bridge."*

"Another necessary risk?"

"Yes. Another necessary risk. You'll need a Bridge you can trust."

"You're placing a large burden on a young boy."

Sadness filled Nadia's eyes. "No, Glorianna. It isn't Lee who will carry the burden."

Glorianna shook her head as if that would clear away the thoughts, the weight of despair.

Its influence. There was too little of her left within these walls to fight against the feelings It coaxed to the mind's surface in order to fill the heart with dark emotions.

She *had* to leave.

Crouching beside the fountain, she studied the tumbled stones in the bottom of the pool. Most of them were just stones without power. But . . .

Pushing up her sleeves, she plunged her hands into the pool, shifting the stones to find the three that contained bridges Lee had created for her.

She'd done what Nadia had asked. She'd found that safe, secret place and made another garden that became her link to the landscapes that were in her keeping. But she came back here, just once, while Lee was in school, and left the three stones. She'd been afraid for him because of his ability to impose one landscape over another. If the Instructors at the Bridges' School had discovered Lee could control even a small piece of a landscape to that degree, they might have handed him over to the wizards for the "good" of Ephemera.

So she'd placed the stones in the fountain to give him a way to escape if the Instructors—or the wizards— turned on him.

She rose to her feet and studied the stones in her hands. The agate provided a bridge to the school. Turning to face the wall, she threw the stone as hard as she could. It arched, met the resistance of the magic that kept each garden private, then disappeared.

She didn't know where the stone had gone. Maybe it dropped on the other side of the wall. Maybe it had ended up somewhere else. Or nowhere else. There was no telling what the wizards' power would do to anything that tried to get over the wall from inside the garden.

The second stone, a piece of red-veined black marble, provided a bridge to the Den of Iniquity. She put that one in her trouser pocket.

The third . . .

She tried to move her hand to put the smooth oval of white marble in her pocket, but she couldn't. Something within her trembled—a kind of knowing the mind couldn't put into words. It was a feeling that went through her whenever Ephemera intervened to stop her from doing something that went against some primal knowledge that lived within her heart.

That was the other part of the answer of how she'd escaped being walled inside her garden. Ephemera had intervened by showing her something irresistible.

She'd been working hard in her garden, creating anchor points to the landscapes that resonated for her, even in distant lands. When that staggering wave of darkness had pressed against her mind, her first thought was that she was coming down with some kind of illness. Then the coaxing whispers began, trying to fill her with desolation, trying to convince her that the desolation sweeping through her was the only thing that belonged in her garden. Desolation. Isolation. Food, clothing, shelter. Yes, those things should be part of her landscapes. But not people. She should always be one step removed from any contact with people.

Alone. Forever alone. That was all she deserved.

But something Dark and powerful had risen up inside her. Something primal that recognized those whispers— and hated them. Before those Dark currents flowing inside her could be shaped and manifested in the world, the ground next to her altered, forming a perfect circle filled with grass and unfamiliar wildflowers—and currents of Light that resonated so strongly they were impossible to resist.

The whispers faded, no longer important, as she stepped into that circle and crossed over from here to there . . .

. . . and found the first of the many Places of Light that would call to her until she brought them together as connected landscapes known as Sanctuary.

She stayed for two days, being given company and solitude as each were needed, until the currents of Dark and Light that flowed in her felt balanced again. Then she returned to her garden, bringing with her an ornamental stone so that she could return to that distant landscape and learn more from the people who cared for the Place of Light.

And then, about a month later, she had used the sundial anchor point to return to her room for the rest of her books and had discovered, instead, what the wizards and Instructors at the school had tried to do.

Glorianna sighed. The wizards hadn't succeeded in sealing her up in tiny, desolate landscapes, but more often than not, she *did* feel one step removed from other people, even when she walked among them. More often than not, she did feel alone.

Get away from this place before it warps something inside you. You may have escaped them, but the resonance of what they tried to do still lingers here.

She dropped the stone that provided a way to Sanctuary back into the pool.

Then she walked away from the fountain, her mind focused on the place she needed to be as she took the step between here and there.

She had to go to Aurora, had to warn Nadia that the Eater of the World was once more hunting in Ephemera.

Long after he'd lost sight of her, Gregor stood on the path that led to the archway, a sludge of fury filling his mind. He wanted to run after her, wanted to pin her to the ground and hammer his fists into that beautiful face, wanted to rip out handfuls of that silky black hair, wanted to . . . wanted to . . .

Vile creature. Nothing but a vessel of power that was a perversion of the magic that provided some stability in their ever-changing world. There had been others like her in the past, and the wizards had done their duty for the good of Ephemera and had sealed those perversions within their gardens, leaving them just enough access to the landscapes that they would be able to find food, clothing, and shelter but creating boundaries around those patches of Ephemera that couldn't be breached.

What the wizards did when the perversion of magic surfaced in a student Landscaper was no different from what the first Landscapers had done to contain . . . contain . . .

Vile creature. Vile, vile creature. The only perversion who had managed to escape the Justice Makers.

He hawked and spit.

Then he stared at the gob of phlegm on the flagstone, feeling queasy, feeling as if he'd just spit out something poisonous. Which was foolish. He was just feeling contaminated by having touched *her*, having spoken to *her*.

But Lukene had believed the Instructors and wizards had made a serious mistake in how they had dealt with the girl. That they had judged without knowledge—and by doing so, had destroyed any chance of learning why a fifteen-year-old girl would create something like the Den of Iniquity.

Fifteen years later, they still didn't know why. And they still didn't know how she had done it.

The wall has been breached.

Ridiculous. That wall would stand forever. *Had* to stand forever.

Warn the Landscapers, Bridge.

She was probably behind the incidents—the unexplained alterations in some of the students' gardens; the girl who woke up screaming each morning because, she said, there were spiderwebs all over her skin, and when her skin was completely covered, the spiders would burrow under her skin and eat her alive; the two boys who had tried to create a bridge to some dark street in a nearby town in order to have a tankard of ale and had, somehow, crossed over to a place so frightening that, after they managed to get back to the school, they were too terrified to use *any* kind of bridge.

But would the girl Lukene feared and yet still believed had a good heart make two students disappear the way Lukene had disappeared?

The wall has been breached.

Probably a lie. *She* had been moving *toward* the archway when he'd stopped her, so how could she know?

But if it wasn't a lie . . . ?

Reluctantly, Gregor moved toward the archway. The daylight seemed to pale with every step he took, but he kept moving forward. He shuddered as he passed under the archway. His body shook as he crossed the ground covered with bloated mushrooms and shadowed by thorn trees. His heart raced as he stared at the broken lock and open gate that meant someone had done the unthinkable and entered that garden.

Unwilling to open the gate any farther, he squeezed through the space. As he stared at the simple stone wall, he had a moment to feel relieved, to think it had been a lie after all.

Then he noticed the stick . . . and the crumbled mortar . . . and the small hole in the wall.

"Guardians of Light and Guides of the Heart, help us," he whispered.

He turned away from the wall, but before he reached the gate, he heard . . .

"Help me. Please. Someone help me."

A familiar voice. A beloved voice.

"Lukene?" He looked at the wall. Icy fear filled his heart. "Lukene?"

"Gregor? Gregor! Help me."

A patch of ground near the gate shifted, lifted just enough to reveal a dark space.

He edged toward the gate, toward the dark space, toward the voice of the woman he loved.

"Gregor!"

A pale hand, scraped and bruised, reached out from the dark space.

Caution and love warred in his chest, making his heart ache. "How . . . ?"

"I saw the breach in the wall and tripped into another landscape when I ran to warn the others. I . . . The tunnel is steep. My leg . . . hurt. I can't . . . Gregor, *please.*"

He reached for her hand. He'd get her away from this garden, away from that wall. Then he'd leave her in the care of the first students he could find while he ran to the school to warn the Landscapers.

For a moment, with her hand clamped in his, she resisted his effort to pull her out of that dark space, as if she needed to savor the contact before gathering her strength.

Then the ground lifted like a trapdoor. Tentacles whipped out and wrapped around him. A head emerged. A sea creature. But the body and other four legs were those of a large spider.

Pain in his belly as It bit deep. Then he stopped thrashing as the toxins in that bite paralyzed his limbs.

It pulled him through the trapdoor, down a steep tunnel. It pulled him into a pool of water at the bottom of the tunnel—his legs, his waist, his chest.

His heart pounded. His lungs still labored to breathe. But he couldn't move his arms or legs. Couldn't struggle to escape.

He screamed when It began to feed.

The meal should have been delicious, but one unpalatable nugget had spoiled it all. While It had feasted on the flesh, It had slipped into the human's mind and filled that mind with terrors that had sweetened the flesh. But even as the mind shattered from the fear, there was one shimmer of Light, one seed of hope. Not for itself, but for its kind. For the world.

The male had sacrificed his sanity in order to lock that seed of hope inside a meaningless word—and had died before It could darken that shimmer of Light, break open that seed of hope, and discover the secret inside.

It would go back to that place where the Dark Ones lived. They would know the answer. And if they did not, they would find the answer.

Then It would know the meaning of the meaningless word that made It feel uneasy—and guarded a seed of hope.

Belladonna.

Chapter Six

Lynnea hunched her shoulders as she studied the land on either side of the road. Pasture, crops, some stands of trees. Not so different from the land she knew, except it looked better tended than ho— the farm where she had lived most of her life.

The farm wasn't home, had never been home. That truth had sliced through her two days ago and had left her heart bleeding.

"Mam should have left you by the side of the road," Ewan muttered. "Should have known you were no good as soon as she laid eyes on you." He slapped the reins against the horse's back. "Get on there, you worthless piece of crowbait!"

The tired animal shifted into a trot. Lynnea grabbed the side of the small farm cart with one hand to keep from falling against Ewan.

"I didn't do anything wrong," Lynnea said, her voice breaking.

"You lift your skirt for a married man while his wife is working to put a meal on the table and you don't think that's wrong? No, I guess *you* wouldn't."

"I went into the barn to see the kittens. That's all. Then Pa—"

"He's not your pa," Ewan snapped.

No, he wasn't. Had never acted like a father, even when she'd been a little girl.

She curled her free hand into a fist and pressed it into her lap to hide the trembling. "I just wanted to see the kittens." *Just to have a minute to cuddle something that wanted to be loved.* She blinked back the tears, and whispered, "Mam didn't believe me."

Ewan snorted. "Why would she? We'd put the kittens in a sack and dropped them in the pond the day before."

Lynnea stared at him, the fear of being turned out that she'd lived with all her life exploding into a beast with claws. "You drowned the kittens? But they were babies!"

"Useless. Like you."

She huddled on her part of the seat, trying not to weep for the dead kittens, trying not to wonder if she was being taken to a similar fate.

Would it have been different if she hadn't struggled, if she hadn't screamed when Pa tried to push her down into the stall and pull up her skirt? Would it have been different if Mam had ignored the scream instead of coming into the barn? Or if, when Mam dragged her back to the house, she hadn't blurted out what Pa had said about the old cow being dried up so she'd have to give him the milk from now on?

It wasn't until she saw the wounded look in Mam's eyes—eyes that had flashed a moment later with jealous fury—that she understood what Pa had meant, and then it was too late.

Which was why she and Ewan were traveling to the Landscapers' School. She was no longer welcome at the farm. Pa had wanted to take her into the village and leave her, but Mam had given him a cold, hard look and said that was keeping temptation too close at hand. So Pa had grudgingly agreed to give Ewan time off the farm to take her to the school, where the Landscapers would send her to another landscape in Ephemera. In a very real sense, she would disappear from the lives of everyone she had known.

They'd been traveling since sunup. The sun was now low in the west. Would they reach the school before full dark? Or were they going to have to find some shelter for the night? From the things he'd muttered all day, she knew what Ewan would like to do to her. Whatever constraints had kept Pa and Ewan at a distance all the years she'd lived with them were broken now. But there had been too many people on the roads throughout the day, and now they were probably—hopefully—too close to the school for him to risk a dark intention that might change things for *him*.

Ewan gave a hard tug on the reins, bringing the weary horse to a stop beside a wooden post that had an R carved into the wood.

"This is it," Ewan said, turning his head to look at her. "Get out."

"What?" Lynnea looked around. The road curved, and trees blocked the view. "Is this the school?"

Ewan gave her a mean smile. "No, but this is as far as I'm taking you. Went up to the village yesterday while Pa and Mam were shouting at each other. Pa figured it was a two-day ride to the school, but I talked to some of the fellows, and they told me about this road."

Her heart pounded. "This isn't the way to the school?"

"There's a resonating bridge on the other side of the bend. That's what the R in the post means. I'm crossing over to another landscape to have some fun. You're getting out here. I got two free days before Pa expects to see me back home, and I'm not going to waste them on a piece of crowbait like you. And I'm not going to have the filth inside you influencing what landscape *I* end up in." He gave her a hard shove, almost knocking her off the cart seat. "Get out."

"But ..." When his hand curled into a fist, she scrambled out of the cart. "How am I supposed to find the school?"

Ewan gathered the reins. "Cross the bridge—and hope you end up in a place that's better than you deserve. Giddyap there!"

Stunned that he had done what she'd always

feared—left her on the side of the road like a piece of trash—she'd almost let him reach the bend before she realized the bag with the change of clothes Mam had allowed her to take was still in the back of the cart. "Ewan!" she shouted. "Ewan! My bag!"

Maybe he heard her, maybe not. Either way, he rounded the bend and was gone.

Moments later he screamed.

She ran down the road. Had the horse shied at something and thrown Ewan from the cart? He had screamed, so he must be hurt. Where could she go to reach help if he was badly injured and the horse had bolted, leaving her with no way to take Ewan anywhere?

She raced around the bend—and staggered to a halt. Goose bumps rose on her arms as she tried to understand what she was seeing.

The cart, overturned and sinking. The horse, frantically struggling in a pool of water that covered half the road. No sign of Ewan, but she thought she could still hear faint screaming.

Wary now, her heart pounding, she approached the water and the struggling horse.

"Easy, boy," she whispered. "Easy."

The horse thrashed, as if spurred by the sound of a familiar voice instead of soothed by it. As its right front leg lifted clear of the water, she saw a strange-looking, fleshy vine coiled around the leg from knee to pastern. Then, in a heartbeat, two other vines, their undersides covered with disks, whipped out of the water and wrapped around the horse's neck and other front leg.

The horse screamed as it was pulled under.

Lynnea stared at the pool, watching the churning water turn red.

She had to go back. She had to get away from this place. How far away was the last farmhouse she'd seen? Didn't matter. The sun was going down. She had to get away from here while she could watch for any traps.

She turned—and froze.

Rust-colored sand covered the road. It hadn't been there when she'd rounded the bend. She couldn't jump across it, and she was afraid of moving into the trees on either side of the road in order to get around it.

Which left the bridge.

Travel lightly.

A few steps back to provide some distance from the sand. Then she turned—and whimpered.

The pool of water had spread. Only a thin strip of road remained, barely wide enough to walk on. Once it disappeared beneath the water, there would be no safe way to reach the bridge.

She'd heard that when you crossed a bridge into another landscape, you thought about what you wanted to find on the other side. Then, if you were favored by the Guides of the Heart, you would end up in the place you needed to be.

What she wanted with all her heart was a place where she felt safe, where she didn't have to be afraid all the time. A place where someone loved her.

And that reminded her of the strange waking dream she'd had last night. She'd been yearning for the things she'd never had . . . and a man's voice had promised to love her, had said . . .

Come to me.

Even if he was real, how could she ever find him?

No time to think. No time to decide. If she didn't go now, she'd be trapped between that pool of water and the rust-colored sand.

Travel lightly.

Come to me.

I want to be safe! I want to be loved! I want to be safe! I want to be loved!

Lifting her skirt, she ran across that narrow piece of road and over the bridge, chanting the two things that mattered the most. When she reached the other side of the bridge, she looked around, trying to get some impression of what kind of place it was. But no matter how hard she looked, she couldn't tell.

Because on this side of the bridge, the sun had already set.

🦎

Waking up groggy and pissed off, Sebastian struggled to extricate himself from the tangled sheets and tangled dreams. He sat on the side of the bed and ran a hand up and down his arm. He felt bloated, starving . . . strange. As if something were trying to birth itself inside him.

Maybe he *was* sick. He hadn't felt quite like himself since he'd gotten away from Wizard City.

Staggering into the bathroom, he turned on the water taps, then took care of morning necessaries while the tub filled with a few inches of water. The water was grudgingly tepid—a reminder that he hadn't tended the little potbelly stove that heated the water tank tucked into one corner of the bathroom.

Cursing softly as he turned off the taps and got into the tub, he took a quick bath, scrubbing off the sour smell the dreams had left on his skin. Too bad soap and water couldn't clean his mood or wash away the jagged edges of whatever was chewing him up inside.

After toweling himself dry, he went back into the bedroom and dressed in a moss-green shirt and black denim pants. The denim, while common enough in other landscapes, was another black-market item in the Den. His cousin Lee had given him two bolts of the stuff, which he'd traded to Mr. Finch in exchange for making a pair of pants and a jacket—and giving him enough credit at the shop for any clothes he might want over the next year.

Stepping out of the bedroom, he stared at Teaser, who was standing by the couch. Then disgust welled up in him as he took a swift look around the room. This wasn't a lair for seduction. This wasn't a place suitable for an incubus. This place was rustic and cozy and so *human* he wanted to puke.

"Good timing," Teaser said. "If I'd had to wait much

longer, I would have gone out and peed in the wide-open."

What difference would it make? Sebastian thought as he strode to the kitchen while Teaser headed for the bathroom. Some of the alleys around the taverns stank like urinals. Why should a tree be any different from a stone wall? Didn't that just prove humans were animals? Were ... prey?

Those thoughts made him uneasy, so he concentrated on measuring out the koffea beans and grinding them. He managed to get the koffee started, but by the time Teaser came into the kitchen, he had his hands braced on the counter and was shaking so hard he thought his skin would split—and something hideous would writhe out of the abandoned cocoon.

"Koffee!" Teaser rubbed his hands together and grinned.

"I want to hunt," Sebastian growled, watching his hands curl into fists.

Teaser's grin faded. "What?"

"I want to hunt!" Sebastian turned his head and glared at Teaser. "That's what we do, isn't it? Find a female who's ripe for the picking and screw her until she's addicted to our kind of sex, then harvest that need for any goods or favors we can wring out of her until she's wrung dry or becomes too boring to tolerate. Isn't that what we do?"

"It's what most of the succutits do, sure. And what a lot of the incubi do. But you don't. You never did."

"Then it's time I started." Sebastian grabbed two mugs and set them on the counter near the stove.

"Sebastian?" Teaser studied him, pale and wary. "What happened when you went to Wizard City?"

"Nothing. I told you when we got to this place. The Justice Makers won't help us."

"Yeah, you said that, but—"

"What difference does it make?" Sebastian shouted. He felt angry, edgy, and he didn't know why. Felt like a part of himself was being ripped up by a vile darkness that wanted to fill him up until there was nothing else. But that part of himself kept struggling to survive. Wanted fiercely to survive. He just didn't know how to help it—or even if he wanted to help it. "I'm an incubus, just like you!"

Teaser looked like a man who had just seen something he valued thrown to the ground and crushed underfoot. He smiled, but it was a sick, pained smile. "Yeah. You're just like me."

Even after a few hours' sleep, she still felt weary to the bone, but Glorianna smiled as Nadia set a plate of sweet rolls on the table and poured koffee into mugs.

"Iced cinnamon rolls," she said, putting one on the small plate in front of her. "And I don't have to fight with Lee this time to get my share."

"We need to talk." Nadia put the koffee pot on a woven mat and sat at the table.

Not at her usual seat, Glorianna noted, but facing the kitchen windows and back door—as if she needed to stay watchful in case anyone tried to approach her home.

"You said that last night." Which was why she had stayed with her mother after telling Nadia that the wall in the forbidden garden had been breached.

The quiet chattering that came from the room that was separated from the kitchen by a screened door increased in volume. A small blue-and-white bird flew to the door, hooked his toes into the screen, and scolded them.

"Not now, Sparky," Nadia said firmly.

The scolding changed to chirps and cajoling whistles.

Glorianna smiled. Nadia did not.

That worried her.

"There are things I must say to you, while I still can," Nadia said quietly.

Glorianna tensed. "While you can? What does that mean?"

"It means I can't take the chance that things that must be remembered will be lost if something should happen to me." Nadia closed her eyes. "My mother died when I was young. I was raised by my grandmother." She paused. Opening her eyes, she stared out the screened back door. "My great-aunt, actually. My real grandmother was like you, Glorianna. And like you, the wizards decided she was a danger to Ephemera and sealed her into her garden at the school, using their magic to create boundaries in the landscapes she had access to in order to isolate her in a kind of living death. They didn't know she was carrying a child when they condemned her, that the power inside her wouldn't be extinguished when she died. They never found out that she and her older sister, who was a Level Five Landscaper, had discovered a place that existed in both their landscapes—a place in the woods that had a large, split stone. The dreaming place, they used to call it. Neither could cross the boundary that separated them, so they were never able to see each other or talk to each other, but they could leave messages tucked into the split stone, or a basket could be left that the other could take.

"One day, when my great-aunt arrived with a basket of food, she found another basket at the meeting place. My mother was inside that basket. And a note that said, 'Love her. Teach her. And don't come back.'

"My great-aunt never found another message from her sister. So she raised her sister's daughter, claiming the girl as her own, and then she raised me. And like her mother before her, she told her daughter, and then me, the family secrets about what we are . . . and what we came from."

Nadia took a long swallow of cold koffee. "And now I must tell you."

"You've told me the family secrets," Glorianna said, covering her mother's hands with hers.

"Not this one. This one is the reason for all the other secrets that the women in our family—and the women in other families like ours, if any others have survived—have held in their hearts for generations." Nadia's eyes filled with tears. "I carried the secrets and the seed of our bloodline, but I was spared the burden of it. You're the one who must carry the burden."

"What burden? I don't understand."

Nadia turned her hands so that she could clasp her daughter's. "What you are, Glorianna, is the reason for all the family secrets."

We will not be found easily in this broken piece of the world. So there is time to hide what must be hidden while we wait to discover who prevailed in the final battle for Ephemera—our enemies . . . or the Eater of the World. Either way, we can no longer walk in the world as we once did. So we must learn how to hide our true nature behind a human mask. And in time, if our enemies were the victors, we will seek them out and embrace them as allies—and they will never realize we are always working to destroy them.

We have ensured our survival by fleeing to this place. We will be well established by the time the shattered pieces of the world are made whole again. By then, no one will look beyond what we pretend to be because our power will be needed to keep Ephemera clean of the human heart's darkest wishes. We will be invaluable to the human world—and we will use our new position to slowly, carefully winnow out the strongest of our enemies, diluting their power generation after generation until they become little more than useful tools.

But there is one fear we dare not speak lest it resonate through the currents of the world.

If the Eater ever finds us, will It realize that we aban-

doned It when It most needed our guidance, that we left
It to fight Its enemies alone?

—The Dark Book of Secrets

Chapter Seven

Koltak braced his hands on the waist-high stone wall that circled the top of the Wizards' Tower and stared at the open land east of the city. Already the sun had risen high enough to vanquish the night's shadows. Already the shadow that had filled him with revulsion and excitement was surrendering to the bright summer light and fading away.

Damn that fool of an apprentice that he'd sent running to fetch Harland. If the boy was too spineless to knock on Harland's door at an unseemly hour, the moment would be lost, and he would be just another fool who had raised an alarm over a shadow caused by natural contours in the land. He couldn't afford to sound like a fool, but if he *was* the one to see the very thing generations of wizards had watched for, that would go a long way toward balancing out his youthful mistake. Wouldn't it?

"I trust you have good reason to send for me at this hour and interrupt my meditations."

Koltak jumped at the sound of Harland's voice, but he didn't take his eyes off the land. His hand trembled as he lifted it and pointed. "Look."

Harland came up beside him. Out of the corner of his eye, Koltak saw the leader of the Wizards' Council stiffen.

"Do you see it?" Koltak asked, keeping his voice low.

"Yes, I see it."

Relief swept through Koltak. He had a witness. No one would doubt Harland. But that meant . . .

A shadow is the warning. That was what he'd been taught all those years ago when he was a third-year apprentice beginning his training for tower duty. *A shadow that ripples. A shadow that seems cast by something below the earth rather than by light shining down upon the earth.*

"Do you think someone should go to the Landscapers' School and ask them to check the hidden garden?" he asked.

Harland looked at Koltak, a feverish glitter in his eyes that was at odds with his solemn expression. "And say what? That we know about the garden they have guarded so vigilantly for generations? A garden they still believe is a secret known only to themselves? A garden only the Landscapers and Bridges can find, despite our years of effort to determine its exact location at the school? They have never acknowledged the existence of that garden, and despite how often we visit the school to help them weed out the dangerous elements among their own kind, we have found no evidence of its existence. No, Koltak. The Landscapers would have sent a message if they had noticed any sign of danger—even though we failed them the last time our help was needed."

Koltak winced at the reminder. He'd resented being excluded from the wizards chosen for the task because of his "family connections." Afterward, he'd been grateful that he wasn't among the wizards disgraced by their failure to seal *that* garden.

"But . . . " He looked around to confirm that they were the only ones on the top of the tower. Still, he lowered his voice. "What about the shadow?"

Harland nodded. "A warning, certainly, that something dark and dangerous has grown powerful enough to threaten Ephemera's landscapes." He paused. "For fifteen years, the council has feared this day would come, but we had hoped she would never become strong enough for this warning to appear. It would seem our hopes were in vain."

Koltak whispered, "Belladonna."

"Yes," Harland said. "Belladonna. An enemy who could destroy everything we have protected—unless she is destroyed first."

"She has eluded us for fifteen years! Most wizards can't even cross over into any landscape under her control, even in the company of a Bridge. How are we supposed to find someone we haven't even *seen* in fifteen years?"

"I don't know," Harland said bitterly. "But we must find a way." He reached out and gripped Koltak's shoulder. "Tell no one about the shadow. Say nothing about what you have seen. I must meditate on this warning before discussing it with the rest of the council. We do not want to spread alarm among the students and younger wizards."

Will you even mention me when you speak with the council? "I understand."

Harland released Koltak and headed for the door that led to the stairs that curved along the inside wall of the tower. Then he paused and looked back. "The apprentice you sent to fetch me. Did he see the shadow?"

Koltak shook his head. "But he's clever enough to realize I wouldn't have sent him to fetch you at this hour if there wasn't a reason."

"Is he trustworthy?"

Koltak hesitated, then shook his head again. "He has a braggart's tongue and a fool's lack of discretion. He had just enough potential to be admitted for formal training, but even after three years, he can barely undo a simple barrier." *Something Sebastian had been able to do with no training at all.* He buried that thought. The power had lain dormant all these years. Sebastian had no reason to believe he *had* that kind of power. Unless something happened that gave the council a reason to demand testing, no one would ever know his offspring was anything more than an incubus.

"I see," Harland said. He studied Koltak. "Why were *you* up here this morning?"

"I couldn't sleep. I came up here to think."

Harland stared at him for a long time. "Fortuitous."

"Yes."

After the tower door closed behind Harland, Koltak turned back to look at the land. Sunlight and natural shadows obscured the warning.

At least the warning had been seen and understood. And the wizards would not fail again. They would find a way to contain—or eliminate—Belladonna before she destroyed Ephemera.

Busy busy busy. Humans were always so *busy*. The Dark currents flowed through so many hearts in this city, but there were enough threads of Light to keep some of the best prey from abandoning this place. Even though It was eager to contact the minds with the darkest resonance, It couldn't resist stretching out Its mental tentacles through the lower part of the city to play with some of the hearts nurtured by those threads of Light.

Yes, It whispered to one of those hearts. *Yes, the butcher has cheated you, put his thumb on the scale to charge you the full price for less meat. But you are nothing, nobody, insignificant. No one will believe you if you accuse him—and if you do accuse him, he will not sell you meat anymore, and your family will go hungry.*

It felt the Light in that heart dim, replaced with the despair that often overtook such hearts when the truth was skewed a little. There would be less kindness in that heart today, and the ripples of unhappiness would be felt by every person the woman encountered. Those hearts would also be dimmed a little. And the threads of Light in the city would become a little weaker, making the Dark more powerful.

It played with Its prey as Its tentacles brushed the minds and hearts of the humans in the marketplace.

Then It brushed against a section of the city where the Dark and Light were woven together in such a way that the currents formed a barrier It couldn't breach. The Dark currents didn't quite resonate with the rest of the city, but the barrier hid the resonance of whatever power controlled that portion.

Tantalized and uneasy, It withdrew from that part of the city and stretched Its mental tentacles toward the two minds It had felt earlier that morning. One mind was barricaded behind walls of self-discipline, but the other was so distracted, slipping inside that mind was as easy as slipping into a dream.

Koltak stared out his sitting room window.

Harland had been so certain that Belladonna and her unnatural power was the reason for the warning. But ...

A shadow is the warning.

Belladonna was an enemy to wizards and Landscapers alike, and certainly a danger to Ephemera, but only for the past fifteen years. Wizards had been keeping watch for generations. The tower was the oldest structure in Wizard City, had been built on this hill so that whoever stood at the top could see all of the surrounding countryside. Could keep watch.

For what? his mind whispered.

Not Belladonna, despite what Harland believed. Wizards had disposed of her kind of Landscaper before. They would find a way to dispose of her, too. No, he didn't believe she and those like her in previous generations were the reason the wizards kept watch year after year after year.

Then why?

Koltak rubbed his forehead, remembering the feverish glitter in Harland's eyes that revealed some strong emotion the man was otherwise able to control. And yet ...

It wasn't like Harland to dismiss the other possibility of danger. And they all *knew* there was another possibility. Every wizard who had walked around the Landscapers' School had felt that core of evil hidden by all the currents of Light that flowed through the school. Every person who lived in Ephemera's shattered landscapes knew the story about how the Guardians of Light and Guides of the Heart had found a way to cage the Eater of the World and the creatures It had shaped. The magic had been powerful, had been meant to last forever. The Guardians and Guides had disappeared in the making of that cage. Not destroyed, but no longer able to walk in the world. People believed they still existed, still listened to the heart's deepest wishes and worked through the currents of power to make those wishes real.

But it was the Landscapers who controlled Ephemera now, keeping the landscapes stable despite the flood of emotions that poured out of human hearts. And somewhere in the maze of gardens and buildings at the school were walls even older than the tower.

Why had Harland refused to consider the possibility?

This possibility must have a name, his mind whispered. *You're not afraid to speak the name, are you?*

No, he wasn't afraid, and he wasn't afraid to look at a truth Harland didn't want to consider. There was only one reason for keeping watch all these years: to see the warning in time to defend themselves if the Eater of the World returned.

Koltak turned away from the window, then rummaged through his desk for a headache powder. It wasn't surprising he felt a little strange after a sleepless night and the events of this morning.

Cursing softly when he realized he had nothing in his room and would have to go down to the dispensary, he sank into his desk chair, still rubbing his forehead.

Harland had been thrown off balance this morning. That was understandable. Given a little time to think, he would realize the necessity of going to the school and discussing the hidden garden with the Landscapers.

After all, if something *had* happened to break the magic that had caged the Eater and Its landscapes, everyone's survival was at stake.

It flowed into the woods north of the city, where Its presence would be lost among other shadows.

It had learned much over the years from the human prey that had stumbled into Its landscapes—especially from the humans who were, themselves, predators. It had learned to take the shape of Its favorite before It had destroyed the sanity of the middle-aged, elegant gentleman who had enjoyed killing women so viciously.

It had learned. And now It understood that the spawn of the Dark Ones had known about the hated stone wall. They had known where the garden was hidden. They had found a way to send prey into Its landscapes, but they had never tried to free It. Caged, It had been a useful tool.

But It was not a tool to be used by the Dark Ones' spawn. It was the Eater of the World. When It returned to the city, they would want to be Its friends.

But before It left this landscape to deal with the enemies at the school, It would show the Dark Ones' spawn *why* they wanted to be Its friends.

With Teaser beside him, Sebastian strode down the Den's main street feeling itchy, angry, ready to hunt. He was dressed for it, primed for it—the bad boy on the strut. As he studied the street, he realized how shabby everything had gotten in the past few years. The windows on the shops and taverns were grimy, the alleys smelled of piss, and the colored lights that had made him think of a carnival when he'd first come to the Den were dulled by layers of dirt. Like an old whore still trying to dress up to prove she was desirable.

But this was his home; this was his life; this was all he had and would ever have. This.

He wanted to smash things, break things, wound and rage, because somehow, after thirty years of living, *this* was all he deserved.

More than anything, he wanted to hurt someone.

That was when he saw the young woman creeping out of an alley, every movement shrieking of fear.

And the small *something* inside him that had been struggling to survive since he'd come back from Wizard City suddenly yearned for her, craved her with enough strength to knock the ugly feelings churning in him off balance for a moment. Then *everything* inside him focused on her. Just her.

Teaser tipped his head and studied her. "Huh. Look at that. A country mouse fresh off the farm."

More like a rabbit who has bolted straight into a pack of wolves. Sebastian's mouth watered at the thought.

Teaser tipped his head to the other side, considering. "Maybe not so fresh. If she smells like she looks, not even the incubi will want a taste before she's washed up. Guess I'll just—"

Sebastian whipped one arm out, forming a barrier in front of Teaser. "Mine."

"On the way here, you said you wanted someone with some kick and bite. You're not going to get much of anything from that one."

"This one is mine."

He approached her slowly, more a stalk than a walk, giving her time to notice him. She glanced at the alley, then back at him, unable to decide if it was safer to stay or run. She didn't want to go back into the alley where it was dark and smelly, but if she stayed he'd be on top of her. Stay or run?

Poor, foolish little rabbit. She didn't realize yet the decision had already been made.

He smiled at her—and put everything he was into that smile.

She didn't smile back. She just stared at him as if he were the vilest demon she had ever seen.

Which was probably true.

"This your first visit?" he asked pleasantly.

"What?"

"Is this your first visit to the Den?" Of course it was. She wouldn't look so bewildered if she'd been here before, but so often the hayseeds liked to pretend they weren't as ignorant as everyone here knew they were. That pretending was one of the reasons some of them didn't survive long enough to go home again.

"Den?"

"The Den of Iniquity." Sebastian bared his teeth in a smile. "Not quite what you expected?"

If she was frightened before, she was terrified now. "I don't belong here. I *can't* belong here. It's a mistake." She looked at him, her blue eyes pleading. "Please. It's a mistake."

He shook his head. "No one comes to the Den by mistake. By accident, certainly, but not by mistake. You got here, which means something inside you resonated with this place."

"No," she whispered. "No."

She looked ready to collapse. If he didn't get her calmed down, she wouldn't be any fun at all.

"My name's Sebastian. What's yours?"

"Lynnea."

"Pretty name." And the way she pronounced it—Lyn*NEA*—gave it a softer, richer sound.

Even exhausted and bedraggled, she was pretty in a wholesome way that made him uneasy. He could picture warming her up enough to enjoy a steaming-hot roll between the sheets—and he could picture holding her in his arms for an easy kiss and a snuggle.

That bothered him. A lot.

"Why don't we go to Philo's?" Sebastian said. "It's just down the street. You look like you could use some food."

"Oh." She raised her hands to her light-brown hair in an automatic, feminine gesture. "Oh, I couldn't. I'm ..." Looking down at the dirty, short-sleeved tunic and ankle-length skirt, she wrinkled her nose.

"It's an open courtyard. You'll be fine." He held out a hand. She shrank away from it, which made him angry, but he kept an easy smile on his face. Before he was finished with her, she would beg him to put his hands on her and have her in any way he wanted.

As he let that thought fill him, the *something* inside him that was struggling against the ugly feelings withered.

"Come on," he said. He shifted just enough to block any attempt she might make to rabbit back down the alley. Seeing no choice, she eased away from the wall and walked down the street, with him a half step behind her so that he could catch her if she tried to bolt.

With this strange mood riding him, he wasn't sure what he'd do to her if she tried to get away from him.

By the time he herded her to Philo's, Teaser was already there, doing a live performance with a succubus. The handful of statues scattered among the tables in the courtyard were all sexually explicit and painted with such detail it took careful study to be sure they *weren't* real. There were also two small platforms for the "live art."

At the moment, Teaser and the succubus were holding a pose. His shirt was open and tugged off his shoulders; his hands were on her hips. One of her legs hooked around his waist, her back was arched, and one hand reached for the zipper of his leather trousers. In a few seconds they would follow through on the moves before striking another pose.

"Those statues look so real," Lynnea said, her eyes wide. "But ... what are they doing?"

Figuring it was better not to shock the little rabbit too much, he guided her to the only available table and pulled out a chair for her that put her back to Teaser's performance.

Philo bustled up to their table, the sleeves of his white shirt rolled up to the elbows in a concession to the warm summer night. His smile of welcome faltered when he looked at Lynnea, and when he turned to Sebastian there was a bleakness in his dark eyes that was too much like Teaser's expression back at the cottage.

Philo was good at assessing his customers, at judging the outcome of a pairing. Which was why the man was dismayed to see him there with a female who was so obviously prey. The kind of female who would get chewed up by the incubi's seductive games and end up throwing herself in a river out of shame or despair.

It rankled that Philo seemed disappointed in him, almost fearful. The man had no right to judge *him*. And it was none of Philo's damn business whom he spent the night with.

He stared at Philo, holding the man's gaze with the force of his will until Philo looked away, uneasy.

Giving them both a weak smile, Philo said, "Will you be having the Phal—"

"Your specialty of bread and warm cheese," Sebastian cut in. If his little rabbit knew what "phallic" meant, she'd probably run down the street screaming. And that wasn't the way he wanted her to scream. "And wine."

Philo hurried away, ignoring calls from other tables.

"Wine?" Lynnea said, shaking her head. "I can't. Only . . . bad women drink liquor."

Well, wasn't she just little miss prissy prig? He'd change that. Oh, yes. Before he let her go, he was going to change a great many things. "Wine isn't liquor; it's wine. No civilized meal is complete without it."

She frowned, and as she tried to wrap her mind around that thought, he noticed how exhausted she was. Not just dirty and scared, but truly exhausted. If it had been that hard to reach the Den, why had she tried at all?

Philo returned with a tray. He set a bowl in front of each of them that contained a small wet cloth, placed a dry hand towel beside the bowls, then put two glasses of red wine on the table and left.

Sebastian felt the tension inside him ease a little. Trust Philo to understand the female ego. The little rabbit wouldn't want to eat with dirty hands, but by providing towels for both of them, he wasn't commenting on Lynnea's appearance.

Plucking his towel from the bowl, Sebastian rubbed it over his hands, the movement releasing a light citrus scent. Lynnea watched for a moment, then copied him. She folded the towel neatly before putting it back in the bowl.

Folding his own towel, Sebastian leaned toward her and said, "You've got a smudge on your cheek." In truth, her whole face was dirty, but he wanted a reason to touch her that would seem innocent—to her mind, anyway. As he stroked the towel down her cheek, he had a lot of thoughts about that touch. None of them were innocent.

With a little coaxing, he got her to take a sip of the wine. By her third sip she didn't need coaxing anymore, and he felt relieved when Philo returned with two small plates, a basket full of chunks of bread, and the bowl of melted cheese. On an empty stomach, it wouldn't take much wine to get his little rabbit thoroughly sloshed, and he wanted her relaxed, not unconscious.

Sebastian looked at the basket and winced—a perfectly understandable response to seeing anything that was usually penis-shaped cut up into chunks.

Since she hesitated, he took a chunk of bread and swirled it in the cheese, then nodded for her to do the same. "Careful. The cheese is hot."

She picked a head out of the basket. Oh, she wouldn't know what it was, wouldn't associate its shape with anything male, but as he watched her swirl the head in the cheese, his pants suddenly felt too tight— and his heart gave a hard bump when her tongue darted out to catch the cheese dripping from the end. And when she blew on the head to cool the cheese enough to eat, he thought his skin would burst into flames.

She had no idea what she was doing—and it was killing him.

"This is good," she said, reaching for another piece.

He stuffed his own piece of bread and cheese in his mouth to keep from saying something erotic, suggestive, lewd. Desperate.

How was he supposed to think when his cock was throbbing and his brain couldn't get past how her mouth closed over the bread, how her mouth could close over his—

Applause from the other tables startled both of them. Lynnea started to turn in her chair to see what people were responding to, but Philo was back, blocking her view as he set a plate on the table.

"Something to go with the house specialty," Philo said. "Stuffed Tits."

"*What?*" Lynnea raised a protective hand to her chest as she stared at the plate.

"Um . . . er . . . " Philo gave Sebastian a panicked look.

Lynnea frowned. "Those look like . . . mushrooms."

"Yes," Philo said quickly. "Stuffed mushrooms. Harmless."

She continued to study the mushrooms. "They do look like tits, don't they? Sort of round but pointy with the stuffing." She took one and put it on her plate. Then she picked up a piece of bread. "What do you call this stuff?"

Beads of sweat popped out on Philo's forehead. "Ah . . . Phallic Delights."

"What's 'phallic'?" she asked. Then she hiccuped.

Sebastian closed his eyes and tried not to moan. His little rabbit was sloshed on half a glass of wine, and watching her inhibitions fall away made him feel very peculiar. He should be reveling in how easy this had been. Instead he wanted to get her away from any bad influences. Which was funny, since he was an incubus, this was the Den, and he intended to be the baddest influence she met during this visit.

"It's a word polite young ladies don't know," Philo replied.

"Oh." Lynnea stared at the bread. "But I'm a bad person, so I can say that word. Phallllic."

Someone from another table called, and Philo fled in response.

Sebastian opened his eyes and watched Lynnea swirl the bread in the cheese—and knew he was in trouble.

"Eat your mushroom," he said. Daylight! Now he sounded like a priggish older brother. What had happened to the desire to hunt, to hurt, to seduce her?

"Stuffed tit," she replied. Then she giggled.

The sound produced a heat inside him that bewildered him. It was like suddenly standing in a beam of sunlight—and that *something* inside him that was struggling to survive fed on the sound.

Having lost his appetite for food, he drank his wine while he watched her eat.

Finally she leaned back, took a sip of wine, and looked around. "This is a strange place."

It's the Den. "Why did you come here, Lynnea?"

"Wasn't supposed to. Was . . . supposed to go to the Landscapers' School, but Ewan left me on the side of the road, and . . ." She shuddered. "Don't want to think about that. Not now."

"All right," Sebastian said soothingly. "We won't talk about that." *Yet.* "Tell me how you got to the Den."

"Went over a bridge. Was trying . . ." Her eyes filled with tears. "He told me to come to him."

Sebastian's heart slammed against his chest. No. It couldn't be. "Who? Ewan?"

She shook her head. "I don't know. A voice inside my head. After Mam told me I was going to be sent away, I was just thinking, and . . ."

A tear rolled down her cheek. She whispered, "I just wanted to find a place where I would feel safe, where I wouldn't be afraid all the time. But I ended up here. So I guess I'm a bad person after all."

The Landscapers will send me to a bad place. I just want—

What? What do you want?

I want to be safe. I want to be loved. I want to be someplace where I'm not afraid all the time.

Come to me.

Guardians and Guides.

Pushing back his chair, Sebastian helped Lynnea to her feet, then led his jelly-legged little rabbit to the brothel that was on a side street two blocks away from Philo's. After getting his key from the clerk behind the counter in the lobby, he half carried Lynnea up the stairs and down the corridor to his room on the third floor.

Dark, heavy furniture. Red velvet curtains around the bed and the windows. The room was big enough to have a sitting area as well as the bed. No fireplace, but he had a connecting bathroom that he shared with Teaser, whose room also had a connecting door.

Masculine. Alien. A room designed for seduction and a sexual feast.

And there was Lynnea, with her torn, dirty clothes, looking more like an exhausted child than a woman ripe for a romp. Looking so out of place it made his heart hurt.

"What are you wearing under that?" he asked, gesturing to the tunic and skirt.

"A shift."

He hoped she was wearing more than that, but he wasn't going to ask.

He led her to the bathroom door, paused a moment to listen, then pushed the door open.

"An indoor privy," she said, sounding impressed. "I'd heard everyone has them in the cities now."

"We may be decadent, but we're not backward. We even have lektricity for the streetlights and in some parts of the buildings." And he'd never wondered until now why a place like the Den would have such things.

"I should take a bath."

She sounded hesitant—not about the bath but about being completely naked with a strange man on the other side of the door.

"You can take a bath later." *When you won't fall asleep in the tub and drown.* "Just take care of your necessaries."

She blushed. He retreated.

He busied himself by pulling back the bedcovers and fluffing the pillows, keeping his mind focused on the simple tasks until he could get out of that room.

Why did he have to get out? In her current haze of exhaustion and wine, it wouldn't take much to have her mindless from sensual pleasure, and then he could feed on the emotions produced by thrilling her body.

That was what he wanted. Wasn't it?

When she came back into the bedroom a few minutes later, her face was clean—and she was wearing nothing but her shift.

Lust swam in his blood as soon as he saw her, but it was flavored by something else, something unfamiliar and delicate. Want and wariness tangled up inside him, making him desperate to get away from her long enough to think.

"Am I supposed to give you sex?" she asked in a small voice. Resigned. As if she expected her body to be used as a commodity.

That made him angry, which made no sense. But nothing was making any sense, so why should this be different?

He wanted to believe she was experienced, wanted to believe she was offering herself, wanted to believe he could unfurl the power of the incubi and feast on the pleasure he could make her feel.

But he couldn't look at her and believe any of those things. He also couldn't leave without doing something to ease the need gnawing inside him, so he walked up to her, cupped her face in his hands, and kissed her softly.

Warm. Sweet. Innocent, but there was a banked sensuality that just needed encouragement in order to bloom.

But not now.

He tucked her into bed the way Nadia used to tuck him in, telling him without words that he was safe and welcome.

"Sleep now," he whispered.

Her eyes drifted shut. She was asleep before he stepped away from the bed.

Returning to Philo's, he ordered whiskey, then sat staring at the liquid in the glass.

I want to be safe. I want to be loved. I want to be someplace where I'm not afraid all the time.

Come to me.

No one came to the Den by mistake. By accident, certainly, but not by mistake.

Except his little rabbit was right—she didn't belong here, would never have found the Den if not for him. Because it was that brief connection with him that had drawn her to the Den, had made it resonate in a way that made it possible for her to cross over.

His fault. His responsibility.

Teaser pulled out a chair and flopped into it. "Where's the country mouse?"

"Sleeping."

"That was quick."

Sebastian stared at Teaser until the other incubus stirred uneasily. "You're going to help me with something. A little game, you could call it."

"Sebastian, I don't think the mouse is ready for something more than a solo—"

He held up his hand. "This is what I want you to do." As he talked, Teaser's expression changed from uneasy to baffled. "Do you understand?"

"No," Teaser replied.

"Will you help?"

"Sure, if that's what you want."

"That's what I want."

Teaser studied him, then stood up. "I'll spread the word."

It didn't take long. Even though he couldn't see it

from where he was sitting, he felt the waves of activity washing over the Den.

She was here because of him, and this much he could do for her. If he were a smart man, he would escort her to the Landscapers' School as soon as she woke up. But he didn't want to be a smart man. He wanted—*needed*—this small pocket of time. He had no influence in any other landscape, but here in the Den he could give her a few hours in a place where she wouldn't be afraid.

After that, he would take her to the school, knowing she would never find her way back to the Den.

Knowing there was something about her that would haunt him the rest of his life.

Chapter Eight

The girl sniffled into a handkerchief and looked up at the two wizards standing in front of her. "He came running down the stairs so fast, I didn't have a chance to warn him they were wet. And he looked so scared, like something terrible was chasing after him. Then he slipped and one foot got tangled in the wash bucket's handle and he ..." She collapsed into the chair behind her, sobbing.

"What were you doing on the stairs so early in the morning?" Harland asked sternly.

The tears dried up, replaced by a hint of angry pride. "My work, sir. When a stairway needs washing, we do it first so it's dry before most other folk are up and about."

"Are you implying that the wizards are lazy?" Harland sounded offended.

"I'm sure that's not what she meant," Koltak said. "The servants are aware that we spend the early hours in meditation or study and don't usually leave our rooms."

"That's true, sir," the girl said, looking earnestly at Harland. "No one's to come knocking to clean a room until after breakfast, so we take care of other cleaning chores until then."

"I see," Harland said, a little mollified.

"Besides," the girl added, "wizards don't use that

stairway. Just the servants. He shouldn't have been using those stairs at all."

"I think that's all we need to know," Koltak said. He glanced at Harland, relieved when the head of the Wizards' Council nodded in agreement.

He led the girl to the door and opened it, not surprised to find the housekeeper hovering in the corridor. She was protective of her girls and had, more than once, publicly berated young wizards for not being able to tell a servant from a slut.

As the housekeeper hurried off with the girl, Koltak closed the door and turned to face Harland. "What do you think?"

Harland stared at the floor. Then he sighed. "The boy had no business on that stairway, but it is a shortcut from the apprentice quarters to the study rooms. So I think you were right about him having a braggart's tongue. He was probably on his way to tell some companion about delivering a message to me."

"If it was nothing more than haste that had him rushing down that stairway, he would have seen the girl and the bucket, would have realized the stairs were wet." Koltak paused. "But the girl said he looked scared."

Some undefinable look came and went over Harland's face. "You think a Dark Guide influenced the boy into taking fright?"

"Don't you believe in the Dark Guides?"

Harland lifted a hand, then let it fall. "If people believe there are Guardians of the Light and Guides of the Heart, how can there *not* be Dark Guides to provide balance, to grant the darker wishes of the heart? Personally, I think people make their own choices, good and bad. If they find comfort in blaming a hardship on something outside of themselves or that some force heard a wish and granted it, then let them believe."

"And so a moment at the wrong place and time ends with a young man tumbling down a flight of wet stairs and breaking his neck?" Koltak said. Why was he arguing this, especially with Harland?

"Yes," Harland said quietly. "Most likely we'll discover some classmates pulled a prank on the boy that frightened him more than they'd intended, and that, in turn, caused the accident that ended the boy's life this morning. I don't think we'll find anything more sinister than that, Koltak. No Dark Guides, no dark presence. Nothing but human weakness."

"I know."

As he went back to his own rooms, he couldn't shake the feeling that Harland was trying to hide something—that Harland didn't believe for one moment this morning's tragedy had been caused by human weakness.

🦋

Nigelle ran all the way to her walled garden. Slipping through the gate, she paused to catch her breath and embrace the glee she felt whenever she stood here.

Secrets. Her garden was full of secrets. Dark landscapes carefully hidden so that a quick look by any of the Instructors would cause no alarm. Not that they were doing the usual inspections lately. Too many strange things had been happening.

And she was the only one who knew why.

She hurried to the far end of her garden, then looked around, impatient. Where was he? Surely he'd come. He *had* to come. He was so splendid, she couldn't stand not seeing him for a whole day.

She'd tried sex with a couple of the boys studying to be Bridges, but she hadn't liked it much. But with *him* . . . It was devastatingly wonderful. Like drowning in sensations. Like being devoured while she crested again and again. It had gotten so that, if a full day went by without sex, she felt jittery, hot, like her skin was too tight and she needed to peel it off in order to breathe.

She'd have sex with him every hour of every day until it killed her. That was how good it was.

Laughing at herself for being so melodramatic, she

rubbed her hands over her arms to ease the jittery, itching feeling.

Where was he?

And it wasn't just the sex, no matter how wonderful. He was showing her things the Instructors *never* would have taught her. And he had entrusted her with guarding the darkest, most dangerous landscapes in Ephemera.

Nigelle frowned. Why *had* he chosen her? If these places were so dangerous and had to be guarded to keep people from stumbling into them, why hadn't he asked one of the stronger Landscapers for help? Why . . . ?

She looked at the garden in front of the patch of grass she stood on. Directly in front of her was a path that ended at the back wall, separating two of the secret landscapes. To her left, hidden by two shrubs and a bed of tall summer flowers, was a patch of rust-colored sand fanning out from the corner. To her right, also fanning out from the corner, was a pool of murky water. Not deep. Even though he'd warned her to stay away from it, she'd used a stick as a measuring rod one day, so she knew it was barely up to her knees.

She'd never seen anyone create a space in a garden that could hold water without enclosing it on all sides to create a small pond.

Can Belladonna do something like that?

She banished the thought. She didn't like thinking about Belladonna anymore. And the other day, when he'd asked her about the sealed gardens, she'd told him about Belladonna, the rogue Landscaper who had escaped from the Justice Makers' magic. But when she'd said she intended to be a Landscaper like Belladonna, he'd gotten the strangest look on his face and murmured, "Perhaps you're not what I thought you were."

He left soon after that, and she hadn't seen him since.

She turned in a slow circle, her eyes scanning every part of her garden. He had to come today. He *had* to.

Then he was there, appearing on the path in front of

her, a handsome, middle-aged man who was carrying a small sack and wearing nothing but a smile.

He pulled her down on the grass, began pulling at her clothes.

"Let me have you," he said, his dark eyes glittering with a feverish excitement. "Let me fill you."

She tried to protest. This was crude. Not at all like him. She didn't like this, even felt . . .

"Yes," he said as he rolled on top of her and thrust into her. "Yes, fear is good. Delicious. Intoxicating."

Then he kissed her. She closed her eyes while that flood of heat and need filled her until all she could think of was having him inside her so she could keep feeling this way.

But things didn't feel . . . right. Her breasts felt enclosed by strange mouths that had a dozen little tongues that rasped the delicate skin and sensitized nipples. Painful. And yet she couldn't bear to have it stop.

And he didn't feel right inside her. Too thick. Too long. Each thrust hurt her, but the pleasure was also building and building and . . .

When she crested, she felt a sting on her shoulder, as if he'd bitten her. Moments later her arms and legs went numb. She couldn't move them, could barely move her fingers enough to scratch at the grass.

Then she crested again—and didn't care.

Still unbearably excited, she opened her eyes. When had he put on that strange cowl that stuck out at the sides and came down so low it shadowed his face? Eyes gleamed at her, and when he smiled . . .

Something wrong with his mouth. What was wrong with his mouth?

Didn't matter. Nothing mattered except him, because he was still moving inside her.

As she crested the third time, she felt him spill inside her and relax. She gasped for air, trying to form words to ask him to move. When he shifted slightly, the salty sweat on his skin burned her raw breasts.

One of his hands clamped down over her mouth before she could draw a full breath. The other hand fumbled inside the sack he'd dropped beside them.

He held the long, thin knife up where she could see it. Then he raised himself up enough to make a slice across her chest just above her breasts.

"Yes," he said, slicing her arm open from shoulder to elbow, "fear is delicious. It will soak into this ground with your blood. Do you know what will happen then?" He smiled at her. "Since this is an access point, the fear will seep through this grass into the pasture it is anchored to. Then it will shiver into anyone who walks through that pasture, and as the fear takes root, those people will be open to the Dark Guides' whispers. Things will happen. Small things at first. But each choice that comes from the dark feelings will make a tiny change in the landscape. And the fear will grow, like a weed among flowers, creating fertile ground for even darker feelings. You will be a seed that helps dim the Light."

No! No no no!

He laughed softly. "Isn't that what you wanted? Isn't that why you opened the wall?" He made another slice down her arm, almost as an afterthought. "I had thought of keeping you for a while, but even though you are far more insignificant than you want to believe, you are still one of the enemies."

As he raised the knife, Nigelle finally understood what she was looking at and what she'd done by poking that hole in the wall inside the forbidden garden, finally understood where the dark, secret landscapes anchored in her garden had come from.

And as the knife came down, she understood one other thing.

It's afraid of Belladonna.

After It had drained every heartbeat of fear It could from the girl, It dragged her across the grass and through the flower bed, leaving the body on the rust-colored sand. The bonelovers would find the remains soon enough.

The Dark Ones' spawn couldn't be trusted, but they could be useful. Discovering that the Landscapers and Bridges didn't remember what they truly were—or had been long ago—had been delightful. They were still the enemy, and even though they didn't have the power the True Enemy controlled, they stood in the way of Its changing the world into an endless hunting ground.

So now was the time to strike, when so many would be in the buildings instead of the gardens. In the gardens there was more chance of them escaping, no matter how quickly Its creatures attacked. But in the buildings they would be nothing more than prey. By the time they realized the Eater of the World was among them, it would be too late.

It walked over to the pool of murky water, changing Its shape to match Its creatures in that landscape.

Moving swiftly through the water, It shuddered as It thought of that one sealed garden. Then It dismissed the thread of fear before the feeling could become a strangling rope.

By the time It was done with this place, that sealed garden would be an island no one could reach.

The ground beneath the circle of sand-colored bricks shifted. Altered. Hot, bubbling mud oozed up, pushed its way through the cracks between the bricks.

One brick tilted. Sank. Another brick tilted toward that empty space. Sank.

Another. And another.

As the change reached the center of the circle, the sundial, that hated reminder of the dance between Dark and Light, wobbled, fell, broke.

Sank.

Chapter Nine

Lynnea woke slowly, the scent of clean linen and cool air giving her a sense of well-being.

Until she opened her eyes. And remembered.

After crossing the bridge, she didn't know how long or how far she had walked before she had caught a glimpse of steady lights that indicated some sort of settlement.

There had been lights before that, the bob and weave of lanterns held by people moving around in the dark. And there had been music, a cheerful sound coming from a distance. She'd almost followed the lights and the music, but a feeling had come over her, as if the ground under her feet were trying to hold on to her, making every step a battle of wills—as if something all around her were whispering, *That's not what you want. That's not what you're looking for.* And then . . .

Come to me.

She remembered the man's voice, and thought, *He needs me.* She didn't know why she was so certain of that—no one had ever needed her—but it had been enough to make her turn away from the lights and the music and keep moving until she'd reached a low rise and had seen the steady lights shining below her.

Then it all became a blur of struggling to reach something that remained out of reach. Maybe it would have been easier to give in, to get swept along with whatever forces were trying to draw her away. And maybe she would have given in, except ...

He needs me!

The world snapped back into focus when she crept out of the alley where *he* had found her.

She'd never seen a man who was storybook handsome, but *he* was. And the clothes he wore. Denim was considered workingman's cloth because it was sturdy, but she'd never seen a pair of pants that fit a man like *that*. And the shirt that made his eyes so impossibly green. And a *leather* jacket. Mam would have called him a bad influence just because of the way he looked.

But he'd been kind. He'd been annoyed about something, angry even, when he'd first seen her. Having lived with Pa and Ewan, she recognized temper in a man's eyes. But he'd taken her to a place where she could eat and had given up his room so she could sleep.

"Sebastian," she whispered. Just the sound of his name warmed her, gave her heart a fluttery lift. "Sebastian."

Then her mood sank. She hadn't found the man who had called to her when her thoughts had been mired in despair and she'd been yearning for something better. She hadn't found the man who needed her. Just looking at Sebastian was enough to tell her he wasn't the kind of man who would need anything from someone like her.

Even worse, she was in the Den of Iniquity. A vile, terrible place. A place decent women shouldn't even know about, let alone ever see.

Which didn't make sense, because Mam and her women friends knew about the Den. Even the younger women in the village knew about the Den. It was probably the most famous dark landscape in Ephemera. But, oddly enough, it wasn't an easy place to find. Some of Ewan's friends had tried to get to the Den last year. They'd crossed over a bridge and found the bad section of a large town, and one of them had gotten beaten and robbed, but they never found the Den.

So what did that say about her?

I guess Mam was right. I must be a bad person.

Why else would she have ended up in the Den when all she'd wanted was to find a safe place? But she did feel safe. Wasn't that a strange way to feel in a place like this?

Pushing aside the sheet and light blanket, Lynnea sat up and looked around the masculine room.

She went into the bathroom, took care of necessaries, then experimented with the water taps on the tub until she figured out how to fill it.

Hot water just by turning a tap. How decadent!

Maybe being a bad person wasn't so bad after all.

She soaked in the bath for a few blissful minutes before remembering the door that connected with another bedroom. Was someone in the other room waiting for her to finish? Using the washcloth and lightly scented soap she'd found along with two clean bath towels, she scrubbed her skin and washed her hair.

After wrapping her hair in one bath towel and drying off with the other, she did her best to clean the tub for the next person's use before she returned to the bedroom.

There was a storage chest at the foot of the bed. On top of it, neatly folded, were clean clothes. Cotton pettipants that would modestly cover her legs from waist to knee, and a cotton undershirt that—

She picked up the undershirt and tried to figure out what the extra layer of material was for. Then she blushed and dropped the undershirt.

Mam had always said only loose city women wore brassieres in order to push up their tits and entice men to act like fools. Or, worse, act like animals after a bitch in heat.

Did Sebastian think she was a loose woman? Probably. She *had* offered to have sex with him. Hadn't she? She'd been so tired when he brought her to the room, she couldn't remember if she'd said it or only thought it.

Or maybe this was the most modest underwear available in the Den. The rest of the clothes didn't look much different from the everyday clothes worn by well-to-do farmers' wives and daughters, even if the material wasn't ordinary.

The long-sleeved blue top was stretchy enough to pull over her head. The sleeveless, dark blue jumper was cut around the neck and shoulders so that a half finger of the top showed above it. It fell to midcalf and buttoned up one side. The socks came up to her knees, and the shoes were sturdy enough for a long tramp through fields.

Country clothes. She wasn't sure why she felt disappointed, since the clothes were new and of nice material, but dressed like she was going to a simple harvest dance made her feel less able to cope with whatever was beyond this room.

Returning the towels to the bathroom, she found a comb inside a small cabinet between the sink and the mirror. When she'd done what she could with her hair, she stared at her reflection and winced. The natural wave in her hair—the wave that had made Mam so angry she'd threatened more than once to cut Lynnea's hair right down to the scalp—seemed to be celebrating its freedom by being wavier than usual. She'd lost all her pins between the bridge and the Den, and nothing short of wetting it down and pulling it back in a tight bun would get rid of the waves—and even that didn't work most of the time.

Nothing to do about it.

Just as she walked back into the bedroom, someone knocked lightly on the outside door. Then Sebastian walked into the room, still dressed like a bad influence and looking more handsome than she remembered.

And her heart made a funny little bounce.

Now he knew what getting kicked in the gut felt like.

His little rabbit cleaned up too damn well. Wholesome and pretty, sweet and a little shy. And uncertain.

Definitely uncertain. As if some part of her that should have bloomed into something glorious had been savagely pruned back over and over again—and had still refused to completely wither and die.

She doesn't belong here. His heart twisted painfully at the thought. When he'd slipped into the room after she'd fallen asleep and taken her old clothes to Mr. Finch to get replacements, he should have chosen garments from the usual racks instead of asking the little man for a "country costume." Maybe dressing her like one of the succubi would have dimmed the wholesomeness, would have made it easier to seduce her and feast on the mindless pleasure he could make her feel.

But he'd selected clothes more suited to the kind of landscape he suspected she'd come from, and now . . .

She scared him. He looked at her and knew that, for all these years, he hadn't played the lover for those lonely women in the other landscapes out of any sense of pity or kindness or even enjoyment. Yes, he'd needed to feast on the feelings brought out from sexual pleasure, and the money and gifts he'd received for his services allowed him to live quite well by the Den's standards, but now he wondered if he'd been drawn to that particular kind of woman because he'd been looking for *her.* Just her.

And now she was here, where she didn't belong, and he . . .

A few hours. Just a few hours with her—and, maybe, the pleasure of being her lover. Just once.

Her fingers brushed the skirt of the jumper. "Thank you," she said softly.

"I'm glad the clothes please you." He crossed the room and lifted a hand to brush his fingertips over her hair. "How did you do that?"

"Oh." She raised her hand to touch the other side of her head. "It just does that. I don't have any hairpins."

"That's good. It's lovely the way it is."

She looked at him as if he'd just threatened her instead of giving her a compliment.

What had her life been like that a compliment made her afraid?

"You've been asleep for a few hours. You must be ready for another meal." He trailed his fingers down her arm until he reached her hand. Linking his fingers with hers, he led her from the room.

The trembling started as soon as they reached the street and she took a good look around. The main street didn't look quite as seedy as it had a few hours ago, but this was the Den, and a place that never saw the sun developed a different kind of character from the bad places in other landscapes where the night and its predators ruled for only a piece of each day.

Dressed in those clothes, which made her stand out rather than blend in, his little rabbit practically screamed "prey," and even with Teaser sending out advance warning, the other incubi couldn't resist drifting into the street to study her. But none of them would approach. Not when he'd so clearly claimed her for himself.

As he led Lynnea to a courtyard table at Philo's, he automatically scanned the other customers, noting the faces that belonged to visitors. When he was younger, he used to take note of the strangers to see which ones would be the most likely to enjoy his kind of fun, and he still did. But over the past few years he took notice because the Den was his home, and there were some kinds of trouble he didn't want here. And, somehow, when someone made him edgy, that person never found a way back to the Den.

"Welcome, welcome," Philo said, bustling up to the table with a full tray. His glance at Lynnea still held wariness, but he relaxed a little after a quick appraisal of her new clothes. He set two cups on the table, along with a small pitcher of cream and a bowl of sugar. "Food, yes?"

He was gone before there was time to say anything.

"He didn't ask what we wanted," Lynnea said, looking timid and uneasy as she studied the courtyard.

"Half the time he doesn't," Sebastian replied. He tipped his head to indicate the cup in front of her. "Philo makes it strong, so you might want to add some cream and sugar."

She picked up her cup and took a sip. Her eyes widened. "Oh, gracious. What *is* this?"

Sebastian grinned. "Koffee."

After taking another sip, she added a sugar cube and a little cream, then sipped again. "Oh, my." She sounded like a woman who had been stroked in just the right way.

Watching her, Sebastian raised his cup to hide a smile. Even the erotic statues in the courtyard couldn't compete for his rabbit's attention when there was koffee.

By the time they'd finished the first cups, Philo returned and set two plates on the table. Slices of steak, buttered toast, and an omelet filled with potatoes, onions, peppers, and sausage. He refilled their cups and went to check on his other customers.

Sebastian picked at his food, just to have something to do. He needed to find some way to set his plan in motion, but Lynnea dug into her meal with such enthusiasm, he didn't want to spoil her appetite by talking about anything that might upset her. So he ate while he watched the incubi and succubi trolling for prey, watched the visitors wandering down the main street looking for a brothel or a gambling house or a tavern where they could drink themselves blind. The Den was a place where the vices frowned upon in the daylight landscapes were openly celebrated. If a man wanted to lose a month's pay drinking, gambling, and whoring, the residents of the Den were more than willing to help him. If a bored, rich wife wanted to buy an incubus's time and particular talents, that was her choice—and if there were repercussions in her own landscape, that was her problem.

Of course, the residents always found it entertaining when a bored, rich wife and her equally bored, rich husband ran into each other in a brothel corridor. And those confrontations confirmed what the Den's residents had known all along: In its own way, the Den was more honest than the daylight landscapes, because the few rules that existed applied to everyone, regardless of gender or species.

When Lynnea finally leaned back and let out a sigh of contentment, Sebastian pushed aside his plate and took her hand. The touch made her tremble, and the little rabbit stared at the wolf who was trying not to drool over the coming feast.

"Tell me what you want, Lynnea," he said. "If you could have anything you wanted for a few hours, what would it be?"

She licked her lips. His pulse spiked, but he didn't allow himself to pull her into his lap and kiss her until they were both too mindless to know or care where they were. He just held her hand and waited.

"I'd like . . ." She closed her eyes. "I'd like to be strong and brave. I'd like to stop being afraid all the time. I don't remember what it feels like not to be afraid."

"Done," Sebastian said softly.

She opened her eyes and looked at him, her expression baffled.

"Did I mention I'm a wizard as well as an incubus?"

The words had barely left his mouth when he felt something snap open inside him, as if a part of him had been waiting to be acknowledged. The truth of it slid through him, filled him.

Guardians and Guides! He was a *wizard*.

Couldn't be. Wasn't possible.

Why not?

Because . . . Wouldn't he have known? Wouldn't Koltak have known?

Or was that the reason Koltak had brought the son he hated back to Wizard City over and over again? What would Koltak have done with a son born of a succubus if that child had shown any sign of having the wizards' kind of magic?

He didn't want to think about it. He'd said it only to give Lynnea a reason to shake off the chains of her past. Instead it had opened a new, and frightening, future for himself.

Power without training. Was there anything more dangerous in a world that altered itself to match the resonance of people's hearts? All he knew about the power wizards claimed came from stories, rumors, things he'd heard they'd done to people. He had to talk to someone, but who could he trust? Lee? Glorianna? Maybe. Or would their intense dislike of wizards make them turn away from him if they found out? Aunt Nadia?

His heart rate settled back to something close to normal. He could talk to Nadia. If anyone could help him understand this, she could.

"Sebastian?"

He put aside his own revelation and focused on the one he'd planned for her.

"Yes," he said. "I'm a wizard as well as an incubus." He stood up, shifted until he was beside her chair, then placed one hand on her head. "By a wizard's power and will, I decree that you, Lynnea, are a tigress. You are strong and brave and powerful. You are a woman of beauty and courage. And whatever you want from this night is yours."

She looked up at him, frightened, confused . . . and hopeful. "Did you put a spell on me?"

"Something like that." Daylight! He hoped he hadn't done anything more than say a few words convincingly enough for her to believe him.

His hand slid down that lovely, wavy brown hair. Then he coaxed her to her feet. Her body brushed against his, and he wanted her with a desperation that bordered on madness. But these hours were hers, and whatever happened between them had to be her choice.

"You need some clothes," he said, his voice rough.

"But I have clothes," she protested, brushing a hand over the jumper.

"Different clothes." Taking her hand, he led her down the street to Mr. Finch's shop.

They were within a step of the door when she stopped and asked in a timid voice, "What's a tigress?"

"A big, beautiful, powerful cat that lives in a distant landscape."

"A cat." She stared at the colored pole-lights. "She wouldn't let anyone hurt her kittens?"

"No, she wouldn't. And she's strong enough and powerful enough to protect them against any fool who tried."

He could almost feel something shift inside her, feel some change in the air around her. When she looked at him, the little rabbit was still there, but so was a hint of tigress.

He could handle the rabbit. He wasn't so sure about dealing with the tigress he was trying to create. And he wished he knew why the mention of kittens produced that response in her.

Mr. Finch greeted them with his usual hums and chirps intermingled with actual words. Every time Sebastian dealt with the small, nervous man, he wondered what was inside Mr. Finch that had brought him to the Den.

"The lady needs strut clothes," Sebastian said.

"Strut clothes?" Lynnea squeaked.

"Strut clothes," he replied firmly. "A tigress wouldn't wear anything else to prowl the Den."

"Tigress," Mr. Finch whispered. His nervous hand flutters stilled, and his eyes, usually so vague behind his gold-rimmed glasses, sharpened with professional interest.

"Yes, yes," Mr. Finch said, his hands fluttering again as he hurried to the door of his work area. "I have just the thing. I call it a catsuit. Designed it last month, just finished hemming this first one. Prim and naughty. Yes, yes."

Returning from the work area, he handed Lynnea a one-piece garment that was prim because it covered a woman's body from her ankles to the top of her breasts, and was definitely naughty because it came just short of fitting like a second skin. The material was dark blue shot with gold, silver, emerald, and ruby threads.

A succubus wearing something like that would become drunk on the emotions she could wring from the men around her.

Seeing Lynnea prowling the Den wearing that thing would kill him. He just knew it.

"What . . ." Lynnea cleared her throat. "What do you wear under it?" She held the material as if it might come alive at any moment and bite her.

"Skin," Mr. Finch chirped happily. He didn't look at Sebastian, but his mouth curved up in a tiny smile. "The incubi like skin."

"Oh, I couldn't—"

Sebastian put his mouth against her ear and whispered, "Tigress."

A succubus came out from behind a rack of clothes, her eyes hot with envy as she looked at the catsuit.

Daylight! Sebastian thought as she approached them. Why did *that* succubitch have to be here right now?

"Sebastian," the succubus purred. "Trying to clean up another stray to make it pass as something desirable?"

"I don't clean up strays," he snapped.

"Ooohhh? I heard you're Teaser's friend, and everyone knows he doesn't have what it takes to be a *real* incubus. He would have been chewed up and spit out long ago if it wasn't for you." Her eyes slid over Lynnea. "Even if you can squeeze those broodmare hips into that delectable outfit, you've still got that face on top of it."

"Perhaps I can help with the face," a cold voice said from the doorway.

It had been over a year since he'd seen her, and he'd never heard her voice sound like *that,* but he knew who stood in the doorway.

So did the succubus, whose face was now twisted into an ugly mask of fear.

Sebastian closed his eyes for a moment to steady himself before he turned to face the door—and Glorianna Belladonna.

Eyes of green ice stared back at him. With her long black hair framing her face, she still looked beautiful, but it was a cold, untouchable beauty—and he wondered if her heart had become just as cold.

This Belladonna was capable of bringing a horror into the Den that killed so viciously.

No. *No!* He wouldn't think it, wouldn't believe it. If she was capable of doing something like that, it would wound something inside him that would never heal.

She walked into the shop and stared at the succubus, who cringed.

"Go," she said.

The succubus bolted out of the shop.

"We need to talk," Sebastian said quietly.

"Later." She studied Lynnea, then smiled. "Sebastian has forgotten his manners. I'm his cousin Glorianna."

"I'm pleased to meet you," Lynnea replied. "I'm Lynnea."

"Glorianna—" Sebastian began.

"Why don't you go out and get some air?" Glorianna suggested.

He recognized a command when he heard one, and, cousin or not, only a fool would disobey Glorianna Belladonna. Despite that, he would have argued with her to give him a minute to explain, but the look in her eyes silenced the protest before he could make one. So he went outside and leaned a shoulder against the building as if nothing of importance were happening inside the shop.

Glorianna watched Sebastian leave the shop. When she'd crossed over near his cottage, she'd felt a dissonance she *knew* was coming from Sebastian. It was as if the dark currents inside him had become glutted to the point of making some essential shift in his heart. Then, as she hurried to the Den to find him and figure out what was wrong, she realized there had been another shift—as if a festering wound were being drained, bringing the Dark and Light inside Sebastian back into balance.

She didn't know what had caused the first change in Sebastian, but the second change had been produced by the woman standing in front of her.

Which made no sense, she thought as she turned to look at Lynnea, who smiled timidly and stared at her with blue eyes shadowed by fear. This woman didn't belong in the Den, shouldn't have been able to cross over into this landscape. But she was here, and there was no dissonance because of her presence.

Glorianna's breath hitched when she realized what she was looking at.

Catalyst.

An ordinary person, but because Lynnea was in a landscape she shouldn't have been able to reach, her presence would be like a pebble dropped into a pond, and the ripples would touch people in large ways or small. Would bring change. Would bring opportunities and choices.

For the catalyst as well as the people around her.

Which could explain why Sebastian was acting like a collie with one lamb to guard. And wasn't that interesting?

It was also interesting that when she'd gone to check on a city in one of her landscapes recently, she'd followed an impulse and stopped at a shop that supplied cosmetics for ladies. The colors she'd picked for cheeks and eyes didn't suit her at all, but she'd been carrying them in the bottom of her pack since she bought them.

The colors suited Lynnea perfectly.

Glorianna glanced at the catsuit in Lynnea's hands, then glanced at the shop's door—and smiled.

"Come on," she said, resting a hand on Lynnea's

shoulder to lead the catalyst to the curtained dressing area. "Let's get you ready for a prowl in the Den."

Sebastian stared at the door of Mr. Finch's shop.

The heart had no secrets from Glorianna Belladonna. She'd know within a minute that Lynnea didn't belong in the Den. But would she look beyond that? She didn't know about his plan to give his little rabbit a chance to be strong and powerful. She didn't know he needed a few hours with a woman who made him feel so much it scared him.

What was happening in the shop?

Teaser loped across the street to join him.

"Well, it's all set," Teaser said. "Although I'd keep this prowl to the main street if I were you. I spread the word, but that's no guarantee that all the incubi and succubi will go along with it."

"They will if they want to remain in the Den," Sebastian growled. If he'd been using the wizard magic inside him unknowingly all these years to keep human visitors he didn't like from returning to the Den, could that magic also prevent a demon from returning? He'd test that out on the succubitch after he took Lynnea to the Landscapers' School. Assuming, of course, that Lynnea was still in the shop.

Teaser gave him a wary look that swiftly gave way to the usual cocky, bouncy energy. There was a light in the incubus's eyes Sebastian hadn't seen in a long time. A tame prowl wasn't the kind of heat and action the incubi looked for, but it was something different, and the novelty of it was reason enough for Teaser's enthusiasm.

"So," Teaser said, looking around and grinning, "where's the country mouse?"

"In the shop. With Glorianna."

The grin vanished. "Belladonna's here?"

Before Sebastian could answer, the shop door opened, and Glorianna walked out. Alone.

He pushed away from the building, wanting to shove her aside and run into the shop to see if there was anyone inside besides Mr. Finch. Instead he stood there, his muscles clenched from the effort to remain still. "We need to talk."

Glorianna gave him a long look, followed by a mischievous smile—and looked like the cousin he loved instead of a dangerous rogue Landscaper. "Later. You're going to have your hands full for a while, Sebastian."

Then she looked at Teaser, who bobbed his head as a salute and said, "I'm helping Sebastian."

"Yes," she said after a long pause. "Yes, you are." She sounded intrigued, as if something had exceeded her expectations.

Then she walked away.

"Well," Teaser said, blowing out a breath and wiping sweat off his forehead. "Well."

He didn't run away, but he headed up the street in the opposite direction at a swift walk that would put some distance between himself and Belladonna.

Which left Sebastian standing alone outside Mr. Finch's shop. Was there any point in waiting? There had been a message in Glorianna's smile, but he couldn't decipher it . . . and wasn't interested in trying.

He turned away from the door, feeling unhappy and discouraged. He'd shaken up the Den to create an illusion for a few hours. And for what? To feel like a child again, encouraged by the other children to think he'd been invited to play, only to discover raising his hope of being accepted *was* the game?

"Sebastian?"

Being part human wasn't human enough. And trying to be human had never gotten him a single damn thing. Why couldn't he give it up, let it go?

"Sebastian? I'm ready. I think."

He turned around and rocked back on his heels. "Lynnea?"

Flustered, she raised one hand to her face. "I don't look that different, do I?"

Daylight, Glorianna! What did you do to my little rabbit? It was Lynnea ... and it wasn't Lynnea. The succubi and human whores—even the city women who visited the Den—wore more paint on their faces, but there was something devastating about seeing wholesome and pretty changed to seductive. And that catsuit ...

Mr. Finch was a wicked, wicked man for designing a piece of clothing that hugged a woman's body like that.

"Sebastian?" Timid. Uncertain. That first taste of feminine power withering under the weight of his silence.

He closed the distance between them and settled his hands on her waist—and congratulated himself for not running his hands up and down her to find out what she was—and wasn't—wearing under that catsuit.

"You look wonderful," he said, leaning a little closer. "Powerful." No perfume, just the light scent of the soap he'd left for her in his room. A scent suitable for a country girl, not this seductress looking at him with innocent bedroom eyes.

Too many conflicting sensory messages. Too much feeling. The only thing he knew for certain was that if he ended up sleeping alone tonight, he was going to curl up and die.

"Kiss me," he whispered.

"Here?" she squeaked, her eyes darting to the people moving up and down the street.

"A tigress wouldn't be afraid to kiss her lover in public."

She stared at him. "Lover?"

"Tonight I'm the lover of Lynnea the tigress."

"Oh, gracious."

He wasn't sure if that translated into something good or bad. Then she lightly pressed her lips against his, and he didn't care how it translated.

Sweet. Warm. He hadn't been this excited about a closemouthed kiss since ... All right. He'd *never* been this excited about a closemouthed kiss. And when her hands curved around the back of his neck and her fingers tangled in his hair, he didn't see any reason for either of them to move until they fell over from exhaustion or starvation.

Then she eased back, looked at him, and frowned. "I don't think that's the way a tigress kisses, but I—"

He didn't give her a chance. He brought his mouth down on hers and showed her how a tigress would kiss a lover, how an incubus would kiss a lover when she really was a lover and not just prey.

A bull demon's bellow from somewhere nearby finally broke through lust's haze. Sebastian stepped back and took her hand. "Let's prowl." *While I can still walk.*

There were musicians on the street corners, jugglers in the street, tables outside the taverns for visitors who wanted to watch the entertainment.

They strolled down one side of the main street, watching everything and everyone. The feel of the Den was festive, with a sharp edge that could turn mean in a heartbeat but was staying on the fun side of that line.

This was how the Den had felt when he'd found it fifteen years ago. This was the feeling it had lost in the past few years, turning harder, crueler. Leaving him feeling dissatisfied with the one place he felt comfortable living.

He looked around and felt breathless. Staggered.

Oh, daylight. What he was thinking couldn't possibly be true.

He didn't realize Lynnea had drifted up the street a little ways until he heard a bull demon's bellow a moment before it lumbered out of a tavern and stopped short of knocking down his little rabbit.

Sebastian held his breath. Lynnea and the bull demon stared at each other.

Finally Lynnea said politely, "How do you do?"

The bull demon pondered the question. "Do good," it rumbled. It shifted its bulk from one foot to the other.

They stared at each other for a few moments more before the bull demon shook its shaggy, horned head and lumbered away, having sufficiently strained its conversational skills.

"Did you see?" Lynnea said when Sebastian hurried up to her and hooked an arm around her waist. Her face glowed with excitement. She turned in his hold and placed her hands on his chest. "I talked to . . . " She paused. Frowned. "What was it I just talked to?"

"A bull demon." He felt the warmth of her hands through his shirt.

"Bull demon?" Another pause. "How much like a bull?"

Guardians and Guides! If they didn't start moving, he was going to do something stupid. Like rip open his shirt and beg her to touch him.

"Nobody but their females knows for sure," he said, taking her hand so he could still have physical contact without being too close.

They slowly made their way back to Philo's place. Holding a plate of nibblies in one hand, Teaser waved them over to a table, then pointed at the bottle of wine waiting for them.

As soon as Sebastian introduced Lynnea to Teaser, Teaser set the plate on the table, looked at Sebastian, and said, "The music's hot tonight. You don't mind if I borrow your lady for a dance, do you?"

Sebastian hesitated a moment. "I don't mind if the lady doesn't."

Teaser gave Lynnea that cocky, boyish grin that had disabled so many women's brains. "Come on," he said, holding out his hand. "I'll show you how to dance in the Den."

"Oh, I don't—" Lynnea caught herself, then looked at Sebastian, who just smiled at her and mouthed, *Tigress.*

Teaser grabbed her hand and led her into the middle of the street. When he began a slow, exaggerated bump and grind, she blushed, shook her head, and took a step back. But he said something that made her sputter and then laugh, and before long she was moving with the music, copying Teaser's movements.

Did she have any idea how blatantly sexual those

movements were? Did she have any awareness of how much male attention was focused on her? No. She was being brave. She was having fun. She was blooming into a sensual woman right before his eyes.

And watching her made him suffer in a way he never had before.

He poured a glass of wine, settled in a chair, and studied the main street. Teaser was right. The music was hot, the energy was hot—and the Den looked like it had all those years ago when a fifteen-year-old boy had been drawn to it, dazzled by the lights and the energy . . . and the feeling that the place welcomed him with open arms.

"You never told me," Sebastian said when Philo came up to the table.

"Told you what?" Philo asked.

"For years I've called the Den a carnal carnival, but I didn't realize until tonight that's exactly what it is. A carnival of vices . . . but tempered somehow."

"I don't know what you mean."

Sebastian took a sip of wine. "Yes, you do. Fifteen years ago I was more innocent than I realized, or would ever admit, and this is that adolescent boy's dream of a dark landscape. Heat and fun and sex. There's a meaner edge. Sure there is." He looked up at Philo. "But it's still a carnival."

"So what if it is?" Philo said, his face and voice solemn. "This is a dark landscape, but it's not a bad place. I've lived in bad places, Sebastian. So has Mr. Finch. So have the rest of the humans who settled here. Finding this place . . . " He sighed. "So, no, I never told that boy he wasn't in a badass landscape like he thought he was. The Den's like you, Sebastian. Hot, dark, a little mean around the edges, but good at the core."

The Den's like you. Sebastian waited until Philo left to check on the other customers before draining his wineglass—and remembered the first time Glorianna had come to visit him in the Den, six months after he'd arrived.

"Quite a place, isn't it?" Sebastian said, his arm linked through hers as they walked down the main street.

"Yes, it is," Glorianna replied. *"You're happy here?"*

"I belong here."

He hadn't realized how tense she was until he felt her relax. Hadn't realized at the time that, while he'd been finding his place, she had lost hers. Hadn't even realized during that first visit that she was the Landscaper who had altered Ephemera to make the Den. And later . . .

"Why did you do it, Glorianna? Why did you create a place like the Den?"

She shrugged. "Even demons need a home."

It had stung that she considered him a demon, but even then, he'd had to admit she was right. The incubi and succubi were the dominant demons in the Den itself, and for the first time they had a place where they could openly be what they were. No more trying to blend in with the humans, no more danger of being hurt or even killed when the nature of their sexuality was discovered. Many who had drifted into the Den during those first months discovered the carnival atmosphere and the lack of danger weren't to their taste. And those who had tried to change the tone of the Den and bring in the kind of danger that would have turned it into a different kind of place . . .

The heart had no secrets from Glorianna Belladonna. Those who wanted a dangerous place ended up in a dangerous place. But not the Den. Those who survived the dark desires of their hearts never came back to the Den.

He'd been seventeen before he'd discovered that the rogue Landscaper called Belladonna was his cousin Glorianna. Might not have discovered it even then if Lee hadn't come stumbling into the Den a few weeks after beginning his formal training at the Bridges' School.

Fifteen years old and running away from a pain he couldn't bear, Lee had come to the Den. Sebastian had turned away from the woman he'd almost lured into bed, in order to keep his younger cousin from getting into too much trouble. He'd helped Lee get beyond drunk, since the boy seemed set on doing something self-destructive, and he'd held his cousin's head later when Lee puked up the liquor and half his stomach.

And he'd listened to the troubled, tearful, painful discovery Lee had made that day—a discovery his mother and sister had withheld from him. Lee had known Glorianna had left the Landscapers' School abruptly and was being trained by their mother. But until he'd taken a walk around the school to find the location of his sister's garden, he hadn't known the Instructors and wizards had tried to seal Glorianna into her garden, hadn't known she'd been declared a rogue Landscaper, a danger to Ephemera, someone the wizards would try to destroy on sight.

Someone now called Belladonna.

All of that Sebastian had learned from a boy trying to come to grips with a truth that had altered his reality. But never why. None of them—not Nadia or Glorianna or Lee—ever told him what Glorianna had done to be declared rogue. Now, after so many years, it no longer mattered. She *was* dangerous . . . and feared—and she was still the girl who had understood his troubled heart better than he did.

A smattering of applause brought Sebastian's attention back to the present. Lynnea was shaking her head and laughing as she stepped away from Teaser. He was grinning, looking carefree and easy—until Lynnea lifted her hair off her neck to cool the heated skin.

Teaser's grin faded. His body went from carefree to tense in a heartbeat. And the look in his blue eyes . . .

Sebastian understood the look. Knew his own eyes revealed the same hunger. He wanted to press his mouth against the back of her neck and taste her skin. He wanted to skim his hands up the front of her, cupping her breasts, rubbing the nipples until they stiffened beneath his touch. He wanted to pull her against him, letting her feel what the sight of her body did to his.

Teaser stared at him, viciously hungry for this particular feast and just as viciously frustrated.

Because the feast had no idea what she was doing to either of them. Her eyes were closed, her fingers were threaded through her hair to keep it up, and her hips were still moving slightly to the music. But not for their benefit. Not to lure or entice or even attract attention. If anyone had told him innocence could make him insane with lust, he would have laughed.

He wasn't laughing now.

Oddly enough, Teaser regained his balance first. Taking a step toward Lynnea, he made a gesture to indicate the table where Sebastian waited, but as she turned in that direction, he glanced down the street. Instead of leading her to the table, he curled a hand around her arm and led her away from the courtyard.

Sebastian stiffened. That son of a succubus! If Teaser thought to have some fun playing a game of rival-rival, he'd find himself looking for another landscape to live in. There wasn't time for games. Lynnea wouldn't be here more than a few hours. And he needed those hours more than he wanted to admit.

As he shifted to set the wineglass on the table, he felt someone approach. The explicit warning to leave him alone never made it past the thought as Glorianna slipped into the chair next to his, her back to the street.

There was so much to tell her, but he blurted out the thing most important to his heart at that moment. "She doesn't belong here."

Glorianna reached for the wine bottle and poured a glass for herself. "No one comes to the Den by mistake."

"She did."

She sipped the wine and studied him. "Are you sure?"

"She was supposed to go to the Landscapers' School, but something happened and she ended up here."

"Then something here must have resonated with something inside her."

Me. But he wasn't going to say that. Not to Glorianna

Belladonna. "I'm going to take her to the Landscapers' School after she's had some sleep."

Glorianna hesitated. "If that's what you need to do."

"It's the right thing to do." His voice sounded harsh, but he heard the plea beneath the harshness. *Tell me I'm wrong, Glorianna. Tell me I can keep her here with me without taking away the life she should have had.*

But Glorianna said nothing, just stared at the wine in her glass. Finally she said quietly, "There may be trouble at the school. Serious trouble, if the Landscapers ignored the warning signs. But it should be safe enough for you and Lynnea to go to the school, since neither of you will be there for long."

He shifted, folding his arms to lean on the table, bringing him closer to her. "What's happened?"

"The Eater of the World is free in the landscapes again."

"The Eater of the World is a myth," Sebastian protested. "An evil that children whisper about to scare one another—or adults use to scare children into behaving."

"It's real, Sebastian," Glorianna replied. "It was confined for so long, most people don't remember It as anything but a story. But now It has escaped. The landscapes that were sealed up with It aren't sealed anymore, and It has the power to connect those places with other landscapes to create access points from which It can emerge to hunt. It will feed on the fear It creates, strengthening Its power over a place until the dark facets of the heart are the only things that shine in that landscape. Until the Light is so dimmed people won't be able to find it in themselves. Hope, happiness, love. Those feelings will fade until they're little more than a memory barely remembered."

Sebastian refilled his glass, then downed half the wine. "Do you think that ... thing ... has been hunting in the Den?"

"I know It came here. It tried to anchor one of Its

landscapes to the alley where the woman was killed. I altered the Den after I saw what It had done."

He told her how the alley had shifted when he, Teaser, and the bull demon had gone in to investigate the body. Then he told her about the other death in the waterhorses' landscape.

"I can understand why this Eater would come hunting in the Den," he said as he poured the rest of the wine into their glasses. "The Den is a dark landscape with plenty of humans and humanlike demons in a small area. But why kill a waterhorse? They're demons that prey on humans when they get the chance. Wouldn't this thing want to ... embrace them?"

Glorianna shook her head. "Like the bull demons and the Merry Makers and some of the others, the waterhorses are a dark aspect of Ephemera—a natural one. The Eater didn't shape them. It can't control them, so It will hunt them, too." She hesitated. "Sebastian, don't stay away from the Den too long. Do what you have to do, but don't stay away too long."

"Why?" There was something she didn't want to tell him, but this wasn't the time for more secrets, not if she was right about this Eater of the World being loose in Ephemera's landscapes.

He didn't like the look in her eyes. Pride and regret—and both those feelings aimed at him.

"Because you're the Den's anchor," she finally said. "The others who live here provide ... texture ... but the Den, at its core, is what you want it to be, what you expect it to be. Because the Den is a reflection of you."

"Are you saying I *let* that thing come into the Den to hunt?"

"No. You couldn't have stopped It from coming into the Den. But It can't *change* the Den if you don't allow the Den to change."

Sebastian laughed harshly. "My will against something so evil and deadly It can change our whole world into a nightmare? Do you really think I can do that?"

"You did it. You did it," she repeated when he just

stared at her in disbelief. "You said it yourself, Sebastian. The alley started to shift and become a different landscape, and *you didn't allow it to happen.* You held on to what the alley was supposed to be, and you got away. You can't stop It from coming into the Den. There are plenty of bridges that connect the Den to other landscapes not in my keeping, and until those are broken, It can find a way in, and It can create small access points. But It can't control the heart of the Den as long as you hold on to this place."

Philo. Mr. Finch. Teaser. All the other residents in the Den. He felt the weight of their lives on his shoulders. He had never bargained for that kind of responsibility.

Then he looked at Glorianna and realized the burden she carried was a thousand times heavier.

He laid his hand over hers. "What are you going to do?"

She sighed. "All I can do right now is hold on to the landscapes in my care and protect them as best I can. Lee can help with that—once I find him."

He heard the worry in her voice. He didn't try to offer false comfort. After what she'd told him, that would be no kindness. So he just kept his hand on hers, offering the connection of family, telling her silently that she wasn't alone.

Glorianna walked up the Den's main street, resisting the urge to rush back to Philo's place and tell Sebastian not to take Lynnea to the Landscapers' School. She didn't think he'd run into any real trouble while he was there, not with all the Instructors who lived at the school and the other Landscapers who were always returning to tend their gardens. Maybe they had already contained the Eater of the World. And if they couldn't contain It by themselves, they'd summon the wizards to help them. After all, wizards were good at containing problems.

No, she didn't think Sebastian would run into trouble, even though she'd made sure he knew of another way out of the school. It was the thrumming of two heart wishes in the currents of power that flowed through the Den that made her want to push him into the decision *she* wanted him to make.

You can guide, but you cannot take control. You cannot take away the choices a person must make in order to fulfill his life's journey.

Opportunities and choices. People were offered opportunities to fulfill heart wishes all the time and either didn't recognize them or couldn't find the courage to reach for the very thing they wanted.

She couldn't interfere with Sebastian's journey, wherever it might lead him. She'd given him an opportunity, an excuse, to back away from the decision to take Lynnea to the school, and he'd chosen to ignore it.

Knowing she was doing the right thing by letting him make the decision didn't stifle the urge to give her darling cousin a swift kick in his newly polished honor.

By the time he said good-bye to Glorianna and went up the street to find Lynnea, Teaser and two younger incubi were finishing up some kind of impromptu skit full of double meanings. Bawdy, yes, but too exaggerated and good-natured to be lewd.

And there was Lynnea, standing at the edge of the crowd, laughing and applauding, shining like starlight.

No, not like starlight. She was too warm to be starlight. Sunlight, then. The kind of warmth that never touched the Den—until she had walked here, laughed here.

He applauded with the rest of the crowd, not because he'd seen the performance but as a way of acknowledging Teaser's help in creating these few hours when his little rabbit could feel like a tigress.

Lynnea turned, as if she recognized the sound of his hands, and smiled at him. "Aren't they wonderful?"

"Yes, they are," he replied, returning the smile.

"Did you have a nice visit with your cousin?"

"It was fine." He slipped a hand into the pocket of his leather jacket and touched the folded linen napkin. Glorianna had insisted on drawing him a crude map of the school. It had seemed silly, since there was only one road into the Landscapers' part of the school grounds, and that led straight to the buildings that housed the classrooms and living quarters. Then he realized the road and buildings were only reference points for the thing she wanted him to be able to reach if he needed to. Her garden.

Mentioning her garden had made her uneasy, but she still made him go over the directions until she was satisfied he could find it. A safe place, if he needed one. And a way to escape, hidden in the fountain in the center of the garden . . . if he needed it.

He'd worry about that once he and Lynnea reached the school. Right now he didn't want to think of anything but her, didn't want to feel anything that wasn't connected to the time they had together. Not enough time. Not nearly enough. But he wouldn't ask for more.

Leaving Teaser, he and Lynnea strolled hand in hand, enjoying the music, the action, the energy. Everything looked different now. They were his people, his responsibility, demons and humans alike. His will and heart were the anchor that would keep the Den safe from encroaching evil. He was needed in a way he'd never been needed before.

And something inside him began resonating in a slightly different way as a response to that knowledge.

As they came up to a side street, two demon cycles zipped around the corner. One, noticing Sebastian, came to an abrupt halt. The other, its attention fixed on Lynnea, rushed forward, waving its arms and roaring, "Blaarrgh!"

Lynnea stared at the demon, with its claws and razored teeth—and she giggled.

The demon stared back at her, its ears lifting at the sound. "Blaarrgh!" it said again.

She giggled again, then wrapped a hand around one of its claw-tipped fingers, and said, "How do you do, Mr. Demon?"

There was a difference between being a tigress and a fool. The demons who had claimed the motored cycles as the spoils of battle could eviscerate a man with one swipe of those claws—and usually started feeding before the first scream died away.

But there it was, *grinning* at her, while its companion looked on as if it had been denied a particular treat. Which was *not* a healthy way for either of them to think about his rabbit.

"We have to go now," Sebastian said. "We have a bit of a walk ahead of us."

The grin was replaced by a scowl. "Where you go?" the demon said in a voice that sounded like gravel rolling in a metal barrel.

They talked? Sure, everyone knew the demon cycles understood human words, but no one had ever heard any of them *talk*.

"We're going to my cottage," Sebastian replied reluctantly. They probably already knew how to find the cottage, since they traveled all over the Den, but that didn't mean he wanted to point it out to them.

"We take you. You ride."

In those moments when he tried to figure out how to refuse without getting hurt, the demons focused their attention on Lynnea.

"Wanna ride?" they asked.

The look on Lynnea's face was answer enough. His little rabbit-tigress wanted to ride. He just wished the excitement he could read on her face had something—anything!—to do with *his* anatomy rather than a demon cycle.

"Okay, let's ride," he said, trying to keep the growl out of his voice that might be misinterpreted as an invitation to a pissing contest. It wasn't a contest he could win, and a gelded incubus wouldn't be much use to anyone, least of all himself.

He straddled one cycle, then had to bite his tongue to keep it from falling out when Lynnea straddled the other one—which made him desperate to find out if she was wearing anything but skin under that catsuit.

Mr. Finch was, without doubt, a wicked, wicked man.

It was less than a mile between his cottage and the streets that made up the Den proper, but the demon cycles couldn't seem to find the lane that was the straight route. They zipped around the countryside, weaving between trees, zooming up a hill and down the other side, making strange sounds that might have been gleeful laughter while Lynnea whooped and squealed and giggled.

Finally, when he insisted that she was too tired to play anymore—and she dutifully agreed with him—the demon cycles found the lane and took them to the cottage.

"Good-bye," Lynnea said, waving at the demons as Sebastian hustled her inside the cottage. "Thank you for the lovely ride."

He closed the door before the demon cycles decided to join them, then tensed when he realized there was a lamp glowing on the table in front of the couch. He never left a lamp burning when he'd be gone for hours. Too much risk of fire.

"Stay here," he whispered, moving cautiously into the room. Then he noticed the package wrapped in brown paper next to the lamp and the slip of paper tucked under the string—and breathed a sigh of relief when he recognized the writing.

Glorianna.

A careful, one-fingered poke at the package gave him the next answer. "I think my cousin brought the rest of your clothes here."

"Was that the wrong thing to do?" Lynnea asked, sounding baffled by his behavior.

"No. It was a kindness." Returning to where she waited, he reached past her and did something he'd never done in the ten years he'd lived there. He locked the door.

"Come in," he said, moving around to light more lamps.

She wandered around the room, looking at everything. Then she stopped and studied two framed sketches on the wall. "Who did these?"

"I did," he replied gruffly, not sure if he was embarrassed to admit it or afraid of her opinion. He'd shown his sketches to Nadia a few years ago, after she'd bullied him into telling her how he spent his time when he wasn't prowling the Den. She'd kept three of them—one for herself, one for Glorianna, and one for Lee—and had these two framed for him.

He'd never told her how much that had meant to him.

"They're lovely," Lynnea said.

And he would never tell *this* woman how much her words meant to him.

"I like your home, Sebastian."

He moved toward her without thinking, too desperate to feel to be able to think. His fingers tangled in her hair and his mouth feasted on hers, wanting anything, everything.

And he could have everything. He knew it by the way her arms wrapped around him, the way she responded to his kisses. He could slake this terrible hunger and give her pleasure she'd remember for a lifetime. All she would forfeit was her virginity.

But he could lose his heart, if he hadn't lost it already. *She doesn't belong here.*

The thought intruded, rankled, savaged desire. He wanted one night with her, but he couldn't have it. Not for her sake, but for his own.

He gentled the kiss, lingering because it would be the last. Then he eased back, out of her arms.

"After we get some sleep, I'll take you to the Landscapers' School."

"But . . ." She stared at him, unfulfilled desire shifting into the pain of rejection. "But I'm a bad person. Mam said so."

He shook his head. "You're one of the finest people I've ever known. If she couldn't see you for who you are, the flaw was in her, not in you. You don't belong in a place where the sun never shines. You don't belong in the Den."

When he took a step forward, intending to ease the sting of rejection, she hunched her shoulders and turned away.

No comfort. No sweet ending to a sweet encounter.

Maybe that was just as well . . . for both of them.

"Bedroom is through that door. You can have the bed."

She didn't ask where he would sleep. She just crossed the room, picked up her parcel of clothing, went into the bedroom, and closed the door.

He stared at the bedroom door for a long time before he pulled off his shoes and stretched out on the couch.

He had done the right thing.

So why did the right thing make him feel so bad?

Chapter Ten

They rode the demon cycle in the fading light of a summer evening, Lynnea snug against his back, her arms wrapped around him. Even here, even now, he hadn't escaped the night. The day was taking its last breaths before surrendering to its rival. Not that it mattered. He belonged to the night. And Lynnea belonged to the Light.

The Landscapers' School spread out over acres of land surrounded by a high stone wall. Borders and boundaries. A world confined in order to be free. Had the first Landscapers envisioned this when they shattered Ephemera? Had they intended for their world to be parceled out and held in pieces, or had they thought their descendants would be able to put the pieces back together?

Don't put all your eggs in one basket, Aunt Nadia had told him once. He hadn't understood the meaning at the time, but now, as the demon cycle skimmed above the road next to the school's wall, he wondered at the wisdom of controlling so much from one place.

Not his decision. Of course, the majority of people in Ephemera didn't have any say in the matter either. Everything was in the hands of the Landscapers. And, perhaps, the wizards, since they decided when a person was too unmanageable to live anywhere but a dark landscape.

Travel lightly, Sebastian thought. Especially when entering *this* place.

"There's the entrance," he said, raising his voice to make sure the demon heard him.

A growl was the only response.

It hadn't been difficult to convince the demon to bring them to the school. All he'd said was that Lynnea might have to walk a long way.

Maybe they should have walked. They'd had to cross through two other landscapes before they found a bridge that would cross over to the Landscapers' piece of Ephemera. If they'd walked through those other landscapes, would they have found a place that would have called to both of them? A new place, a new start. With Lynnea.

But the Den needed him, and every day he was gone could make the Den susceptible to another will. An evil will.

They turned off the main road and went through the entrance to the school. The demon cycle slowed down as they passed empty pastureland.

"Where are the animals?" Lynnea said, looking around.

"Maybe they put them up for the night," Sebastian replied. But something didn't feel right. The silence was too heavy, too ... expectant.

They were halfway between the buildings and the school's entrance when the demon cycle stopped abruptly and began gliding backward.

Sebastian dropped his feet to the ground, dragging his heels. "No. Stop."

The demon growled and kept gliding back toward the main road.

"Stop!" He tapped Lynnea's hand to tell her to dismount once the demon came to a shuddering halt. "Daylight! What's wrong with you?"

"Sebastian?" Lynnea hugged herself. "Where are the people?"

"Probably inside the buildings. It's almost dark." But

something was making his skin crawl. Probably just the typical response when someone like him entered this place. After all, Landscapers didn't think of demons as people. Aunt Nadia and Glorianna were the exceptions in thinking demons were entitled to their own little pieces of the world.

"Here," he said, "give me that." He took the pack Lynnea had on her back. Glorianna had done a little more shopping on her way to the cottage. The trousers, shirt, and lightweight jacket Lynnea wore were good traveling clothes. Her other clothes were in his pack.

Had she kept the catsuit?

He slipped one strap over his shoulder, then took Lynnea's hand and linked his fingers with hers. Giving the demon cycle a hard stare, he said, "Wait for me."

Did the school always feel like it was stretching and moving even when a person stood still?

"I don't like this place," Lynnea whispered.

Neither did he, and if he still felt uneasy after talking to the Landscapers, he'd make some excuse, get them both out of there, and take Lynnea to Aunt Nadia's house.

Which is what I should have done in the first place.

"Come on," he said, leading her toward the buildings. "Let's find someone who can take us to whoever is in charge."

The closest building was two stories and square. Probably the classrooms. Not a promising place to find anyone at this time of day, but it was better than wandering around.

He thought he saw movement above the first-floor windows, then decided it was nothing more than a bird or small critter moving in the branches of a tree that almost brushed against the building. But his nerves were humming, and the desire to get on the demon cycle and get away from this place was growing stronger.

The building's double doors were partially open, which didn't seem right. Would they be that careless about closing up after lessons were over for the day?

Maybe it meant someone *was* in the building—a student running in for a forgotten book and not checking that the door was closed because she'd be coming back out in a minute.

A shiver went down his spine as he pushed one door all the way open.

Lynnea grabbed her jacket and pulled the material over her nose and mouth as soon as they stepped into the building. "Oh. It smells bad in here."

It did smell bad. Which was why he had to look. If someone was alone and injured in here, he had to do what he could to help—or go and find help if there was nothing else he could do.

He almost told Lynnea to stay by the door. After all, the first classroom wasn't more than ten paces from the doorway. But even ten paces felt too far.

Giving her hand a squeeze, he walked to the first classroom door, letting her trail a step behind him, their linked hands providing a tether. The door was ajar, but it resisted opening further when he gave it a light push, so he put his shoulder to the wood and shoved.

And wished with everything in him that he'd left the door alone.

"Sebastian?" Lynnea whispered from behind him.

This time he gave her hand a hard squeeze, a command for silence. His heart pounded as he stared at what the room contained.

They hadn't had a chance. Something had attacked them so fast, most of the girls hadn't had time to try to run.

He shook his head, as if that would erase the carnage in the room. This couldn't be real. These were the Landscapers, the women who were supposed to be able to protect the rest of Ephemera's people until the Eater of the World was destroyed. For him to be looking at the aftermath of a slaughter inside their school . . .

Then it hit him. The bodies weren't fresh. Unless they were holed up in another part of the school and were still under attack, the other people who lived here should have removed the bodies by now instead of leaving them to decay.

If there was anyone left.

Cold conviction wrapped around him. This wasn't an isolated attack. If he dared spend the time checking more rooms in this building or the other buildings, it would be the same. Death. Slaughter. Maybe most of the Landscapers escaped to their gardens and crossed over to other landscapes. Maybe the Bridges were able to get away before whatever swept over this part of the school reached them. Maybe.

It didn't matter if most of them had escaped or were still here among the dead. Right now, the absence of other people meant one thing: He and Lynnea might be the only people alive at the school.

Which meant they were the only available prey.

Spinning around, he pulled Lynnea to the outside door, desperate to get out of an enclosed space where they could be cut off from any chance of escape. Once they reached the demon cycle, they'd be able to outrun whatever was here before it sensed their presence. And once they got away from the school . . .

They were out the door and running toward the demon cycle when they both jerked to a stop, frozen by the sight in front of them.

The front end of the cycle was submerged in a pool of murky water. There was no sign of the demon, but something floated belly-up, just visible below the water. In the dusky light, the creature was too dark in color to make out its size or shape, but the paler belly was still visible and showed the lethal slashes of sharp claws.

The demon cycle had fought, but it hadn't won.

"It's like the horse," Lynnea whispered. "When Ewan left me on the road, I ran after him. By the time I got to the bend in the road near the bridge, the horse was struggling in a pool of water and . . . something pulled it under."

The ground looked solid enough around the pool.

They could skirt around the water and make a run to the main gate. Except ...

"That funny-colored sand," Lynnea said, her voice barely audible. "I saw that sand on the road, too. It wasn't there when I first ran to the bridge. It just appeared while I was trying to decide if I should cross the bridge or go back down the road to find help."

For a moment he was back in the alley in the Den, feeling sand beneath his feet.

"The Eater of the World is free in the landscapes again. . . . The landscapes that were sealed up with It aren't sealed anymore."

The Eater of the World was *here,* right now, changing the Landscapers' School into pieces of Its own dark landscapes. But It hadn't changed everything yet. As long as he and Lynnea stayed on ground that was still part of the school, they had a chance of getting away.

Even as the thought formed, he watched the land beyond the sand and pool of water change into a bog that stretched back to the stone walls that enclosed the school.

A feeling too primitive for words made him look back at the building. *Was* that just a shadow on the wall? Or was it a predator that blended in so well it was almost invisible?

Releasing Lynnea's hand, he eased the pack's other strap over his shoulder to settle it on his back. More sensible to drop it, but he didn't want to leave anything behind that might be used to trace them.

Guardians and Guides! How were they supposed to get out of here?

Sebastian's breath caught as the answer came to him: Glorianna's garden.

They'd have to go deeper into the school, run straight into the enemy's lair.

Rustling sounds of things moving closer, hidden by the fading light.

Only one chance.

He reached for Lynnea's hand. Both of them would

get out of here or neither of them. He wasn't going to let her fall behind and die like the people he'd seen in that classroom.

He led her back toward the building. "We've got to reach my cousin's garden," he said quietly. "When I tell you to go, you run like a rabbit. Understand me?"

Staring straight ahead, she nodded. "Something's coming."

"I know." He gave himself a moment to picture the map Glorianna had drawn, not daring to take the time to pull the linen napkin out of his jacket pocket. The sundial was the first marker.

Glorianna. He focused his will, focused on the need to find her garden . . . and hoped that something—Guardian, Guide, or Ephemera itself—would respond to his heartfelt call for help in finding the piece of ground that resonated with her. *Glorianna. Glorianna.* "Ready?"

Lynnea tightened her fingers around his in answer.

"Run!"

Things out of nightmares ran after them. Ants as long as his forearm. Spiders as big as dogs. And things he had no name for.

The flagstone path beneath their feet felt spongy, fluid, as if the stones were about to change into something else between one step and the next.

We're in the school. We're in the school. We're in the school. Underneath that chant he hoped would keep them from stumbling into one of the Eater's landscapes was another chant that came from his heart: *Glorianna, Glorianna, Glorianna.*

The sundial should be there, right in front of them. But there was nothing but a circle of bubbling mud.

No markers anymore. Nothing to guide them.

"Where . . . ?" Lynnea gasped.

They had to keep moving or die.

Glorianna, Glorianna, Glorianna. "This way."

He ran, pulling Lynnea with him, letting instinct—or something more—guide him. A maze of gardens, all the same. Walls and walls and walls. The light almost gone.

They'd never find their way through this maze once the light was completely gone.

But he turned from one path and followed another and another as if a string had been attached to his chest and were reeling him in.

Glorianna, Glorianna.

Then he saw it. No different on the outside from any of the others, but he knew it was hers.

"Here," he panted, rattling the wrought-iron gate as if that would be enough to break the lock. Even if he did break it, there was a wooden door behind the gate that was probably locked from the inside, since he couldn't see any way to open it from this side.

He didn't have time to figure out if wizard magic could open doors. Somewhere in the twists and turns of the paths, they'd lost the predators, but the creatures wouldn't stay lost for long. Not with fresh prey available.

"Climb." He clamped his hands on her waist and gave her a boost up to get her feet on a crossbar. "Pull yourself over." Sounds coming from the intersection of two paths. *"Now!"*

He took a step back to avoid getting kicked in the face as Lynnea swung her legs over the top of the gate and the wooden door. His foot came down on a stone, making him stumble. He grabbed the gate to keep his balance—which brought his face level with the brass plaque attached to the stone wall next to the locked gate.

Etched into the plaque was a date and the wizard's symbol, indicating that this was a forbidden place.

He forgot about the danger coming toward him. Everything faded to insignificance as he stared at the date on that plaque.

Then Lynnea screamed, "Sebastian!"

Jolted back to the immediate danger, he snatched up the stone he'd stumbled on.

Giant ants and spiders raced toward him, and in front of them was something that looked like an elongated spider with two black eyes and jaws powerful enough to crush his legs.

A deadly part of the magic wizards wielded was something they called "the lightning of justice." Bolts of magic that could kill a man. It was used when a person was deemed so dangerous he or she had to be destroyed instead of being sent to a dark landscape as punishment.

Unfortunately, he had no idea how to call that kind of magic or control it. But raw power swelled inside him now, so he channeled it—and his anger—as best he could into the stone in his hand.

The spidery thing rushed toward him with terrifying speed. The others weren't far behind.

With a yell that was part fury, part desperation, he threw the stone at the spidery thing. It struck between the creature's eyes, then—

Sebastian threw his arms up to protect his eyes as bolts of light exploded out of the stone, searing the spidery thing and the other creatures near it.

He blinked, shook his head, then scrambled over the gate. Coming down on the other side, he leaned back against the solid stone wall.

"Sebastian?" Lynnea rushed toward him.

"Don't!" His hand still tingled from the released magic. Since he was pretty sure the wizards' lightning didn't usually splinter like that, he didn't want her to touch him until he felt more confident that he wouldn't sizzle her, too.

"There's no door on this side of the wall," Lynnea said, looking at the solid stone. "Why isn't there a door?"

Because they tried to seal her in. Because . . . Damn you, Lee! You never told me why. All these years, and you never told me why.

He pushed away from the wall and looked around. An overgrown, abandoned garden—with a way to escape hidden in the fountain at its center.

"This way. Hurry." Still not daring to touch her, he

followed a path to the center of the garden, Lynnea right behind him.

When he reached the fountain, he circled it, looking for whatever was hidden here that would get them out of this place. Moss on the stones that shaped the fountain's pool, green scum covering most of the water.

Nothing! But something here tugged at him.

Crouching, he thrust a hand into the water. His fingers brushed over stones—and his heart jumped as he heard the sounds of creatures fighting over the remains of those he had killed. But charred corpses wouldn't interest them long if they sensed living prey nearby.

His hand moved through the water. Then he felt a tingle, a tug, a sense of warmth right ... there.

His hand hovered over the stone—and he remembered something Lee had told him during a visit to the Den.

"People expect bridges to be large enough to physically walk over," Lee said. *"But a one-shot bridge can be small enough to fit in your hand."*

Sebastian stopped picking at the remains of his dinner and frowned at his cousin. "One-shot?"

"A small object, filled with just enough of a Bridge's power for one crossing to a specific landscape."

"Doesn't sound like it would be much use."

Lee hesitated, then said quietly, "Sometimes it gives a person the only chance to escape where they are."

Too bad Lee hadn't told him how these one-shot bridges worked. Was there something he needed to do? Or would he be pulled into another landscape the moment his hand closed over the stone?

"Sebastian," Lynnea whispered.

He looked up. Saw a spider coming over the wall.

"Take my hand," he said. He didn't dare look around to see what else might be coming over the walls.

Holding on to Lynnea with one hand, he closed his other hand over the stone. He stood up and turned away from the fountain at the same time the spider reached the ground inside the garden.

He took a step, pulling Lynnea with him.

The spider ran toward them.

He didn't know where this bridge would take them, but he trusted Lee, who was the only Bridge who would have put an escape route in *this* garden. And he trusted Glorianna Belladonna.

As Glorianna's name echoed in his mind, he and Lynnea took another step—and disappeared a moment before the spider reached them.

We look human, but we are not. Ephemera shaped us, manifested us, brought us into the world in answer to the cries of human hearts for guidance.

Some of us have gathered in the places where the currents of Light are the strongest. These Guardians will keep their distance from the chattering of the human heart, will live simple, peaceful lives that will feed the Light and keep those currents flowing in the world. And those currents, in turn, will nourish hope, courage, love.

The rest of us are Guides. We walk among people and feel as they do—glittering moments of joy, warm moments of contentment, moments full of the jagged shards of envy, anger, disappointment. We drink from the wells of sorrow and feast at the banquet of love.

But we understand what Ephemera cannot: That the human heart is as fluid as itself, that a heart is touched by the winds of emotions, bending with them for a moment, sometimes breaking beneath the violence of a storm. But those feelings are the wind, not the bedrock of a heart.

And yet, even bedrock is malleable. A seed can find its way into a crevice, root itself in the dark while it grows toward the light. Given time and the things it needs to grow, the plant's roots can widen that crevice, become strong enough to break stone. And things change.

So it is the bedrock of the heart that resonates for us, not the winds of changing feelings. It is the true desires, the deepest yearnings, the heart's need to make its journey through life that calls to us.

Be careful what you wish for, because Ephemera will manifest that wish—but not necessarily in the way you intended ... or even wanted. People hear the words, but they're full of wind wishes—things they want now, are desperate to have now, only to forget about those same things tomorrow because those things did not truly feed the heart.

So we walk among them, feeling the resonance of the bedrock wishes, the true dreams of the heart. And we whisper to Ephemera, *Don't listen to that wish. It's not a true wish.* Or, *Yes, that's a true wish. Alter the currents around that person to provide the chance for him to take the first steps of the journey that will end with the heart having what it desires.*

One of us would resonate with that yearning heart for a moment, showing it the possibility, giving it the chance to take those first steps.

Some hearts will back away from the journey, too fearful to leave the familiar even though it withers. Others will leap forward and never look back, bruising the hearts left behind. Pain will force some to begin the journey. For others, love will be a beacon that keeps them moving forward.

We walk among the people. So do the others. As we are drawn to the Light and the feelings that resonate with the Light, the others are drawn to the darkness that dwells within the human heart.

The people call them the Dark Guides.

Ephemera manifested them, too, because we who follow the Light could not resonate with the hearts that yearned for the Dark.

There will always be such hearts. There will always be

that choice. If that wasn't true, then a heart that walks in the Light has made no choice at all.

—*The Lost Archives*

Chapter Eleven

Simple stone markers stood sentry at the beginning of a dirt path that curved down the hill. A step away from those markers, Sebastian pulled Lynnea into his arms.

He watched. Waited.

No nightmarish creatures appeared between the stone markers.

Weak with relief, he closed his eyes and rested his cheek against Lynnea's head, rubbing one hand up and down her back to offer comfort.

"You're all right?" he asked quietly. "You're not hurt?"

"I'm all right, but ..." Lynnea turned enough to look at the markers. "Where are we?"

"I don't know. Whatever landscape this was connected to." He opened his hand and stared at the piece of smooth, white marble.

Peace folded around him like a warm, soft blanket. Fear diminished with every breath.

He could almost see the air shimmer like a veil between the sentry stones. If he stepped through them in the other direction to enter whatever landscape lay beyond, fear would have a savage bite, and the world beyond the veil might be filled with things that would rape courage and murder hope. But here ...

Slipping the piece of white marble into his jacket pocket, he looked at Lynnea. "We'd better find out where we are."

She nodded, but he wasn't sure she'd heard him. She seemed quietly dazzled by the feel of this place.

They started down the hill. The trees that had blocked the view on their left ended at the curve in the path, revealing a small lake. A handful of tiny islands dotted the lake, and a light shone on each one. Another light moved steadily away from one island, and in the day's last breath, he saw a man walking across a bridge back to the shore.

"Hey-a," Sebastian called, using the folksy greeting that was commonplace in the landscape Nadia called home. Even in a friendly tone, a raised voice sounded wrong here—disruptive, almost obscene—but the man stopped on the shore, lifted a hand in greeting, and followed the path around the lake that connected with the path down the hill.

"Welcome, welcome," the man said when Sebastian and Lynnea reached the bottom of the hill. "I am Yoshani, a fellow visitor in this part of the landscape. You have missed the evening meal, but there is always something in the kitchen for late travelers. Come. We'll get you settled in the guesthouse, and then you may wander as the heart wills." He turned and led them up another hill. "Have you traveled far?"

"In some ways," Sebastian replied.

Yoshani nodded. "So it is with many who find their way to Sanctuary."

Sanctuary. "I never thought I'd see this place," Sebastian said, the words barely voiced.

But Lynnea heard him and squeezed his hand to indicate she understood.

She didn't understand. How could she? She was human, and someone like her could have found her way here at any time.

But she hadn't. When her heart was looking for a safe place, she found the Den—and you.

"We have many guests in this part of Sanctuary," Yoshani said. "They come to renew the spirit so they are stronger when they go back to their journey in the world."

"There are other parts of Sanctuary?" Lynnea asked.

"Yes. There are many Places of Light in the world, but we were islands, each alone in the sea of the world until the Landscaper brought us together, creating borders that connect these places with one another. Her brother, who is a Bridge, also helped by making bridges between our landscapes so that we may visit and better understand the other caretakers of the Light." Yoshani raised a hand in greeting. "And there he is now."

At the top of the hill stood a three-story stone building. A man stepped out into the light of the lanterns hung by the doorway.

"Hey-a, Lee!" Yoshani said. "We have visitors."

In that moment, everything else vanished for Sebastian. His mind and heart were filled with one image—a brass plaque with a wizards' seal . . . and a date that had revealed a secret.

Shrugging off the blanket of peace, he strode toward the familiar figure, whose mouth was curving into a smile of surprised pleasure.

"Sebastian!" Lee said. "What brings you—"

A shove pushed Lee back a step. Then Sebastian grabbed Lee's shirt, pulling his cousin close as his hands curled into fists.

"You never told me," Sebastian growled. "I had a right to know, and *you never told me.*"

No blankness in Lee's eyes to indicate he didn't know what Sebastian was talking about. No surprise at the anger. And no apology.

"Hey-a, hey!" Yoshani said. "Don't be spilling your troubles on the ground for other people to trip over. Not in Sanctuary."

Sebastian felt heat flood his face—the same heat he used to feel as a boy when he'd done something that felt natural to him but wasn't acceptable to everyone else.

He opened his fists, releasing Lee's shirt.

Yoshani studied them, then shook his head. "Tch. Here. Take the lantern. Go down to one of the islands and speak your angry words if you must. Let the water wash them away. I will look after the sensible one among you," he added, making a graceful gesture with his hand to indicate Lynnea.

Sebastian took a step back. "No, it's—"

"Yes," Lee said. He took the lantern from Yoshani. "It's time things were said."

Sebastian followed Lee down the hill to the lake. They crossed a bridge to the first island, which had a stone bench and a hollowed rock that sheltered another lantern.

Lee swung a leg over one end of the bench and sat down, straddling it. Sebastian mirrored the move, settling at the other end of the bench.

On one of the other islands, wind chimes rang softly, stirred by puffs of air, the clear notes blending with the rustle of leaves and the lazy sound of water lapping the edges of the islands.

Sebastian closed his eyes. The sounds pulled at him, urging him to let go of anger and surround himself once more in that blanket of peace.

Then Lee moved, setting the lantern aside. It was a quiet sound that didn't intrude on the leaves and wind chimes and water, but it was enough to make Sebastian remember—and hold on to—the anger.

"I saw the plaque on Glorianna's garden," Sebastian said. "I saw the date. That was shortly after she created the Den, wasn't it? *Wasn't it?*"

"So what if it was?" Lee replied.

"*Damn you!* She was fifteen years old, and she was declared rogue because she made the Den!"

"No, she was declared rogue because she escaped being sealed into her garden, and by the time the wizards and Instructors realized that, she had disappeared into the landscapes."

Sebastian bobbed his head. Not to agree with anything, just to indicate he'd heard. "So the crime she committed that was great enough to be walled in was creating a place called the Den of Iniquity. For me."

"You aren't the only one who has benefited from the Den," Lee countered.

"But I was the reason she created it. She made that place so that I would have a home."

"Whether that's true or not doesn't matter," Lee said, his voice sharp. "They never knew about you. The Instructors never asked why she made the Den, and Glorianna never told them, so they never knew about you. I doubt there's any among them that know even now why she altered the landscapes to make the Den."

"So you decided not to tell me that Glorianna had sacrificed her future for my sake."

"Don't blame me," Lee snapped. "By the time I found out what had happened, it was two years too late to make any difference. What could you have done, Sebastian? I was fifteen; you were seventeen. What could either of us have done? The wizards had condemned her. The other Landscapers had condemned her. All I could do was get through my formal training as fast as I could so that I could be a Bridge for her, since you can be damn certain no one else would do it knowingly. And I had to be careful, always so careful, because I was Glorianna's brother, and they were always watching me to see if my gift had any unacceptable . . . flourishes."

"Like being able to impose one landscape over another?"

"Exactly. Which is something only my family knows about me."

Sebastian hesitated, absorbing the importance of that statement tossed out in anger. When Lee had told him about this rare ability, he'd understood his cousin was sharing something very private, but he hadn't realized how much trust Lee was offering by telling him at all.

Only my family knows about me.

And he hadn't realized how difficult all those years at the school had been for Lee. "Why did you stay?"

"Because I needed the official training. Oh, I didn't need most of the training itself. I'd done more just playing with Glorianna when we were children than I learned in the first three years at the school. But if I hadn't gone through the formal training to prove my talents weren't a potential danger to Ephemera, I would have been declared rogue, too, and that wouldn't have done Mother or Glorianna any good."

Sebastian hung his head. "I'm sorry things were hard for all of you, that things went bad for Glorianna ... because of me."

"It wasn't you, so stop feeling sorry for yourself."

That stung his temper and his pride. He raised his head and stared at his cousin.

Lee looked out over the water. "It wasn't you, and it wasn't the Den. Not really. I overheard some things while I was in training that make me think it was just an excuse. Before she ever got to the school, the wizards suspected that Glorianna's power might eclipse what was considered 'natural' in a Landscaper, and they *wanted* to seal her in, confine her, isolate her. If it hadn't been the Den, it would have been something else at some other time, when it might have been harder for her to break free."

"What makes you say that?"

"Like I said, things I overheard. The wizards come by several times a year, right after students are evaluated for advancement. They always want to know about the strongest student Landscapers, the ones who might become a 'problem' in the future once they're away from watchful eyes." Lee looked at Sebastian. "Glorianna wasn't the first, you know. Whenever I had a free day, I would wander all over the school. There were other sealed gardens, some dating back a hundred years or more. Some going back so far the date had been etched in the stone wall instead of on a brass plaque. I think . . ." He lowered his voice and leaned forward. "I think the wizards have been culling the strongest Landscapers for generations. I think they find some excuse to get that girl declared a threat to Ephemera, then seal her up in a cage of her own making. In theory, the girl can reach the things she needs to survive—food, clothing, shelter—through the access points in her garden, but she's alone. She can reach *things* but not people. Even if one of her access points is a street in the middle of a city, she's still isolated from any direct contact with other people. That's the real punishment of being walled in by the Justice Makers. The girl lives alone—and she dies alone. And her line is extinguished."

Sebastian braced his hands on the bench and leaned forward so he wouldn't have to raise his voice above a whisper. Daylight! He felt as if he were exchanging vile secrets that would be worth his life if anyone else heard what Lee was saying.

And maybe that's true.

"You can't know that's what happens to the girls, that they're left alone like that," Sebastian said.

"Yes, I can. Because I found one of them two years ago." Lee shook his head. "A calling so strong, I created a bridge to answer it. And I found her. She was very old and quite mad, but it was a lucid madness. She was in a woods, gathering leaves and twigs. I don't know if she thought they were edible or if she was just doing it for something to do. She was wearing rags that barely covered her and looked so frail. . . .

"Then she saw me. And she told me about being sealed in her garden and what the wizards' justice meant for the girl who was condemned."

"But she was mad," Sebastian protested. "You don't know if any of it was true."

Even in the lantern light, with his face half in shadows, Sebastian could see the pain in Lee's eyes.

"She talked about her sister. How her sister would take care of the baby. And how the daughter of that baby would carry the seeds of the Dark as well as the Light—and would be an enemy not even the Eater of the World could survive if the Dark Guides didn't destroy her before she bloomed into her full power.

"Then she broke off pieces of two plants and held them out to me. When I reached out to take them, I felt my hand pass through a barrier of power—and she disappeared." Lee rubbed the back of his neck. "Somehow my bridge had pierced the barrier enough for me to see her and talk to her but not enough for her to feel the touch of a human hand. I wandered those woods for an hour. Same land, but not the same landscape. Except . . . the plants were there, and I think I understood the message. I never told Mother or Glorianna about seeing that old woman because of that message."

"Message?" What kind of message could be made out of two plants?

"What she tried to give me was heart's hope . . . and belladonna."

Sebastian felt his breath catch, felt his heart bump hard against his chest. But "belladonna" made his thoughts circle back to how this talk began.

"Why would the wizards eliminate the best Landscapers? And why would the Landscapers at the school agree with it?"

"How did the wizards become the Justice Makers, Sebastian?" Lee asked. "Why are they the ones who decide when a person is too . . . damaged . . . in some way to live in the daylight landscapes and must be sent to the darkest place that resonates within that person? No one remembers. The Landscapers are the ones who actually perform Heart's Justice and shift a person to another landscape, but it's the wizards who decide when it needs to be done. How did they become such a powerful force in our world?"

Sebastian leaned back, feeling uneasy about what he'd heard. If it were true that the wizards had been systematically eliminating the Landscapers with superior skills, it meant the Justice Makers had an agenda for Ephemera no one else knew about. But what? And why?

"Well," Lee said, reaching for the lantern, "I don't know what part of the day you're in, but I need to get some sleep before I go to the school to record my working log."

The school. For this little while, his personal discovery had blocked out the horror. Now it came flooding back. "You can't."

"Have to. I don't have an established circuit of landscapes—at least, not that the Bridges' School is aware of—so I'm required to report in once each season to log the locations of any bridges I created and the landscapes they connect."

Sebastian grabbed Lee's forearm. "You can't go back to the school. Everyone's dead."

Lee stiffened. "What are you talking about?"

"The Eater of the World escaped. It's loose in the landscapes."

"Who told you that?"

"Glorianna." He felt Lee tremble beneath his hand. "I think It attacked the school. There were creatures there—giant ants, giant spiders, other things—and I found a classroom full of bodies." Parts of bodies, but he didn't say that.

"Everyone?"

Hearing the shock in Lee's voice, Sebastian hesitated. "I don't know. We ran, made it to Glorianna's garden, and got away to here." Releasing Lee's arm, he pulled the piece of marble out of his pocket. "Using this."

"A one-shot bridge," Lee said, brushing a thumb over the marble. "I made this for Glorianna on one of my visits home." He looked at Sebastian, his face hard. "I made three, to different landscapes. This was the bridge to Sanctuary."

"When I put my hand in the fountain, I didn't feel anything from the other stones. Just this one." He hesitated. "There was a stone just outside the gate of Glorianna's garden."

"Black marble?"

"No, just a polished stone. I stepped on it, stumbled. If I hadn't, I wouldn't have noticed the plaque."

Lee rubbed the back of his neck. "Then maybe the Guides of the Heart meant for you to find out about this now. Sometimes it's a small thing that can make a difference in someone's life." He sighed. "You must have stepped on the agate. It was a bridge to the entrance at the Bridges part of the school. The black marble connected to the Den. If it had still been hidden in the fountain, you would have felt it. Which means Glorianna must have gone back to the school at some point and taken it. Damn foolish of her to take the risk."

"She knew there was trouble at the school." Sebastian heard the hesitation in his voice and hated it, but he knew Lee understood the question beneath the statement.

"Glorianna believes in letting people make their own choices, good or bad, but if she'd suspected the Eater could make *this* kind of attack, she would have told you straight out not to go to the school. And if she decided not to tell you straight out, she has a connection with Ephemera no other Landscaper can match. You would have started out on the journey, but she would have made sure you couldn't reach the school."

Sebastian felt one knot of tension ease inside him, swiftly replaced by another. "What's going to happen to Ephemera?"

"Most of the Landscapers and Bridges don't live at the school. They wouldn't have been caught in the attack. Even if the Landscapers came back to their gardens, as soon as they realized they were in danger, they'd be only a step away from escaping into another of their landscapes."

Sebastian studied his cousin. "You should never lie to

someone who has played cards with you. You give too much away."

"Then I'm lucky I've never played cards with anyone at the school, since I've had a lifetime's worth of experience lying to *them*," Lee snapped. Then he looked out over the water. "The school is a focal point because the gardens are there. If a Landscaper comes back to the school through her garden and realizes something bad has happened, she'll probably be able to get out again before she's attacked, but . . ."

"She won't have access to all the landscapes in her keeping, will she?"

"I'm not sure. My mother can step from one of her landscapes to another without going back to her garden, but she's a Level Five Landscaper. Landscapers below that level don't have the skill to do that. They're dependent on having access to their gardens."

"So what happens to Ephemera?"

Lee closed his eyes. "The Landscapers' resonance will last a few weeks, maybe a month, without being renewed. After that . . ." He swallowed hard. "After that, there won't be anyone standing between Ephemera and the human heart, so it will begin manifesting everything in response to all those emotions. A child will have a temper tantrum, and the family's well will go dry. A farmer will have an argument with his wife, and when he goes out to work in the fields, his plow horse will step into a hole that suddenly appears and break a leg. People will blame one another for their troubles, and everything will get worse and worse because the Dark currents will get stronger and stronger—and the Eater of the World will be able to use all those dark emotions to shape terrors made from people's deepest fears."

"Guardians and Guides," Sebastian whispered.

Lee opened his eyes and stood up. "I have to go."

Sebastian stood as well. "Go where? You can't go to the school."

"We have to assume all the Landscapers who were

at the school are dead. And all the Bridges who were there as well. But that means the Eater has access to all the landscapes connected to those gardens."

"So where are you going?" Sebastian asked, hurrying after his cousin as Lee left the island and strode across the bridge.

"I have to break the bridges between Glorianna's landscapes and the rest of Ephemera. I have to break as many as I can, as fast as I can. I can start with the ones that cross over into Sanctuary."

As they reached the shore, Sebastian grabbed Lee's arm, pulling his cousin around to face him. "You're going to cut people off with no way to escape that thing?"

"I'm going to do what I can to save what I can," Lee replied. "Guardians and Guides, Sebastian! We need some safe ground that the Eater can't reach, or we'll never be able to gather enough force to fight It."

It made sense, but . . . "So you're going to save Sanctuary." He felt cold . . . and so alone.

Lee gave him a strange look. "I'm going to close off Glorianna's landscapes. I'll break the bridges that connect them to outside landscapes. We'll be isolated from the rest of Ephemera, but the landscapes are diverse enough to provide people with everything they really need."

"But you said . . . Sanctuary."

Lee smiled with bitter humor. "This is one of Belladonna's landscapes. Sanctuary and the Den are connected. Not directly, but they're connected."

The Den. Sebastian shook his head. "There are dozens of ways into the Den, and the Eater has already attacked there." He swallowed the lump in his throat and felt it lodge in his heart. When he went back to the Den, Lynnea could stay here in Sanctuary. Lynnea would be safe. "You have to let the Den go, or you won't have your safe ground."

"There are ten stationary bridges that cross over into the Den. I created them, and they all connect with landscapes held by Glorianna or Nadia. It's the resonating bridges and any stationary ones other Bridges established since the last time I made a circuit around the Den that I have to find and break."

"Didn't you hear me? The Den is already compromised!"

"Then the only thing I can suggest, cousin, is that you gather whoever you can to help you defend it. Because Glorianna isn't going to abandon the Den, and neither am I."

We're not going to abandon you. That was the message. They didn't care if he was human or demon. He was family. That was all that mattered.

"All right," Sebastian said. "I'll hold on to the Den." *Somehow.*

They climbed the hill in silence. When they reached the door into the building, Lee paused. "Could you stop at my mother's house on your way back to the Den? Just to make sure everything's . . ." He closed his eyes. "There's a saying I learned in school. 'Despair made the deserts.' That's what the Eater of the World really does, you know. It's not the landscapes It twisted or the creatures It twisted into monsters; it's the loss of hope, the seeds of fear that almost gave It control of the world long ago. It feeds on those feelings, cultivates the dark aspects of our hearts. It's going to try to kill all the Landscapers. That's the only way to keep the world from holding on to the Light."

"I'll check on Aunt Nadia."

Lee nodded.

They went inside, Lee to pack his things and begin his own kind of fight against the Eater of the World, and Sebastian to find Lynnea and tell her he was going back to the Den in a few hours. Alone.

"There's something you need to see," Nadia said. She opened a kitchen drawer, removed two folded pieces of paper, and set them on the kitchen table in front of Glorianna.

"Where did you find these?" Glorianna asked as she opened the papers and saw the heavy lines of masculine handwriting.

"In the attic." Nadia latched the kitchen's screen door, locked the wood door, then walked over to one of the windows. "I didn't go up for anything in particular. Just to sort things out, I suppose, for something to do, since I was feeling restless. I found those at the bottom of a trunk of children's clothes, wrapped in your old baby blanket."

Glorianna looked up. "You told me a dog stole my blanket."

Nadia closed the window, then closed the shutters over it. "What was I supposed to tell you? It was so worn and tattered—and got more tattered every time I washed it. But you didn't want to let it go."

"So you lied to me?"

"I told you a lie that gave the loss meaning. You used to find comfort from thinking a small orphan dog was snuggled up in that blanket on cold nights."

Glorianna watched her mother close the other kitchen window. "Why are you doing that? It'll be stifling in here."

"For a little while. Read, Glorianna."

So she read, and what she read chilled her to the marrow.

"Guardians and Guides, can this be true?"

Nadia sat down opposite Glorianna and said nothing for a long time. Then, "It makes a frightening kind of sense. Both sides lost some abilities, some aspects of their magic after the Eater of the World was fought and defeated long ago. But one side forgot its roots, except for the families who passed the truth down from mother to daughter; the other side did not. It hid in plain sight, keeping its bloodlines strong while depleting the strength of its enemy."

Glorianna looked at the papers lying on the table between them. "Who . . . ?"

"Your father. Peter. Shortly before he . . ."

"Disappeared."

"Yes." Nadia closed her eyes. "I thought he left because he was dissatisfied with his life, or with me. I thought he left because he'd grown tired of the secrets he'd insisted we keep—and because of the secrets he knew I kept from him about my family. I thought he left because he crossed into a strange landscape and couldn't find his way back—or didn't want to find his way back. I thought a lot of things during the months after he disappeared." She opened her eyes. "After reading that, I don't know what to think anymore."

Glorianna looked at the papers, at the strong handwriting that looked as if the hand had trembled a little while it held the pen. Out of haste? Fear?

"You think the Wizards' Council killed him, or had him killed, because he found out about this?"

"It's possible."

"But . . ." Despite the closed door and windows, despite their being alone, Glorianna lowered her voice. "Females kept in secret as breeders? Females who aren't . . . human? Even if it's true, he didn't say where he saw these females or who was mating with them. He didn't accuse any particular group of being the—"

"Peter was a wizard," Nadia interrupted. "If he'd seen this place anywhere but in Wizard City, he would have reported it, and the wizards would have been the first to rally against some dark aspect gathering strength in secret. They've always been the most vocal about keeping humankind away from the demons who share this world."

"Exactly."

Nadia looked at Glorianna. Her face, even in the soft glow of the lamp on the table, appeared older than her years. "If the power that your kind had shaped in order to control the world had been defeated by your enemies, by the ones who stood for the

Light, what better way to survive than to transform into a shape that would blend in? What better way to survive than to build a fortress city in which to hide the females who, for whatever reason, weren't able to transform but who held the dark legacy in their wombs?"

"I don't believe this. I don't believe any of this." But Glorianna stared at the words on the papers and felt sick.

The Dark Guides are not just an unseen force that flows through Ephemera, providing an opportunity for a person to follow the baser feelings in his heart. And they are not figures so malformed that they slink in the dark corners of cities or hide in caves in the countryside, appearing as a black-cloaked shape that whispers lies or helps bring about misfortune.

I have seen the creche, the breeding grounds. I watched males who wear the mask of human faces mate with females who are not human.

The Dark Guides exist. They are real. They wear human faces, but they are not human under the skin.

And, perhaps, neither am I. If the power I was born with comes from this dark place, neither am I.

"I told you the family secrets," Nadia said softly. "Things I never told your father. We can trace our line back to the first Landscapers, who were the Guides of the Heart. Human in form, but not human. They had such a strong connection with Ephemera, they could alter the landscapes, actually change the shape of the world."

"Like me," Glorianna whispered.

"Like you."

Nadia got up, rummaged through the cupboards, then returned to the table with a bottle of brandy and two glasses. She filled the glasses and set one beside Glorianna's hand. Then she drained half her glass before sitting down again.

"I have no marriage lines," Nadia said. "I wanted them, but Peter said it was enough that we were married in our hearts, and I loved him enough to be content with that. Even when I became pregnant with you, he still refused to consider a formal marriage. But that's when he told me one of the wizards' secrets.

"It was, and is, taboo for a wizard to have carnal relations with a Landscaper, and if the Wizards' Council had found out he'd been with me and I carried a child that mingled the bloodlines of wizard and Landscaper, at best they would have punished him. At worst, they would have sealed both of us in a dark landscape.

"He loved you, Glorianna, but he was also terrified of you."

Glorianna licked her lips, which felt painfully dry. "If the wizards are the descendants of the Dark Guides and the Landscapers are the descendants of the Guides of the Heart . . ."

"You are the mingling of the Dark and the Light, and you are the only known Landscaper in our time who can alter landscapes. Truly alter them. I think the kind of Landscaper you are is the reason for the taboo. The wizards didn't want to give Dark power back to the Light— because I think that mingling is the only kind of power that can defeat the Eater of the World."

Glorianna gulped some brandy. "I can't do this alone. You think I can go up against the Eater of the World?"

"I don't know. Can you?"

The question froze her blood. But another thought unfurled. "Sebastian," she whispered.

"Yes," Nadia agreed. "Sebastian. Your uncle Koltak's scandal. Living testament that wizards and the succubi can mate and have offspring. Dark power mating with dark power."

"Which means he might have all the power of a wizard as well as the power of an incubus."

"The seed resides in him, but he's never shown any ability for wizards' magic. If he had, I imagine the council would have taken him in and trained him."

"But Koltak's not pure wizard."

Nadia nodded. "Koltak and Peter didn't come from Wizard City. I suspect the human marriages in that family line are the reason Koltak never achieved the power he craved. Not if it's the Wizards' Council and their handpicked protégés who are mating with those females to keep some bloodlines of the Dark Guides pure."

"What about Sebastian? Is there any human in him at all?"

"A little." Nadia paused, then sighed. "He is human in his heart, Glorianna, even if he's no longer willing to acknowledge it."

Relief shuddered through her. It would break her heart to have Sebastian as an enemy.

"You have to leave, daughter. If the wizards manage to find you and destroy you, we have no hope of defeating the Eater of the World. You have to hide until you're ready to fight."

"I'll go if you come with me."

Nadia shook her head. "I can't abandon the landscapes in my care. Not now."

"Mother—"

Nadia rested her hand over Glorianna's. "We are not the whole world. Maybe there are other Landscapers in faraway lands, even if they're known by a different name. Ephemera didn't shatter as much in those faraway places as it did here where the battle was fought, Dark against Light. We are not the whole world. If that were not so, you and Lee would not have discovered a southern land where koffea beans grow."

"Merchant ships have been bringing koffea beans into ports of call for many years," Glorianna said.

"And yet those beans were unknown in many landscapes here. Our world is very large, and it is very small. We see only what our hearts can hold, whether we sail the seas to distant lands or live out the whole of our lives in the village where we were born. But the people here live on the bones of the battleground, and the Landscapers who care for this part of Ephemera may be the only ones who know this *was* a battleground—and they're the only ones who can see with their own eyes that this will be a battleground again."

"So if we win, most of Ephemera will never know. And if we lose . . ."

"The Eater of the World will be able to unleash the horrors It created and alter the world into a dark hunting ground." Nadia leaned back in her chair and dropped her hands to her lap. "Despair made the deserts."

"And hope shaped the oasis. I know the saying."

"You're our oasis, Glorianna. I'll look after myself. You look after Ephemera."

Unbearably weary, Glorianna nodded and pushed her chair back. "I'll go."

"May the Guardians of Light go with you, daughter."

After Nadia unlocked the kitchen door, Glorianna wrapped her arms around her mother and held on tight.

"I'll see you again," she whispered.

"You're always in my heart," Nadia whispered back. "You and Lee . . . and Sebastian."

Just tired, Glorianna told herself as she hurried along the familiar garden paths, blinking back tears. Just tired. And afraid. So very afraid.

Which was why she doubled back to a particular part of Nadia's gardens and took a small statue of a sitting woman. She, Lee, and Sebastian had worked at odd jobs an entire summer in order to earn the money to buy the statue for Nadia's birthday. Her mother cherished it because of that. And because it was cherished, it was a powerful anchor to this place.

Nadia wouldn't approve of her taking on the added burden. Most Landscapers held a handful of landscapes. She held thrice that many. And she was about to add a dozen more. Because once she altered the landscapes and shifted the borders and boundaries, she would make all the landscapes in Nadia's garden a single landscape within her own. Until Lee could establish more bridges between Nadia's landscapes and hers, it would isolate the people living in those places from the rest of Ephemera.

But it would keep her mother safe.

Chapter Twelve

Sebastian and Lynnea crossed over the bridge that connected Sanctuary to Nadia's home landscape and stepped into a clearing filled with sunlight.

Sebastian threw an arm up over his eyes and blinked away the tears caused by the unexpected brightness.

"Daylight," he muttered, lowering his arm a little so he could squint at the land around them.

"Yes," Lynnea said, looking up at the sky. "It's a lovely day, even if it is a bit overcast."

Overcast? This wasn't bright?

With his face still safely hidden by his arm, he grimaced at the prim tone in her voice. She'd been sounding like that since they woke up—as if they'd slept on opposite sides of the bed instead of being twined around each other.

And did she appreciate the fact that he had untwined himself instead of rolling that little bit necessary to bring her under him and feed the hunger she stirred in him? No, apparently she did not.

And the way she'd pulled his underwear out of the pack, with thumb and forefinger, as if it were encrusted with who knew what instead of being clean—and then calling it his "unmentionables." When he pointed out it was called underwear, she told him it wasn't made out of enough material to mention.

He'd never had any complaints. In fact, most women liked that next-to-nothing he wore under his pants.

And she wouldn't have said anything either if you'd made love to her last night instead of acting like some prissy prig human. "I can't," *you said. As if being a virgin meant the country girl couldn't figure out what was making that lump in your pants. And you let her curl up on her side of the bed without explaining that it wasn't your body that was having trouble where she was concerned. Not that you're ever going to explain that—for both your sakes.*

She'd gotten back at him, even if she didn't know it. After she'd fallen asleep and he'd cuddled up against her, her dreams had shifted to a sweet erotica that didn't go nearly far enough to satisfy the hunger in him—and left him panting with the effort to remain a passive participant instead of sliding deeper into the dream, as he'd done with so many other women, and taking her to the limits of his experience rather than remaining confined by the limits of hers.

But he hadn't done that. Being so close to her physically, he couldn't resist the lure of her dreams, but he'd held himself at the edge. Because she was innocent. Because she belonged in a landscape that saw the sun rise and set.

Because he was scared to death that if he had her once he wouldn't be able to let her go.

"Are you still mad at me?" he asked, lowering his arm the rest of the way now that he could squint at the light without feeling like his eyeballs would cook.

"I'm not mad at you."

The words said one thing; the tone of voice said something else. Definitely still mad at him. And it was funny, in a tear-your-hair-out kind of way. For all his experience with women, he'd never had to deal with moods. When the woman got moody, it was time to leave and become someone else's fantasy lover.

But human men lived with female moods day after day, month after month, year after year.

They were out of their minds.

And he envied every one of them.

He looked around the clearing. In Sanctuary, the bridge that crossed over to this landscape was a simple wooden bridge that spanned a piece of a water garden. Lee had called it a one-way stationary bridge, which he hadn't understood at the time. Now he did.

In *this* landscape, the bridge was just the space between two large stones set in the middle of the clearing—a space wide enough for a handcart but nothing bigger. And on this side, it was a resonating bridge.

Since he'd never heard of a bridge being stationary on one side and resonating on the other, he wondered if this was another unique aspect of Lee's gift.

"Lee said to take the right-hand path when it forks," Sebastian said, taking Lynnea's stiff hand and leading her toward the edge of the clearing. "That will take us to Aunt Nadia's house. She'll be up by now." He hoped.

The path out of the clearing was plain to see, but he wasn't sure he would have found the fork if it hadn't been for the sign nailed to a tree—a plain piece of wood with a bird etched into it.

"Don't you ever visit your auntie?" Lynnea asked, censure now added to that prim tone.

"Three or four times a year," Sebastian replied, feeling testy as they followed the barely visible path. "But I've never come here from that particular bridge."

They walked in silence until the path ended at a break in the stone wall that separated the woodland from Nadia's lawn and gardens. Releasing Lynnea's hand, Sebastian stepped over the knee-high stones, then watched to make sure she didn't stumble when she stepped through the break.

"Did something damage the wall?" Lynnea asked, sounding worried.

"Not as far as I know," Sebastian replied, taking her hand again as he walked toward the house. "It's been like that for as long as I can remember."

"And you never offered to fix it for her? She's your auntie."

Another offense laid at his feet—as if he knew any-thing about fixing walls. Maybe Aunt Nadia knew how to deal with a woman in a snit. After all, she had a daughter, and, being older and sensible, she'd under-stand that by not becoming Lynnea's lover, he was just doing what was right for once in his life.

The kitchen's wood door was open to let in the fresh summer air. So were the windows. It looked dark inside the house compared to the daylight, but through the screen door, he thought he saw two people standing close together.

And something about the *way* they were standing . . .

"Hey-a!" he called. "Aunt Nadia!"

The figures jumped apart. One disappeared into an-other part of the house.

Sebastian strode up to the kitchen's screen door and grabbed the handle just as Nadia hurried up to the door from the other side.

"Oh," she said, looking—and sounding—flustered. "Sebastian. What a pleasant surprise."

A surprise, anyway.

"You going to let me in?" Sebastian asked.

"Oh. Yes. Of course."

As she unlatched the screen door and pushed it open, he kept his eyes on her face. But damn it all, he *was* an incubus, and she *was* wearing a summer dress, and it wasn't *his* fault her nipples were acting perky enough to make little bumps in the thin material— and they were both going to get through this visit by pretending he didn't know she wasn't wearing any-thing under that dress.

"This is Lynnea," Sebastian said, hauling his little rabbit into the kitchen. Maybe Lynnea, being another woman, could suggest that Nadia put a coat on over that dress.

"I'm pleased to meet you," Nadia said.

"It's early to be dropping in so sudden-like . . ." Lyn-nea stammered.

"Nonsense. I was just starting breakfast. Sit down. Be at home."

"Can I help?"

"You could—"

A small blue-and-white bird hit the screen door between the kitchen and the adjoining room and started scolding.

"—entertain Sparky," Nadia finished, walking over to that door. "Sebastian, make sure that outside door is closed properly."

"You could always leave him there," Sebastian said as he made sure the kitchen's screen door was secured.

"He'll just keep scolding if I do that, and then he'll get the rest of them started and we'll have to shout to hear one another."

"Come on," Sebastian said, cupping Lynnea's elbow in his hand. "It's safer sitting down."

"What? Why?" Lynnea kept her eyes on the inside screen door while Sebastian guided her to a chair at the kitchen table.

Dropping into another chair, he watched Nadia open the door just enough to offer a hand for the bird to perch on. The scolding changed to excited chatter.

Did the chatterhead just stay on Nadia's finger and look cute? Of course not. The moment the bird spotted him, Sparky zipped across the kitchen to land on top of Sebastian's head.

"Pretty boy," Sparky said, digging his sharp little nails into Sebastian's scalp as he walked back and forth. Then he stopped and made kissy noises.

Sebastian raised his hand slowly, hoping the bird would take the hint and hop on his finger. He liked Sparky. He really did. But he liked the little chatterhead better when he could see what the bird was up to.

But the moment Sparky saw the hand, he began beating Sebastian's head with his wings and scolding in a volume that made all the humans wince.

"Fine," Sebastian grumbled, lowering his hand. "Have it your way."

The scolding stopped; the wings were folded back.

Sparky marched to the top of Sebastian's forehead, leaned over, and said, "Behave."

"Oh," Lynnea said. "He's adorable. Do you think he'd come to me?" She held up a hand.

With an extra dig of his nails that Sebastian *knew* was deliberate, Sparky flew over to Lynnea to be properly admired. While woman and bird exchanged "Pretty birds," Sebastian started to ease out of his chair, intending to give Nadia a hand with breakfast.

Then Sparky said, "Kismrz."

Settling back in his chair, Sebastian said, "Sparky is a keet. The species originally came from a distant landscape. Isn't that right, Aunt Nadia?"

"Yes, that's right," Nadia replied as she laid strips of bacon into a skillet.

"They're bright little birds," Sebastian continued. "And they can talk. Some things they learn because a person teaches them. And sometimes they hear something often enough that they just pick it up. Thing is, if the words aren't enunciated clearly, the bird might not pick up all the sounds."

Lynnea gave Sparky a delighted smile. "Do you think he was trying to say something?"

Nadia, who was busy pouring egg batter into another skillet, didn't answer.

Oh, yeah, Sebastian thought, watching his aunt. *I think he was trying to say something. What I want to know is why Sparky would hear "kiss me" often enough to have learned it.*

As if in answer, someone tapped on the screen door—and Nadia dropped the fork she was using to turn the bacon.

"Jeb," Nadia said as she picked up the dirty fork. "Come in. You're just in time for breakfast." She put the fork in the sink, got a clean one out of the drawer, then turned back to her cooking.

Sebastian swiveled in his chair as the screen door opened, noticing how Jeb pulled the door open just enough to slip inside and paused to make sure it was properly latched. A frequent visitor, then. One who didn't need to be told that some of Nadia's birds might be loose in the house.

"Hey-a," Jeb said as he removed his cap and put it on a peg next to the door.

"Hey-a," Sebastian replied.

"Ah . . . Jeb, this is my nephew, Sebastian, and his friend Lynnea," Nadia said.

Sebastian gave Jeb a smile that was brilliant and insincere. "You're getting a lot of company for breakfast this morning," he said, glancing at his aunt. He didn't think the heat from the stove was the reason her face was flushed.

"Jeb is a neighbor," Nadia said, taking plates and mugs out of the cupboards.

Taking the plates and mugs from her, Jeb set the table. "I help Nadia with some chores from time to time. I'm a woodworker by trade, so I'm handy with my hands."

"I'm sure you are," Sebastian said pleasantly. And wasn't it interesting that this neighbor had been in such a hurry to help out with some chores that he hadn't taken the time to button his shirt properly.

Nadia thumped a rack of toast on the table, which startled Sparky into another scold.

"Feed him some toast," Nadia snapped. "Maybe that will keep him quiet."

Taking the hint, Sebastian helped himself to a piece of toast, breaking off a corner for Lynnea to feed to Sparky, while Jeb poured koffee for all of them and Nadia dished out the bacon and eggs.

He'd managed to put two women in a snit before breakfast. Was that some kind of record?

He filled Lynnea's plate, since Sparky was perched on her wrist and didn't seem interested in going anywhere—and smiled at her when the stiff silence of the other two people at the table finally broke through her enchantment with the bird.

They didn't linger over the meal. When Jeb pushed

his chair back, thanked Nadia for breakfast, and offered to take care of a few of the chores, Sebastian said, "I'll give you a hand"—and ignored the sharp look Nadia gave him as he followed Jeb out the door.

Lynnea kept her eyes on the bird dozing on her wrist. Such a small creature, but joyful and loving. What would it be like to have something that would love her just for being there, just for loving it in return? A companion that wouldn't criticize or think her inadequate?

She'd felt the tension during breakfast, but she hadn't known the cause. She hadn't known what to do or say. And she'd been afraid that the tension would change to anger funneled toward her if she didn't stay quiet.

But now Sebastian was outside helping Jeb, and a tigress wouldn't cower at the thought of saying something to a nice woman.

"You have a lovely home," she said, looking around the kitchen. And it was lovely. Comfortable and warm. Welcoming. It reminded her of Sebastian's cottage. A place she'd probably never see again.

"Thank you. It's been in my family for several generations." Nadia stood up and began scraping the remains of their meal onto a single plate.

"Can I help?"

Nadia smiled and looked at Sparky. "You are." She stacked the plates. "Have you known Sebastian long?"

"Not long. And, I guess, not for much longer."

"What makes you say that?"

Her face burned with the shame of failure—and the shame of wanting. So she kept her eyes on the bird when she said, "He won't have sex with me."

Nadia bobbled the dishes, almost dropping the stack. "What do you mean, he won't have sex with you?"

"He won't. He says he can't, but he could if he wanted to. I may not know a lot about . . . sex things . . .

but I know enough to know that when a man's . . . stuff . . . sticks out like that, he wants sex."

Nadia set the dishes back down on the table. "And Sebastian's . . . stuff . . . sticks out when he's around you?"

Lynnea nodded. "But he won't do anything, even though I'm a trollop."

Nadia sank into the chair. "Trollop?"

"I'm a bad person. That's why I ended up in the Den. If I'm a bad person, why can't I have sex with a man who makes my heart feel so strange? When he kissed me, it felt wonderful. I felt wonderful. Like the tigress spell he put on me was still working, and I was still strong and powerful."

"I think," Nadia said slowly, "that I should put on another pot of koffee. Then you can tell me the whole story of how you came to the Den and about this spell Sebastian put on you."

Sebastian waited until they'd fallen into the rhythm of filling the watering cans from the buckets drawn from the well.

"So," he said while he watched Jeb carefully soak the ground in one of the flower beds, "how long have you been sleeping with Aunt Nadia?"

Jeb hesitated a moment, then moved over to the next part of the bed. "Don't rightly know that it's any of your business."

"What about Lee? Is it his business?"

"No, I don't reckon it is. Nadia is a grown woman, well able to make up her own mind about such things."

"So you just sneak over here a couple times a week for some—"

Jeb dropped the watering can and straightened up. "You've no call to be saying things that would shame your auntie. *No call.* She's a fine woman. The best I've ever known."

Sebastian gauged the anger in Jeb's eyes. Not the bluster of a man caught doing something he shouldn't but the anger of a man defending something—or someone—that mattered to him. "Do you love her?"

"I do." With a mild curse, Jeb reached down and righted the watering can, which had spilled out too much water on that flower bed. "I'm content with the way things are between us. I'd like more, but until Nadia's ready, I'm content with how things are." He took off his cap, slapped it against his thigh, then settled it on his head again. "I can't say what Lee does or doesn't know, but if it sets your mind at ease, Glorianna is . . . aware . . . of how things stand between Nadia and me."

"And you're still here," Sebastian murmured.

"I'm still here."

It wasn't that he objected to two people—two *humans*—having sex without marriage. And it wasn't as if he didn't know what men and women did together—and why. But he couldn't quite wrap his mind around *Aunt Nadia* panting and moaning under a man—or over a man.

"What about you?" Jeb demanded. "You sleeping with that girl?"

Already off balance, he felt as if the question mentally knocked him on his ass. "We slept together," he stammered. "There was only one bed in the room, so we slept together. But we didn't . . . we haven't . . ." He raised a hand as if to gesture, then let it fall back to his side. "Daylight," he muttered. "I never thought I'd be having *this* conversation."

"Comes as a surprise to me, too," Jeb admitted. He scratched the back of his neck. "Thought you were an incubus."

"So did I."

"Ah."

Flustered and embarrassed, Sebastian looked around the garden . . . and remembered why he'd come here.

"You live far from here, Jeb?"

"Just a few minutes' walk along that path," Jeb replied, pointing in the general direction. "Have a nice little cottage. Too small for someone thinking of raising a family, but it suits me. And I took it on because the barn makes a good workshop, gives me plenty of room to store my wood and build things."

"But it's still a distance from here." Sebastian hesitated. Jeb had a bit of a drawl, which indicated that he'd come to this landscape from another place at some point in his life. But his manner still said "country" rather than "city," and folks from a country landscape could be earthy and easy or as prim and starched as an old spinster's knickers when it came to men and women. "You should move in with Nadia. You should live here."

"Now, wait up a minute."

"Trouble's coming." Sebastian glanced toward the kitchen windows and lowered his voice. "Bad trouble. Landscapers have died. That's what I came to tell Aunt Nadia."

"And you think something will try to hurt Nadia?"

He nodded. "Not only is she a strong Landscaper in her own right; she's Belladonna's mother. So I'm asking you, Jeb. What if being a few minutes away is too far away?"

"I . . . I have my work. Wouldn't be easy to move my workshop. At least, not quickly. And Nadia has to tend her landscapes. I can't be with her then."

"But at night," Sebastian persisted. "Here, at night."

Jeb looked uncomfortable. "Aurora is a small village. What people suspect and what they *know* can make a difference. It's your auntie's reputation we're talking about."

"It's my aunt's *life* we're talking about."

Jeb nodded. "All right, then. I'll talk to Nadia. That's all I can promise to do." He paused, then added, "What about you and the girl?"

"I belong in the Den. She belongs someplace else."

"And you can live with that?"

"I *have* to live with that," he snapped.

Jeb took off his cap and turned it round and round in his hands. "You asked me a question, and I know how my heart wants to answer. So I'll ask you the same question. If you send her off to some landscape you think is the right place for her, someplace that's more than a few minutes' walk down a path . . ."

"This is different. The Den isn't safe!"

"Will any place be safe?" Jeb asked quietly. "How will you feel if this trouble skips over the Den and lands square in the middle of this place you think is so safe and you can't reach her?"

The thought made him sick. "I'm trying to do the right thing."

"I can see that. But Sebastian? Sometimes doing the right thing isn't the right thing to do."

"Here," Nadia said, caging the keet between her hands. "It's time for him to go back in his cage."

"Oh," Lynnea said. It had been easier to tell Nadia about her life with Mam, Pa, and Ewan while she kept her eyes on the bird. Much easier to admit the thing Pa had tried to do that had led to her being sent away. When she'd told Nadia about the water and the sand, the older woman's hands had trembled. But what had her stumbling was talking about Sebastian and those hours when he'd made her a tigress and she'd seen what it could be like to live without fear.

But even Sebastian was trying to send her away. He'd wanted her to stay in Sanctuary. He hadn't argued when she'd told him she wanted to go with him to his aunt's house, but he'd made it clear enough that he didn't want her going back to the Den with him.

"Now," Nadia said, returning to the table, "what do you want, Lynnea?"

I want Sebastian. "I don't understand."

"You're free of the life you had. You have a chance at a new beginning. Where would you like to go?"

"I want to go back to the Den." She didn't have to think about that. It was a dark place, and a strange place, but she felt safe there. "But Sebastian doesn't want—"

"Darling, Sebastian *does* want. That's what has him tangled up in knots where you're concerned." Nadia smiled. "Don't you see? If you'd been nothing more than a woman who had aroused his body, he would have been your lover by now."

"But he knows I'm not . . . that I haven't . . ."

"He's an incubus. That wouldn't have mattered in the least. But you've done more than arouse his body, Lynnea. You've touched his heart, and that's something I've hoped would happen to him—that he would find someone who touched his heart." Nadia patted Lynnea's hand. "Frustrating for you, I know, and doubly so for him, I imagine."

"He still doesn't want me to go back to the Den."

"That's not his decision, is it?"

Lynnea looked at Nadia. She'd always been told where to go and what to do. "But—"

"Your life, your journey, your choice. Your opportunity." Nadia leaned back. "Have you ever tossed a coin into a wish well?"

"Once. Just a penny."

"The amount doesn't matter," Nadia said. "It's how much heart is put into the wish."

"But nothing happened."

"Oh? And just how do you think the wish wells work?"

"You hold a coin, make a wish, toss the coin in the well as a tribute to the Guides. And then if you're meant to have it, your wish will come true."

Nadia sighed. "Yes, I suppose that's how most people think it works. This is how it *does* work. You make a wish and toss a coin in the well as a declaration of your intention to have something in your life. Then what do you do?"

Lynnea shook her head to indicate that she didn't know.

Nadia's voice took on the tartness of impatience. "You roll up your sleeves and you work to make it happen."

"But I don't know how to make it happen!"

"Opportunity and choice, Lynnea. What the heart truly desires doesn't come to you overnight, and it doesn't always come in the way you imagined."

Lynnea nibbled on her thumbnail. "Maybe I could find work in the Den. Maybe I could work for Philo. I know how to cook and bake. I know how to clean, wash dishes. I'd need to find a place to live."

"I don't think that will be a problem," Nadia said dryly. She pushed her chair back and stood up. "I'd better put something on under this dress before I shock my nephew more than I already have. Then, I think, it's time to find out why Sebastian is here."

Thank all the Guardians of the Light, Sebastian thought when he saw Nadia and Lynnea walk out of the house. Nadia had put something on under that dress. He'd already seen more of his aunt than he wanted to.

"Jeb?" Nadia called. "Why don't you show Lynnea the flower gardens?" After giving Lynnea a friendly push, she walked off in the opposite direction, toward the back of her personal garden.

Figuring that was his cue to have a private talk with Nadia, Sebastian set the watering can down and followed his aunt. He caught up to her when she stopped at the fountain and frowned.

"The statue is gone," she said, sounding annoyed and resigned but not terribly worried.

"Statue?"

"The statue the three of you bought me for my birthday one year. It's gone."

Being related to Nadia and Glorianna, he knew more about how the Landscapers' magic worked than most people. His heart raced as too many awful possibilities leaped through his mind. "Someone stole it?"

" 'Stole' is a harsh word, since I know Glorianna took it. I told her it wasn't necessary, but I think she's going to alter the landscapes to bring Aurora and all my other landscapes into her garden."

His heart still raced, but the feeling of relief that swept through him left him shaky. "Good. That's good."

"It's not good. She has enough to deal with without taking on more."

"Aunt Nadia. There's something I have to tell you."

Nadia stared at the fountain. "The Eater of the World is loose among the landscapes. I know, Sebastian. Glorianna already warned me."

"Does she know about the school?"

Frowning, Nadia looked at him. "What about the school?"

He rested his hands on her shoulders, offering silent comfort. "The Eater has taken over the school. The place is crawling with Its creatures." Even through the thin material, he felt her skin growing cold beneath his hands as her face paled. "The Landscapers are dead, Aunt Nadia. The Bridges are dead. Everyone who was at the school—"

"Lee?"

"We saw him in Sanctuary. He knows. He said he was going to break the bridges that linked Glorianna's landscapes to any others."

Nadia sank to the ground. Sebastian dropped to his knees with her, holding her upright while she swayed.

"Aunt Nadia?" he asked sharply. He wouldn't like it if she fainted, but he could deal with it. What brought him close to panic was the fear that he'd shocked her so much she was having some kind of attack.

"We're the only ones left?" Nadia whispered. "Glorianna and I are the only Landscapers left?"

Sebastian rubbed her arms. "Maybe not. Plenty of Landscapers would have been traveling, checking up on their landscapes, so—"

"But they don't know!" Nadia's voice rose.

Out of the corner of his eye, Sebastian saw Jeb look

in their direction and take a step toward them. Saw Lynnea reach out and stop him.

"The Landscapers who are traveling won't know about the danger." Nadia sounded panicked.

"If the Eater tries to connect one of Its bad landscapes to a daylight one, people will notice. Word will spread, right?" He wasn't sure why he was arguing, since Lee had already told him what could happen to Ephemera without the Landscapers, but seeing Nadia distraught had him grasping for anything that might steady her.

Then something occurred to him. "Even if the surviving Landscapers have to use bridges to avoid going back to the school, and even if the Eater *has* been in a landscape, the Landscaper who controls that piece of Ephemera will be able to alter it back to—"

"No."

"Glorianna did it," Sebastian insisted. "The Eater had connected one of Its landscapes to the Den, and she altered the Den to break that connection."

Nadia looked at him, her dark eyes full of despair. "Glorianna is the only Landscaper who can alter landscapes like that. The only one who can rearrange pieces of the world, bringing them together to form a new pattern. *The only one,* Sebastian."

He sat back on his heels. "Then she's the only real enemy this thing has, isn't she?"

"Yes, she is. And the landscapes she holds will be islands connected with one another but no longer quite part of the world, like a reflection you can see in a pool of still water, but when you turn to look at it directly, it isn't there."

Food, clothing, metal for tools, wood for building and fuel. How many of those things were in Glorianna's landscapes?

"Well," Nadia said. "There's nothing we can do right this moment, so we'd best get on with the business of living."

Rising swiftly, Sebastian helped her to her feet.

"Aunt Nadia, about Lynnea . . ."

"She wants to go back to the Den."

"No."

"Her life, her journey, her choice."

"I won't take her back to the Den."

"Then she'll have to find her own way back."

Let Lynnea stumble around trying to find a bridge back to the Den? Unthinkable. Even if Nadia escorted Lynnea to the bridge he'd always taken to go back home after visiting here, there was no guarantee Lynnea would arrive at the Den.

Doing his best to look and sound menacing, he said, "If I take her back, I'll *take her.*" Surely Nadia understood *that* message.

"It's about time you stopped dithering and got down to it."

His mouth fell open.

Amused, Nadia patted his cheek, then headed toward the part of her garden where Lynnea and Jeb were pretending to admire the flowers.

He ran to catch up to her, then grabbed her arm to slow her down.

"Aunt Nadia, I don't think you understood—"

"I'm a grown woman, and I've had my share of lovers. I know exactly what you meant."

"Lovers? *Lovers?*"

"Well, no one else since Jeb and I—"

"Have pity on me."

Nadia laughed. "Very well. If you don't ask about my sex life, I won't ask about yours."

"Right now, I don't have one."

She stopped before they got close enough to be overheard. "Tell me something, Sebastian. How long has it been since you've walked in daylight?"

"I . . . don't know. A few years."

She nodded. "That's a long time. Even when you came to visit, you never showed up until the sun set— and you never stayed long enough to see the sun rise."

Couldn't. Especially in the last year or so. He *wanted*

to see it, but it was the cruelest reminder of what he'd left behind when he'd turned his back on the daylight landscapes—because it was the one thing he'd truly loved about those landscapes.

"You may want to consider why you're standing here in daylight," Nadia said quietly. "Opportunity and choice, Sebastian. Lynnea isn't the only one making a journey."

He looked over at his little rabbit, who raised her chin as if getting ready to fight.

You started this, he thought. *You're the one who gave her a taste of being a tigress.*

He walked over to her.

"I'm going back to the Den," she said, sounding scared and defiant.

"I know." He still thought she was making a bad choice, but he was too glad to have her with him a little while longer to argue about it anymore.

It moved through the landscapes, smothering the flickers of Light It found in the places Its lesser enemies, the Landscapers, hadn't valued enough to give more than token protection. So easy to create an anchor for one of Its landscapes. Ephemera barely resisted when It imposed Its will in those places. But the shining landscapes, the places that would be such a feast when It destroyed the Light . . . It couldn't find a way into those places. No matter how It twisted and turned through the landscapes, It couldn't find a way in. And that dark landscape, that delicious hunting ground. It could feel the edges of that place, but no matter how hard It tried, It couldn't breach the wall that surrounded the Den of Iniquity.

So many thoughts focused on a single thing, so sure that single thing would keep them safe.

Sebastian. Sebastian. Sebastian.

Humans and demons alike believed in this thing

called *Sebastian* that kept It away from the Den itself, leaving It with no access except for the two anchors It had already established in the dark landscape that bordered the hunting ground.

What enraged It even more was the certainty that the choicest hunting grounds were landscapes controlled by the True Enemy. What troubled It was the feel of the Dark currents in the spots where It had managed to create anchor points in those landscapes. The old Enemies, the Guides, that had fought and caged It so long ago had resonated with the Light and held only a thread of the Dark. But *this* one held the Light and the Dark in equal measure. *This* one could do what the old Enemies never could: she could control Its dark landscapes.

She had to be destroyed before she realized how powerful she truly was.

But this time It wouldn't be the one fighting against the Enemy. This time It would have friends.

It moved along the steep northern slope of Wizard City, a rippling shadow. It had found the Dark Ones' weakness, the thing they feared to lose. In spider form, It had climbed the wall of the building to be sure anyone standing at a particular window would see what It wanted him to see.

Ready now, It reached out with a mental tentacle for the Dark One. It didn't try to slip into that mind unobserved. It made Its presence felt—and relished the fear that flooded that mind before the feeling was controlled.

Come to the window, It whispered. *Look at the steep land. Watch.* It withdrew the tentacle, knowing the Dark One would obey.

Choosing ground that was a short distance from a flock of sheep grazing on the hillside, It altered the grass into a large patch of rust-colored sand, changing that piece of Wizard City into the bonelovers' landscape.

Then It waited until It sensed the Dark One's presence.

The simpleminded animals began to bleat and move away as It rippled beneath them. Already primed to bolt, they panicked when It transformed part of Itself and tentacles burst out of the ground in the middle of the flock. The ones in front of It ran straight into the patch of sand—and disappeared.

Satisfied, It pulled the tentacles into the earth, changing them back into Its natural form.

It felt the Dark One's mind reaching out. Hesitant. Afraid.

We helped you, the Dark One said. *All these years, we sent you prey.*

More prey found its own way into my landscapes, It replied. *You never freed me. Never tried.*

We couldn't! We didn't know where the Landscapers had hidden—

Lies. It waited, savoring the fear.

What do you want?

The True Enemy must be destroyed. She is one; you are many. It will be easy for you to destroy her.

We've tried to destroy Belladonna!

A shudder went through It. Belladonna. The first male It had killed at the Landscapers' School had used that word as a shield for a kernel of hope. Now It knew what the word meant.

Destroy the True Enemy, It insisted.

Why can't you destroy her?

A thread of hope flowed through the words, enraging It. The Dark One was too fearful to hide his thoughts completely. He hoped It and the True Enemy would destroy each other. Foolish creature, to think that It had learned nothing from Its prey when It had spent so much time absorbing Its prey's deepest fears.

Don't you want to be friends?

We are your friends!

Prove it. It projected an image of the females It had found—the females that had been hidden for generations. *Destroy the True Enemy—or something besides sheep will disappear in the bonelovers' landscape.*

It felt the Dark One's fear spike.

We . . . We will find a way to destroy Belladonna. The Dark One hesitated. *Is there anything else we must do to prove we are friends?*

It considered for a moment, thought about the dark hunting ground It wanted to claim for Itself. *Yes. Destroy the thing called Sebastian.*

🜚

Glorianna walked the paths in her walled garden, the statue of the sitting woman cradled in her arms, an old piece of towel tossed over her shoulder. Fifteen years ago, she had done what Nadia had asked—she had removed all the access points from her garden at the school and had rebuilt her garden on this small island. Then she had altered the landscapes, hiding this place so well it could not be found by conventional means.

Its existence was known in Sanctuary, but the Keepers of the Light did not talk to outsiders about the Island in the Mist—unless heart's need compelled them to speak.

The wizards could not find her here. The Eater of the World could not find her here. The only way to reach this island was through Sanctuary, and Sanctuary was held, protected, within the walls of her garden.

She could feel the connection between her landscapes and the rest of Ephemera breaking, setting these pieces of the world adrift, anchored only to one another.

Ephemera. As solid and strong as stone, as delicate as a dream.

And if she was successful, the dream would not become a nightmare.

She just didn't know how she was supposed to fight something like the Eater of the World. And if she did manage to find It and fight It, she didn't know how a single Landscaper could win that fight when it had taken so many like her to contain the Eater the first time.

"Stop dithering," she muttered. "You'll reach that battle when you reach it. You know what needs to be done now." She turned around and walked to the front part of her gardens.

She hadn't spent the past hour wandering the paths in order to decide where to put the statue that would anchor Nadia's home. She already had an access point to her family home—a bed of flowers she had grown from seeds and cuttings from Nadia's personal gardens. Near the front of the bed was a large piece of slate. She'd always intended to use the slate as a foundation for some kind of decorative ornament, but she'd never found anything that felt right.

Going down on her knees, she set the statue on the slate, turning it this way and that until she had it positioned exactly the way she wanted it. Then, with her hands resting on the statue, she called to Ephemera and altered the landscapes, breaking some bonds and forming others, rearranging the pieces and shaping new borders and boundaries.

The sun was low in the sky when she finally sat back.

Some strange pairings. Some unexpected borders. She didn't always know why two seemingly different landscapes resonated with each other, but she didn't doubt what she'd done.

Getting to her feet, she took a deep breath, then clamped a hand over her mouth when the exhalation came out as a sob. No. She couldn't waver. This next task made her sick at heart, but she couldn't waver.

Clenching her fists, she strode deep into her gardens to an odd little bed that sat alone and contained nothing but one heart's hope plant and a brick.

She rested her fingers on the brick and felt the Dark nibbling around the edges of this small landscape. The Eater didn't recognize what this was or why the Dark currents didn't quite resonate with the Dark in the rest of the city, but given enough time, It would.

Pulling the piece of towel off her shoulder, she spread it on the ground in front of the bed, then picked up the brick and wrapped it in the towel.

Racing to finish this task before the sun set, she picked up the wrapped brick and ran to the sheltered horseshoe of rock where she kept the boat the River Guardians had made for her. Theirs were the only boats that could survive this part of the river.

Getting into the boat, she sat on the front seat, the wrapped brick in her lap, and emptied her mind of everything but the boat and the river.

The boat had no oars, no sails, no tiller. The will and the heart supplied those things.

Slowly, smoothly, the boat slipped out of the horseshoe of calm water into the churning power of the river. It cut across some currents, followed others, balanced and driven by the task of the person it held.

At the edge of that tangle of currents, she willed the boat to stop. Immediately a circle of calm water spread out around it.

Picking up the brick with both hands, she held it over the water.

It had been a foolish thing to do, decided in a moment of youthful anger and seasoned by the need to answer a need.

Opportunities and choices. A bitter farmer who still had a seed of kindness in him. She'd fed that seed a glimmer of Light, a ray of hope. He'd taken that glimmer back to a place in the city that was full of dark emotions and had sparked another glimmer. And another. And another. Kindness fed on kindness, and the Light grew. A few months later, when the resonance of that little piece of the city called to her, she'd crossed over and taken the brick to be her access point so she could continue to guide the currents of Light. She'd gone back a few times over the years to keep the resonance of that small landscape balanced, gambling that she wouldn't run into Sebastian's father, who was the only wizard who might recognize her.

Now . . .

She had to let them go—those people, that beacon of Light. Having a landscape within the walls of Wizard City had always been risky. Now it could endanger all the landscapes in her care. It could be the chink in the wall that gave the Eater of the World a chance to attack the stronghold of Light.

Her hands shook as she lowered the wrapped brick into the water.

"I'm sorry," she whispered. Tears ran down her face. "I'm sorry."

Why? something whispered. *Why give them up? You worked so hard to help them. Don't you want to help them?*

Of course she wanted to help those people.

Then let them stay protected. Let them stay in the garden.

She felt it then—a Dark current that didn't resonate with her. A malice behind the words assuring her she didn't need to do this.

With a cry of anguish, she let go of the brick.

It sank fast, but the river's currents cleansed it of all trace of her before it reached the bottom.

She huddled in the boat for a while, scared to the point of feeling sick.

She'd almost wavered. Even knowing that little landscape could be a danger to all her other landscapes, she'd almost wavered. Because something had gotten in just far enough to try to lure her into making an error. It had arrowed in on her own reluctance to abandon those people, sending them back to the mean existence they'd known when only the wizards' influence had touched that part of the city. If she'd taken the brick back to her garden, the Eater might have found a way to use that small landscape to attack Sanctuary.

Weary to the bone and half-blinded by tears, she sat up and focused her will on guiding the boat, allowing no other thoughts until the boat was safely moored in the horseshoe of calm water.

As she stumbled her way to her house, she kept wondering if she'd truly done the right thing by letting that landscape go—or if this was her first failure in the battle to save the Light.

Chapter Thirteen

The moment he opened the back door and stepped into his kitchen, Sebastian felt uneasy. He put a hand back to stop Lynnea, then stood still, listening. A rhythmic *plink . . . plink* coming from somewhere inside the cottage, but that was an ordinary sound. It was the feral muskiness that troubled him. Not a bad smell. Alluring in its own way. Seductive, even. But not familiar. Not something that belonged in his home.

Moving warily, he went to the small table, found the box of matches, and lit the oil lamp.

Nothing in the kitchen looked out of place, but he couldn't shake the feeling that things had been lifted and put back almost where he'd left them.

He put a finger to his lips, then crooked that finger to tell Lynnea to come in. When she reached him, he cupped a hand around the back of her head and brought his mouth close to her ear.

"I think someone's been in the cottage. I have to look around. If I tell you to run, you get out of here, go back up the path. Focus on reaching Nadia. Nothing but Nadia. Understand me?" He waited until she nodded before he stepped back, his lips brushing against her cheek as he moved away from her.

After taking the biggest kitchen knife from the wood block, he moved into the living area.

Plink ... plink.

The lamp in the kitchen didn't offer much light, but it was enough for him to make out the shapes of the furniture. Pausing at the table in front of the couch, he lit another lamp.

Nothing there that shouldn't be there.

With the lamp in one hand and the knife in the other, he approached the bedroom, not sure he'd be able to hear anything over the pounding of his heart.

Nothing looked out of place there, either, except . . .

The bed was neatly made—exactly as Lynnea had left it before they'd headed out to the Landscapers' School. But the bedroom reeked of that muskiness, and there was an indentation in the middle of the bed, like someone had lain there.

Staring at it, he had the oddest sensation, as if something inside him recognized the intruder. Something that came from instinct, from blood and bone, not the intellect.

One thing he knew with absolute certainty: He didn't want Lynnea anywhere near that bed.

Plink ... plink.

He followed the sound into the bathroom, watched the water drops fall into the sink. After a long moment, he set the lamp down and turned the faucet to stop the drip.

The little stove that heated the water tank was cold, as it should be, and nothing was out of place. And yet . . .

We can't stay here. The cottage was less than a mile from the streets that made up the Den. Distant enough to give him the separation he'd needed but still an easy walk. Now the isolation weighed on him. They were alone out here, too far away from help of any kind.

Maybe he would have risked himself and stayed here, but he wouldn't risk Lynnea.

Coming out of the bedroom, he saw Lynnea standing in the doorway between the living area and the kitchen. She was trembling, but she held a knife in one hand.

"What is it?" she whispered.

He shook his head and checked the other downstairs room, then climbed the stairs to check the empty
rooms on the second floor. Bedrooms, but he hadn't
needed the space, so he'd done nothing with the rooms
except sweep the floors and wash the windows twice a
year.

Hurrying back down the stairs, he said, "Whatever it
was, it's gone now." He paused. "But we can't stay here."

"Do you have a carry basket? I can put the food
Nadia gave us in that, and you can use the travel bag she
loaned us for your clothes."

"There's a basket in one of the bottom cupboards.
I'll—" As he looked at the wall, the pain in his chest was
so fierce he struggled to breathe.

His framed sketches. If he had to give up the cottage
and never come back, it would hurt. He would miss it,
and the home he'd made here, but the sketches were a
part of him.

"You have to take them with you," Lynnea said.

Her words were a balm and yet scraped his heart
raw. "Can't. We've already got all we can carry."

"You can't leave them here, not knowing what might
happen to them."

"We can't carry them!"

She got a look on her face that reminded him of bull
demons at their most stubborn.

"We're taking them."

His heart was bleeding already, and that stubborn
look combined with that prissy tone of voice made him
want to scream.

She huffed. "Don't you have a handcart?"

"No, I don't have a handcart," he replied in a nasty
imitation of her tone.

"Then how do you haul wood for the fires or take
care of chores?"

"There's the—" He stopped. Thought. "There's a
wheeled barrow in the shed out back." One wheel and
long handles. They could load it up, and he could pull it
behind him.

"Fine," Lynnea said. "You get the barrow, and I'll find something to wrap the sketches in."

She went into the kitchen, then came out with the lamp and marched into the bedroom.

"Don't use the linens on the bed," Sebastian said.

The look she gave him was sharp enough to strip off several layers of skin.

"Daylight," he muttered as he stomped out to the shed. Women were definitely easier to deal with when sex was all you wanted to give and take.

By the time he pulled the barrow out of the shed and returned to the cottage, she'd already taken the sketches off the wall and wrapped them in a sheet. The package looked bulky to him, but he wasn't about to say anything that would add to her snit, so he unpacked the food from the travel bag Nadia had given him and went into the bedroom to pack up whatever clothes he could fit into the bag.

Returning to the kitchen with the bag, he discovered she'd packed the food into the carry basket along with his perk-pot, grinder, two mugs, and the bag of koffea beans.

"The barrow's not that big," he grumbled.

She just sniffed.

The weight of the basket surprised a grunt out of him as he lifted it off the table, which made him grateful he wasn't going to have to carry the thing all the way to the Den.

Not that he would tell *her* that.

It took some shifting, but he got the travel bag, the carry basket, and Lynnea's pack into the barrow. Which left the sketches to balance precariously on top of the pile.

Lynnea came to the kitchen door, her arms wrapped tightly around the bulky package.

"Here," he said, reaching for the package, "I'll—"

"No!" She twisted her body, blocking his attempt to take the sketches. "They could get damaged in the barrow. I'll carry them."

"Don't be foolish," he snapped, reaching for the package again.

"No! I'll. Carry. Them."

"Suit yourself. But don't start whining when your arms are aching."

Her lower lip quivered, and he thought she was going to give in. Then she stiffened up and gave him another of those skin-scraping looks.

Why couldn't she be a rabbit again for a little while? "Could you at least get out of the way so I can extinguish the lamps?"

He waited until she stood beside the barrow before he went into the kitchen. He snuffed out the lamps, then stood in the dark.

"I'll come back," he whispered. "If we're both still standing when this fight is done, I'll come back."

Then he walked out of the cottage, locked the door, lifted the barrow's handles, and began trudging down the dirt road toward the Den with Lynnea walking beside him.

By the time she saw the lights of the Den, Lynnea's arms were aching. The framed sketches would have been awkward enough to carry over any distance, but the other things she'd wrapped in the sheet made the package bulky in a way that defied any attempt to shift her arms to another position.

But she refused to let Sebastian see any hint of her discomfort. He'd argue to leave the bundle behind, maybe promising to come back for it after they got settled into his room at the bordello. Maybe he would have gone back for the bundle, and maybe it would have been there when he did go back, but she wasn't about to trust something so important to "maybe."

Did he think she hadn't seen how much the thought of leaving the sketches had hurt him? They were more than pencil markings on paper. He would have been leaving a piece of his heart behind—and he might never have gotten it back.

So she kept her chin up, ignored the looks Sebastian kept giving her, and repeated over and over, *I am a tigress.*

Until that day when Pa had tried to force her to do the sex thing, she had never disobeyed an order. Wouldn't have dared disobey an order. Now here she was defying Sebastian, a man who made her feel things that were both wonderful and scary, because she knew in her heart that she was right.

Funny how something inside a person could change in so short a time.

A moment after they reached the Den's main street, someone shouted, "Sebastian!" And there was Teaser, loping toward them, looking happy and relieved—until he saw her. Then he skidded to a stop.

"I'll meet you at Philo's as soon as I have Lynnea settled in our room," Sebastian said.

Teaser glanced at her. "But . . . I thought—"

"Things changed," Sebastian snapped.

Something flickered across Teaser's face—uneasiness? doubt?—but was gone before she could put a name to that feeling.

"Right," Teaser said. "You got your room key?"

Sebastian nodded. "But there's an extra key at the desk."

"I took that one." Teaser shrugged, as if it meant nothing. "Been keeping the door of my room locked. Yours, too. If you need to put anything into the chiller, you can get into my room through the bathroom."

Sebastian gave Teaser a long look, then nodded again.

After giving her a hesitant smile, Teaser headed down the street.

She and Sebastian followed at a slower pace. Now that she was almost to a place where she could set it down, the bundle weighed more with each step.

When they reached the bordello, Sebastian shouldered the pack, then opened the front door for her before hefting the travel bag and carry basket.

The man behind the desk just watched them as they crossed the lobby and started climbing the stairs.

"Don't you usually lock your doors?" Lynnea asked as she watched Sebastian fish the key out of his pocket and turn the lock.

"For privacy, but not to keep someone out when I'm not here."

As soon as he pushed the door open, she hurried to the bed and, with a quiet groan, set down her bundle. Then she turned to face him, hoping her smile looked genuine.

He just stood in the doorway, staring at her. Then he brought their bags and baskets far enough into the room to close the door.

"You have to talk to Teaser and Philo," she said, becoming more and more nervous about the way his green eyes stared at her. "If you just tell me what a chiller is so I don't go looking at things I shouldn't, I can get things put away here." Especially the things she didn't want him to find just yet.

He walked up to the bed and, firmly but gently, pushed her aside.

"Sebastian."

He unwrapped the sheet . . . and said nothing. Her heart pounded as he brushed his fingers over a wooden box and the leather carry case that held the sketching paper.

He opened the box, then closed it again.

"My cousins gave me this box a few years ago. Charcoals and leaded pencils in different weights. Aunt Nadia gave me the colored chalks." His fingers brushed the leather case. "Can't get this kind of paper in the Den. Not even on the black market. Aunt Nadia or Lee used to get it for me from one of the big cities, but there's no telling if that place is within reach anymore."

He looked at her, and in his eyes she saw the struggle to hold back a flood of emotion. Even the trickle that was breaking through the dam of self-control left her breathless.

"Thank you," he said, his voice barely above a whisper. He brushed his lips over her forehead, over her cheek, over her lips. "Thank you."

Something was happening here. More than a sexual wanting. Something that made her afraid ... and made her feel as if she could fly.

"You have to talk to Philo and Teaser," she said.

He rested his forehead against hers. "Yes."

"Before you go, could you ..."

He raised his head. His eyes were full of heat, hunger. Something more.

"... show me what the chiller is?"

Sebastian pulled out a chair at one of Philo's indoor tables. Since the indoor room wasn't used except in bad weather, they had the place to themselves.

Teaser came around the small bar at the back of the room, carrying a bottle of whiskey and glasses. "Philo will be along in a minute. Just has to finish up the last order."

While Teaser poured the whiskey, Sebastian thought about Lynnea arguing with him to bring his sketches, carrying his art supplies in secret. Carrying his heart.

And all he'd done was made it harder for her by being difficult.

"How do you apologize to a woman for being stupid?" Sebastian muttered.

"Great sex?" Teaser replied with a cocky grin—which changed into something close to panic. "Not sex. Box of sweets. That's better. Much better. Or flowers. If you can find any."

Daylight, Sebastian thought, *he's like a boy who's just realized his mother has done the same things he's trying to get his sweetheart to do. What is it about Lynnea that brings that out in him?*

Philo came through the swinging door that led into the kitchen, sparing the two incubi from saying anything more about the woman getting settled in Sebastian's room.

"Last customer served," Philo said, setting down a tray that held a basket of Phallic Delights and a bowl of melted cheese. "Not that there have been many customers today. Didn't do much cooking, so there's not much left, but I can make you a cold beef sandwich."

"Not for me, thanks," Sebastian replied, "but I'll take something back to the room for Lynnea."

Philo bobbled the tray, almost knocking over the whiskey bottle. "But . . . I thought you were taking her to the Landscapers' School."

Sebastian knocked back his whiskey. The room was warm and stuffy, but he needed the liquor's heat. "The school is gone."

This was why he'd wanted to talk to them in private, but it was hard to tell them what he'd seen at the school, and reliving those minutes when he and Lynnea were running for their lives put a chill down his spine even whiskey couldn't thaw.

Philo left the table long enough to fetch another glass. After pouring a generous measure for himself, he refilled Sebastian's and Teaser's glasses. "So the Bridge is going to cut us off from the rest of Ephemera."

Sebastian nodded. "From everything except the other landscapes Belladonna holds."

"That's going to cut down on business," Teaser muttered.

"Business isn't the problem." Philo rolled his glass between his hands. "What about us? The folks who live in the Den? Where's the food going to come from? We can't grow our own, and if things are going bad in the daylight landscapes, folks there might not be willing to sell their surplus, especially to the likes of us."

Had Lee considered that when making the decision to break the bridges that connected Glorianna's landscapes to the rest of Ephemera?

"What about the lektricity?" Philo added. "I have a meat freezer and a big chiller for other kinds of food. If the lektricity goes, we won't even be able to store up much."

"We'll take it a step at a time," Sebastian said. "First we spread the word to everyone who runs a business in the Den—brothels, taverns, gambling houses, shops. Everyone. If anyone sees a change in the landscape, especially pools of water or that sand, they're to report it."

"To you?" Philo asked.

Sebastian hesitated, then nodded. "I promised Lee I'd do what I could to hold the Den."

The other men shifted uneasily.

"What else?" Teaser asked.

"We need to locate the bridges that connect the Den with other landscapes," Sebastian said. He knew the location of one, and it worried him. The bridge he and Lynnea had used to cross over to the Den from Nadia's house had been two boulders set on either side of a woodland trail that ended at the open ground at the back of his cottage. If whatever had been inside his home returned, would it be able to follow that path back to Aunt Nadia's house? The people who had died in the school were proof enough that Landscapers were as vulnerable as anyone else to the creatures the Eater of the World could bring into a landscape. "And I want to know about any strangers who come into the Den. Especially if they don't feel . . . right."

Philo and Teaser exchanged a glance, but before either could speak, someone knocked frantically on the closed door.

When Philo got up to answer the door, Teaser said, "I'll get a demon cycle and ride around to locate the bridges. But I'm not going to cross over."

"We'll have to eventually to find out what landscapes they connect to," Sebastian replied. "Especially since Philo's right. We're going to need food."

Philo returned to the table with Mr. Finch trailing behind him.

"Oh," Mr. Finch said, wringing his hands. "Sebastian. Teaser." He glanced at Philo. "You're busy."

"What's wrong?" Sebastian asked, regretting the sharpness in his voice when Mr. Finch flinched and looked ready to bolt.

"I closed my shop," Mr. Finch said, looking at Philo pleadingly. "I said I had to meet you. Is that all right?"

"That's fine," Philo said, "but why did you close your shop?"

Mr. Finch shuddered. "One of *them* came in, and she made me feel so . . . strange."

Sebastian looked at Teaser.

"Two succutits and three incubi strolled into the Den after you and Lynnea left. They're . . . different." Teaser took a deep breath and blew it out slowly. "Don't know how to describe it."

"They smell musky," Mr. Finch said, his voice trembling. "Like wild animals."

Sebastian tensed. Musky. Had one or more of these newcomers spent time in his cottage?

"Yeah," Teaser said. "Saw one of the incubi snare a woman. I spent a little time with her last moon. She's a hard-edged bitch and not generous in any way. But even from where I was standing, watching him reel her in, I could tell there was something about him that scared her but she just couldn't resist the lure."

"What happened?" Sebastian asked.

Teaser shrugged. "Dunno. I saw him trolling again a few hours later, but I didn't see her."

"They've been asking about you, Sebastian," Philo said, refilling his glass and handing it to Mr. Finch, who gulped down the whiskey.

"Yes," Mr. Finch said, gasping. "When is Sebastian coming back? That's what they ask."

"Why the interest in me?"

"Dunno," Teaser replied. "I found one of them rubbing her hands over the door of your room and licking her lips like a cat that's cornered a particularly tasty bird. She seemed amused when I asked her what she was doing. She said something about wondering if you'd had any interesting dreams. When I went downstairs later, I found the other succubitch trying to persuade the desk clerk to give her the spare key to your room. That's when I took your spare and mine off the hooks and made sure the doors were always locked."

Sebastian drained his glass and set it aside. "If you could make those sandwiches, Philo, I'd be grateful."

Philo nodded, then looked at Mr. Finch. "I'm closing down for a few hours of rest time. I've got a spare room if you'd rather not stay at your place alone."

"Thank you, Philo," Mr. Finch said.

Time crawled while Sebastian waited for Philo. Teaser dug in to the bread and cheese, but the thought of food knotted Sebastian's stomach. He wouldn't feel easy enough to eat—or do anything else—until he was back in his room with Lynnea.

As soon as Philo came back with a basket, Sebastian took his leave and strode to the bordello, watching the street, watching the people. Not as many visitors as usual, and all of them moved with hurried purpose, as if they sensed danger but couldn't locate the source.

When he reached his room, he saw Lynnea standing in the open doorway, looking confused and stubborn . . . and blurry. As if he couldn't quite bring her into focus, not when the gorgeous woman standing on the other side of the door turned and smiled at him. But there was something about the succubus's smile that made his skin crawl—and also made him want to unfurl the power of the incubi and take her.

"Sebastian," the succubus purred.

The sound of her voice shivered through him, full of hot promises.

She gave Lynnea a scathing look. "Is that the best you can do?"

Anger burned out lust when Lynnea winced at the insult.

"What do you want?" Sebastian snapped.

The succubus's smile sharpened, became surly and

yet malevolent. "I can give you dreams you can't even imagine."

He looked her up and down. "I can imagine just fine what kind of dreams I'd get with the likes of you."

Fury flashed in her eyes. This one wasn't used to being resisted. She moved, which brought her a little closer to Lynnea.

Sebastian raised his hand, felt the rush and tingle of power flowing through him. Wizard's power. He didn't want to call the lightning, not when he still didn't know how to control it, not with Lynnea standing so close. But the succubus must have sensed the power—or understood she was being threatened in some way. She bared her teeth like a predator who had just discovered its prey wasn't as helpless as it had thought. Then she backed away.

Sebastian watched her until she was far enough away for him to get into the room and lock the door. Leaning against the door, he waited for his heart to slow to a normal beat.

Lynnea looked uncertain. "It was rude not to let her in, but—"

"No, it was smart." Sebastian set the basket down. "I'm betting she's one of the newcomers who showed up recently."

Lynnea frowned. "She smelled . . . odd. That's what made me uncomfortable about letting her in. She smelled . . ." Her eyes widened. "Like the cottage."

He nodded. "If it wasn't her, one of the others had spent some time in the cottage."

"Why would they enter someone else's home?"

"I don't know." Closing the distance between them, he put his arms around her. *Like holding sunlight,* he thought, the feel of her cleansing him of the lust the succubus had drawn from him—and filling him with a different kind of lust. Just as hot, but sweeter.

"Don't wander around the Den without me," he said.

"I can't live pinned to your shirttails."

He eased back enough to look at her. Stubborn rabbit. "Just until I find out where these newcomers came from and what they want. They're not like the other incubi and succubi, Lynnea. Look, you don't have to stay pinned to my shirttails, as you put it. You could give Philo a hand or . . . or spend time with Teaser." Did she have any idea what it cost him to surrender his prize to another incubus, even temporarily? "Please."

She studied his face for so long. "All right," she finally said, but she didn't stop studying him. "Can you all do that?"

"Do what?"

"Change your face. It was subtle, but I was sure her face didn't look the same when she was talking to you as it did when I first opened the door." She shrugged. "Maybe it was a trick of the light."

"And maybe it wasn't." Uneasy again, he stepped back. "There are stories—old stories—about the incubi and succubi, about how they lure men and women by appearing to be a friend or lover." Hand in hand with those stories were the ones about incubi and succubi providing such intense pleasure the sex was lethal.

"Do you know me?" he demanded suddenly. "Can you *feel* me?"

"If you're asking if I could tell the difference between you and someone wearing your face, then, yes, I know you. I would always know you, Sebastian. Even if the face was the same, that other person couldn't be you."

He hadn't realized how much he'd needed that answer until he felt the tension drain out of him. Weary now, he rubbed his hands over his face. "I brought some food. Let's eat. Then we'll consider what comes next."

While they shared the food in companionable silence, Sebastian chewed on one thought: Why were these newcomers so interested in him?

Chapter Fourteen

Koltak rapped on the door, then barely waited for an acknowledgment before rushing into the room.

"You sent for me, Harland?" he asked.

Harland turned away from the window. "The council has received news. It is terrible—and terrifying."

A chill went through Koltak, but he just waited, saying nothing.

"Belladonna has shown her true nature. She attacked the Landscapers' School, Koltak. She killed all of the Landscapers and Bridges who were at the school, leaving Ephemera's landscapes vulnerable to her malevolence."

Koltak staggered to a chair and sank into it. "How is that possible?"

"Her power has turned vicious, and she's far stronger than any of us imagined." Harland moved away from the window. "Already the dark feelings in human hearts are forming a veil over some of the landscapes."

"But . . . what will killing the other Landscapers gain her? She can't control a landscape if she doesn't resonate with it."

"What she can't control will be torn apart by the storm of human emotions," Harland replied. "Unless we stop her, Ephemera will become an insane world that will destroy everything humans have built. Music, literature, cultured society. All lost. Crushed by the desperate need to survive in a world that keeps changing so fast there will be no chance to survive in those landscapes. And what is left will belong to Belladonna and will be a dark place full of terrors." He paused. "There is evidence that she's pulled some of the darkest landscapes back into the world. You know the ones I mean."

Koltak struggled for any coherent thought like a drowning man flailing to grab hold of anything that will keep him from going under. "Nadia. What about Nadia? Surely she's not trying to protect—"

"We will try to reach Nadia. Right now, we cannot confirm that she and her son, Lee, are still living—or if they, too, were victims of the rogue Landscaper's viciousness." Harland looked at Koltak with an expression of harsh sympathy. "Belladonna must be destroyed."

"But we can't find her!"

"We *must* find her," Harland said. "Since we don't know what happened to her mother and brother, there's only one person left who might be able to draw Belladonna to Wizard City, where the council will be able to gather its full strength and destroy her. There's only one person left, Koltak, and you're the only person who can reach him."

Stunned, Koltak stared at Harland. "Sebastian? What do you expect Sebastian to do against Belladonna?"

Harland smiled a terrible smile. "Nothing."

❧

"You don't have to stay," Lynnea said. "I'm just going to sit here for a while."

"Uh-huh," Teaser replied, following her to a table at the back of Philo's courtyard. "Sebastian told me to stay with you." He flashed a cocky grin. "Besides, you won't tell me what you've got in the box."

Lynnea sighed. She should have told him what was in

the box the first time he'd asked. But she'd felt so flustered and guilty about doing something idle that her denials that the box held anything important had only sharpened the incubus's curiosity.

Setting the box on the table, she chose the seat that put her back to the courtyard's wall and let her watch the courtyard and the street beyond. Let her watch for Sebastian's return.

Philo came up to the table. "What'll you have?"

"Ale for me," Teaser replied. He looked inquiringly at Lynnea.

"I'll find something for the lady," Philo said when she hesitated. He tipped his head to one side. "What's in the box?"

"She won't tell anyone," Teaser said.

Lynnea huffed. "It's just a game a friend of Sebastian's auntie made." She opened the box and carefully poured out the pieces of thin wood. "It's called a puzzle. See? There's a picture painted on one side. You put all the pieces together in the correct way, and you get to see the picture."

Teaser picked up a piece and studied it. "It's got bumps sticking out of it on two sides and round bites taken out of the other two."

"That's part of the puzzle. The bumps of one piece fit into the openings of another."

"Oh, I know *that* game."

"Mind who you're talking to," Philo said sharply.

"What?" Teaser looked at Lynnea. "Oh. Right."

Lynnea kept her eyes on the puzzle pieces she was turning over so that the painted side was on top. "If I'm going to live in the Den, there's no reason why everyone should avoid talking about . . . sex stuff . . . when I'm around."

Loooong pause.

"I'll see what's in the kitchen," Philo said, hurrying away from the table.

Feeling like an outsider, and resenting it, Lynnea concentrated on righting all the pieces so she could begin putting the puzzle together, aware that Teaser seemed to be concentrating equally hard.

Finally Teaser said quietly, "You're different. That's why it feels all right to be a little bit naughty around you, but not bad, not . . . blatant."

Pondering that, Lynnea fit two blue pieces together. Sky? Water? "Why?"

"Dunno, exactly. No one like you has ever come to the Den before."

She couldn't think of anything to say, so she nibbled on the food Philo brought to the table, focused on the puzzle—and waited for Sebastian.

Tired and hungry, Sebastian thanked the demon cycle for its assistance, then scanned Philo's courtyard. He didn't see Lynnea, but one of the people crowded around the table in the back would be able to tell him where she and Teaser had gone.

As he made his way to the back of the courtyard, he wondered if failure, in this case, equaled success. He hadn't seen any sign of rust-colored sand, hadn't spotted any pools of water that were located in places they didn't belong. He'd made note of any physical bridges, but he hadn't crossed over any of them—and wouldn't until he'd talked to Lee and found out which of them his cousin had created.

At least he'd managed to find residents of some of the dark landscapes that bordered the Den and warn them about the creatures that might prey on them. They would spread the word among their own.

He'd done all he could do for now, so it was time to take something for himself. He needed to feel the warmth of her presence, feel the sound of her voice wash over his skin. Just needed to be with her. That, in itself, was a wonder to him. He wanted sex. Of course he did. But that wasn't all he wanted, wasn't all he needed.

She dreamed of him at night, and he found the lure

of those dreams irresistible. But it was like being given a taste of a banquet, then having the door shut in his face before he could feast. Problem was, he had a nagging feeling that if he pushed the door open instead of waiting to be invited into her dreams, the very best of that banquet would disappear and he'd never quite know what he'd missed.

But those were thoughts for another time. Right now, a full belly held more appeal than a hot bed—which, for an incubus, was a sad state of affairs.

Finding Lynnea turned out to be easy. Getting to her was a different matter. As he pushed his way through the crowd gathered around the table, he heard Mr. Finch say, "They fit, and they're both blue, but not the same blue. This one is sky, I think, and this one . . . water? Philo, can't we have more light?"

He heard Lynnea say, "Teaser! You're doing it wrong."

And Teaser replying, "The pieces fit."

Lynnea, sounding exasperated, "But they aren't the right colors. They're just a jumble."

That was when he nudged himself into the space between Teaser's chair and Mr. Finch's and got a look at the table—and felt a jolt go through his body.

Then Teaser said, "All right, then. I'll do it proper," and reached out to break apart the puzzle pieces that fit but didn't belong together.

Without thought, simply reacting to churning emotions, Sebastian reached out and clamped a hand around Teaser's wrist. Ignoring the other incubus's startled yelp, he stared at the table. Even Lynnea's delighted greeting couldn't pull his focus away from the scattered pieces of painted wood—especially the pieces that had been put together again.

"It's Ephemera," he said quietly. Everyone around him became silent, waiting. "It's like Ephemera, in the old stories." In that moment he was a child again, sitting at the kitchen table with Glorianna and Lee, listening to Aunt Nadia tell the story of why Ephemera was the way it was.

"The world was whole once." Releasing Teaser's wrist, he moved his hand above the table to indicate all the pieces of wood. "Different lands, different people, but all of it connected. Then the Eater of the World came along. It had the ability to reshape pieces of the world, making them more attuned to the dark feelings in the human heart. It could take a person's deepest, darkest fears and use those feelings to change creatures that were part of the natural world into something terrible. Something that would then prey on humans."

Sebastian picked up Teaser's glass and drained the last inch of ale to ease the dryness in his throat. Setting the glass down on the table, he continued the story. "It roamed the world, and as people drowned in despair, the world changed to become a reflection of their hearts. Fertile land turned into deserts, and the people suffered even more.

"In a desperate act of love for Ephemera and its people, the Guides of the Heart shattered the world, then shattered those pieces into more pieces." Sebastian separated the pieces of the puzzle Mr. Finch had put together, spreading them out just enough so they no longer touched. "Finally, those who stood for the Light contained the Eater of the World in one small piece. There they fought, Light against Dark, driving the Eater to the place they'd chosen for a trap. Furious, It drew all the landscapes It had created to that place so that the creatures It had created would help It fight.

"And that's when the Guides sprang the trap. They poured their power into stone and created a cage that locked the Eater of the World inside Its own landscapes.

"Ephemera was saved, but it remained a world of shattered landscapes."

"Why didn't they put Ephemera back together?" Teaser asked.

Sebastian stared at the puzzle. He'd lived with the nature of Ephemera all his life, had felt the frustration, like everyone else, of finding a different landscape once and never being able to find it again, even when he walked the same path, crossed over the same bridge. Sometimes a person could be certain only of where he was—and sometimes there wasn't even that much certainty.

"The Guardians of the Light closed themselves away from the human world and the Guides disappeared, no longer able to walk in this world," he said. "The Landscapers and Bridges who came after them were able to stabilize Ephemera enough to stop it from manifesting every emotion, but they couldn't put the world back together."

He nudged the puzzle pieces he'd separated until they were close together but still not fully connected. "Different landscapes resonated for each of them, so those were the ones each Landscaper took under her control and care, while the Bridges found a way to provide a link between the landscapes so that people weren't trapped in one small piece of the world."

Philo rubbed his chin. "It's true that the landscapes held by a Landscaper have the same feel, for good or bad. If you get stuck in a place where your heart doesn't feel easy, your life never feels easy, whether you become prosperous or not."

Sebastian nodded. "And if you find the place where you belong, you can weather the hardships as well as the good times—because life will give you both."

"What's this, then?" Teaser waved a hand over his jumble of pieces. "You can't have a jumble of landscapes like this."

Sebastian felt that jolt again. "Yes, you can. Those are Belladonna's landscapes."

People had begun whispering among themselves, but that statement produced another wave of silence.

Seeing things Lee had said to him mirrored now in a simple human amusement, Sebastian placed his thumb on one of the dark pieces. "She brought some of Ephemera's dark landscapes together"—he stretched his hand and rested a finger on the bright blue piece of sky—"and she brought together places of Light. In between are the landscapes that are a bit of both. Neither dark or light, just . . . human. The human landscapes stand between us, but the Den and Sanctuary are connected. Because of her. Which means we each have something to offer the world." *And if one is lost, the other won't survive.*

"Enough stories," he said, easing between the people and the table to reach Lynnea. When she started to rise, he rested a hand on her shoulder. "No, sit. Finish the puzzle. I'd like to see it finished."

"That's enough now," Philo said, making shooing motions at the crowd. "That's enough. Find a chair for Sebastian so he can sit with his lady and have something to eat."

A chair was found, the crowd dispersed to fill the other tables, and Philo brought him a bowl of stew and pieces of bread.

As he watched Lynnea, Teaser, and Mr. Finch put the puzzle together, Sebastian couldn't shake the feeling that he was watching a promise being made—the promise that, someday, Ephemera would be whole again.

Chapter Fifteen

"That's enough," Glorianna said. As she reached for the papers her brother held, she noticed his hands trembled from exhaustion. "Lee, that's enough."

He pulled the papers toward him, his fingers tightening convulsively. "There are so many," he muttered as he stared at the papers that held the careful notations of every bridge he'd created over the years, as well as the location of bridges other Bridges had formed that provided access to one of Glorianna's or Nadia's landscapes. "With the other landscapes unprotected, there are so many ways the Eater of the World can—"

"*Enough.*" She laid her hands over his. Doubt could form heavy chains around the mind, making each decision weigh so much, no decision, no action would be taken for fear it was the wrong one. She could see him bending from the responsibility he now carried. With the weight of doubt added to the burden, she worried he might break under the strain. "Did you or did you not break the stationary bridges between Sanctuary and the landscapes in this part of Ephemera?"

Lee nodded. "Except the ones that connect with landscapes controlled by you or Mother."

"And did you not break the stationary bridges that

would provide a way into Mother's landscapes from Wizard City or the Landscapers' School?" She waited for him to nod again. "And you broke the stationary bridges that would lead to the Den from any place but my landscapes."

He flinched, which made her narrow her eyes.

"There's the bridge in the woods by Mother's house that crosses over from the Den to Aurora," he said.

"That one stays. If something happens at home and Mother is blocked from reaching Sanctuary, I want her to be able to reach Sebastian." She studied her brother. "What else?"

"I . . . connected one of Mother's landscapes to the Den. There was a stationary bridge in that landscape that led to Wizard City. When I broke the connection between those two landscapes, I felt a . . . hole, an emptiness that needed to be filled, but none of the landscapes I would have normally connected with that one felt right, so I had to leave it. Then, when I went to the Den to change the resonating bridge into a stationary one . . . something in those two landscapes resonated so strongly with each other, my presence was enough of a conduit to make a connection. Took a fair amount of stubbornness on my part to hold them apart long enough to link them properly."

"Then it was meant," Glorianna said. Before he guessed her intention, she pulled the papers out of his hands, tapped them into a neat stack, and put them in the document box Jeb had made for Lee a few years ago. She took the box to the desk and set it in the bottom drawer. After locking the drawer, she slipped the key's chain over her head and tucked it into her shirt.

This suite of rooms in the guesthouse at Sanctuary was the closest thing Lee had to a home of his own. Oh, he had a sitting room and bedroom in her house on the island, and his bedroom at their mother's house, but that wasn't the same as having his own place.

He was twenty-eight and had never had a sweetheart. Because of her. Not that he'd ever admit that, but she knew whatever liaisons he enjoyed were kept casual because he hadn't trusted those women enough to expose his strong connection with his sister, the rogue Landscaper.

It made her sad. He should have a wife to come home to, children to play with. He wanted those things. She knew he did. After all, no heart held secrets from Glorianna Belladonna.

But sadness and doubt weren't what he needed from her right now, so she held out her hand and said, "Let's take a walk."

He gave her a weary smile. "Do you know how many miles I've walked in the past few days?"

"You should rent a horse when you can."

He just grunted, pushed himself to his feet, and took her hand. "A short walk."

She led him through the gardens and felt him begin to relax when he realized where she was taking him.

Lee might not have a home, but he did have a place of his own.

A stream separated the gardens from the open land beyond. Two bridges spanned the water at different points to provide access to the countryside. A third bridge went to a small island that had been formed by the stream splitting around that rough circle of land. Trees guarded the circle of stone that sheltered the heart of that small place.

No flowers bloomed here. This was the silence, the peace at the heart of a wood. Ferns grew in the dappled light, and in the center was the fountain—a bowl of black stone that was fed by a length of hollowed-out cane. The mechanics of bringing water from the stream to the fountain were cleverly hidden, just as the drainage pipe that gave the water back to the stream was cleverly hidden. A bench provided an invitation to sit and linger, to listen to the song of water and stone, to breathe in the green of silence.

The people from the various Places of Light that

made up Sanctuary had helped her build this place as a private sanctuary, but the little island had resonated with Lee from the moment he'd set foot within the stone circle.

And it was this place he could impose over any other landscape. A safe place because, when he shifted it, it existed nowhere except on the bridge of his will and yet was still rooted in Sanctuary. He could walk among the trees and see what lay beyond, but another person's eyes couldn't see the island. Only the right kind of heart could find it when it was imposed over another landscape.

They settled on the bench and, for a while, did nothing but listen to the water and breathe in the green of silence.

Finally Glorianna said, "For today, you'll eat and rest. Tomorrow we'll go to my island and walk through the gardens, and we'll consider how to protect what we can of Ephemera."

Lee got up and took a few steps away from the bench. "And what if the Eater of the World finds a way into these landscapes through a stationary bridge I missed somewhere along the way? Or through a resonating bridge in a landscape I can't reach?"

"Then we'll deal with it."

"You mean you'll deal with it. That's what it comes down to, doesn't it?"

It did, but he already sounded troubled, and she wasn't going to let him chew on blame that was undeserved.

She walked over to him and placed a hand on his cheek. "We'll take each day as it comes, and if we can't destroy the Eater of the World, we'll find a way to close It back into Its own landscapes."

He placed his hands on her shoulders. "Will you promise to keep yourself safe?"

"I don't make promises if I'm not sure I can keep them."

His eyes were bleak as he wrapped his arms around

her. "I know. That's why I hoped you could give me that promise."

Hand in hand, Sebastian and Lynnea left the bordello and strolled down to Philo's.

He missed his cottage, missed making koffee for himself when he woke up, missed cooking a simple meal he could eat in private.

"We could get a meal at the bordello if you'd prefer," Sebastian said.

"If you'd wanted to do that, you would have mentioned it sooner," Lynnea replied.

He shrugged. Meals at the bordello had been another way of trolling or were part of the seduction. He'd done plenty of trolling at Philo's, too, but he'd also sat at one of those tables just to while away some time talking to people, so he felt more comfortable being there with Lynnea.

"It's a delicious night, isn't it?" Lynnea said, smiling.

He wished she wouldn't use words like "delicious." A quick glance at her was enough to make him want to lick his chops and start nibbling. "You're bright and cheerful."

"I had a dream last night that . . . Well. Hmm."

I know. That dream had churned him up so much he'd gotten up to take a cold bath to cool the fever in his blood. Daylight! Why couldn't he just give in? Resisting his own libido was hard enough—especially when he'd never felt the need to resist it before—but resisting hers was going to kill him. He'd never had this problem with any other woman.

She's not just another woman.

Lynnea stopped and looked up at the sky. "There's no moon."

"It will rise later."

"Will it?" She cocked her head. "I wonder if that means it's day in the other landscapes."

He shrugged. "It's always night here, so it makes no difference." But it did. The endless night had delighted the youth he had been—and wearied the man he now was.

"It might make a difference," Lynnea said. "If the moon rises and sets, that means it follows the same rhythm as it does in the rest of the landscapes. So when it's not in the sky, most likely it's daytime in other places."

"You mean it's morning outside the Den?"

Lynnea breathed in slowly, then shook her head. "The air doesn't have that early-morning quality of being fresh and cool before the sun bakes the land."

Sebastian released Lynnea's hand, then draped an arm around her shoulders to nudge her into walking again. "You should explain this moon rising and setting to Philo."

"Why?"

"Might give him a reason to serve different dishes at different times. Just for variety. Not that he doesn't have variety, but—"

"Is that your way of saying you want bacon and eggs?"

"And biscuits." Nadia hadn't made biscuits when he and Lynnea had shown up unexpectedly, but he relished the treat whenever Glorianna or Lee left a few of them at the cottage for him. Fresh, sometimes still a little warm, slathered with butter or fruit jam . . .

"Why are you licking your lips like that?" Lynnea asked.

"What? I'm not." At least, he hoped he hadn't been.

"If you want bacon and eggs, I'll make them for you. If Philo has bacon and eggs."

Sebastian snorted. "Philo doesn't let anyone else in his kitchen."

"Want to bet on it?"

There was a sparkle in her eyes and a hint of a smug female smile curving her lips. "Have you already talked Philo into using the kitchen?"

"I have not. It wouldn't be proper to wager if I already knew the outcome."

"That's usually called having an ace up your sleeve," he muttered.

"So you're not going to bet?"

"Not in this lifetime."

She pouted a little. "Don't you gamble? I thought that's one of the things people were supposed to do in the Den."

"I gamble enough to know when to fold. And you, joy of my heart, already know you've got the winning hand."

Joy of my heart. He felt the jolt go through her as the words sank in, felt that same jolt go through him. The words said too much, gave away too much. She didn't belong here. Even though she'd returned to the Den by her own choice, she didn't belong here. If he wasn't careful, words could chain her to this place.

"So," he said, desperate to turn the mood back to light and friendly, "what were you going to wager?"

She sniffed. "Since you didn't take the bet, I don't see why I should tell you."

"Ah, Lynnea—"

The sound of wheels rattling toward them caught his attention. People came to the Den by horse and buggy or by bicycle, but most left the animals and conveyances at one of the liveries at the edge of the Den so the animals wouldn't be leaving piles in the street. Having a big farm wagon clomping up the Den's main street wasn't usual—and anything that wasn't usual was suspect.

Apparently he wasn't the only one who felt suspicious. By the time the wagon pulled up close to Philo's, the male residents of the Den had formed a circle around the wagon—and none of them looked willing to give the newcomers a friendly welcome.

As he hurried toward the wagon, he heard the driver say in a loud voice, "Hoo-whee! Looks like we took a wrong turn, boys. Yes, sirree, looks like I got misdirected and took a wrong turn."

Daylight, Sebastian thought, *what's he doing here?*

Teaser stepped forward, his cocky grin just shy of malicious. "No one comes to the Den of Iniquity by mistake."

"The Den!" The man trembled. "Guardians and Guides!"

"What's in the wagon, hayseed?" Teaser asked.

"His name is William Farmer, and he's not a hayseed," Sebastian said, stepping through the circle. "There's no need for pretense here."

William studied him. "I know you."

Sebastian nodded. "You gave me a ride up to Wizard City."

"Well, now. Well. If you'll just explain to these fine gentlemen that—"

"Been traveling long?"

William hesitated, then nodded.

"Then step down and rest a bit. We can't offer any feed for the horses at the moment, but we can provide a bucket of water."

"That would be a kindness."

"You boys get down from there," Sebastian said. He recognized the hard look in their eyes, that blend of arrogance and fear. He'd seen it often enough in a mirror at that age.

The boy up on the driver's seat opened his mouth to say something Sebastian was certain would get him into trouble, but William put a hand on the boy's arm and said, "Mind your manners."

The farmer set the brake and climbed down from the driver's seat. After a moment's hesitation, the boys climbed down too.

"Teaser," Sebastian said as he eased around the horses, "keep the boys company and see they get something to eat." He shifted his focus to the farmer. "You come with me."

As the circle opened to let them through, he asked, "Is it morning in the landscape you came from?"

"After midday now," William replied.

"Breakfast is the first meal of the day," Lynnea said, falling into step with them. "So you can still have bacon and eggs. If Philo has bacon and eggs."

Philo reached the table at the same time they did—and just in time to hear that comment. "He wants bacon and eggs?"

"He does," Lynnea said.

Philo scowled at Sebastian.

"Why don't I give you a hand?" Lynnea said, smiling brightly.

Philo continued to scowl at Sebastian. "If the man is going to start getting fussy about what's put before him, I suppose he'll have to have his own cook."

"I didn't say . . ." Since Lynnea and Philo had already headed for the kitchen and he was talking to their backs, he turned to William. "I didn't say I had to have bacon and eggs."

William's smile was sympathetic, but his eyes twinkled. "All good women have a measure of grit and sass."

"Do they?" Sebastian said sourly.

"That they do. Or so my dear wife tells me often enough."

He laughed, since the alternative was banging his head against the table. Pulling out a chair, he sat down where he could keep an eye on the street. "So now that we've settled that much, what brings you here?"

William settled his bulk in a chair on the other side of the table. "Didn't mean to come here. Didn't know I'd end up here. But—" He stopped when Lynnea approached the table and set down two cups of koffee along with sugar and cream.

"There's not much besides koffee to give to boys that age," Lynnea said, indicating the other cups on her tray. "I hope that's all right."

"They'll drink whatever is put before them," William replied.

"Well, they're too young to be drinking whiskey or ale," Lynnea said primly.

Sebastian brushed a finger over her wrist. "Never tell

a boy he's too young for whiskey or ale. He'll need to prove you wrong and drink himself sick."

"I'm not going to tell them anything. They're just not getting any." She headed for the other table, where Teaser was keeping an eye on the boys.

"She used to be a little rabbit," Sebastian muttered. "I *liked* the little rabbit."

"I'm thinking you like the side of her that nips and nudges even more."

The truth of that pinched a bit, so Sebastian just drank his koffee.

"It's like this," William said. "I was on my way to Wizard City, like usual, but . . ." He lifted the cup, then set it down without drinking. "I couldn't get there. Took the same road, crossed over the same bridge, but as soon as I crossed the bridge, day turned to night and . . . I ended up here."

Lee's doing, Sebastian thought. Had to be. "If you managed to reach the Den, I don't think you'll be able to get to Wizard City. The landscapes have been altered."

William paled. "Altered?"

"Places you could go before may no longer be within reach."

"Home," William whispered. "My wife. My children." He clamped a hand over Sebastian's. "Can I get home?"

"I think so." He hoped so. He didn't know how long it would take Lee to break the bridges that connected Glorianna's landscapes to any landscapes beyond her and Nadia's keeping, but since William had managed to reach the Den, the odds were good the farmer lived in a landscape controlled by one of them.

Lynnea came back with two plates of bacon, eggs, and fried potatoes, gave him a told-you-so smile, then was gone again.

"What about the boys?" Sebastian asked as he dug into his meal.

"That's another thing." William tasted the eggs, made a sound of approval, and spent the next few minutes concentrating on the food. "Found them along the road, just before I reached the bridge. Whole pack of them. Recognized most of them by sight, if not by name. Something's happening in Wizard City that's making folks uneasy. Remember I told you about that part of the city that was different?"

"I remember."

William tipped his head to indicate the table where the boys were sitting. "They said the good feeling was going away, like someone was blowing out candles one by one and pretty soon there would be only darkness left. Some of the older folks gave the children what coin and food they could spare and told them to get away from the city. So they left because they were more afraid of staying than going. Slipped out among the other travelers and met up down the road a ways. By the time our paths crossed, they'd been traveling for a few days, sleeping out in the open and scared to death to do it, but there was no going back."

William pushed a piece of potato around his plate. "I didn't know the landscapes had changed, hadn't realized things were different, so I pointed out the road that would lead to Kennett, my home village, and told them to follow it. May the Guardians of the Light watch over them and get them to the village safely."

"And those three?" Sebastian asked.

William sighed. "Kennett is a small village. I think the other children will be able to find a place there and settle in, but those three have a bit too much ... grit ... if you understand me. They grew up fast and hard in order to survive. They'd be troublemakers in a place like Kennett, and that might sour folks on the other children. I think they knew that. I think that's why they offered to come with me, even though they thought it would take them back to Wizard City. Not that they put it that way."

No, they wouldn't put it that way, Sebastian thought. But they'd know there was something inside them that would never fit in with the rhythm of a country village.

Opportunities and choices.

"They'll fit in here," Sebastian said. "The Den was made for badass boys."

"Well, now," William blustered. "Well, I don't know." Then he looked into Sebastian's eyes. "Would you have been one of those boys?"

"You could say I was the first."

William pursed his lips. "They'd find charity hard to swallow."

"That's good, because they won't find any here. If they're going to live here, they'll work to earn their keep."

William nodded. "I never got your name."

"Sebastian."

William held out his hand.

He clasped the hand, then released it, surprised at how a simple handshake could sometimes bridge two very different lives.

Opportunities and choices.

Pushing his plate aside, Sebastian folded his arms and leaned on the table. "So, William Farmer, since you can't get to Wizard City, what are you going to do with all that food in the wagon?"

William studied him for a moment, then smiled. "I suppose you have some ideas about what I can do with it?"

"I do," Sebastian replied, returning the smile. "I certainly do."

🕮

Koltak ground his teeth in frustration. He wasn't used to riding horses, and the daylong ride was turning into a misery. Worse than the physical discomfort was his growing uneasiness.

The road went on too long, too far. He'd been there only once, but he knew the way to that foul landscape Sebastian called home. The main road curved and went on to a bridge that led to another landscape and another bridge that crossed over near Nadia's home village. He'd traveled that road enough times when he'd gone to fetch Sebastian and bring the whelp back to Wizard City. The cart path that branched off the main road led to another bridge— and the Den of Iniquity.

But when the road had curved, he hadn't seen any sign of a cart path. Thinking he'd misremembered the spot, he and the guards Harland had sent with him had continued riding along the main road.

On and on. Too long. Too far. The guards offered no opinions, offered no company, although they'd talked quietly among themselves. So he couldn't express any doubt, couldn't afford to admit he was no longer sure where they were.

Harland had entrusted him with this task. He alone had the means of bringing Belladonna out into the open, where the Wizards' Council could deal with her. He wasn't going to fail Harland or the council, not when Harland had all but promised him a seat on the council as acknowledgment of this accomplishment.

One act to wipe out a mistake made thirty years ago. One act that would be the perfect balance of the other.

"Wizard Koltak." Dalton, the guard captain, brought his horse alongside Koltak's. "Are you certain this is the way to the landscape you need to reach?"

"Why do you ask?" Koltak said, hedging.

"It looks familiar, and that troubles me." Dalton looked up, even though the trees that crowded the road blocked the sun. "And I don't think we're heading south anymore."

Before Koltak could think of an evasive response, a guard scouting up ahead shouted and raised an arm to attract attention.

Dalton kicked his horse into a canter, heading for the guard. Koltak's horse followed, leaving the wizard no choice but to cling to the saddle, since he lacked the skill to control the animal.

It was a pity Harland had considered the details of

this task so well and had overruled Koltak's riding in the comfort of a carriage. A horse and rider lent more credence to the story of urgency than a carriage and driver.

He saw the logic in that, but it didn't make his body ache any less.

When its companions were in sight, the horse slowed to a walk, allowing Koltak to gather the reins again and provide the illusion of being in command.

Dalton stared at the large stone that stood like a sentry where two roads met, then swore softly.

As Koltak looked at the stone, a sick feeling filled his belly and rose up to clog his throat.

"Well," Dalton said when Koltak reached him, "there's nothing more we can do today. We'll start out again at first light tomorrow and hope for luck on the roads."

At Dalton's signal, two of the guards headed down the east road. The captain looked at Koltak, shook his head, then followed his men.

With the sting of failure heating his face, Koltak followed Dalton, trailed by the other two guards.

The road that had seemed to go on and on perversely became shorter. Far too soon, they rode out of the trees and looked on the open land—and the steep northern side of Wizard City.

"This can't be," Koltak muttered. "It *can't* be. We rode south. We *can't* end up on the northern side of Wizard City."

"Sometimes Ephemera is as perverse as a woman," Dalton said. He let out a gusty sigh. "We'll have to find another road with a bridge that crosses over into a different landscape."

"But the road south was the way to the landscape I need to reach!" Koltak protested.

Dalton looked annoyed, then smoothed out his expression as if suddenly remembering he was dealing with a wizard. "There's no way around it, Wizard Koltak. Right now the south road just circles back to the city.

We'll try again tomorrow. Maybe strike out across country, see if we can find another bridge. Many's the time when a bridge between landscapes isn't set in an obvious place, especially if it's a resonating bridge, and there's more of them than the stationary bridges you'll find on well-traveled roads."

Koltak waited until they reached the northern gate before broaching the subject that had weighed more heavily on him as the city loomed nearer and nearer.

"Perhaps it would be best if I remained at the guardhouse tonight," Koltak said, keeping his gaze fixed on the space between his horse's ears. "It would save time if we're to be on the road again at first light."

Dalton remained silent a moment, then nodded. "It would be more convenient. In fact, it's probably best to stay at one of the guard stations in the lower circle. The lodgings may be rougher than you're used to, and we'll probably have to share quarters, but you should be able to have a bed to yourself."

Koltak winced at the thought of making do with rough lodgings when he was so close to his own comfortable rooms, but he nodded agreement. Then he glanced at Dalton and wondered if the man's expression was a little too blank. Had the captain figured out the real reason he didn't want to go up to the Wizards' Hall? Was that why the suggestion had been made to stay in the lower circle?

If he returned to his own rooms, Harland would know he'd failed on his first attempt to reach Sebastian. If he stayed in the lower circle, the head of the Wizards' Council might not realize he'd returned to Wizard City. Better to endure rough lodgings than see the groundwork for his ambitions crumble again.

Yes, he thought as they rode through the lower circle, he could endure physical discomfort much easier than failure.

"So I'm going to be waiting on tables at Philo's a few hours each day," Lynnea said happily. "Philo said if he was going to train Brandon to work at his place, I could help, too."

"You're going to wait tables?" Sebastian asked, startled by this revelation.

"I am. In exchange for my meals."

"You don't have to do that."

"Of course I do. I heard you when you were talking to the boys, and I agree. Visitors come for the drinking and the gambling and the . . . other things . . . and they pay for those things with coin or goods that can be bartered. But those who live in the Den have to earn their keep."

Wondering if she was aware that she was swinging their linked hands like a happy child, he choked back the denial that she lived in the Den. He didn't want her to settle in and make a place for herself. It would be harder for her to leave and find the landscape where she truly belonged if she started thinking of herself as a resident of the Den.

And the more she acted like she was settling in, the easier it would be for him to believe she meant to stay, not just in the Den but with him. And the deeper it would slice his heart when she realized she wasn't meant for this ever-night and left.

"So I'll be serving food and helping with the clearing and washing up, and . . . ." Lynnea paused. "If Philo blushes over serving Phallic Delights, why does he make them?"

In the fifteen years he'd lived in the Den, he'd never seen Philo blush once, but he didn't think it would help any to tell her it was handing over the basket to his new helper and not the basket's contents that had caused the blush.

"Then Brandon snickered and said if men were really built like that, women wouldn't want to do anything but have sex."

"Brandon talks too much," Sebastian growled.

She laughed.

Daylight! She was going to be serving Phallic Delights and Stuffed Tits in a courtyard full of erotic statues. Once awareness filtered into dreams, she was going to drive him stark raving mad.

Her mood changed by the time they reached the bordello; she'd become quiet, thoughtful. She didn't say anything when he unlocked the door to their room, just walked in and lit the lamp on the table by the window. Then she took her nightgown, which she neatly folded and tucked under her pillow each morning, and went into the bathroom.

He blew out a breath, locked the door, and wondered what he was going to do with himself until it was time to try to sleep.

Then she came out of the bathroom and hesitated a moment before walking up to him.

"Sebastian."

Looking at her, hearing the blend of hesitation and determination in her voice, was enough for the power of the incubus to unfurl inside him.

"Sebastian, I don't know how to say this, don't know how to ask. . . ."

"Ask what?"

"I want to be with you. In bed."

It would change things for you in a way that could never be undone. The thought was there, but he couldn't quite remember why it mattered when he saw nerves and desire mingled in her eyes. No longer a rabbit, not quite a tigress. Woman. His woman.

He was too hungry, needed the seduction and the feast too much to turn away from what she offered.

But when his lips brushed hers, something besides the power of the incubus burned inside him, something bright and powerful. As his mouth softly devoured and his hands gently explored, that bright power tempered the incubus hunger into something he'd never felt before, something he craved and couldn't quite name.

Then he took her to bed, finally to bed. And while he showed her the pleasures of sex, she taught him the mysteries of love.

Chapter Sixteen

Lynnea glanced at the closed bathroom door as she laced up her shoes. Sebastian had been amused by her reluctance to get dressed in front of him. After all, he'd pointed out, he'd seen her naked—and she'd seen him. But that was a different kind of naked, and getting into her underwear while he lay back in the rumpled bed with the covers barely covering his interesting bits was more than the new-found tigress inside her could handle. So she'd grabbed her clothes and scampered into the bathroom to dress in private.

Since she'd expected to find him dressed when she came out of the bathroom, which was how things had worked since they'd started sharing this room in the bordello, she'd been surprised to find him lounging in bed, still rumpled and naked. And looking so delicious she wanted to lick his skin just to have another taste of him.

Whatever he'd seen on her face had made him smile, push back the covers, gather up his clothes . . . and stroll into the bathroom. The look he gave her before he closed the door made her want to hit him—or drag him back into bed.

"Idle hands give the mind time for mischief," she muttered as she looked around the room for something to do. She looked at the bed, hesitated, then squared her shoulders. It was just a bed. It wasn't any different now than it had been when they'd just slept together.

Except it was. As she smoothed out the sheets, she remembered the feel of his hands on her skin, and the way his skin had warmed as she touched him. The delicious tugs in the belly when he suckled her breast. The way he'd caressed her with his fingers until she was drowning in sensation and didn't care if she ever surfaced.

The joining had hurt, and that had dimmed the pleasure—until she'd fallen asleep and slid into the dreams.

The bordello, the room, the bed—and Sebastian. This time the dreams didn't stop with hugs and long kisses. This time the dreams seemed more intense, more . . . real. *He* seemed more real than he'd been in the other dreams. He'd done all the things he'd done to her earlier, but now she knew what a man felt like when he was hard and hungry. And instead of pain when his body slid into hers, there was pleasure—waves and waves of it, cresting and receding as one dream faded, rising again as the next dream filled her, and she and Sebastian did things she couldn't even think about now without blushing.

But her body responded to those memories, producing a fluttery feeling in her belly and a wet heat between her legs.

"What are you thinking about?"

Jolted by the sound of his voice, Lynnea turned. Sebastian stood close to her. He was dressed, but he hadn't bothered to button his shirt, and she found that glimpse of bare skin more disturbingly sensual than if he hadn't put on a shirt at all. "What?"

"You're hugging a pillow."

"What?" When he just smiled at her, she felt her face heat. "I was just thinking about . . . about . . ."

"Pleasant dreams?"

"No, I—" She stared at him. Remembered the bits and pieces she'd heard about incubi and how they usually linked with their prey. "You . . . You can see my dreams?"

He took a step closer. "Only when you invite me in. And you did invite me in, sweet Lynnea." Something hot and hungry flashed in his eyes.

Oh, gracious. She was going to have to think about this.

Turning away from him, she set the pillow in its place and began straightening the covers. "I should be at Philo's soon. I don't want to be late for my first day of work."

"And I need to make a circuit around the Den to check the bridges." Silence. Then, "Miss me a little, all right?"

Wondering what kind of teasing reply women were expected to make in response to that kind of request, she gave the covers on that side of the bed one more smoothing brush of her hand before she looked at Sebastian—and felt the ground shift under her feet.

Nothing hot and hungry in those green eyes now. Just vulnerability . . . and yearning.

Had anyone ever missed him? Not the incubus and the sex he provided, but Sebastian the man? Had any woman ever welcomed him simply because she was glad to see him?

He needs me. Her heart filled with the wonder of that discovery.

Closing the distance between them, she said, "I'll miss you more than a little." Then she slipped her hands under his shirt, wrapped her arms around him, and rested her head on his shoulder.

A moment of stiff hesitation as his mind and body translated the feel of her against him as affection and not prelude. His arms came around her, pulling her closer. He rubbed his cheek against her hair. His body relaxed, and his sigh of contentment was the finest sound she'd ever heard.

"You have to go," he said. "Philo will be waiting."

"Yes." But she didn't make any move to let go of him.

He was the one who finally eased back. "Lynnea?"

"Yes?"

He brushed his lips over hers. "I'll miss you, too."

❧

Koltak and Captain Dalton studied the two planks of wood across the narrow creek.

Dalton swore. "A bridge this close to the city, and no kind of marker to indicate where it leads."

"That is not the nature of resonating bridges," Koltak replied, but so softly it was more a thought voiced for himself. Oh, plenty of times, if you kept your mind focused, you could cross over a resonating bridge and reach a particular destination. But there were other times when the bridge ignored the will's intent and resonated only with the heart. When that happened, a person could end up anywhere.

"I know that," Dalton said. "Doesn't mean I have to like it." He paused. "Well, it's your decision, Wizard Koltak. Our orders are to wait for you on this side of the bridge and give you escort back to the city." He looked over his shoulder at the city still visible in the distance.

Koltak shivered. It was a sensible plan. After all, he couldn't go into the Den with armed guards. But he didn't want to cross that bridge alone, not knowing what was on the other side.

Maybe Dalton sensed his hesitation, or maybe it was a standard move whenever a bridge had to be crossed.

"Faran," Dalton said, "cross over the bridge with Wizard Koltak." He looked at Koltak. "If the bridge crosses over to a daylight landscape, Faran will report back and the rest of us will cross over to continue providing escort. If it's a dark landscape, he'll simply come back to this side and wait with the rest of us."

And I'll go on alone, in unfamiliar land, to find a man I'd rather not set eyes on. But if this works, it will be the last time I have to see him—and my place in the council will be assured.

"Faran will lead your horse over those planks," Dalton said.

Koltak watched the guard dismount, hand his reins to a fellow guard, and rummage in his saddlebags before approaching Koltak with a small lantern in one hand. "What about his own horse?"

"He won't need it," Dalton said. "He's just crossing over with you and reporting back."

Faran stood at the horse's head and looked up at him, waiting.

Koltak closed his eyes and focused his will. *I need to reach Sebastian. I need to reach the Den.* Keeping his eyes closed, he nodded to indicate he was ready.

He felt the horse resist going over the planks, heard Faran's murmurs of encouragement and command. Feet and hooves on wood. Barely enough length for man and horse to stand on the planks at the same time. But he couldn't think about that, couldn't think about anything but what he needed to achieve. *I need to reach Sebastian. I need to reach the Den.*

The horse shied. Koltak opened his eyes and grabbed the saddle to keep from being thrown. Faran ran with the horse for a few steps before bringing the animal under control.

"Easy, boy," Faran said. "Easy."

"What happened?" Koltak demanded.

"Something spooked him just as we crossed to this side of the bridge, but I didn't see anything." Faran looked around. "Land looks a bit different here. I'm thinking we're not close to Wizard City anymore."

"No, I don't think we are," Koltak replied.

"So we missed the mark?"

He shook his head. "Despite the daylight, this is a dark landscape. They feel different." He just wished he knew *where* he was. But somewhere in this land, there had to be a bridge that would lead him to the Den. There *had* to be.

"No roads here," Faran said. "How will you know which way to go?"

Sebastian. Sebastian. Sebastian.

He gathered the reins and turned the horse's head without conscious thought. "I'll have to follow my heart."

"All right, then." Faran stepped away from the horse. "I'll tell Captain Dalton you're on your way. We'll be waiting for you on the other side of the bridge."

Koltak nodded, banged his heels against the horse's sides, and set off at a rough trot that promised to bruise more than his pride.

It would be over soon. He wouldn't fail the council. All he had to do was keep his will focused on finding what he didn't want to find.

Sebastian. Sebastian. Sebastian.

Faran shook his head as he watched the wizard ride off. Not a horseman, that was for sure. He just hoped the man was fit enough at the end of the journey to do what needed to be done.

No point lingering here. And truth to tell, something about the place made him uneasy, even though there wasn't anything around him that looked dangerous.

His steps slowed as he neared the bridge.

But *something* had spooked the horse.

He started to draw his short sword, then hesitated and pulled out the long knife tucked in his boot. As he straightened up, his eyes caught a movement barely a stride away from the planks and off to the side. Had the ground shifted a little, or was it just the air stirring the grass?

He moved toward the bridge, setting each foot with care, unable to shake the feeling that something was waiting.

Nothing stirred. Nothing moved.

Clear your mind, he thought. *Get back to Captain Dalton and the fellows. Cross over the bridge. Wizard City, Wizard City, Wizard City.*

He turned to face the bridge straight on. Lifted a foot to set it on the planks of wood. A few moments more and he'd be safe.

It burst out of the ground, all legs and jaws. A familiar shape, if it had been the size of his thumbnail, now grown into a nightmare.

He screamed as it grabbed him and bit into his leg. He went down hard, his legs already numb from the venom, but he held on to the knife. Before the nightmare could pull him into the tunnel beneath the trapdoor, he reared up and, using both hands and what strength was left in his arms, drove the knife into the spider's head.

Its legs flailed and its jaws bit deeper as the creature died. Then it lay still.

Panting, sweating, Faran turned his body as best he could. If he could stretch out his arm, he could reach the bridge. Had to reach the bridge. Had to get to the other side. Help was across . . . the . . .

Lynnea hummed a little tune while she cleaned off a table. She'd done pretty well for her first day of work. True, she'd forgotten part of one order, but she'd made up for it by calming down a bull demon bellowing for food.

Grinning, she wondered if she'd get to be the first to tell Sebastian about the new addition to Philo's menu: the Sebastian Special. Who would have guessed a vegetable omelet could impress a demon?

She took her tray of dirty dishes back to the kitchen, gave Brandon a cheerful smile, since he was the one stuck with the washing up, grabbed another tray, and headed back out to the courtyard to clear off another table.

Despite the Eater of the World being loose in the landscapes and the very real possibility that terrible things could happen in the Den, she had never been happier. She had work she found interesting, she was with a good man who was also an incredible lover, and—noticing the blond man across the street, she smiled—she was making friends.

The Den wasn't the place she would have picked if she could have chosen a landscape, but here she'd found all the things she'd yearned for, so it had turned out to be the right place for her after all.

She picked up the full tray, then waited for Teaser to cross the street so she could tell him she needed a few more minutes to finish up before she could go back to the bordello. She'd promised Sebastian that she'd stay at Philo's until he or Teaser escorted her back to the room.

Problem was, there wasn't anything to do when she got there. She wasn't used to having idle time, and it seemed wasteful to sit and do nothing. Well, she'd just have to think about what skills she had and how she could make use of them. If she could find the supplies she needed, she could knit some scarves. The Den's visitors would have no use for such simple things, but the residents might appreciate them when the weather turned cold. If it did turn cold. She'd ask Teaser as soon as he . . .

She watched a woman walk up to Teaser, watched the body language that plainly indicated a flirtation—or something more—was going on between them.

Watched him walk away with the woman without so much as a glance in her direction.

So that was how well promises were kept in the Den.

He's an incubus. This is what he does. I suppose it's silly to feel hurt that he chose to go off with a bed partner instead of keeping a promise to me . . . or Sebastian.

"Isn't it time for you to be going?" Philo asked, glancing in her direction when she brought the tray into the kitchen. "I thought Teaser was coming for you."

"Apparently not," she replied, just sharply enough to have him turn away from his pots and pans to look at her.

She shrugged to indicate it was nothing. "Got more customers. I'll take the order." She was out of the kitchen before Philo could ask any questions.

She'd just taken the order and was heading back to give it to Philo when Teaser walked into the courtyard, rubbing his hands and looking gleeful.

"You ready to go?" he asked. "Or do I have time for a bowl of whatever Philo's serving?"

"Finish your business so soon?" she replied tartly.

"Just in time, I'd say. Was down at Hastings playing a few hands of cards while I waited for you. Won the last hand, scooped up my winnings, and said I had to be off to give Sebastian's lady an escort. Bull demon at the table didn't even bellow about me leaving before he had a chance to win a few coins back. He just rumbled, 'om . . . e . . . let good'—whatever that means."

Lynnea stared at him. "Teaser, I saw you just now. You went off to the bordello with a woman."

"Didn't." He looked baffled and a little hurt. "Said I'd be here, and here I am."

"But I *saw* you."

He shook his head. "Must have been someone else."

"There's someone else in the Den who looks just like you?"

"Wasn't me. Although . . ." He rubbed the back of his neck. "Hastings said he saw me in the tavern a couple of days ago making time with the succubitch, which is a load of horse . . . stuff, since he knows I can't stand her." He turned and looked in the direction of the bordello. "But he also said no one has seen her since then." He looked back at Lynnea. "Come on. I'll take you to the room. Then I'm going to see what I can find out about this . . . twin . . . people have been seeing."

"All right. Let me give Philo this order; then I can go."

As she started to walk away, Teaser grabbed her arm. "How much did this other fellow look like me?"

She hesitated, more because he seemed upset than because she wasn't sure of what she'd seen. "Well," she hedged, "he *was* across the street, and he wasn't directly under one of the lights, so I *could* have been mistak—"

"If he'd come over here, would you have gone with him?" Teaser demanded.

A chill went through her as she stared into his blue eyes. "Yes," she whispered. "I would have gone with him, thinking he was you." And if the man she'd seen *wasn't* Teaser, what might have happened to her once she was away from Philo's? There were plenty of dark alleys where she might have been taken and . . . hurt.

She knew two women had died in the Den before she'd arrived. Sebastian had told her about them. That was one of the reasons he didn't want her walking around alone.

"I have to give this order to Philo," she said, holding on to something simple and ordinary. As soon as Teaser released her arm, she hurried to the kitchen. She must have looked as shaky as she felt, because both Brandon and Philo stopped working to stare at her.

She ignored the stares, gave Philo the order, and told him she had to go now.

"Teaser is here?" Philo asked.

"Yes." But was she certain the man waiting for her was Teaser? She'd met the incubus only a few days ago and didn't know him that well.

Maybe she should tell Teaser she was going to wait for Sebastian, even if it hurt his feelings. But what if a man approached her wearing Sebastian's face? Would she be able to tell the difference?

Yes. Definitely, yes. She knew the feel of Sebastian, would be able to pick him out in a crowd of men all wearing his face. Because none of them would be able to imitate the feel of his heart.

But there was still the question of Teaser. Go or stay? The hesitation must have shown in her face, because he cocked his head when she walked toward him.

"If I promise not to leave wet towels on the bathroom floor anymore, will you let me escort you to the bordello?"

Relief surged through her. No one but the real Teaser would think to say that to her. "I'll hold you to that promise." She linked her arm through his as they left Philo's courtyard. "So how much did you win off the bull demon?"

He grinned and relaxed—and asked her about her first day working for Philo instead of answering.

Yes, that felt like the real Teaser. Smiling, she told him about the bull demon and the Sebastian Special while they walked to the bordello.

Sebastian planted his feet on either side of the demon cycle when it stopped halfway down the Den's main street. Since it floated on air, he didn't need to do that to keep the cycle upright. He just wanted to see if his legs still stretched to the ground.

Why had he spent the past few hours riding around, looking for signs that the Eater of the World had found a way into one of the dark landscapes that bordered the Den? Why had he studied every bridge as if he could tell what he might find if he crossed over?

Part of it was his promise to Lee to do what he could to protect the Den. The other part was that he needed something to do while Lynnea was working at Philo's. Hovering around the courtyard would have made her nervous—and might have given too much of an impression that he was waiting for the right company to come along. And in a way that was true, since he'd be waiting for Lynnea.

He felt no desire to troll the streets for a woman. Hadn't felt the need since he'd met his little rabbit. Just living with her fed the incubus's hunger in ways the hottest sex with other women had never done. He craved her company, the sound of her voice, the feel of her skin beneath his hands.

Besides his own lack of interest in being some other woman's dream lover, he didn't think Lynnea would see his carnal attentions to another woman as anything but a betrayal—the kind of betrayal that would break a woman's heart. So if he wasn't going to troll the Den and provide sex as a commodity, what could he do to earn his keep?

He lifted one hand, rubbed his thumb over his fingertips. He felt the tingle of power that marked him as a wizard. Since "wizard" was a dirty word in the Den, he still hadn't told anyone about the power that had awakened in him. But sooner or later people would find out. Sooner or later he'd have to decide what he was going to do with that power.

Which led his thoughts back to why he'd spent the past few hours roaming the boundaries of the Den.

Defender. Protector. A few weeks ago he would have laughed if anyone had used those words to describe him. Now, knowing he was the one who anchored the Den made a difference. Lynnea made a difference. This was his place. These were his people. She was his woman.

Could that really be enough for her, to be his woman? Could the Den give her enough of what she needed so that she'd be content to stay? Even if they couldn't live in the cottage right now, he could take her to visit Aunt Nadia. She could shop in Aurora, talk to the kind of people she was used to. Spend a few hours in sunlight. Would it be enough to keep her coming back to him and the kind of loving he could offer a woman?

But in the village . . . How would Aunt Nadia introduce her? As a young friend visiting from another landscape? As her nephew's companion? Oh, that would produce plenty of knife-edged smiles and whispers as soon as Lynnea turned her back. But what else could Nadia call her? His wife?

Sebastian's heart gave a hard bump before settling back into its usual rhythm.

Wife. Friend, lover, companion.

No. Oh, no. "Wife" was a human word, not one to be bandied about in a place like the Den. Besides, "wife" went with "marriage," and that was too . . . permanent. He'd known Lynnea only a few days. His craving for her could diminish, could disappear altogether. The temptation to feast on another woman's emotions and flesh could rise up at any moment. After all, he *was* an incubus. Constancy wasn't part of what he was.

Then he saw her with Teaser, heading for the bordello, and he knew his craving for her wouldn't diminish, wouldn't disappear. This was more than a craving. This was love. So he'd find some way of giving her what she needed so that she would be willing to stay.

"There's Lynnea," he said.

The demon cycle growled what might have been a happy sound and zipped forward so fast Sebastian was sure he'd scraped off half the soles of his boots before he managed to lift his feet.

"Slow down before you knock someone over," Sebastian snapped. Not that his order made a bit of difference. The demon cycle tore around the corner and into the side street with no regard for anything that might have been in the way.

Of course, Lynnea had gone inside by the time they reached the building, which left him promising a sulky demon that he'd ask if she wanted to go for a ride later.

What was it about his little rabbit-turned-tigress that made demons act besotted?

Best not to think too hard about that, since you're one of those demons, he chided himself as he walked into the building.

"Better keep your eyes on Teaser," the desk clerk called as Sebastian headed for the stairs. "Your lady is the second one he's brought here in the past hour."

He paused. "Up to our rooms?"

The clerk shook his head and gave a room number on the second floor.

Sebastian took the steps two at a time. Daylight! What was Teaser up to? Why take Lynnea to one of the rooms that were rented for a "night" of pleasure when an incubus or succubus didn't want to bring the prey home? He'd trusted Teaser to look after Lynnea because he and Teaser had been friends for so many years—and because he'd had the feeling that, while the other incubus was drawn to Lynnea, Teaser didn't see her as prey.

Bounding up the last steps, he turned into the corridor just in time to see Teaser backing away from an open door.

"It's not me," Teaser said as he hit the wall opposite the door and slid to the floor. "*It's not me!*"

Lynnea dropped to her knees and wrapped her arms around Teaser, who sounded hysterical.

Sebastian didn't know if she'd heard him or just sensed him, but she turned her head and looked at him, her eyes full of worry and relief.

He strode to the door, stepped into the room—and froze.

The woman on the bed was so ensnared in a sexual haze she wasn't aware of anything else. Her hands were fisted in the sheets and her hips pumped with the desperation of someone whose release was being held just out of reach, but her breathing sounded painfully harsh and her eyes were chillingly blank.

The man was too busy pounding himself into her to either notice or care that he had an audience.

The woman's breathing became more labored, but her hips kept up the desperate pumping.

Save the woman. Get that bastard off of her.

But as he took another step, the man turned his head and looked at him.

Teaser's face. But there was a sharp cruelty in the smile and a viciousness in the eyes that he'd never seen in his friend—not even when Teaser *was* being cruel.

The humping continued, hard and fast, the last thrusts before release. The woman moaned, but it was impossible to tell if the sound was a response to pain or pleasure.

As Sebastian breathed in the feral, musky scent that

filled the room, the power of the incubus unfurled inside him, a sharp-edged hunger honed by the other male.

Yes. Take her. She was only human, only prey. Feed desire until it became insatiable, then feast on the flood of feelings, working the body until the mind was helpless to do anything but respond and provide more meat for the feast. Feast and feast until the prey was incapable of fighting to survive.

Kill with pleasure.

One last thrust. The woman cried out—a liquid, unhealthy sound, as if something had broken inside her. The male with Teaser's face closed his eyes and sighed with pleasure.

Sebastian's heart pounded. He felt hot, hard—and sick with a desperate hunger he had never felt in quite that way before.

Then he heard Lynnea's voice, just a murmur of comfort to Teaser, and he gasped for air, feeling as if he'd almost been pulled into a dark, ugly place. He had *never* hunted like this, had no desire to hunt like this.

But in a dark corner of his heart, he understood the power of this kind of hunt, understood the cruel pleasure. And he understood that without Nadia, Glorianna, and Lee, he might have become a hunter like the male now rolling off the bed.

The male moved to the center of the room—Teaser's body but not his eyes. There was nothing of Teaser in those eyes.

"Diluted spawn," the male said, sneering. "One-faced mongrel who does its tricks to win a few scraps of emotion. We starved, locked away in that landscape, while the ones we had driven out because they had become tainted by feelings survived by hiding in the human landscapes. They *mated* with *prey* and ended up producing things like *you*."

"What are you?" Sebastian said, even though he already knew. In his blood, in the marrow of his bones, he knew.

The male's body changed. The blond hair darkened. The blue eyes turned green.

Sebastian stared at his own face.

"I'm what you should have been," the male replied. He looked over Sebastian's shoulder. "I'm more than you'll ever be. She won't be able to resist me," he added in Sebastian's voice.

Lynnea.

The hunger of the incubus withered inside Sebastian as another power flared, fed by fear and fury.

He threw himself at the incubus, sent them crashing to the floor. It fought viciously, with animalistic savagery. But hearing Lynnea shouting his name made him just as vicious, just as savage in his desperation to save her from what this male would do to her.

It rolled, pinning him beneath it, its hands around his throat, choking him.

Then Lynnea darted into the room, grabbed the male by the hair, and yanked. That provided enough of a distraction for Sebastian to break the choke hold and roll away.

The other male rolled, too, trying to grab her, but Teaser dashed into the room and pulled Lynnea back to the doorway.

Sebastian scrambled to his feet, gasping for air. The other male got to his feet with more grace—and changed again.

Sebastian stared at the bull demon. It didn't have the height or muscle of a real bull demon, but the horns could gore him just as effectively.

He felt the tingle of power, but he still hesitated to reveal the wizard side of his nature.

Then the male roared, lowered his head, and charged—not at Sebastian but at Teaser, the rival male who was holding the female prey.

Sebastian leaped on the male, one hand grabbing a horn while the other hand clamped on the male's throat. As they twisted and fell, he let the wizard's lightning surge through him and into his hands.

The male screamed as the lightning ripped through it, burned it, razored through brain and heart.

Finally it stopped moving. The smell of burned flesh hung in the air.

Sebastian rolled away from the male and lay on the floor, staring at the ceiling, sickened by what he'd just done. And sickened even more by a loss of innocence—not just because he'd killed, but because he'd seen a truth about himself.

"Sebastian?"

Lynnea.

The sound of her voice got him to his feet. Thank the Light, Teaser had pulled her into the corridor and had blocked her view of the last of the fight.

He moved to the doorway. "It's dead," he said in a flat voice.

She looked at him, studied his face, his eyes—and relaxed.

"I have some things to take care of here. Can you get Teaser back to his room?"

Teaser looked about to protest, then realized what Sebastian wanted. "Yeah." He leaned on Lynnea, who immediately wrapped her arms around him. "Yeah, I'm a little shaky."

"Of course you are," Lynnea said. "That was horrible, seeing someone wearing your face."

Sebastian wanted to touch her, hold her, let her warmth cleanse what was churning inside him. But he felt too vile, too filthy to get even another step closer. So he watched her lead Teaser to the stairs. Then he turned and walked back into the room.

The male was dead. Unquestionably dead. Sebastian's stomach rolled as he looked at the body.

It must have tried to change again, or maybe that had been its body's reaction to being burned inside by the wizard's lightning. It was now a twisted blend of bull demon, his own face, and something dark-skinned that might have been the male's natural form.

The woman was dead. Not knowing what else to do,

he pulled the sheet up over her. She might have crossed over with a friend, might have someone looking for her. If not . . .

Humans who came to the Den seldom gave their real names or told anyone which landscape they called home. If there was no one here who knew her, they would bury her in the fields—and her friends and family back home would eventually accept that she was one of those people who had gotten lost in Ephemera's landscapes.

Pulling the blanket off the bed, he wrapped the male's body so no one else would have to look at it.

When he was finished, he just stood there, rubbing his thumbs over his fingertips. He, too, had the power to kill.

And he was going to make sure that . . . thing . . . *stayed* dead.

He walked out of the room, closed the door, and went down to the clerk's desk to give his orders.

🦎

Dalton stared at the wooden planks that crossed the narrow creek and counted to one hundred for the tenth time.

Too long. Even if Faran had decided to check the saddle on Koltak's horse or had been listening to further instructions, the guard had been gone too long.

"Henley, Addison," he called without taking his eyes off the bridge. "Cross over and find out what's delaying Faran." As the two men handed their reins to the two remaining guards, Dalton held up a hand to detain them. Walking over to his own horse, he removed a lead rope secured to his saddle. "Tie this to your belts. Henley, you cross over the bridge to the other landscape. Addison, you stay on this side of wherever that bridge leads. If there's trouble, Henley will pull the rope twice. That's the signal to pull him out."

Watching the two men tie the lead rope to their belts,

Dalton felt the heat of embarrassment stain his face. He knew it was foolish. No amount of rope would make any difference once a person crossed over to another landscape. But he wasn't going to let another man cross that bridge without trying to find out what was happening on the other side.

Henley and Addison moved across the planks that made up the bridge, keeping the length of the lead rope between them. The wood looked sturdy enough, but if the planks broke, the bridge would be gone, and there would be no way for Koltak to come back to Wizard City from that direction. No way to find out what had happened to Faran.

Henley's right foot stepped off the planks of wood. The man was still visible, still in the landscape that contained Wizard City. Then Henley's left foot lifted off the plank—and he was gone.

A few heartbeats later, a yank on the lead rope threw Addison off balance, had him stumbling forward.

"Jump, man! Jump!" Dalton shouted.

Not a controlled jump, but Addison managed to stumble off the bridge and land feet-first in the creek. Another jerk on the lead rope had him dropping to his hands and knees.

"What is it?" Dalton fought the urge to race across those planks to reach his men.

"Don't know, Cap'n," Addison said. "It's not the signal, but I—"

Dalton watched the rope jerk once. Twice. That *was* the signal. "Move back this way, Addison. Keep steady pressure on the rope. Guide him back." He struggled to keep his voice controlled and encouraging as Addison waded to the near side of the creek.

The rope disappeared into nothing, but they followed its movement. Not the steady movement of a man walking, but the stuttering struggle of someone moving with care and desperation.

Was it a man coming back over the bridge? They didn't know what was on the other side.

"Addison! Get that rope off your belt. Now! *Now!*"

While Addison struggled to untie the lead rope, Dalton grabbed his arm and hauled him up to dry land.

Addison dropped the rope and backed away from the bridge. Dalton unsheathed his short sword and waited for whatever was about to cross over into their landscape.

"Do you hear that, Cap'n?" Addison asked, cocking his head.

Something faint but getting clearer. A voice panting over and over, "Guardians of Light and Guides of the Heart, please let me get him to the captain."

Henley appeared suddenly, hunched over, his hands fisted on the lead rope he'd tied around Faran's chest. "I found him, Captain," he panted as he dragged Faran the rest of the way off the bridge. "He's hurt bad."

Dalton stared at the thing that had been dragged into this landscape along with Faran.

Almost every night for the past week, his daughter, his sweet little girl, had had nightmares about giant spiders creeping around the corners of her room, ready to eat her. Those nightmares had given him and his wife sleepless nights, because what the heart believed could change the resonance of a person and bring that person into contact with the landscape that matched that belief.

Now he was staring at his daughter's nightmare. It existed. It was real. And far too close to home.

"Captain?" Henley said, his voice full of uncertainty.

Dalton shook himself. He couldn't think of his family now. His men needed him.

Approaching cautiously, he went down on one knee next to Faran's shoulder.

Faran opened his eyes. His breathing was harsh, as if it took all of his will to keep his lungs moving. "Can't feel . . . my arms . . . or legs. Trapdoor . . . near bridge."

Pressing a hand on Faran's shoulder, Dalton studied the dead spider that was as big as a dog. The hilt of a knife stuck out of its head. "Hold on, Faran. You just hold on."

Dalton stood up. "Guy, you ride back to the city, fetch a healer and a wagon. Henley, Addison, you wade across the creek and see if there are saplings or branches over in that wooded area that we can use as poles to make a litter."

He watched his men scatter to follow his orders. Then he tried to will his pounding heart to calm back down to a steady pace. But his heart wasn't fooled as he walked around Faran to take a position near the guard's leg.

Maybe the best thing would be to cut the fangs away from the jaw. That would separate the spider from the man. But that would bring his hands, his body too close to those jaws, and even though he *knew* the spider was dead, his body didn't believe it.

Cut the creature in half? That would ease the weight and drag on Faran. But his hands were shaking, and there was a chance of slicing into Faran's leg. The guard couldn't afford to lose more blood.

He felt his courage withering, and he wanted to ride away, wanted to get stinking drunk, wanted to shrug off the weight of being responsible for other men's lives. And he could almost hear something whispering at the edges of his mind, feeding the shame and the fear.

"Cap'n? We found a couple saplings. Think they'll do?"

Addison's voice snapped him back. How long had he stood there, doing nothing to help a man who had followed his orders because his men trusted him with their lives?

Dalton took a step back before turning his head to look at the two men splashing across the creek. He swallowed his fear and gathered what was left of his courage.

"They'll do," he said when Addison and Henley reached him.

He sheathed his sword and took the cut sapling from Addison. His heart pounded as he used the wood to push Faran's legs apart and gingerly push the spider's body in the space between. Then he handed the sapling back to Addison, drew his sword, and hacked at the spider's abdomen.

The spider didn't move, didn't twitch.

Encouraged, he shifted position to slice the spider's body, working carefully, always aware that a careless move with the sword could harm his own man.

Finally he stepped back and nodded at Henley, who grabbed Faran under the arms and dragged the man away from the remains. The head, part of the torso, and four legs remained attached to the guard.

Addison studied him. "It's a hard thing, Cap'n, to know the bad things in the world are close enough to touch us. I reckon we've got some evil days ahead of us."

Dalton rubbed his sleeve over his face, wiping off sweat. "I know." Using the bottom of his jacket, he wiped off his sword, then sheathed it. "Come on; let's make that litter."

🙊

Sebastian watched everyone who had gathered at his command—the bull demons, who had dug the deep fire pit; Hastings and Mr. Finch, who covered the bottom of the pit with kindling; two other residents, who gingerly lifted the blanket-wrapped bundle and lowered it into the pit; Philo, who opened a jar of lamp oil and poured it over the blanket.

He watched everyone—and wondered if the people he knew were behind those familiar faces.

When Philo stepped back, Sebastian held out his hand. He didn't see who handed him the torch. It didn't matter. He walked up to the pit, stared at the bundle for a long moment, then dropped the torch onto the oil-soaked blanket.

Despite his efforts to keep the creature covered up, a few of them had seen its face, frozen by death in the process of change. No one had asked how the thing had died—but all of them were acting wary around him.

They had more reasons than they knew to be wary.

"Daylight," Philo said as he took a handkerchief from his pocket and wiped his face. "I didn't know there was a demon that could change shape and disguise itself as human."

You've known, Sebastian thought. *You just never realized it.*

"What kind of demon was that?" Mr. Finch asked.

Sebastian watched the fire, trying to ignore the sick churning in his guts. He had to tell them. They had to be warned. A few days ago Teaser had told him five newcomers had arrived at the Den. Which meant there were four more of those things out there, able to wear anyone's face.

"Sebastian?" Philo shifted his feet, then glanced at Hastings and Mr. Finch. "What kind of demon was it?"

He had to tell them. But it would change things.

He turned away from the fire and looked into Philo's eyes. "It was an incubus. A pureblood incubus."

Koltak let the horse wander. Maybe the animal would have better luck finding its way out of this thrice-cursed landscape. Where were the towns, the roads, even a farmhouse with some doltish landgrubber who might have enough wits to point him in a direction?

How many miles had he traveled? How many hours had he wandered around these green, rolling hills?

He should have made some inquiries in Wizard City. There were bound to be a few citizens who knew how to find the Den. Of course, none of them would have been willing to admit it to a wizard, but if he'd sensed any evasion, he could have brought them up to the Wizards' Hall for questioning.

Too late for such thoughts. He had to find his way, alone, and bring Sebastian back to Wizard City. And once he'd accomplished his part of the plan to save Ephemera, the wizards in the council wouldn't look at him as if he'd stepped in manure and hadn't wiped all the stink of it off his boots.

The horse snorted, pricked its ears, changed its stride from an amble to an active walk.

Koltak tensed as he gathered the reins, then relaxed again when he spotted the black horse standing at the top of a rise, just watching him. He'd seen a handful of these horses since he'd crossed the bridge. The first two times he'd expected to find a farmhouse or some kind of estate, some indication that the animal belonged to someone. After that, he'd come to the sour conclusion that whoever lived in this landscape just let their animals run wild.

Or had already been crushed by the monsters Belladonna had unleashed in the world.

Prodding the horse with his heels, he deliberately turned away from the wild horse standing on the rise—and from the west, where the sun was making its journey toward the horizon. He had a bedroll and some food, and there was grain for the horse, but he hadn't considered that he might not find the Den quickly or, barring that, find accommodations in a village. He didn't want to sleep out in the wild.

Shelter, he thought. *An inn with warm food and a bed with clean sheets. That's all I ask. All I ask.*

A few minutes later he found a bridge. Not just planks over a stream, but a proper wooden bridge wide enough and sturdy enough to take a farm wagon.

Which made no sense, since there was no road leading to it or away from it. But he wasn't about to ponder the logic of a bridge that had no purpose. It was the first sign of civilization, the first hint that he might find a place to stay before the sun went down.

The horse crossed the bridge . . . and stepped onto a dirt road that followed the curves of the land.

Koltak jerked the reins, bringing the horse to an annoyed stop. Twisting in the saddle, he looked back over the bridge. The dirt road continued on the other side.

But it hadn't been there before.

He'd crossed over into another landscape. But he hadn't felt the warning tingle of magic, hadn't had any warning that the bridge was more than a bridge.

His heart raced as he straightened in the saddle, wincing at the protest of muscles that had spent too many hours riding.

Urging the horse to a trot, he followed the road and felt relief when, a few minutes later, he caught a glimpse of rooftops and the smoke from chimneys.

By the time he reached the village, the shops had closed for the day, and most of the people had gone home to have their dinners, but he followed the sounds of voices and laughter to what was, undoubtedly, some kind of inn.

He groaned when he dismounted, then felt a flash of annoyance when no one hurried out to take his saddlebags so he wouldn't have to carry them himself. Leaving the horse tied to a post, he hauled the saddlebags over his shoulder, stepped into the main room, then walked up to the bar, bumping into people who didn't have the sense to step aside for him, as was proper.

The man behind the bar gave him a hard look and a cold smile. "Good evening to you."

Koltak grunted. "What's the name of this village?"

"Dunberry."

Not a familiar name. "Give me a glass of your best ale."

The man drew a glass of ale and set it on the bar. But he didn't release the glass. "Let's see your coin first."

Deeply insulted, Koltak gave the man his most formidable stare. Then he tapped the badge pinned to his robe. "You dare insult someone who wears this badge?"

The man leaned a little closer to get a better look, then shrugged. "Could be a family trinket, for all I can tell. If it's not but brass or copper, it might fetch enough to equal two glasses of ale and a plate of whatever is left in the kitchen. If it's gold, it's worth that and a room for the night, plus stabling for your horse, if you have one."

"You think I would barter this?" Koltak shouted. "I am a wizard!"

The man cocked his head to one side and considered. "A wizard, is it? And what would that be?"

Koltak stared at the man, then turned and studied the other men standing at the bar and sitting at the tables.

"A wizard," he repeated, growing uneasy when the blank looks didn't change. "A Justice Maker."

"Like a magistrate, you mean?" someone asked. "You set the fine if someone's pig gets out of the pen and tramples the neighbor's garden?"

"How dare you insult me?" Koltak whirled toward the sound of the voice but couldn't tell who had spoken. "I am a Justice Maker. I can call down the lightning of justice and kill you where you stand!"

"Well, Mr. Wizard, sir," said the man behind the bar, "around here we call that murder. And we don't care if you do murder with a knife or with this lightning of yours. You kill a man here, we'll hang you good and proper."

A sharp-edged ball of fear rolled in Koltak's belly. Not his part of the world. Not any of the landscapes he knew. He was powerless here, because any use of the power he controlled would have them hunting him like a common criminal.

"I have some money." He fumbled with the money pouch tied to his belt and put three gold coins on the bar.

The man behind the bar moved one coin away from the others. "This will get you a meal, two glasses of ale, and a room." He moved another coin. "This will get you a bath and stabling for your horse."

"Yes," Koltak said softly, humbly. "The horse is outside and . . . a bath would be welcome."

"Most likely you'd like to have the meal in your room."

Most likely you'd prefer me out of the way. "Thank you."

"I'll show you the room." The man went to the open end of the bar. "Patrick! See to the gentleman's horse."

A youth, who looked enough like the barman to be family, stepped forward and shot Koltak a cold look. "I'll see the poor creature gets a good feed and is tended properly."

As Koltak followed the barman up the stairs to the rooms, he heard a man in the room below say, "That one thinks well of himself, doesn't he?"

"That he does," another answered. "And there's no kindness in him. You can see it in his eyes."

"That you can," the first one replied. "Has me thinking that no one would miss him if a waterhorse took him for a fast ride and a long sleep."

Then the barman opened a door and entered the room to light a lamp. "I'll bring up your dinner as soon as it can be put together. Bath is down the other set of stairs, along with the indoor privies."

Koltak set the saddlebags down at the foot of the bed and waited for the man to leave before sinking down on the bed.

They didn't know about wizards. Did they know about the landscapes? If they didn't, how did they survive?

They had no respect, no courtesy. They treated him like some common traveler.

He hadn't felt this lost, this lonely, since he and Peter made the journey to Wizard City to become apprentice wizards. But he'd had his brother then, even though they hadn't liked each other much. Now he was far from home, and the status that made even the wealthiest gentry careful to show respect meant nothing to anyone.

And that was another stone he would hang around Sebastian's neck when the time came.

🦋

All the way back to the bordello, Sebastian told himself to expect any kind of reaction from Lynnea, to accept any disgust or revulsion she might feel toward him after seeing that thing. He'd prepared himself for any kind of response—except to have her throw her arms around him as soon as he walked into their room.

"You're all right?" she asked, squeezing him hard enough to shift his ribs. "You're not hurt?"

He didn't complain about his ribs or the feeling that he couldn't quite breathe. He just held on to the warmth of her, the love inside her—knowing he couldn't hold on to it much longer. That was something else he'd prepared for on the walk back to the bordello.

"I'm all right," he said, finally shifting her back enough to give himself breathing room. "How's Teaser?"

Lynnea looked back at the door that led into the bathroom. "He said he wanted to be alone. Wouldn't let me sit with him in his room, and he didn't want to stay in here. I think he's drinking."

Giving her a light kiss on the forehead, Sebastian stepped aside. "I'd be worried about him if he weren't trying to get drunk."

Lynnea narrowed her eyes. "Is that your way of telling me you're planning to get drunk too?"

"I guess it is." He edged toward the bathroom door. "I'd better talk to him."

Since it hadn't occurred to Teaser to lock anyone out from that direction, Sebastian simply walked through the bathroom and opened the other door. He found Teaser sitting on the floor, back braced against the side of the bed, cuddling a half-full bottle of whiskey.

Settling on the floor next to his friend, he took the whiskey bottle, helped himself to a long swallow, then handed it back.

"That's not me," Teaser said. "That's not me."

Feeling like he'd aged a decade in the past few hours, Sebastian rested his head against the bed. "Yes, it is."

Teaser looked at him with wounded eyes. "You think I'm like that? You think this is a mask I can take off? You think . . ." He raised one hand to his forehead, his nails digging in as if he could peel the skin off.

Sebastian grabbed Teaser's hand and pulled it away

from his face. "It's what we are, Teaser. That's what's inside us. You know it is. When our power unfurls, that's the feel of it. Diluted, but that's the feel of it."

"I know," Teaser whispered. "I wanted . . . When it was on her, it made me so hungry, I wanted . . . And then I saw its face. My face."

"It wore my face for a little while, too." And he would never forget the fear that had filled him when it had looked at Lynnea.

They passed the whiskey bottle back and forth a couple of times.

"Then that thing really was . . ."

"An incubus." Sebastian sighed. "A pureblood. The real thing."

"Then what are we?"

"Mongrels." Sebastian forced himself to smile. "The result of incubi and succubi mating with humans and having the seed take hold."

Teaser stared at the whiskey bottle. "So . . . I'm part human?"

"Looks like it."

"Do you know why I wanted to be your friend?"

Sebastian shrugged. "When I first came to the Den, there weren't many incubi and succubi here, and you and I were the youngest ones. Since we liked each other and had fun trolling together, I didn't give it any thought."

"I wanted to be your friend because you knew how to be human," Teaser said softly. "We learn how to imitate humans in order to blend in enough to stay in a place for a while and hunt, but you *knew*. The first time we ate at Philo's, you said 'please' and 'thank you.' "

He shifted, feeling embarrassed. "Well, my aunt is a stickler for good manners."

Teaser nodded. "You knew those things. You knew how to do more than hunt. You knew how to have fun living in the Den. I wanted to know those things, too. Not that I didn't like you," he added, letting his head roll so he could give Sebastian an earnest look, "but you were more than any incubus I'd run across. And the times when Lee came to visit, and the three of us would strut on the streets . . . I saw how it must be for humans, having friends, being foolish, just having fun."

"Were you lonely before you came to the Den?" Sebastian didn't expect a reply. Teaser never spoke of where he grew up or what it was like or how the incubi and succubi lived, or even if there was some landscape that was "home" for them.

"Lynnea hugged me," Teaser said softly. "I've never been hugged before, just for a hug."

If it wasn't for the times he'd lived with Nadia, he wouldn't have known the warmth and comfort of a hug, either. What kind of man would he have become without Nadia and Glorianna and Lee?

"One day soon I'm going to have to take you to my aunt's house for a couple of hours."

Teaser's eyes were filled with a blend of panic and hope. "Your aunt? But I'm . . . and she's . . . Won't she mind?"

Now he could smile and mean it. "Aunt Nadia has a soft spot in her heart for bad boys. She'll put you to work and make you feel human in no time."

Teaser chuckled. His eyes started to close.

Sebastian stood up, put the whiskey bottle on the table by the bed, and hauled Teaser to a somewhat vertical position. "Go to bed and get some sleep. You won't wake up happy if you end up sleeping on the floor."

Teaser swayed gently as he studied his shoes. "My feet are way down there. How'd they do that?"

"It's a mystery." The barest push had Teaser flopping on the bed. Sebastian took off the shoes, rolled Teaser closer to the center of the bed, and tossed a blanket over him.

Then he went back to his own room.

He made excuses for not touching Lynnea. He needed a bath. He was tired. By the time she came out of the bathroom, he pretended to be asleep.

I'm doing this for her. I know what's inside me now. Really know. I can't let the stain of it dim her life.

When she cuddled up against his back, he didn't turn to let her rest her head on his shoulder. And when her dreams invited him in, he stayed away—and had never felt so lonely.

Chapter Seventeen

A light breeze softened the summer heat, and the combination of wind chimes, stirring leaves, and water trickling into the koi pond made a kind of music no human-made instrument could match.

Glorianna sat on the stone bench and watched the flashes of gold as the koi went about life in their own small world, fearful of nothing but the occasional heron that might decide to go fishing in the pond.

A feeling of change brushed her skin, whispered in the air. Turning her head toward the wooden bridge that arched over a "stream" of decorative stones, she watched the man who suddenly appeared a step beyond the bridge.

Seeing her, he smiled and raised a hand in greeting.

Returning the smile, she shifted on the bench to make room for him. "Good morning, Honorable Yoshani."

"Good morning, Glorianna Dark and Wise." He sat on the bench, put a glazed, covered jar between them, and continued to smile. "I woke this morning and had a feeling that if I came to this part of Sanctuary before the sun rose too high, I would find you here. So I heeded my feeling, and here you are."

"And here I am."

"Where is your brother?"

"Gone to visit our mother. Or, more to the point, trying to decide how he feels about our mother's lover moving into the family home."

"Ah. The lover is a fortunate man to have earned your mother's regard."

"I don't think Lee has your wisdom."

"He is her son. I am not. It is easier for me to have wisdom," Yoshani said, grinning.

Glorianna laughed. "There is truth in what you say." She looked at the dark eyes she thought of as wells that went all the way down to the great pool of wisdom that lay at the heart of the world. "But you didn't come to this part of Sanctuary to share that wisdom."

"I came to give you this." He handed her a smooth white stone that lay warm in the palm of her hand. "And to show you this." He picked up the jar.

"What is it?"

"It is a jar of sorrows," Yoshani replied softly. "Every season, in my part of the world, those who serve the Light go out into the villages with these jars and a large bag of white stones—enough stones for every man, woman, and child. In the morning each person in the village takes a stone and carries it with them. Throughout the day each finds quiet moments to hold the stone and whisper the things that weigh on the heart. Small hurts, large regrets. The stones hear the sorrows and absorb them. Before the sun sets, everyone drops the stones into the jar, and the jar's keeper pours clean water over the stones and closes the lid. The next morning, as the sun is rising, the villagers bring jugs and buckets of water with them and follow the keeper to the spot they have chosen as 'sorrow's ground.' The keeper opens the jar and pours out the water, which has turned black. The jar is refilled with water again and again until it finally pours out clean. That's when the people know the sorrows have been cleansed, and they return to their lives with lighter hearts."

"Is there something in the jar that turns the water black?" Glorianna asked, rubbing the white stone in her hand.

"Only sorrows," Yoshani said, smiling. "That is the magic those who serve the Light in my homeland can give to our people. The people in your part of the world have a saying: Travel lightly. It does not mean the burden a man can carry on his back, but the burdens he carries in here." He tapped his chest. "Is that not so?"

"That is so."

"Your heart does not travel lightly these days. So I offer you the magic of my people: a stone ... and the jar of sorrows."

Glorianna looked at the white stone, warm and smooth in her hand. What would it be like to let go of the weight of memories, to still the echoes of hurt that remained inside her from the day she'd realized the Instructors and wizards had tried to wall her inside her garden? How would it feel to whisper her secret fear—that loneliness might one day darken her heart so much she could no longer touch the Light? Wouldn't life be easier if she let stone be the vessel for those feelings, if she let those feelings be washed away?

She closed her eyes and listened to the resonance of Light and Dark that lived inside her and made her another kind of vessel.

With a sigh of regret, she handed the stone back to Yoshani.

"Why will you not accept this gift, Glorianna Dark and Wise?" Yoshani asked. "Why do you hold on to your sorrows?"

His hand was open. It would be so easy to take the stone back.

Glorianna gently closed his fingers over the stone, hiding it from sight. "Because, Honorable Yoshani, I think I'll need them."

After finishing what he considered a meager breakfast, Koltak pushed back his chair, picked up his saddlebags, and headed toward the door. The barman, the only other person in the tavern's main room, was pretending to clean the bar with a rag instead of clearing away the dirty dishes left by the other travelers.

Probably trying to avoid talking to me. The thought was surprisingly bitter, since, back home, he would have felt insulted if a mere innkeeper or tavern owner attempted conversation with him.

"You'll be going then?" the barman asked, keeping his eyes on the rag he rubbed over the bar's wood.

"I am," Koltak replied coldly, reaching the door.

"Your horse is saddled. Stable is around back." The man hesitated. "Which way are you headed?"

Why do you want to know? But he turned back to face the man. After all, this was a strange place, and a day's ride had taken him a long way from home. "Back over the bridge."

The hand holding the rag stuttered to a halt. After a moment, the barman picked up the rhythm of his polishing. "Well now, most folks have no trouble crossing that bridge, and the road will take you all the way to Kendall, which is a fair-sized town on the coast. But there's some wild country between here and there, and it's said that if a man's heart isn't in the right place, he can cross paths with one of the waterhorses that live in that part of the land."

Koltak took a step toward the bar. "Waterhorses?"

The barman nodded. "Beautiful black horses. They'll come right up to you, as tame as some spoiled darling of a pet. But they're demons, the waterhorses are, and if you give in to the urge to take a ride on one of them ... Well, you'll get a sweet ride, so I've heard. They run like the wind and move so smooth you think you're skating over ice. But as soon as you get on one of them, it's got you caught in its magic, and you can't get off. So they run as they please, with you helpless to do anything but go with them. And then, when they come to one of the small lakes or ponds that are all over the land there, they'll run straight into it, run right down to the bottom. Doesn't bother the waterhorse any, so they stay down on the bottom while the person who was foolish enough to take a ride struggles and flails . . . and drowns."

The barman shook his head. "Some say they release the magic then and let the body float to the surface to be found by any who come looking for him. And some say the waterhorses take those drowned men back to the edge of the lake and feed on the flesh."

Koltak felt a surge of excitement. Waterhorses! A demon landscape. He'd seen those black horses but hadn't recognized them as demons. That didn't mean this particular dark landscape was connected to the Den, but Sebastian had come to Wizard City and slipped away again, so it seemed likely that any dark landscape that had a bridge connecting it to Wizard City would also have some connection to the dark landscapes that were closer to home.

"Thank you for the information," Koltak said, now eager to be on his way. If the Guardians and Guides were watching over his journey, he might be on his way back to Wizard City by this evening.

As Koltak opened the door, the barman said, "Travel lightly."

Anger flared hot, turning excitement to ash. He turned and stared at the barman. "What did you say?" Had this all been some bold scheme to play a trick on a wizard? Had they understood what he was all along and pretended ignorance?

Looking uncomfortable, the barman shrugged. "It's sorry I am if it offends you, but it's just a saying. Traveler's Blessing, we call it. Been said around these parts for as long as anyone can remember, but I doubt there's a soul living—or dead back five generations, come to that—who can tell you what it means."

No, they hadn't pretended ignorance, Koltak decided as the anger trickled away. They *were* ignorant. Perhaps when the threat to Ephemera was ended, he would recommend to the Wizards' Council that a more substantial bridge be made to connect this landscape with Wizard City. The people here deserved to be educated about their world—and he would be happy to oversee their education.

He left the tavern, found his horse waiting in the stable yard behind the building, and rode away, retracing his path from the previous day.

He saw the bridge and focused his mind on what he needed to find on the other side: taverns, gambling houses, whores of both sexes.

Certain he would find what he sought, he banged his heels against the horse's sides and sent the animal clattering over the bridge . . . and several lengths down the road before he managed to rein it in.

There had been no road in the dark landscape he'd wandered through the day before. So this must be the road to Kendall, a town on the coast where, no doubt, he'd find the kinds of places that catered to men who spent their lives on the sea—taverns, gambling houses, and brothels.

But he wouldn't find the Den of Iniquity by following this road. He wouldn't find Sebastian.

So he turned the horse and went over the bridge and up the road a little ways toward Dunberry. Then he returned to the bridge, which was his only way to find his ungrateful whelp of a son who would finally, finally, *finally* do something right for his father. He crossed the bridge . . . and found the road to Kendall.

And found the road on his next attempt. And the one after that.

Travel lightly.

Either the Guardians of the Light had abandoned him or the Dark Guides were playing with him. No matter how hard he tried to focus on the things that made up the Den, he couldn't reach the landscape where the waterhorses dwelled. Even if the people here were ignorant of the ways of their world, Ephemera worked the same way. The land would look the same, the landmarks wouldn't change, but there were layers of landscapes here. Perhaps there were only two accessible from this bridge, but he couldn't get to the one he wanted. He couldn't cross over to the dark landscape.

Koltak closed his eyes. There was no eagerness left, no anger left. All he wanted right now was to find Sebastian, to talk to Sebastian.

Sebastian. Sebastian. Sebastian.

Prodding the horse, he crossed the bridge ... and into a countryside unmarred by any road.

Relief shuddered through him. He had crossed over into this dark landscape from Wizard City. He was sure of it. But did it connect to the Den? Only one way to find out.

Sebastian. Sebastian. Sebastian.

With no reason to choose one direction over another, Koltak turned the horse and rode south.

Sebastian began another circuit around the Den's main street. He'd been on the move since dropping Lynnea off at Philo's, and the trolling without pleasure, combined with an unsatisfying night and fitful sleep, had left him on edge, itchy. On top of that was the sense that he was a jagged puzzle, just like the landscapes, except there wasn't the equivalent of a Landscaper to shift the pieces until they resonated in harmony with one another.

Seeing the undiluted power of the incubus had sickened him. Realizing that the wizard power that had lain dormant in him was now trying to find some way to fit—or dominate—the rest of him made him feel vulnerable.

Who was he when he talked to Philo, gave orders to Teaser, craved the feel of Lynnea's body brushing against his? Was he a human making plans with other humans to defend the Den, a wizard giving orders because no one would dare disobey him, or an incubus who craved whatever warmth he could get from a woman who had been an innocent before she'd stumbled into the Den?

Who was Sebastian? Why didn't he know anymore? Wasn't he a little old for this kind of soul-searching?

He did know one thing with absolute certainty: If the other newcomers who had come to the Den were pure-blood incubi and succubi like the one he'd killed, he would die before he let any of them near Lynnea.

He would kill before he let any of them near Lynnea.

Which was why he'd spent the past few hours on the street, hunting. He'd recognize the feel of them. He was sure of that. But if they kept that power contained, they could hide behind any face, maybe even cross over to a daylight landscape where no one would recognize the danger until it was much, much too late.

As he passed Mr. Finch's shop, which was locked tight, Mr. Finch and Wayne, the boy he'd taken in as an apprentice, paused in their reorganization of the shop to wave at him—just as they'd done each time he'd passed by. He wasn't sure if they were doing that to assure him they were who he thought they were or if they were paying attention to how long it took him to make a full circuit so they could raise an alarm if he didn't appear within a reasonable time.

Daylight! Was he going to spend the rest of his life walking the streets, watching for trouble, protecting the people and making sure the Den remained as it should be?

And what did it say about him that he found the prospect of such a life appealing?

At the end of the street, where the cobblestones changed abruptly to the dirt lane that led to his cottage, he paused for a moment, then started back down the street. He'd take a break when he reached Philo's, have a cup of koffee and a plate of whatever was being served, talk to Teaser, flirt with Lynnea. Especially flirt with Lynnea.

And do what? he thought unhappily. Stir up the juices, the wants and needs, and then pretend to be asleep again tonight so he didn't have to wonder if he was taking more from her than he should?

But he *wanted* to flirt with her, make love to her, hold her. Just hold her. Was it the incubus or the man who wanted those things? Did knowing what was inside him really make him any different from the person he'd been a few weeks ago?

He lengthened his stride, moving down the street with no other thought than to spend a few minutes with Lynnea. She was safe there. Teaser had volunteered to keep an eye on her—and all of them knew the offer had been made, in part, because Teaser was still shaken up over seeing a pureblood incubus wearing his face. So Teaser was watching over Lynnea—and Philo was watching Teaser.

As he approached, he saw Teaser step up to the edge of the courtyard. The incubus raised a hand in greeting and almost had his usual cocky smile.

"Was told to keep watch for you," Teaser said, his blue eyes twinkling. "There's a lady here who thinks you should rest your feet and have a bite to eat."

"The lady is right," Sebastian replied, looking past Teaser to watch Lynnea come into the courtyard to serve a table of four bull demons.

Teaser looked over his shoulder and grinned. "Guess she didn't have a chance to tell you about that. The Sebastian Special is a treat, as far as the bull demons are concerned. And since they paid for the meal with a jar of ripe olives swimming in oil, I thought Philo was going to weep with gratitude."

Olives? You couldn't even buy them on the black market most of the time. And how many times had he heard Philo grumble that a particular dish just didn't have quite the right flavor because he couldn't get his hands on any olive oil? What had the man concocted that the bull demons liked so much?

"Sebastian Special?" That part finally sank in.

Teaser grinned. "Vegetable omelet. Apparently Lynnea told the first bull demon who got one that it was a special dish she made only for you. Therefore, the Sebastian Special. But the bull demon liked it, and now he's gone and told all his friends, so—"

"We're never going to get another omelet, are we?" Sebastian said, suddenly feeling wistful about eggs he'd never know. "If the bull demons are willing to pay for them with olives, Philo won't give up a single egg to the rest of us."

"Well, you might still get some, since Lynnea's the one who makes the omelets. As for the rest of us, I'm hoping your farmer friend can add eggs to the supplies he's already promised to bring to the Den."

Sebastian grinned. "I wonder if William Farmer has ever tasted olives. This might end up as a very good deal for us."

That was the moment when Lynnea, having delivered her tray of omelets and toast, turned and saw him—and everything about her lit up with pleasure.

The warmth of her feelings flowed through him, and he dropped his guard, just a little, to fully embrace those feelings.

That was when a different kind of feeling flooded through him. This had claws that tried to pull him under, drown him in sensation. He felt the power of the incubus unfurl inside him, but it was primitive, furious, viciously hungry.

Lynnea froze and stared at him. Teaser made some inarticulate sound and took a step back.

"Protect Lynnea," he whispered to Teaser. Then he turned to face the street.

All four of them were moving toward him. All of them hammered at his emotions, at his wants and needs, trying to find a way in that would leave him seduced by their power, vulnerable to whatever they intended to do to him.

"Sebastian," one of the succubi purred. "Join us. Rule the Den with us. This is your only chance."

Sweat beaded his forehead. They moved toward him, shoulder-to-shoulder, their matched steps a sinuous dance humans could never imitate. And behind them a crowd was growing, their faces dark with ugly emotions.

"I already rule the Den," Sebastian said, each word

an effort of will. How long could he hold out against them? How long before the lure of being glutted by emotions became impossible to resist?

"He rules the Den," an incubus said, mocking. Its eyes glittered with malice as it turned its head slightly to address the crowd. "*He's* the one standing in the way of your pleasure. *He's* the one preventing you from getting what you deserve." The incubus looked at Sebastian. "*He's* the one who needs to be eliminated."

Mutters from the crowd as the men moved closer, spreading out to surround him. "Run him off!" "Show him who's really in charge!" "Bastard thinks he can make the rules and tell me what to do? Bury him!"

Sebastian stared at the four purebloods. During the hours he'd spent searching for them, they had fed the dark emotions of the Den's visitors. Now those men were convinced there was nothing wrong with killing him in return for all the pleasures that had been promised to them. Pleasures that would end up killing them.

He felt the crowd stir, glanced around quickly. Some of the men were holding broken chair legs as clubs. Some held pocketknives. All it would take was one lunging at him to have them all trying to tear him apart. Even if the Den's residents jumped into the fight to help him, people would get hurt. Some might even die.

The purebloods knew he'd killed one of them. They wouldn't risk themselves when the humans would do this ugly bit of work for them. But they were still trying to lure him in, make him vulnerable to every kind of attack.

Sebastian.

Why was he resisting? He couldn't quite remember.

He took a step toward the purebloods.

Sebastian!

Love turned fierce in its desperation to reach him blazed through him, freeing him from the purebloods' thrall. He knew the feel of that love, the heat of it, the passion that came from that heart.

Lynnea!

The wizard's power rose up in him, tingled in his fingertips—a cold fire that came from an icy clarity of mind rather than the heat of emotions.

"I protect the Den," he said, raising his voice to reach the crowd as he stared at the purebloods. "You are a threat to the people here, to all the people of Ephemera. You are killers and must be destroyed. Justice demands it."

The purebloods snarled. The crowd surged toward him.

He raised his hand, pointed at the purebloods—and unleashed the lightning.

Jagged streaks of power, blinding white, hit all four of them. Enveloped them. Blazed through them.

Burned them.

They screamed, unable to escape the power. The men who had been surging toward him suddenly fell over one another in their haste to get away from him.

Even after the purebloods lay dead in the street, an echo of their screams seemed to linger.

No one spoke; no one moved.

He looked at the crowd. The thrall had died with the purebloods. Now the men's faces held nothing but fear—of him.

"Leave the Den," he told them. "Don't come back."

They scrambled to their feet, scurried in the direction of whatever bridge would take them back to their home landscapes. He watched them until the last man was out of sight. Then he turned to face the courtyard.

Fear in Teaser's eyes, in Philo's. Even the bull demons looked at him in fear. But Lynnea . . .

Maybe she didn't understand what he was. Maybe she didn't care. All he felt from her was relief . . . and love.

"Daylight, Sebastian," Teaser finally said, his voice rising to a pitch close to hysterical. "You're a wizard!"

He rubbed his right thumb over the tips of his fingers, feeling the slight tingle of that cold magic. And he remembered something Aunt Nadia had said once.

There are two kinds of wizards. Many enjoy the fawning and attention that is given them out of fear. But there are others who use their power in the name of justice to protect people from the things that would truly do them harm.

"No," he said, looking at Philo, then at Teaser. "I'm not a wizard. I'm a Justice Maker."

Chapter Eighteen

Dalton watched Henley and Addison set up the tents near the wagon that held their supplies. No point sleeping on the ground, exposed to the whims of weather, when they didn't have to. And they were close enough to Wizard City that he could send a man back every other day for fresh food.

Faran would live. The surgeon was hopeful that the man wouldn't lose the leg and that the rest of the limbs, numbed by the venom, would fully recover. But the surgeon was less hopeful that the injured leg would ever be strong enough to support the demands of a guard's duties. So Faran would be given a season's pay as compensation and would be cast out to build a new life suitable for a partially crippled man.

"Cap'n?" Addison said, approaching him. "Tents are up. We're going to water the horses, then picket them to let them graze."

Dalton looked past Addison's shoulder, unwilling to look the man in the eye. "That's fine."

Addison sighed. "You did what you could, Cap'n. We all know you argued to keep Faran on the ledger, leastwise until he was healed up and could know for sure if he had to give up the guards. But maybe it's for the best. Bad times are coming. We all know it. So maybe Faran will be better off going back to some country village and taking up a different line of work. He's a good man with horses. Has a way with them. And he was never comfortable with the rough side of a guard's life. Too much a gentleman." He paused, then added, "Like you."

Flattered and embarrassed, Dalton looked at the other man. "Thank you."

Addison scuffed the ground with one foot. "I'd best go help Henley with the horses."

Dalton waited until the guard walked away before turning to study the planks of wood that crossed the little creek. Guy and Darby had the first watch. He'd keep the watches short in the daylight hours to relieve the fatigue of boredom. The night watch . . . He'd take the night watch. Not alone. He wasn't a fool. But he could relieve his men of some of the tedium of waiting for Koltak's return—and share their fear that something besides Koltak would cross over that bridge.

Sebastian wrapped his arms around Lynnea, pulling her up against him.

Laughing, she pushed at his chest in a halfhearted effort to get away. "Haven't you had enough?"

"I'll never have enough of you."

When they'd gotten back to the bordello, they'd made love for hours. She hadn't given him a chance to evade. And what choice did he have when she'd squirmed on top of him, wearing nothing but her skin and a smile—a combination of sultry and wholesome that sent his libido into a fever of lust? He took, he gave. She took, she gave.

And somehow, in the hours when he'd slept after the loving, the jagged pieces of himself had shifted until they fit together instead of scraping against one another.

"Well, you've had enough of me for the moment," Lynnea said, giving him her best no-nonsense look.

"I've got to get to work, and you've got to meet with Philo."

His contentment faded as he thought about the folded piece of paper that had been pushed under his door, requesting a meeting. He knew why Philo wanted to talk to him.

"What's the matter?" Lynnea asked. "What's wrong with Philo wanting to talk to you?"

He rested his forehead against hers. "Incubi are welcome in the Den of Iniquity. Wizards aren't."

She stiffened. Did she finally realize why everyone had become so uneasy after he'd killed the purebloods?

When she pushed at his chest, he let her go, let her step back from him.

Then he looked at her face and took a step back himself. Outrage. Fury. His little rabbit was spitting mad and ready to take a swing at someone. Anyone.

"Lynnea." He tried for soothing, placating. If that didn't work, he'd sink to pleading. Maybe.

She bounced. Her hands curled into fists, and she ... bounced.

Oh, damn the daylight.

"You're the same person you were before. Now they want you to leave because you have a power that can defend them against bad things? What kind of idiots run the businesses in this place? What kind of morons live here?"

She marched to the door and flung it open before he gathered his wits enough to try to stop her.

Unfortunately, Teaser picked exactly the wrong moment to open his door and step into the corridor.

"Are you an idiot?" Lynnea shouted, jabbing a finger into the incubus's chest. "Are you a moron? Have you exchanged your brains for a bag of manure?"

"What'd I do?" Teaser said, raising his hands in surrender. Since Lynnea was already marching for the stairs at a fast clip, he turned to Sebastian. "What'd I do?"

"She's on a tear."

"What'd *you* do?"

"Nothing. Just . . ." He dug in his pocket and handed his key to Teaser. "Lock up the room for me, will you? I've got to stop her before she does something stupid."

"Like punch a bull demon in the nose?"

He wasn't going to consider the possibility.

He raced down the stairs—and still wasn't fast enough to stop her before she got out of the building.

He caught up to her before she got to Philo's but couldn't think of any way to stop her without causing a scene that would be the talk of the Den for years to come.

"Lynnea, wait."

She marched through the courtyard, flung open the door to the indoor dining room, and stopped so abruptly he rammed into her back and had to grab her shoulders to keep her from falling.

At least, that was the excuse he was going to use for holding on to her.

Philo wasn't the only one waiting for him. Hastings and Mr. Finch also sat at a table. Wasn't that wonderful? Exile by committee. Not that Philo or anyone else really had a choice about his staying. He anchored the Den. Didn't matter if they considered him incubus, wizard, or human, he had to stay. And they had to accept it. The Den's survival depended on it.

"Lynnea," Philo said, "maybe you'd like to go into the kitchen and—"

She bounced.

"You want her to go into the kitchen?" Sebastian said, unable to hide his disbelief. "Where there are sharp things?"

Philo looked at Lynnea—and paled. "Ah. A chair, perhaps?" He pointed at the empty chair at the table.

Sebastian shook his head—one sharp little movement. Until his rabbit calmed down, he wasn't letting her near anything she could pick up and use as a weapon.

"Well, then." Philo pulled a handkerchief out of his pocket and dabbed his forehead. He looked at Hastings and Mr. Finch, who both nodded. "Well. The thing is, Sebastian, after those ... creatures ... were disposed of, the merchants and business owners got together and talked things over. If you're going to be protecting the Den from now on, you should be compensated. Like ... wages."

"All the businesses would put in a percentage of their take each month," Hastings added. "Some credit slips, some coin. A place like the bordello would just reduce the rent on your room for their share."

"Besides," Philo said, glancing nervously at Lynnea, "we all sort of figured you'd retired from your previous occupation."

That was the truth. If he'd had any doubts about being Lynnea's exclusive lover, he was sure of it now after seeing her in a full-blown mad.

Suddenly her body relaxed. She cocked her head. "You want Sebastian to be like a law enforcer in a village?"

"Yes," Mr. Finch chirped. "Exactly."

Sebastian reluctantly let go of her as she turned to face him.

Her blue eyes still flashed with temper. "They wanted to talk to you about protecting the Den, and you thought they wanted you to leave. You moron."

He yelped when she reached up and pulled his ears to bring his head down. The hard kiss on the mouth was nice, but didn't quite make up for getting his ears pulled.

Then she walked out of the dining room.

"Any bets that she'll scare the customers into eating all their vegetables?" Sebastian asked.

"Wouldn't take the bet," Hastings replied. "Not today." He looked at Sebastian and frowned. "Why did you think we'd want you to leave?"

"I'm a wizard."

"Justice Maker," Mr. Finch chirped.

He studied the three men. "Are you serious about this offer?"

Philo chuckled. "A badass incubus wizard as the Den's law enforcer and Justice Maker. What could be more perfect?"

Chapter Nineteen

With Jeb beside her, carrying a carpetbag and grumbling about the foolishness of making this visit, Nadia switched the basket she'd brought from one hand to the other and continued walking up the main street of the Den of Iniquity. Bursts of music and voices came from various buildings as the doors of taverns and music halls opened and closed. The colored globes on the poles turned the streetlights into something festive instead of providing mundane illumination. It made her think of the seedier part of a harvest fair—the tents and booths that most of the people who attended a fair didn't realize existed. There was an edginess here, and enough resonance of mean to rub at the grain of doubt that had lodged in her heart during the past few days.

"Don't see why we couldn't have left this at the cottage," Jeb grumbled.

"It didn't look like anyone was staying at the cottage," Nadia replied, trying to ignore the uneasiness she'd felt when she'd realized Sebastian had abandoned the place he'd called home for the past ten years. "I want to see how Lynnea is getting on, that's all. And I wanted to see the Den."

"It's been here a few years now," Jeb said, looking at her with the awareness of a man who'd been awakened too many times in the past few nights when the dreams had plagued her. "Any reason you felt the need to see it now?"

Every reason. But she wouldn't say those words out loud, wouldn't give them that much weight. For fifteen years, she had maintained an unshakable faith that Glorianna was not a deadly, dangerous creature, as the wizards claimed. When Glorianna had shaped the Den of Iniquity and altered the way Ephemera's landscapes flowed into one another so that several of the demon landscapes were connected to one another, Nadia had trusted that her daughter, so gifted in her power, had seen some need other Landscapers couldn't.

For fifteen years she had trusted, because to do less might have shaken Glorianna's faith that she had her mother's support—and Glorianna was already too alone in the world. Now a grain of doubt was wearing away at that trust, and she had to see, had to know what kind of dark landscape had been made of this place.

"First-timers?" a voice asked, pulling Nadia out of her thoughts.

The blond-haired man watching them had the cocky grin of an appealing troublemaker, but when she got close enough, she detected a bruised wariness in his blue eyes.

"Why do you think we're first-timers?" Jeb asked, sounding defensive.

The cocky grin took on a hint of mean. "Got the look of it. So . . ."

Those blue eyes never left her face, but she could have sworn she'd been stroked from breasts to hips, and his hands knew every curve she had. Except for Sebastian, she'd never met an incubus, but she was certain she was looking at one now. The experience was . . . unsettling . . . in a way that made her feel ripe and female.

"Who's your friend?" the incubus asked.

"I'm the lady's *friend*," Jeb growled.

Nadia blinked. Had she just heard Jeb—solid, reliable Jeb—claim her like some meaty bone? As if some young man, even if he was an incubus, would have any interest in having a romp between the sheets with a woman old enough to be his mother.

She looked into those blue eyes again—and felt her heart flutter and her face heat. Guardians and Guides, he *was* interested!

"We're here to visit my nephew," she said firmly, ready to blame the streetlights or the walk here to justify any blaze of embarrassment coloring her face. When he smirked, making it clear he heard variations of that statement all the time, she added, "Sebastian."

The incubus jumped as if she'd whacked him with a broom.

"You're Sebastian's auntie?" His voice rose to a squeak.

"I am."

"Daylight!"

"Who are you?"

"Teaser. Ma'am. Auntie, ma'am." He looked around, his expression on the edge of desperate. "Here, now, why don't I take you up to Philo's, and then I'll have a look around for Sebastian. He's here somewhere. Better be," he added under his breath.

He was even more appealing when he was flustered, Nadia decided as she and Jeb followed the incubus down the street. More . . . human in a way she understood. And more comfortable to be around.

"What about Lynnea?" Nadia asked. "Where is she?"

"At Philo's," Teaser replied.

"Is she well?"

"She's doing fine. Gets pretty scrappy if I leave the towels on the bathroom floor or forget to rinse out the tub. Do all human women get scrappy about things like that if you're not giving them sex?" Teaser paused. "Of course, she gets scrappy about those things with Sebastian, and he *is* giving her sex. Uh . . ."

Nadia sighed. Before he'd known she was Sebastian's aunt, he would have said all kinds of things to her. Now just the mention of sex had him blushing like a schoolboy. "Being an aunt doesn't make me less of a woman," she muttered.

"It's different," Teaser muttered in return.

"How?"

"I don't know. It just is."

It was astonishing to discover incubi could be . . . What was the phrase she'd heard Sebastian mutter on occasion? Prissy prigs. Yes, that was it. Prissy prigs.

Maybe in another day or two she'd see the humor in that.

"What are *those*?" Jeb asked as they approached four large, shaggy, horned creatures standing just beyond a courtyard filled with tables and chairs.

"Bull demons," Teaser replied, then added, "I hope William Farmer brought eggs in that last wagon of supplies."

Before Nadia could ask what eggs had to do with such dangerous-looking creatures, Teaser raised his voice and said, "This is Sebastian's auntie, who's come for a visit and a bite to eat. So you just find a table and wait your turn—and don't go bellowing and give her a sour stomach."

The shaggy creatures stared at her.

"Om-e-let?" one rumbled.

"She doesn't want your omelet," Teaser said. "Just go sit down." He pulled out a chair at an unoccupied table and smiled at Nadia. "This is a good spot."

For what? she wondered, noticing the closest statue. And also noticing that Jeb's face was turning bright red as he looked around. The carpetbag slipped from his hand and landed on the flagstones with a thump.

Nadia set her basket on the table and just stared at the statues. All those years when Lee had come to the Den and had laughed at her concern that he might be too young . . .

Mother, if I wanted to be wild and wicked, I wouldn't go to the Den. Sebastian's worse than a spinster aunt twice over when it comes to my doing anything you might disapprove of.

She should have known a son would be less than truthful about things like that. And it didn't look like a young man of tender years would have to do anything but look around in order to have an interesting education.

Dark. Decadent. But . . .

Her heart jumped into her throat when a bellow was abruptly cut off. "Oh, dear. That bull demon just smacked another one on the nose."

The people at the other tables tensed, ready to flee at the first sign of a fight breaking out.

Then Lynnea stepped out of a doorway. Four shaggy heads turned and stared at her. She held up four fingers. Four heads bobbed up and down.

"How did she do that?" Jeb asked.

"She won't make them omelets if they don't behave," Teaser replied, raising a hand to catch Lynnea's attention.

When she turned and saw them, she darted between the tables, her face lit with delight, her hands reaching out to grasp Nadia's.

"You're here!" Lynnea said. "I'm so glad!" Then the delight changed to concern. "Is everything all right at home?"

"Everything's fine." Nadia gave Lynnea's hands a friendly squeeze before letting go and turning toward the basket. "I just wanted to bring you a few things. I would have left them at the cottage, but it seemed . . . unoccupied."

"Oh. Yes. Sebastian thought it would be safer to stay here for a while. There's been a bit of trouble, you see, and—"

"How'd you get here?" Teaser said, focusing on Jeb.

"Took the bridge that crosses over in the woods behind the cottage," Jeb replied.

"But how did you get *here*?"

"Walked."

"What's wrong?" Nadia asked when Teaser started swearing and Lynnea looked upset.

"Sebastian's going to have a thing or two to say about that," Teaser muttered.

"Why should Sebastian have anything to say about it?" Nadia said, irritated. If she dismissed the sculptures, shaggy demons, and the fact that it was middle-of-the-night dark instead of morning sunshine, she might very well have stepped into some squabble in her own village. And to her way of thinking, the only thing worse than getting caught between two sides of a family squabble was being one of the participants.

"He'll have a lot to say about it, you being his auntie and all," Teaser said hotly. "Besides, he's the—"

"Here now!" A round man with receding dark hair hurried over to the table. "Teaser, let our visitors sit down and have some refreshment before you start jawing at them. And, Lynnea, darling . . ." He tipped his head toward the bull demons. "There's an order waiting for your attention."

"Yes, Philo, you're right," Lynnea said. Then she added in a rush, "Nadia, Jeb, please stay. I'll get you something to eat, and you can catch your breath. And Teaser? Don't be a moron." She wove through the tables and dashed into the building.

"How does being concerned about Sebastian's auntie make me a moron?" Teaser shouted, causing all the people in the courtyard to turn in his direction.

Siblings of the heart, Nadia thought, feeling the sting of sentimental tears. Lynnea was blooming here, changing from a frightened girl to a strong-minded woman. And the baffled, annoyed young man standing beside her was part of the reason for that change.

"Aunt Nadia?"

Turning, she felt her heart jolt when she saw Sebastian.

He's changed.

Maturity cloaked him like a new coat that needed time to become a comfortable fit. But it was more than that. There was a feeling of strength in him, of . . . power.

"Justice Maker," Nadia said.

His body tightened, as if bracing for a blow, while he inclined his head slightly to acknowledge the truth of what she'd said.

Wizard. Justice Maker. One was supposed to be the same as the other, but they weren't the same. Sebastian's father, Koltak, was a wizard. But Koltak's brother, Peter, the husband of her heart and father of her children, had been a Justice Maker. She thought if Peter had survived, he would have understood Sebastian far better than Koltak ever could.

"Is the Justice Maker embarrassed to give his aunt a hug in public?" Nadia asked, pleased to see Sebastian relax as he walked up to the table and enveloped her in warm, strong arms.

Teaser snorted. "This is the Den. There's nothing you do in public that will embarrass us."

Sebastian eased back but left an arm around Nadia's shoulders. "Jeb is the man who made that puzzle."

"Is he?" Teaser's eyes lit up. "I've had a couple of thoughts that could bring in a few coin."

"Then why don't you take Jeb over to another table while I talk to Aunt Nadia," Sebastian said.

Just that simply and quickly, Teaser led Jeb to another table, Nadia was seated with Sebastian, and a youth who didn't look old enough to know about the Den, let alone live there, took the carpetbag and basket, saying that Philo would tuck them out of the way. Before Nadia could catch her breath, Philo was filling the table with dishes of food, two glasses of wine, and two cups of koffee.

"Looks like Philo wanted to give you a sampling of his specialties," Sebastian said. "There are Stuffed Tits, Phallic Delights, and olives."

Nadia picked up a roll, realized how it was shaped, and dropped it.

"It's just bread, Aunt Nadia," Sebastian said.

She wanted to smack him for looking so amused.

"Here." He took another Phallic Delight, broke it into three pieces, and put it on her plate.

Nadia narrowed her eyes. "Are your hands clean?"

"Yes, Auntie, my hands are clean. And I still remember to wash them after I pee. Most of the time."

She laughed. How could she not laugh? "All right. So you all think I'm being foolish."

Sebastian smiled as he dipped a Delight into the melted cheese. "You're a first-timer. It would be a keen disappointment to all of us if there wasn't something in the Den that shocked you."

Nadia picked up a chunk of bread and dipped it in the cheese. "This is just a strange little village, isn't it? It's wicked with a sense of humor, naughty for the fun of it."

"Yes, exactly."

She set the bread and cheese down without tasting it. "Then the Den isn't the problem. May the Guides of the Heart forgive me, I had hoped it was."

He tensed. "You came to check out the Den?"

"Yes."

"You think it's the weak spot in the landscapes Glorianna holds?"

"No, Sebastian. I think I'm the weak spot."

A long silence. Then Sebastian said gently, "Drink your koffee. It's getting cold."

Obediently, she pulled the cup and saucer closer—and noticed that he reached for a glass of wine.

"A few days ago," she began hesitantly, "the resonance of a town within one of my landscapes changed, became discordant. I couldn't tell if that discordance came from some hearts that needed to move on to a different landscape or if it was a change in the town overall. So I crossed over to the marketplace in that town.

"Uneasiness and worry resonated from many of the people who went about their daily business, but it was the malicious glee of a few, thinly disguised as shock and disgust, that disturbed me. Even in the daylight landscapes, there are hearts that are nourished by dark feelings. They're like weeds in a flower bed, except they can't be plucked out. It's more like they get trimmed back so that the good plants around them grow strong enough to overshadow them."

"I understand that, I guess. If you sent everyone who had cheated or lied or had done something spiteful at some time in their lives to a dark landscape, there wouldn't be anyone left in the daylight landscapes."

"Exactly. The heart is capable of the most noble feelings and the most vile. The possibilities are inside each of us. It's the feelings we embrace, as well as the ones we turn away from, that shape who we are."

"So what happened in the marketplace that disturbed you so much?"

Nadia sipped her koffee. "Stories about bad things happening in the next town over. A boy killing his younger sister with an ax, screaming that she turned into a big spider at night and crawled on him while he slept. A man beating his wife to death because she'd been late serving his dinner. Whispers about families having a run of bad luck. It felt like the words had smeared something vile over me, and when I left the marketplace to find a quiet spot where I could resonate with feelings that belong to the Light, I realized I was resonating in tune with that vileness. I was reinforcing it, helping it become stronger."

Sebastian put his hand over hers. She held on to that warmth, that connection.

"The dreams began that night," she said, her voice barely above a whisper. "Not dreams in the usual sense. Almost like someone whispering in the dark. But I didn't want to listen, and the one image I can remember from those dreams is me pushing and pushing a heavy wooden door, fighting to get it closed and lock out whatever was on the other side. Except I'd lost the key, so the door wouldn't stay closed."

Sebastian sat back, picked up his wine, and drained the glass. "Sounds like something is trying to reach you through the twilight of waking dreams."

"The what?"

He gave her a grim smile. "That's how the incubi and

succubi hunt their prey most of the time. We don't have to cross into another landscape, don't need physical contact. Oh, we like real sex, but it's the feelings we feed on. So we send out a tendril of our power, searching for a receptive mind, and we weave a fantasy—or participate in a fantasy. We're dream lovers who can make a dream feel so real there's physical gratification."

Nadia cleared her throat. "I see. I never . . . I never asked you about that part of your life."

"And I wouldn't have told you even if you'd asked."

"I think . . . I've been contaminated. Maybe by a Dark Guide. Maybe by the Eater of the World. That's why I'm here, Sebastian. I never doubted Glorianna's reason for shaping the Den. Until these dreams started."

"What do you feel compelled to do, Aunt Nadia?" Sebastian asked, his voice stripped of all emotion.

Nadia shivered. "Go to the wizards and tell them how to find her. Take them to Sanctuary—a place none of them have been able to reach on their own."

"But you didn't." Now his voice was sharp, alarmed.

"No, I didn't. Instead I came here. Glorianna can do things no one else can. She embraces the Dark and still walks in the Light. I needed to see this place . . . to reaffirm my faith in Belladonna."

Sebastian took a deep breath, then let it out slowly. "Let me tell you about the dreams Lynnea's been having lately."

She could feel the heat rise in her face. "Oh, no, Sebastian. I don't think that's—"

"She's been rearranging furniture. Or I should say, she's been pointing and I've been rearranging furniture, hauling things I couldn't possibly lift in the real world. And it's a mix of furniture, some from our room at the bordello, some from the cottage. So I'm moving the bed and the couch and tables and chairs while Lynnea keeps saying, 'No, that's not the way it should be.' Each morning she wakes up and looks at the furniture with this gleam in her eyes, and I wake up with a sore back.

"Last night I was rearranging windows. I'd grab the wooden frame and lift the whole thing out. There wouldn't be a hole in the wall where it had been, and every time I pressed it against the wall, a hole would open exactly the right size for the window.

"But Lynnea kept saying it wasn't where it should be. Then she wanted me to put it against an inside wall. I argued that we wouldn't see anything but the person in the next room, but it was her dream and I was just the labor, so I did what I was told."

Nadia tipped her head to the side. "And did you see into the next room?"

"No," he replied softly. "I couldn't see anything. The window was full of sunlight. The room was washed in it. And when I looked back at Lynnea, it was Glorianna standing there. She smiled at me and said, 'Yes. Now it's where it should be.'"

He reached across the table, picked up her glass of wine, and drank half of it. "I don't know what it means, or even why I told you this now."

"I know why you told me," Nadia replied softly. "You believe in Glorianna—and you trust Belladonna. I'm going to fight very hard to do the same."

Sebastian pushed his chair back. "Come on. Teaser's had enough time to make Jeb blush right down to his toes, and I think it's best if you went home. And stayed home."

Nadia shivered. "You think I'm a danger, don't you?"

"I think you've been poisoned." He tapped his chest. "In here."

He was right. She could feel the resonance of his words and knew he was right.

"Yes, we should be getting back." She squared her shoulders. "And the walk will do me good."

Sebastian draped an arm over her shoulders. "That's too bad, because you're riding back on the demon cycles."

"Demon . . . Oh, no, I . . ."

Paying no attention to her protests and blustering, he

rounded up Teaser and Jeb, gave her a moment to say good-bye to Lynnea, and had her riding behind him on something that was a combination of a thick bicycle with no wheels and a demon with lots of sharp teeth and wickedly curved claws.

It wasn't too bad while they were on the Den's main street, but once they reached the dirt lane that led to the cottage . . .

"You can let go now, Aunt Nadia."

That was what he thought. She felt him patting her hands and trying to loosen the fists that had a death-hold on his shirt.

"We're not moving anymore."

"Then I'll just wait for my insides to catch up with us."

Sebastian laughed. That wicked boy actually laughed. Which annoyed her so much she managed to let go of his shirt and get off the cycle.

Jeb, she noticed, didn't seem the least bit shaken. She couldn't see him clearly, since there was only starlight, but he was rubbing his chin in that way he had when something had caught his interest.

Teaser grinned at Jeb and cocked his head.

"I'll think about it," Jeb said. He walked over to her and cupped her elbow in one of his big, strong hands. "Come along, darling. I'll make you a cup of tea when we get home and you can have a bit of a lie-down."

"Don't talk to me like I'm old and decrepit," Nadia snapped. Since the demon cycles had brought them right to the edge of the woods behind Sebastian's cottage, it was no more than a few minutes' walk before she'd be home.

She looked back at Sebastian. "The next time you come to visit, I hope Sparky poops in your hair."

Jeb's chuckles didn't cover up Sebastian's sputters. That made her feel better, so she hooked her arm through Jeb's, and the two of them followed the path that led home.

Sebastian stared at the dark path in the woods, his heart aching.

"Do you want to check the cottage while we're here?" Teaser asked.

He shook his head. "No one has been around." He was certain of that because he stopped at the cottage each day when he checked the bridges leading to the Den. "Let's get back."

"Jeb said he'd think about my idea."

"Where's he going to find an artist to paint erotic pictures to make into a puzzle?"

"Well, he did say that might be a sticking point." Teaser paused, then asked, "Who's Sparky?"

On the way back to the Den, Sebastian thought about Nadia. Why would she have doubts about Glorianna now? Why would she consider telling the wizards where to find Belladonna? Unless, as he'd said, she had been poisoned by a mind strong enough to plant doubts and thoughts where none had been before. How was he supposed to tell Glorianna and Lee that something dangerous might have been locked in Nadia's landscapes when Glorianna had altered Ephemera to isolate those places and keep her mother safe?

And how was he supposed to tell his cousins that their mother could no longer be trusted?

*S*hadows in the garden.

It is the hardest lesson for a Landscaper to learn.

The gardens are not just access points put together in a pleasing manner. They also reveal the heart of the Landscaper, the signature resonance that will overlie the landscapes in her care. It is a reflection of who the Landscaper is, and her innermost self will be manifested into plants and stones and water for everyone to see.

If the heart tries to lie, the garden will reveal that, too.

But every student's first attempt tends to be a pretty lie. All the plants are the ones that symbolize kindness and generosity, patience and understanding. Love. Despite the student's best efforts, the garden struggles to survive because the dark feelings that are denied also resonate in that confined space and have no patch of ground to call their own. So they interfere, tangle up the currents of power, thrusting up where they don't belong. And the garden fails.

It takes time to find the courage to display the parts of yourself that aren't bright and shining. But you have to see them, have to know they're inside you, because they *will* resonate in the landscapes you control. Because you, as a Landscaper, are the sieve through which all the human hearts in your landscapes touch Ephemera—and none of those hearts lives completely in the Light.

So every Landscaper has to learn, and acknowledge, the dark side of her own heart in order to keep our world balanced.

Shadows in the garden.

They are a part of all of us.

—The Book of Lessons

Chapter Twenty

"Perverse beast," Koltak grumbled when the horse suddenly stopped a few strides away from the large pond. "Nearly pulled my arm out of the socket to get to the water, and now you don't want to drink?"

He didn't know much about horses, but the animal seemed uneasy about something, so he looked around. Just rolling green hills that looked the same as the ones he'd seen yesterday—and the day before that. What was happening in Wizard City? Was anyone concerned about the length of time he'd been away? Was he trapped in this landscape, doomed to wander in a place where he was nothing more than a bumbling traveler?

The horse took a step forward, then stopped again.

"Stay thirsty, then." Koltak removed the canteen from the saddle. Keeping a firm grip on the reins, he moved toward the water.

Apparently reassured by his action, the horse moved with him. But it still hesitated at the edge of the pond before it finally lowered its head and began to drink.

The dusky light had turned the water an opaque gray, but the pond looked clean enough. He would let the animal drink its fill, and then—

The creature broke the surface of the water right beside the horse's head. Brownish gray. Bumpy. The open jaws, filled with serrated teeth, clamped onto the horse's neck. A twist of its large body dragged the horse into the pond. A savage shake of its head severed the horse's head, leaving it to bob in the bloody water.

Another of the creatures suddenly appeared and ripped off a hind leg, while another one bit into the horse's belly and spun, churning the water until the sharp teeth and the spinning motion tore off a chunk of meat.

Gasping for breath, his body shaking with fear, Koltak stared at the pond. He didn't remember moving, but now he stood several man-lengths from the carnage.

He knew what they were. Every wizard had to study descriptions and rough sketches of the creatures that had been locked away with the Eater of the World. Bonelovers, trap spiders, and wind runners were some of the creatures that had been taken out of the world.

These were the death rollers. Crocodileans bloated by human fear. A larger, more savage version of one of Ephemera's natural predators.

His hands were full. Puzzled, Koltak lifted them. One fist gripped the strap of the canteen. The other still held reins.

His eyes followed those strips of leather. Then he screamed, dropped reins and canteen, and stumbled back a few steps to get away from the severed head he must have dragged from the pond. He fell to his hands and knees, was violently sick, then crawled away from the mess and lay on his back, staring at the first stars to shine in the darkening sky.

The terrors that had been manifested from human fears were no longer contained. The landscapes where those terrors dwelled had been reconnected to the rest of the world. If a connection had been made that allowed the death rollers to intrude in this landscape, had other landscapes been altered to give those creatures access? And what about the other terrors? Would a child on a family outing to the beach walk across a patch of rust-colored sand and disappear, caught in the bonelovers' landscape?

It could happen. Fed by grief and fear, those landscapes could encroach on all others, changing the resonance, consuming hope. And the nightmare the Eater of the World had tried to create once before would become fully realized, and all that was good in the world would shrivel away until there was nothing left.

For one shining moment, as he stared up at the stars, his heart and mind were swept clean of ambition and personal grievances and only one thought resonated: He had to find Sebastian. Ephemera's survival was at stake, and finding Sebastian was the key to saving the world.

Shaky but determined, Koltak got to his feet and began walking.

Sebastian was the key to saving the world.

Reaching into the inner pocket of his robe, he felt the reassuring crackle of paper.

Sebastian . . . and the message he'd brought with him from Wizard City.

༄

Dalton leaned against a tree and wondered, again, what he could have done to change things.

"Cap'n?" Addison walked up to him, then looked toward the creek where Guy and Henley were standing watch. "What happened to Darby wasn't your fault. You sent him to the city to pick up supplies and leave a report at the guard station to be taken up to the wizards. You didn't tell him to stop at a tavern, get into some piss-assed fight, and end up knife-stuck enough times to die."

"He wasn't a hot-tempered man," Dalton said, his voice full of baffled anger and regret.

"No, he wasn't. But something's been bringing out the mean in people lately. Surely does seem that way."

"I know."

Addison rubbed the back of his neck. "It's none of my business, Cap'n, but maybe you should be thinking of another place for you and yours."

"I've thought about it," Dalton said softly. "My current contract is finished in a few months, and my wife has said more than once that she wouldn't mind leaving Wizard City. So I've thought about it. But where would we go? What kind of landscape could we reach?"

Addison shifted from one foot to the other. "I've spent time in a few landscapes over the years, and I've served under several guard captains. Even the ones who were good captains weren't always good men. You're a good man. You don't belong here. Knew that after the first week of being assigned to your fist. Haven't changed my mind in the years since. It's not a kind city, Cap'n. Never was. You keep on rubbing elbows with the wizards, you might start forgetting what it means to be a good man."

Addison was coming too close to the bone, giving voice to things Dalton tried not to think about—especially in the darkest hours of the night.

"What about you, Addison? You came here from another landscape and stayed. You've been here more years than I have. Why aren't you thinking of leaving?"

Addison's smile was sweet and bitter. "I never said I was a good man."

🦂

Glorianna walked toward the source of the dissonance in the waterhorses' landscape—the dissonance that had set her teeth on edge when she'd walked through her garden to check the feel of her landscapes. This dissonance had made her angry. The other "weed" in her garden left the taste of despair burning at the back of her throat.

Lee would find out what had thrown their mother's heart into such confusion. Nadia would talk to him, would tell him what was wrong, and he would do what he could to ease the trouble. Or at least find out the source of the trouble. Because she didn't want to consider the unthinkable—that her mother's heart was no longer attuned with hers, that something in Nadia had changed so much she no longer fit in a landscape held by Glorianna Belladonna.

Lee would take care of whatever trouble waited at home. Whatever had made the wrongness in *this* landscape was a task only she could deal with.

Whatever? She knew what had left Its mark on the waterhorses' landscape. She just didn't know how It had gotten here.

When Sebastian had told her about the waterhorse being killed, she'd gone to the pond. There had been a stain of Dark that didn't fit with this landscape, that didn't resonate with her. But she'd found no sign of an anchor that could be used as an access point, so she'd sent her resonance out over the land, concentrating the power on the pond and the land around it until it was in harmony with her once more. The stain of Dark hadn't been completely washed away, but it should have faded by now—unless someone full of dark emotions that resonated with that Dark had passed by this pond often enough to feed the Dark, providing the Eater with just enough of an opening to alter the pond again to be an access point for one of Its landscapes.

Wishing she hadn't ignored Lee's sharp order to bring a lantern with her, she hurried toward the pond until, in the waning light, she spotted what she thought was a dark, oddly shaped rock. Then the smell of blood and vomit made her gag.

Fighting to control her churning stomach, she approached warily and stared at the severed horse's head a long time before shifting her focus to the pond a few man-lengths away. There was only one thing that had been locked away in the Eater's landscapes that could bite through muscle and bone like that. Death rollers.

A freshwater pond would suit them, but the waterhorses came from a northern climate, so this landscape should have been too cold for death rollers. Unless the creatures had changed in the long years they'd been taken out of the world and were no longer dependent on the heat of the sun to warm their bodies.

Or the pond was nothing more than a place where they would hunt for prey and then go back to their own, warmer landscape. Either way, the Eater needed a way to reach this landscape in order to alter the pond, which meant It had an anchor nearby that was small enough to escape detection—or there was a bridge Lee didn't know about that was giving It access.

And if It had access to *this* landscape, it could reach the Den or take the bridge to . . .

Oh, Guardians of the Light, was that why there was something wrong with Nadia? Had the Eater of the World crossed over the bridge to Aurora? Was it already altering the village, changing streets into rust-colored sand so that anyone who walked there would be pulled into the bonelovers' landscape? Would the pond where children swam in the summertime become a hunting ground for death rollers? Or what if It hadn't reached the village? It wasn't that far between the border of this landscape and Sebastian's cottage—and the bridge that crossed over to the path that led to Nadia's home was behind the cottage. What if she was under attack? What if Lee stumbled into trouble and was seriously injured before he had time to impose his island over whatever was happening at home and get himself, Nadia, and Jeb to safety? And what about Nadia's gardens? Every one of those landscapes had a bridge that crossed over to Sanctuary. And that was the Eater's ultimate goal: to crush the places that were beacons of Light, the places people, simply by knowing they existed, used to hold on to feelings of love and kindness and hope.

So why was she worried about horse-shaped demons being fodder for death rollers and bonelovers and whatever else the Eater was bringing back into the world? She could alter the landscape. She had the power to rip this chunk of the world away, to take it out of the world so completely it would be lost forever. It wouldn't move, not physically, but the eye wouldn't see it, the mind wouldn't recognize it, and the heart wouldn't acknowledge it. No access. No bridge to cross over. And if a heart did acknowledge that dark place ... No way out once the person stumbled into that landscape.

Are you going to give up another piece, Glorianna? Are you going to become like the other Landscapers who thought demons didn't matter, didn't deserve a place of their own in the world, didn't need that breathless moment when something beautiful catches the eye and dazzles the heart? Are you going to give them up because they aren't human? Neither are you. Not completely. You don't have that comforting lie anymore. Whatever you came from might have bred with humans so that, all these generations later, you live in a human body, but your power isn't human. Was never human. Landscapers focus on humans because the human heart can create so much—and destroy so much.

But other beings shouldn't be forgotten. You knew that when you were a student, felt that need from those no one else wanted to think about. Even demons need a home. Even a dark landscape should feel the warmth of the Light. Why have you forgotten that?

Glorianna stopped. Turned around. Night had fallen, and she had no sense of how far she'd walked or in what direction. Her emotions were so churned up, she had no idea where the pond was in relation to where she stood.

"Insidious bastard," she whispered. "I don't know how you gave me that gut-jab of fear, but I won't forget you can use my own heart as a weapon against me. I won't give up the landscapes in my care. Not even this one. And I won't let you have any of them. I'll find a way to defeat you. I'll find a way to do alone what it took hundreds like me to do the last time. And by the time I'm finished, I will lock you in a landscape even *you* will find unbearable."

She closed her eyes and began to breathe slowly, evenly, until she could feel the resonance in the land. Until she could feel the dissonance once more.

And something else, drawn to the strength of her feelings.

Ephemera. Ready to manifest her feelings and make them real.

Wait, she told it, sending gentle restraint as she walked back to the pond. *Wait.*

When she smelled the blood and vomit, she stopped. In her mind, she pictured lines of power—red with anger, black with despair—running from where she stood straight into the heart of the pond. Then she let her feelings flood through her and become a channel for the world.

"Despair makes a desert," she whispered, watching grass and rich earth turn to sand, sensing the water in the pond changing to sand. "And anger . . . makes . . . stone."

Boulders pushed up from the earth, forming a cage around what had been the pond. Smaller stones edged the sand, separating it from the grass. As the last stone formed beneath her feet, Glorianna stepped back.

Altered landscapes. A piece of desert in a place that knew nothing of deserts. A one-way border . . . but not a boundary. This place would be visible to the eye and could be avoided. Anyone who crossed the border of stones would find sand and heat and little else. And no way back to the waterhorses' landscape.

The death rollers would die there.

But there was still an anchor—or a bridge—somewhere in this landscape that had allowed the Eater of the World to return.

Enough, she thought. *Lee can locate a bridge a mile away from where he's standing, but you can't. That's not your gift. It's time to go home.*

She walked for a little while, not caring about the direction, just wanting to feel the land. It was a dark landscape, but it was good land. Rich land. Oh, human fears had seeped into it, but also relief and joy.

She smiled. The waterhorses were changing, weren't thinking of all humans as prey or the enemy anymore. They were beginning to realize it was as much fun to scare a drunken fool by giving him a fast ride and a cold dunk as it was to kill a man. And the man, given that moment to see that his life could end and have that life given back, was also given a chance to change. Opportunities and choices. For some it would change nothing. For others it would take them on a different path, lead them to another landscape, bring a little more Light into the world.

Calm again, she focused on her heart and will, took the step between here and there, and stepped into her garden a moment later.

It wasn't until she'd gone back to her house to wait for Lee to return that she thought about the horse's head again—and wondered what had happened to the traveler.

Sitting alone on a bench in her personal garden, Nadia watched Lee stop and study the plants that had turned brown overnight.

"Frost?" Lee asked as he walked to the bench. "At this time of year?"

"Frost," Nadia agreed sadly. She tapped her chest. "That came from here."

Lee sat down beside her. Looked at her.

He had his father's eyes, that green that could be soft and dreamy at times or darken toward stormy gray with a mood—or, like now, be clear and penetrating.

Her boy. But he wasn't really hers. Not for a lot of years now.

"What's troubling you, Mother?" Lee asked gently.

No, not her boy. As much as he loved her—and she knew he did—he wasn't hers. "Did Glorianna send you?"

"She knows something is wrong. Something strong enough to resonate through your landscapes."

"She's right." After all, the heart held no secrets from Glorianna Belladonna. "When I went to a town in one of my landscapes, something touched me, contaminated me."

Lee stiffened. "A Dark Guide? You think one of *them* is in your landscapes?"

Had there been one of *them* in the marketplace? "Maybe. Or maybe it was the pleasure coming from some of the people because of other people's misfortunes. A Dark Guide nurtures feelings that are already inside a person. It can't create doubt if the seed of doubt doesn't exist."

"I see." Lee pulled on his lower lip. "So you're the one Landscaper out of all them for all the generations who doesn't have the full range of emotions."

"What?"

"You never get angry or sad or grouchy or wonder if you made a good decision or just feel pissed off because it's been that kind of day. No, you're nothing but happy, kind, generous, sweet, loyal, loving. Yep. You're just a puddle of goodness."

Deeply insulted, Nadia sprang to her feet, sure she'd burst if she didn't move. "I can't decide if I should whack you upside the head or wash your mouth out with soap."

"Before you try doing either, remember what you taught us," Lee said quietly. "The human heart is capable of every feeling imaginable—good and bad—and it's part of our journey through life to decide, day after day, which of those feelings we will nurture so they grow stronger within us and which feelings we'll turn from because we don't want them to dominate our lives. But those feelings still exist inside us. The shadows in the garden. Isn't that what the Landscapers call them?"

She felt as if he'd thrown cold water in her face, waking her out of some foggy dream. She sat down on the bench. "Shadows in the garden," she said softly, the echo of the feeling she'd had as a student when that phrase began to have meaning welling up inside her. "Yes, that's what we call them."

"And now, when things are turning bad and the whole world depends on the choices she makes, you're wondering what's inside Glorianna that makes her Belladonna."

Shame stained Nadia's cheeks. "Yes."

Lee shifted on the bench to get more comfortable. "Do you know where the koffea beans come from?"

Nadia frowned at him, puzzled by the change in subject. "They come from a land far south of here. A—"

"Demon landscape."

She stared at him—and wondered why his smile was a blend of amusement and sadness.

"Not all of them," Lee said. "The ships that come in to trading ports from those southern lands carry koffea beans grown on farms—no, that's not the word for them, but that doesn't matter. Those other places are human. But the koffea beans that find their way to some of your landscapes as well as Glorianna's come from the piece of that land inhabited by a race of demons."

"You never told me."

"You love her and you'd fight to your last breath to protect her from the wizards, but you've never been comfortable with the fact that Glorianna resonates with the dark landscapes inhabited by demons. So I'd like to tell you about this one."

She looked into his eyes and knew that if she refused to listen, couldn't find it in herself to try to understand, she would lose her children. Both of them.

Her throat felt so tight she couldn't speak, so she just nodded.

"I was with Glorianna the day that demon landscape resonated so strongly she had to answer. She'd been working in her garden, turning the soil in one of her 'waiting' spaces, and I was there to keep her company and rest, since I'd done a lot of traveling over the previous few weeks. I saw her pale, saw the shock in her eyes as her hands pressed flat against that newly turned earth. She had to go, right then, with dirt on her hands and wearing the old clothes she keeps for the times when she's going to be grubbing around in the garden. I held on to her, and we took that step between here and there.

"I'm not sure who was more shocked when we appeared in that landscape—Glorianna and me ... or the spirit men from the various clans who had gathered to ask the Sacred Mother for help. They were asking for protection against their enemies, and two of the enemy suddenly appeared inside their circle of power.

"But they recognized what she was. They had old stories, passed down through the spirit men, of women like her. Heart-walkers, they called them." Lee paused for a moment. "Do you know what they wanted, Mother? Peace. There are veins of gold and silver in parts of their land. And there's the land itself. The humans, who already control all the land around them, wanted to drive them out. But that place is all they have in the world. It's their roots, their life. They just want to live there and tend the land. They've had enough contact with humans to know there are 'pretties' they'd like to have and are willing to trade for. But the human traders who had found a way into their land weren't honest and brought in other men who were willing to burn out villages and kill everyone they could before they, in turn, were killed."

"She took them out of the world," Nadia said softly.

"Yes. She altered the landscape so that its boundaries no longer touched the human land in that part of Ephemera."

"But ... you said the koffea beans come from there."

Lee nodded. "For a few months, the only access to that landscape was through Glorianna's garden, and she was the only one who could reach that place. Then, one day, she came with me when I went to check on the bridges in one of her landscapes, and she headed off down this road that led to a little village. When we got there, we ended up in a merchant store. The two brothers who ran the store were grumbling about a promised shipment that had been sold to someone else in another town who could pay a thieves' ransom for a bag of koffea beans. They had a grinder and two perk-pots and had dreams of adding a room to their store, making it into the village koffee shop, but the traders who brought bags of koffee inland from the seaports and had to cross over bridges to reach various landscapes tended to sell what they had to whoever would pay the price. Less time traveling meant more profit—and less chance of crossing a bridge and ending up somewhere the trader didn't want to be."

Guessing where the story was going, Nadia smiled, even though tears welled in her eyes.

"Well, the sum of it is, Glorianna said this was a place for opportunities and choices, so I made a bridge between those two landscapes. Now the merchants, who were willing to trade with demons in order to have a steady supply of koffea beans, have their koffee shop and have expanded their store as well, since they can sell bags of koffea beans to merchants in the bigger towns near them. More trade means providing the people in their village with more variety of goods—as well as establishing sources for the goods the demons want in exchange for the koffea beans. And there's a man, a teacher by training and an adventurer at heart, who now lives in the demon landscape, teaching the demons human language and acting as a translator when they cross over the bridge to barter with the merchant brothers."

Lee paused. Nadia watched his throat working, as if he needed to swallow some strong emotion.

"Do you know what those demons say when someone asks them where they come from? 'I come from a piece of Belladonna's heart.' So tell me, Mother. How do we judge a dark landscape? Is it dark because the ones who already live there won't let humans have their piece of the world? Do we judge who is good and who is bad by the color and shape of their skin—or by what resonates in their hearts?"

The tears fell, washing away the stain on her heart. *I should have asked about those landscapes a long time ago.*

She wiped the tears from her face. "I went to see the Den the other day."

Stunned silence. Then Lee burst out laughing. "Oh,

Sebastian must have sweated bricks when you showed up."

Annoyed humor filled her. "He took it better than that other boy, Teaser. Acting all flirty until he found out I was Sebastian's auntie, and then—"

Lee howled.

Nadia gave her son a hard smack on the shoulder. "It's not funny. For pity's sake, Lee, he's an incubus, and he *blushed.*"

He laughed so hard he fell off the bench.

Nadia huffed and waited for him to regain some semblance of composure. When he finally sat upright, albeit on the ground, red-faced and gasping for breath, she leaned forward and looked him in the eyes. "You shouldn't laugh at him. *You* can't say 'mother' and 'sex' in the same sentence."

Sputtering, he raised his hands in surrender. "No, I can't, but we aren't talking about me."

"You're grown men. You've had sex. I don't see why you get so huffy about someone else having some."

"Can we go back to talking about Sebastian and Teaser? Please?"

Looking at his face, she laughed—and felt something shift inside her, felt her heart regain its balance.

When her laughter faded, she sighed. "She really is a Guide of the Heart, isn't she?"

Lee sobered. "Heart-walker. Yes, she is. It's what she's always been."

"I know. I keep hoping there are others like her, somewhere in the world beyond the landscapes we know. But even if there are others, Glorianna is the one who is here—and the Eater of the World is going to do everything It can to destroy her."

Lee held out his hand. She took it, welcoming the warmth and connection, while she thought about the daughter who held Ephemera's fate in her hands.

They sat that way, silent, for a long time.

❧

Koltak stumbled, although there was nothing to trip his feet. Then he realized the endless grass had changed to a dirt lane. The air felt different—warmer, drier—and he could hear the sound of waves rolling in to shore.

He hadn't felt the resonance of a bridge, but he was so tired, he might not have sensed it. More likely he'd crossed a border between similar landscapes rather than a boundary that required a bridge. Still, a lane would have a destination, so he followed it until he came to a cottage.

The place looked human-made. He could knock on the door and ask for food and shelter.

Of course, just because the cottage was human-made didn't mean the occupants were human.

He hesitated, then continued following the lane. If there was one cottage, there would be others. Maybe even a village.

He had no sense of how long or far he walked before he saw the colored lights. His heart lifted. Had he finally reached the end of the journey?

Hope battled exhaustion, winning long enough to get him to the edge of a cobblestone street he'd seen once before, years ago.

Determined to finish the journey, Koltak walked down the main street of the Den of Iniquity.

The Eater of the World has been sealed away and can no longer touch anything in Ephemera except the landscapes It shaped. And they, too, have been taken out of the world. But the Dark Guides, who brought the Eater into being, who rejoiced in Its destruction of the world, are still out there in the landscapes. Somewhere.

They are clever. And they are cruel.

They nurture the dark desires of the heart. It is said they can slip into a mind to whisper things that can turn a heart away from the Light.

Yes, they'll tell someone, *it isn't fair that you are poor and can't afford that pretty trinket. You deserve to have the pretty trinket. If you take it . . . The merchant is wealthy. What's the loss of a few coins?*

Yes, they'll whisper, *you're right to be angry. She was cruel to break your heart. She deserves to feel your fist . . . that knife . . . that ax.*

They nurture the dark feelings in the heart and help them grow.

But the worst thing they can do is use truth to destroy something good, to use truth as a lie in order to dim the Light inside someone—or even within a landscape.

No one is immune to the Dark Guides. Not even Landscapers. So beware. If someone tries to persuade you to turn away from something you know is right in order to do a greater good ... sometimes it really will be the truth and is the right thing to do.

And sometimes it will be a lie.

—The First Teachings

Chapter Twenty-one

Sebastian and Teaser stood at the edge of Philo's courtyard, looking over the customers. Or, in Sebastian's case, watching Lynnea take orders and clear tables.

"Is it love," Sebastian wondered, "when a particular woman complaining that you hog the bed makes you feel happier than a dozen other women undressing you with their eyes?"

"Don't ask me," Teaser grumbled. "I'm not the one sighing and moaning every night."

"Lynnea doesn't sigh and moan." Not loudly enough to be heard in the next room, anyway.

"Wasn't talking about Lynnea." Teaser gave Sebastian a long look to make his point, then a quick once-over. "You're dressing hot these days. More than you've done in quite a while."

Sebastian smiled. "I've got a reason to—and I don't want her to forget it."

Oh, yeah. Despite being a one-woman incubus and the Den's Justice Maker, he was dressing hot these days. Tight black denim pants and a black denim jacket, a green shirt to enhance the color of his eyes, and a pendant—a flat green stone on a gold chain that Glorianna had given him years ago—that he'd found in the back of a dresser drawer when he went rummaging for something interesting to catch a woman's eye. He wasn't sure if there was something about the stone or something about him wearing it, but Lynnea—

"You keep thinking what you're thinking, you're going to sproing in public," Teaser said.

"That's crude."

"I'm just saying. And since we all know who you sproing for these days—"

"Why aren't you out trolling?"

Teaser shifted his weight from one foot to the other. "Because the last time I saw an attractive woman who looked safe enough to nibble on, it turned out to be your auntie."

"I'm trying to forget that."

"Me too."

"Really trying to forget that."

"Me too." Teaser sighed and started to turn toward the street. "All right, then. I'll take a stroll and—Daylight! What's one of *them* doing here?"

Sebastian looked in the same direction and felt the heat of anger and the chill of fear run through him. "Have a word with the bull demons," he said quietly as he watched the wizard stagger down the street. "Tell them to watch over Lynnea and keep her safe."

"You going to get testy if they start goring people or bashing in skulls?"

"No."

"Right." Teaser looked at Sebastian. "He can call the lightning, too. Remember that. If it comes down to it, you need to be the one standing when it's done."

"Don't worry," Sebastian growled. "I will be."

He strode up the street, knew the wizard recognized him the moment he started moving—which was more than he could say about recognizing the wizard. He'd never seen Koltak so dirty and exhausted. Obviously reaching the Den had been a long, hard journey.

But Koltak shouldn't have been able to reach the Den. Not anymore. Which was something Sebastian needed to tell Lee at the first opportunity. If Koltak could find his way to the Den, what else might be wandering through Glorianna's landscapes?

He stopped and waited for the wizard to get within a man's length of him. "You're not welcome here."

"Sebastian," Koltak gasped. "There's danger. Great danger. We need your help. You have to listen."

"The way you listened when I came to you for help? Go back where you came from. You'll get nothing from us."

"You have to listen." Koltak started to raise his hand, perhaps in supplication, perhaps for a different reason.

Sebastian didn't wait to find out. His hand shot up, the power crackling through him, balling in his fingertips, waiting for release.

Koltak stared at the hand, then slowly lowered his own. "So. The power awoke in you. You're a wizard."

"Justice Maker," Sebastian snapped. "I wouldn't expect you to understand the difference."

"But I do," Koltak cried. "I do! I—" He swayed. "Sebastian, if there's anything human in you, show a little pity."

"Don't throw that in my face, old man. You've always said there was nothing human in me, never wanted to see anything human in me. So now—"

"Do you think this is easy for me?" Koltak said, the familiar, angry venom back in his voice. "Do you think I want to grovel for your help? To be *here*? But I'm willing to put aside our differences to save Ephemera. Are you enough of a *Justice Maker* to do the same? Or are you going to let everything be destroyed as a way of farting in my face?"

To save Ephemera. Which, for him, meant saving Glorianna's and Nadia's landscapes. Which meant saving the Den, the place he'd promised to protect. Which meant keeping Lynnea safe.

"Come on," Sebastian said. "We'll get you some food—and I'll listen."

Leading Koltak back to Philo's, Sebastian hurried along the edge of the courtyard until he reached the door to the interior dining room. Koltak smelled ripe enough to put anyone but the bull demons off their food, so getting the man away from Philo's customers as quickly as possible was a kindness. He held the door for Koltak, took a deep breath of fresh air, and went into the dining room.

Koltak staggered to the nearest chair and collapsed into it.

Thinking there were benefits to having a head cold and wishing he could have one for the next hour, Sebastian reluctantly pulled out the chair on the other side of the table and sat down.

"Long journey?" Sebastian asked too politely, making it plain that no matter how long the journey had been, it hadn't been long enough. Which, judging by the flash of anger in Koltak's eyes, the wizard understood.

"Yes," Koltak replied in a restrained voice, "it was a long journey."

What does he want from me that he's making an effort to be civil? And why did the words "a long journey" make him uneasy, as if something important was just out of memory's reach?

The inner door swung open. Teaser walked in with a tray, set out two steaming bowls of water, two towels, and a plate with two pieces of soap that had been cut off a bar, then walked out again.

Sebastian eyed the pieces of soap and hoped someone made Brandon wash the knife before the boy went back to cutting up meat or vegetables.

"Is this . . . customary?" Koltak asked, embarrassment coloring his face.

"No," Sebastian replied, reaching for a piece of soap. "But it's appreciated when it's offered." He washed his hands, dried them, set everything to one side, and smiled at his father—a dare to turn down an amenity just because everyone knew it was needed.

By the time Koltak finished scrubbing the grime off his hands, Teaser was back with a pitcher of water, a bottle of red wine, and various glasses that looked like they'd been grabbed because they were clean and handy, since they weren't the ones Philo usually used for water and wine.

"Not very well trained, is he?" Koltak grumbled as he poured a glass of water and drank it greedily.

"He's just helping out." And Teaser *had* remembered to take the bowls of dirty water and the towels away. Sebastian wasn't sure if leaving the soap on the table was an oversight or a comment.

"The wench doesn't serve the tables in here?"

The wench is going to be my wife. But the less Koltak—and every other wizard—knew about Lynnea, the better. Still, he wondered what it said about Koltak as a man that a woman on the other side of the courtyard had caught his eye when it was supposedly so vital that he talk to his son—and what it said about the man that he'd seriously use the word "wench," which, in the Den, was said only as a good-natured tease.

"No, she doesn't serve tables in here."

Teaser swung into the room for the third time. After dropping two spoons in the middle of the table, he emptied the tray, which held two bowls of beef stew, a plate of cubed cheese instead of the usual bowl of melted cheese, and a basket of Phallic Delights. No butter.

Sebastian looked at Teaser. Teaser shrugged and walked away. Obviously Philo didn't think their visitor deserved a delicacy like butter. Or olives.

Probably just as well, Sebastian decided as he took a Delight out of the basket. This wasn't a meal he wanted to linger over.

"That's disgusting," Koltak said, staring at the Delight in Sebastian's hand.

"It's bread," Sebastian snapped. "If you don't want to eat it because of how it's shaped, then don't eat it." Dropping the bread into the bowl of stew, he poured a glass of wine and sat back. It scraped something inside him to know he still wanted his father's acceptance. Pointless, useless way to feel, since he'd done without that acceptance all his life. Especially when the "wench" comment pricked something that was less than a memory, more like a faded impression of the times Koltak had come to Nadia's home to drag him back to Wizard City and the journey had required staying overnight at an inn.

If Koltak hadn't been a wizard, if he hadn't had that authority to hide behind, he would have been nothing more than a crude, unlikable man. Maybe, by refusing to accept an incubus for a son, he's done me more of a favor than I'd realized. Instead of learning from him, I'd had Aunt Nadia showing me what it meant to be a good person.

Koltak hesitated. Then hunger overcame disgust and he grabbed a Delight from the basket and took a big bite. He dug into the stew with the same mixture of disapproval and hunger on his face.

His own appetite gone, Sebastian drank wine and watched his father devour the meal. While Koltak mopped up the last of the stew with a piece of bread, he drained his glass, pushed his own untouched meal aside, and leaned forward, resting his arms on the table.

"What do you want?" he asked.

Koltak belched. Then he sighed. "Your report of violent deaths was just the first of many. If the council had listened—"

"If *you* had listened!"

Anger flashed in Koltak's eyes before he fixed his gaze on the table. "Yes, all right. If *I* had listened. It's worse than you realize, Sebastian. The Landscapers' School was attacked."

"I know." Remembering what he'd seen soured the wine in his belly. "I had ... business ... at the school, but it was too late. I didn't see anyone alive. Barely got out of there myself."

"Then you saw. You *know*."

"That the Eater of the World has escaped and is loose in the landscapes? Yes, I know."

The shock he saw in Koltak's face couldn't have been an act.

"No," Koltak said. "Not the Eater of the World. Even—" He stopped, made an effort to regain control. "The Wizards' Council is aware that some of the dark landscapes that were taken out of the world have been ... appearing ... in other landscapes, that a Dark force is manipulating the landscapes to allow these places access to the rest of the world again. It has to be stopped, has to be destroyed. You can see that, can't you?"

"I can see that," Sebastian said.

"Then you must come with me to Wizard City and talk to the council."

"No." He shook his head. "I'll tell you everything I can about the deaths here in the Den. I'll tell you everything I saw at the Landscapers' School. But I won't go to Wizard City. I won't." His voice sharpened when Koltak began to protest. "There's no reason for me to go and every reason to stay. I gave my word I'd protect the Den."

"Then protect it!" Koltak pressed the heels of his hands against his temples, as if trying to squeeze out the right words. "Don't you realize what's going to happen to Ephemera without the Landscapers?"

"The landscapes will be vulnerable. The Eater will be able to alter—"

"You fool! It's worse than that." Koltak clenched his hands and banged them on the table. "Without the Landscapers, there is nothing that stands between Ephemera and the human heart. The dark landscapes will only add to the madness. Picture it, Sebastian. A baby cries and the family's well changes to salt water— undrinkable. Two girls, who consider themselves rivals, run into each other in front of a sweetshop and argue— and boulders suddenly push up through the street, stranding wagons and carriages that can't get through, possibly even hurting people. *Ephemera manifests feelings.* It always has. The Landscapers are the only ones able to restrain the manifestations."

Sebastian sat back, stunned. Was that what Glorianna had meant when she'd said he was an anchor? That his feelings for the Den, his affection for the place, kept it in balance? But not just his feelings. Her feelings, too. Glorianna Belladonna resonated through the Den.

But something wasn't quite right about what Koltak was saying. If the Den had a person as its anchor, wouldn't other places have anchors as well? After all, the Landscapers' signature resonances might set the "flavor" of their particular landscapes, but they couldn't be everywhere all the time.

And why did his head suddenly feel stuffy, as if something were pushing at him from inside his skull? Could wishing for a head cold actually produce one? If *that* was the case, he was going to think healthy thoughts from now on.

"You think you're safe here," Koltak said. "And maybe you are for a while. But if the rest of Ephemera becomes unstable, how long will this place last? The turmoil will break through—and will pull everyone down with it."

"How . . ." Sebastian poured more wine and gulped it down, trying to clear his throat, hoping to clear his head. "How am I supposed to help you stop that?"

"We're trying to find any of the Landscapers who are still out there, trying to get word to them to avoid going back to the school. We knew something had happened at the school, something bad, but we couldn't find out what it was. Every wizard who had gone to investigate didn't come back. We're fighting blind, Sebastian. Some of the bridges have been broken, leaving us with no access to a number of landscapes. Leaving us with no way to reach or help the people who may be struggling to survive. The council wanted to talk to you because you could tell us about the deaths that had taken place here, give us some idea of what was coming out of those hidden, dark landscapes. But you've also seen the school. You're the only one who has. You're the only one who can tell us what we're facing. You *must* come with me!"

"No." Sebastian rubbed his forehead. Koltak was making sense. Why was he being so stubborn? Going with Koltak to report what he'd seen was the right thing to do. Wasn't it?

Koltak sighed. "I volunteered to try to find you. To make up for not having listened when you came to me for help. If another wizard had come here instead, telling you all the things I've just told you, would you have been willing to do what is right? You call yourself a Justice Maker. Does your justice—and mercy—begin and end with the streets of this place? I wasn't a good father. I know that. But what I did or didn't do in the past doesn't matter now. *Can't* matter now. Saving Ephemera is all that matters, and in that, I think, we're brothers on the same side of a war."

Truth rang through Koltak's words, resonated inside Sebastian. But something in him still resisted. If he'd been playing cards with Koltak, he would have walked away from the table long before now, following gut instinct that the man was somehow a cheat. He just couldn't figure out why he kept feeling the truth was somehow a lie.

But there was something Koltak hadn't considered: Anything he learned from the wizards he would pass on to Nadia, Glorianna, and Lee.

"Where did you cross over?" he asked.

"A plank bridge within sight of Wizard City. Crossed over to a dark landscape. Demons in the guise of horses."

"I know the place." He'd crossed that same bridge when he'd gotten out of Wizard City. Obviously Lee hadn't found every bridge that could provide access between Wizard City and any of Belladonna's landscapes.

"All right," Sebastian said. "I'll go with you. At least as far as the bridge. I'll decide if I'm going on to Wizard City at that point." He frowned. There was something about Ephemera, something he should remember. But the thought kept dancing just out of reach. "I'll find you a place to sleep for a few hours, then—"

"There's no time!" Desperation rang in Koltak's voice. "It took days to find you. Who knows what's happened in the other landscapes while I've been searching for you."

There it was again. That feeling that something wasn't right. "You spent days wandering through the waterhorses' landscape?"

"I crossed over bridges, hoping one of them would lead to you. Ended up in places called Dunberry and Foggy Downs and the like in some other part of the world."

He'd never heard of those places. "And you left Wizard City on foot? With no supplies?"

"There was an ... attack," Koltak replied. "The horse was killed. I escaped. Finally found my way here after that."

If he had a little more time, maybe he could figure out what was bothering him about all this. "You need to rest."

"I'll rest when the task is done. When I've done what I can to make Ephemera safe again."

The quiet dignity in Koltak's voice lanced Sebastian's heart, turning aside all doubts.

"I need to go back to the bordello to pack a few things. Leave some instructions," Sebastian said.

Koltak pushed back his chair and rose to his feet. "I'll go with you, if you have no objections."

Sebastian just nodded. "Wait here a minute."

He caught Lynnea just as she entered the courtyard with another order.

"Sebastian, who is that man? Teaser said he's a wizard, that he's not a good man."

He's my father. And I don't think he is a good man. "I have to leave for a couple of days. Three at the most. Bad things are happening in the other landscapes. The wizards—the other Justice Makers—have asked for my help. I have to go, Lynnea."

Worry filled her eyes.

Sebastian brushed a finger down her cheek. "You stay safe, all right? Ask one of the bull demons to escort you back to the bordello if Teaser isn't around."

"I will."

"Miss me a little?"

"I already do."

He stepped aside to let her deliver the food on her tray. Then he found Teaser.

"Did that wizard whore scoop out half your brains and fill your head with sand?" Teaser said before Sebastian finished telling him why he was leaving.

That was pretty much how his head felt, but he didn't tell Teaser that. "I'm doing what's right."

"For them, maybe."

"Teaser."

"I'm just saying."

"I have to go."

"Why? We don't deal with those landscapes anyway."

Frustration filled Sebastian. He hadn't expected Teaser to get scrappy about this. "Are you sure we don't deal with them? Are you sure we can survive if those other landscapes are destroyed? I'm *not* sure."

Teaser looked away.

"I'm going to leave a message for Lee, telling him about the bridge and the places Koltak was able to reach through the waterhorses' landscape. I'll leave it in your room. If he shows up before I get back, you make sure he gets the message. And look after Lynnea."

"We'll look after each other, I guess. Kind of like family."

Looking at Teaser's wistful smile, Sebastian felt a shimmer of rightness go through him. "We are family."

Pleased and embarrassed, Teaser tipped his head toward the dining room door. "That one is impatient."

How long had Koltak been standing at the door, watching him?

"Sebastian?" Teaser said. "Travel lightly."

"I'll be back as soon as I can." As he walked away

from Teaser and passed the doorway, he said to Koltak, "Let's go."

Watching Sebastian was like seeing his brother, Peter, again. The same indefinable quality that drew people to him, made them listen. The same combination of charm and steel. Peter Justice Maker. Never Peter, Wizard Third Level, or Wizard Peter. It had never been about being Somebody—not for Peter. It had always been about justice.

But believing in justice hadn't prevented Peter from disappearing into the landscapes, never to return.

Of course, no one in Wizard City had known darling Peter had sired two children with a Landscaper. So maybe his disappearance *had* been a kind of justice— the punishment for having done the forbidden.

Koltak pushed the thoughts away as Sebastian finished a discussion with some kind of demons that were a combination of flesh and a thick bicycle without wheels.

"The demon cycles will take us as far as the bridge that crosses over to Wizard City," Sebastian said when he returned to the corner where Koltak waited. "After that, Guardians and Guides willing, we'll find someone to give us a ride."

We. Sebastian had said *we.* The mind control was working.

To save Ephemera, Koltak chanted silently. *For the good of Ephemera.*

They went down a side street and entered a building halfway down the block.

Plush. Well-kept. He'd seen places like this in the cities of many landscapes—he had needs like any other man—but the only times he'd been in a place that looked this expensive was when a well-to-do family paid for the room and the woman in return for a favor. All very discreetly, of course.

Sebastian paused at the foot of the stairs, as if something was troubling him. Koltak resumed his silent chant. *To save Ephemera. For the good of Ephemera.*

The room on the third floor was large enough to have a separate sitting area and didn't shout "whore." It would seem Sebastian had done well for himself.

The room felt masculine, but there were touches of femininity.

"You live with a woman?" Koltak asked, wondering how an incubus did business with a female in residence.

"None of your business," Sebastian snapped, pulling a pack out of the bottom of the wardrobe.

"No, it's not." He saw the hesitation again. The boy had always had a will of steel. *For the good of Ephemera. To save Ephemera.*

Two changes of underwear went into the pack. Two shirts.

Then Sebastian went through a door, closing it behind him. A moment later Koltak heard the bang and grumble of old water pipes.

Not sure how long Sebastian would be occupied, Koltak scanned the room as he reached into the inner pocket of his robe and withdrew the folded, sealed paper that contained Ephemera's salvation. He'd worried that he wouldn't find a good place to leave the document—a place where he could be certain it would be found, but not too quickly. Sebastian had conveniently solved the problem for him by having a female living with him.

The water pipes stopped grumbling.

Koltak tucked the paper between the seat cushion and the arm of one of the sitting room chairs, leaving enough of it visible to catch the eye.

"Ready?" Koltak asked when Sebastian walked back into the room, shifting slightly to hide the chair and keep Sebastian from noticing the paper.

"Let's go."

When they reached the street and Koltak saw the two demons waiting for them, he balked. "No."

Sebastian adjusted the pack on his back, then swung

a leg over the creature's leather seat. "You're the one insisting that we get there as soon as possible. The demon cycles are the fastest way to travel."

Reluctant but unable to think of how to refuse when he *had* been insisting they needed to reach Wizard City as quickly as possible, Koltak mounted the other demon cycle, setting his feet on the footrests the way Sebastian had done.

"Hold on," Sebastian said.

Koltak's hands ached from gripping the handlebars so hard. As the cycles moved sedately up the main street, he relaxed a little. They weren't going any faster than a horse could walk. Why couldn't they have used a natural beast instead of *these* creatures?

"How many days do you think it will take to reach the bridge?" he asked.

Sebastian looked at him, his expression hesitant and puzzled.

Had to stop asking about time. The boy wasn't stupid. Given enough time to consider the nature of Ephemera, Sebastian would come to the correct conclusion, which would be disastrous. *Need to move quickly to save Ephemera. Need to find the bridge to protect Ephemera.*

Sebastian grinned wickedly. "It won't take that long."

They moved sedately up the main street until they reached the dirt lane. Then . . .

Koltak screamed as the demon cycles surged forward, whipping above the dirt lane at speeds a galloping horse couldn't match or sustain. The cottage flashed by. Sebastian shouted, "Border ahead."

The cycles lifted like a horse jumping a fence. Koltak had no idea if it was necessary to cross the border from this side or if it was the demon's perverse attempt to scare him into pissing himself.

The ground he'd toiled to cross flowed under him, and the moon, almost full now, illuminated the land, giving it a strange beauty and peace he hadn't noticed or felt in all the days he'd been trapped in this landscape.

The demons rumbled and slowed down as they approached what looked like pale, barren earth that had a ring of boulders at the center of the fan-shaped area.

"It's sand," Sebastian said. Leaning forward, he tapped the demon on the shoulder. "Get us a little closer, but go slow. Be careful."

The cycles edged up to within an arm's length of the place.

"We've gone the wrong way," Koltak said. "I don't remember seeing a place like this."

"No," Sebastian said in an odd voice, raising a hand to point at something half-buried in the sand. "I think this is the right way. Look."

Koltak gasped when he realized he was looking at the severed horse's head. "But . . . it wasn't like this before."

"It's been altered. I'm thinking if you cross the stones outlining the sand, you'll end up in another landscape a long way from here." Sebastian looked at Koltak, wariness in every line of his body. "What killed the horse?"

"What does it matter?" Koltak replied, trying to hammer the fear back with righteous anger. *She* had done this. Must have done this. Had she altered an unprotected landscape into this wasteland? Were there towns out there, suddenly awash in sand?

"What killed the horse?" Sebastian demanded.

"Death rollers. There were death rollers in the pond."

Sebastian took a deep breath. Blew it out slowly. "Doesn't look like they're going to find any water where they are now. Come on. If this was the same pond, we're not that far from the bridge. I couldn't have walked more than a couple of hours before I met the waterhorse." He paused, then added softly, "I wonder what happened to it."

For the good of Ephemera, Koltak chanted silently. *To save Ephemera.*

They headed north. One hill looked like another, as far as Koltak was concerned, just as one stand of trees looked much the same as all the others, but Sebastian slowed at each stand of trees, circling each one to study it from every direction.

"It's this one," Sebastian said. "After crossing the bridge and walking for a while, I turned south at a stand of trees. I think it's this one."

Koltak bit his tongue to keep from saying something imprudent. He couldn't risk saying anything that would jar Sebastian's focused thought of reaching the bridge.

They turned west, and in less time than Koltak would have thought possible, they reached a narrow creek.

But not a bridge. No sign of the wood planks.

The demon cycles drifted north, following the creek.

"I see the planks!" Koltak said, his heart pounding with excitement. Almost there. Almost done. If Dalton didn't fail him ...

Suddenly the cycles swung away from the creek, snarling viciously. They circled back, ending up north of the planks, facing the way they'd come.

"Something was here," Sebastian said quietly. "Something bad." He looked at the two demons, who finally stopped snarling. "But I don't think it's there anymore." He looked east—the direction that would take him back to the Den.

No, Koltak thought. *No. Not now. To save Ephemera. For the good of Ephemera.*

Sebastian leaned forward and whispered in the demon's ear—and kept whispering until the demon bobbed its head in agreement. Then he swung off the cycle and adjusted his pack.

Koltak hurried to do the same. Uneasiness rippled through him when the demon cycles didn't go away, just moved off a couple of man-lengths from the bridge.

"They'll stay a little while, in case we need them," Sebastian said. "If there's something bad on the other side of the bridge, we need to get away from it fast."

It scraped at his pride, but he made his voice sound weary and weak. "Would you mind crossing first, Sebastian? If there *is* trouble, you're younger and . . . more fit . . . to get back across the bridge."

Hesitation. Wariness.

For the good of Ephemera. To save Ephemera.

Sebastian moved toward the bridge, testing the ground with each step, keeping his eyes on the spot the demon cycles didn't like. One foot on the wooden planks. Both feet. One step toward the other side of the bridge. Another step.

Koltak hurried to the bridge, stepped on the planks. Sebastian was at the other end of the bridge. One more step and he'd cross over.

He didn't take that step. Just stood there.

Koltak rushed across the bridge and gave Sebastian a hard shove, sending the younger man stumbling off the bridge.

"Seize him!" Koltak shouted as he took the last step to bring him back to the landscape where all his ambitions would finally bear fruit.

His heart filled with glee as he watched Sebastian trying to fight off two guards. A knee to the groin had one guard rolling away, retching. The other guard seemed more capable but wasn't trying to do more than restrain Sebastian.

"You lying bastard!" Sebastian shouted, almost shaking off the guard before Dalton and another guard could reach the bridge.

In the light of the flickering torches that were planted on either side of the bridge, Koltak saw the intent in Sebastian's eyes, but couldn't move fast enough to prevent being struck.

Lightning lashed out from Sebastian's hand. It would have been a killing strike if the guard hadn't hit Sebastian in the head, ruining his aim.

Koltak felt the power rip through his left foot as Sebastian fell to the ground, stunned by the blow.

"Truss him up before he can do any more damage," Dalton snapped.

One of the guards untied a rope hanging from his

belt while the other stripped off Sebastian's pack. Koltak waited until Sebastian's hands were tied behind his back and his feet bound before taking a limping step toward his son.

The pain was hideous, and he suspected he'd lost the toes on that foot. But he took another limping step forward, raised his hand . . .

. . . and Dalton stepped in front of him.

"No," Dalton said. "You can't strike down a defenseless man."

"He'll be less trouble without his legs," Koltak snarled.

He saw the shock in Dalton's eyes and knew he'd made an error. This guard captain wasn't suitable for serving the power in Wizard City. But that was something Harland would rectify. For now, he needed Dalton and his men.

"You're right," Koltak said. "I wasn't thinking. A reaction to the pain."

Dalton nodded, but it was clear the man wasn't convinced.

"Tell me why," Sebastian gasped.

Dalton hesitated, then stepped aside.

Koltak stared at his son. The blood smearing Sebastian's hair and face gave him some satisfaction, but not enough. Not nearly enough.

"I'm no use to you," Sebastian said. "Why go through all the trouble to bring me here?"

"But you are of use to us," Koltak said. "You're going to deliver the enemy into our hands. There was no way for us to reach Nadia or Lee, so you're the only one she'd come here to save."

"No." Sebastian groaned. "No."

"Yes." Koltak smiled. "So you see? I didn't lie. By bringing Belladonna here, where we can destroy her, you *will* save Ephemera."

I do not know how things are done in other places in the world, but here in the landscapes there are three kinds of justice: common justice, Wizards' Justice, and Heart's Justice.

Common justice is performed by law enforcers and the magistrates who hold court to settle minor wrong-doing and disputes that arise wherever people gather to live.

Whenever violence has been done, a wizard is summoned to decide the penalty. Sometimes it is Wizards' Justice—the lightning they can summon that, while inflicting agony, is a quick death.

But sometimes the penalty requires something less, and more, than death, and the wizard will send word that a Landscaper is needed for Heart's Justice.

Nothing produces more fear—and more hope—than Heart's Justice. The Landscaper forges a direct link between Ephemera and the accused, and that person is sent to the darkest landscape that resonates in his heart. It is an inescapable punishment, because no matter what landscape the person ends up in, he must live with the knowledge that this reflects who he is, and whatever hardships he endures in that place have come from his own heart.

But there is also the hope that a person will learn from his past and change enough so that, one day, he'll be able to cross over to another, gentler landscape.

Most of the time, though, the person disappears into some desolate part of the world and is never seen again.

—*The Magistrate's Book of Justice*

Chapter Twenty-two

L ynnea closed the door, then leaned her forehead
against it, not quite ready to face the empty room.
She'd spent plenty of hours alone here, but it felt
different this time—because Sebastian wasn't just out
and about somewhere in the Den. He was going to another landscape—the *wizards'* landscape—traveling
with a man who made her uneasy, even though she'd
gotten only glimpses of him. There had been something
about the wizard that made her glad the bull demons
had wanted a second helping of omelets and had lingered at the table while the man had talked to Sebastian.

Turning, she walked to the pale squares in the opposite wall. With the curtains open, the streetlights cut
through the darkness enough for her to cross the room
and light the oil lamp on the table by the window instead of fumbling with the candle on the stand next to
the door.

Feeling sorry for herself because Sebastian had to go
away for a couple of days was foolish and selfish. She
had plenty to do. The bag Nadia had left for her contained skeins of yarn—so much softer and finer than the
coarse wool Mam used to give her—and knitting nee-
dles in different sizes. She didn't know if the Den had a
particular celebration around the winter solstice, but

most landscapes had some kind of festivities. So the blue skeins would be a scarf for Teaser and the green skeins would be a scarf for Sebastian. There were enough undyed skeins to make herself a shawl—maybe with bands of blue and green at the ends. And Teaser had offered to take her to one of the little music holes where the musicians were developing some style of music he swore was going to outrage the prissy prigs in the daylight landscapes—and make all the humans with heat and sass wild to hear it. Or they could both enjoy a frustrating hour of him trying to teach her to play cards.

Since she'd lost the coin toss with Teaser over which of them would use the bathroom first, she could knit a few rows of the scarf she was making for him while waiting her turn. For a man who complained about how much time *she* spent in the bathroom, he certainly did his share of primping.

She walked over to the bed to retrieve the yarn bag she kept tucked under it, then paused. She pulled back the covers and lifted her pillow. Sebastian sometimes left little sketches under her pillow—sometimes flowers as he remembered them or faces of the people who lived in the Den.

Nothing there. Of course, there wouldn't be. The wizard had been impatient to leave. Sebastian wouldn't have stayed in the room any longer than was needed to pack a few things.

She pulled out the yarn bag, turned toward the stuffed chairs that made up their sitting area—and saw something white sticking up between the cushion and the arm of the chair.

Smiling, she dropped the bag and hurried over to the chair. Maybe this was like a treasure hunt. Mam hadn't allowed her to attend parties where she might start thinking too much of herself, so she'd never participated in a treasure hunt, but she'd heard other girls talking about them. Would she start finding little sketches tucked here and there in the room?

She stopped smiling when she picked up the paper. It

wasn't sketching paper, and it wasn't new. It was a bit crumpled and dirty, as if it had been carried a long way, and the word on the front of it . . .

She could read a little and do her numbers enough to make sure she wasn't cheated at the market, and she was getting better at reading now that she could read printed books that had stories—something else Mam had forbidden her to have—but handwriting was still a struggle for her.

She went back to the lamp, turning the paper to see the writing better.

A chill went through her as she sounded out the word. *Belladonna.*

Her hands shook as she turned the paper over. It had been folded to form a packet that would keep the message private, closed with red wax that had been pressed with an ornate, official-looking seal.

It could be nothing more than a message Sebastian had been asked to deliver. But something inside her knew it wasn't an innocent message.

Dread shuddered through her as she pried up the wax seal and unfolded the paper.

The handwriting inside was neat and precise, probably done by someone who made a living writing out important documents.

She stumbled over some of the words, but the message was clear enough.

"No," she moaned. "Oh, no."

She didn't think, didn't knock. She simply rushed into the bathroom. Finding it empty, she crossed the room and flung open the other door.

Stripped for his bath, Teaser yelped when he saw her. Then he dove for the bed, grabbed a pillow, and held it in front of him.

"I'm naked!" he shouted. "You can't be in here when I'm naked."

Thrown by the near-panic in his voice, she stared at him. "For pity's sake. You're an incubus. You *like* being naked in front of women."

"You're not a woman. You're Sebastian's lady. Go away."

Sebastian. She stepped into the room and held out the paper. "That wizard left a message for Belladonna. Read it." She took a step toward him.

He skipped back a step. "If the message is for Belladonna, I shouldn't be reading it. Neither should you."

"*Teaser!* The wizards are saying Sebastian killed the woman who died here a few weeks ago. *They're going to hurt him.*"

"What?"

"*Read it!*"

He took the paper, backed up until he reached the oil lamp he'd lit, then read. As he read, the pillow slipped from his grasp, forgotten.

"Daylight," he whispered. "They're summoning the strongest Landscapers to come to Wizard City to administer Heart's Justice, but they'll perform Wizards' Justice if they receive no response to the summons." He frowned, then shook his head. "That doesn't make sense. They must know the school was attacked. How do they expect any—" He stopped. Stared at the paper. "It's her. The wizards have never been able to find Belladonna, so they're threatening Sebastian to get her to come to them."

"We have to do something," Lynnea cried. "Sebastian didn't kill that woman. You know he didn't."

Teaser looked at her, his eyes bleak. "What are we supposed to do? Sebastian has been gone for hours. Went off with the wizard on a couple of demon cycles. They've probably already crossed over to the landscape that holds Wizard City. No way to catch up with them even if we knew where to find the bridge. And nobody knows how to find Belladonna. She comes to a landscape when she feels like it."

"Nadia will know how to find her, and I know how to find Nadia." She snatched the paper out of his hand and headed out the door.

"Wait!" Teaser leaped, closing the distance between

them, and grabbed her arm. "Don't you understand? This is what those maggot-filled bastards want. They *want* someone to find Belladonna. And once she's in reach of the Wizards' Council, they'll kill her *and* Sebastian."

Lynnea tried to shake him off. "I have to do something. I won't let them hurt Sebastian. I won't."

Teaser started to argue, then just shook his head. "All right. She has to be told about this, so we have to find Belladonna. But taking a few minutes won't matter at this point."

"But—"

"Listen, will you? We both need a quick wash and fresh clothes. If we have to talk to anyone in the daylight landscapes besides Sebastian's auntie, it's best to look respectable."

She swallowed hard to push her heart out of her throat. "We?"

Teaser looked uneasy, but he shrugged. "I'll go with you."

"Why?"

He released her arm and stepped back. "Because we're family."

🙢

Dalton walked out of the Wizards' Hall, then stopped and stared blindly at the courtyard and gardens in front of him.

He'd expected a reprimand for failing to protect Wizard Koltak from the stranger's attack. But this?

Stripped of his command and captain's rank. Exiled from Wizard City. Not because he had failed to protect Koltak but because he'd stopped Koltak from harming a man who was bound and defenseless.

A man who believed he had been betrayed.

You're making a mistake, Koltak! the stranger had shouted as they rode back to Wizard City. *The Eater of the World is out there! Belladonna's the only hope you have of saving Ephemera!*

The stranger's fate was in the hands of the wizards now. He couldn't help the man, wasn't even sure if he could help himself at this point. He had to get his wife and children out of the city before tomorrow's sunset, along with whatever household goods they could take with them in the big merchant wagon that had belonged to Aldys's father.

But where were they supposed to go? And who could he ask about other landscapes whose answer he could trust?

As if pulled by an invisible string, Dalton's head turned in the direction of the detention rooms.

There was one person who might know.

A quick glance around the courtyard. Addison was standing by the wrought-iron gate that led to the street. No sign of Guy or Henley. They must have gone back to the barracks.

Dalton headed for that part of the courtyard, walking past the locked doors and shuttered windows of the detention rooms until he came to the last one. When he'd left the prisoner there, he'd noticed a fist-sized piece of window glass had been broken out of the far-thest window. Maybe the last person who had been de-tained in that room had broken the glass in a futile effort to escape. Or maybe he'd been desperate to hear something besides the silence of his own heart. What-ever the reason, the opening was there, and Dalton thanked the Guides of the Heart for this chance to talk to the man.

He leaned against the wall, close to that corner of the shuttered window. "Psst. Can you hear me?" He kept his voice low to avoid being overheard by anyone who might pass by. If another guard saw him, he could say he was keeping watch on the prisoner. But if a wizard no-ticed him, he had no doubt he'd be occupying another of those locked rooms and would never see his wife and children again.

A shuffling sound. The thump of someone collapsing against the wall.

"What do you want?" The voice sounded rough, exhausted.

What did he want? To go back to that moment when the stranger had stumbled off the bridge. To have a chance to follow the gut feeling he'd had when he'd seen Koltak step off the bridge.

"If I could do it over, I would have let you escape and go back to wherever you came from."

"Why?"

"When Koltak stepped off the bridge, everything felt wrong. *He* felt wrong. You didn't." *And you didn't use the lightning to harm my men. You could have. Any wizard here would have.* "What you said to Koltak about the Eater of the World. Is it true?"

Silence. Then, "It's true."

Not much time. Someone could come along at any moment. "I've been exiled from the city. I have to get my family to another landscape. Is there any place I can take them where they'll be safe?"

"Why are you asking me?"

"I don't think you would harm the innocent. Whatever wrong I did you by following orders, my family is innocent."

A long silence. "Heart's hope lies within Belladonna. Her landscapes . . . the only safe places. Resonating bridge . . . might get you . . . to one of them. But if the wizards destroy her . . . no hope at all. For anyone."

He had to go. He'd already lingered too long. But . . . "I'm sorry for the part I played in this."

Another silence.

As Dalton stepped away from the window, he heard, "Travel lightly."

Addison was still waiting for him when he reached the gate.

"Best not to linger here, Cap'n," Addison said. "This place has got a bad feel to it today. More than usual."

"I'm not your captain," Dalton said as he opened the gate and walked out. "I've been exiled."

"I'm sorry for the trouble of it, but I can't say I'm

sorry you'll be going." Addison shook his head and sighed. "Maybe this is just the Guardians' way of telling you it's time to go."

Maybe, Dalton thought. But deep down in his heart, he didn't think his exile had anything to do with the Light.

Sebastian shuffled back to the wobbly table and chair, the only pieces of furniture in the room. No candle or oil lamp. The slats in the closed shutters let in a little daylight, but this room would hold a bleak darkness once the sun went down.

Bracing his hands on the table, he lowered himself into the chair and waited until he felt fairly steady before reaching for the canteen of water—and wondered if the guard captain had provided the water as a kindness. He took a mouthful of water, then closed the canteen and set it aside. Shutting his eyes, he sat very still, waiting for the pain in his head to subside again to a dull throb.

Daylight, he hurt! But despite the lump on his head and the shallow cut from the first blow that had soaked part of his hair with blood, he didn't think he was badly injured. Hurt, certainly, but there didn't seem to be anything wrong with him that couldn't be put right with a headache powder and some sleep.

Except for the feeling of rough fingers lightly scratching inside his head. Except for the whispering voices that were close enough for him to hear but too far away for him to make out what they were saying— voices that seemed to creep closer whenever his mind lost focus.

Could wizards do that? Creep into a mind? Was that the way they determined whether someone was truly innocent? Not by the questions that were asked for the sake of formality, but by this intrusion?

He wouldn't be able to keep them out forever. His

body craved sleep—and sleep would leave him vulnerable to the voices. The light scratching would become a torment soon. But he could choose now what those voices would find when they finally breached his mind and what would stay hidden in the core of his heart.

He should have insisted on having an hour to consider Koltak's request/command/plea. He should have given himself that hour to consider the good and bad of leaving the Den to come to Wizard City. If he had, he would have realized what had troubled him about Koltak's journey to the Den.

Koltak had wanted him as bait for a trap but hadn't *really* wanted to find him, because Koltak had *never* wanted to be around him. Ephemera had responded to that heart conflict by making the journey difficult.

That was what had troubled him—the fact that Koltak had spent days trying to find the Den. But the words "to save Ephemera" had swept away the thought before it could form, before it could become solid enough to resist being influenced.

Sebastian opened his eyes and stared at the wall. Was that what Koltak had done? Influenced his decision with the plea to save the world? But he hadn't felt this scratching, this sense of intrusion.

Maybe that was why the council had chosen Koltak. Maybe there was enough similarity in resonance between a father and son, despite their animosity, that he wouldn't sense the intrusion. When Koltak talked about saving the world, the words had rung true.

Liar. Deceiver. Raper of truth.

If Ephemera truly gave each person what the heart deserved, Koltak would receive the reward of his ambitions—and the reward would be bitter.

Now wasn't the time to think about Koltak. While he could, he had to take what was most precious to him and hide it away, deep inside his heart . . . where the wizards would never find her.

He didn't dare let her name echo in his mind, but he pictured her—the blue eyes, the wavy brown hair, the expressive face that looked the most innocent when she was trying to learn how to be naughty. How she looked wearing that catsuit. How she felt when he made love with her.

His rabbit, who was changing a little more every day into a tigress.

For a moment he could feel her resonating inside him. Then he tucked away all his memories, all his feelings for her.

Glorianna wouldn't come for him. He didn't want her to come for him. There was too much at stake to throw it away trying to save one man.

So the wizards would kill him.

But even as he died, he would keep what he cherished the most away from them.

Chapter Twenty-three

Standing at the edge of the woods behind Sebastian's cottage, Lynnea tried to clear her mind and heart of everything that wasn't good, wasn't positive. To travel lightly. Now, more than ever, it was important for her to travel lightly. Despite being in a different landscape, Nadia's house wasn't far from here, but to get there she needed positive thoughts. A gentle heart. They were going to cross the bridge that was on this path in the woods. They were going to find Nadia, find Glorianna, find some way to free Sebastian from those wizards.

And if Teaser didn't stop taking forever to light the candle in the lantern he'd brought with him, she was going to find a large branch—or uproot a small tree—and give him a whack for every minute she'd stood there waiting.

No, no, no. She couldn't think that way. It might be an honest feeling, but it wouldn't help them cross the bridge.

Travel lightly. Travel lightly. Travel—

Finally! "Ready?" she asked.

"Guess so."

But he was still crouched, staring at the lit candle. Not moving.

Bristling with impatience, certain that every minute they delayed might change her life in ways she didn't

want to imagine, she opened her mouth to yell at him.
Then she took a good look at his face.

"Are you afraid to cross the bridge?" she asked.

"Maybe," Teaser mumbled. "Some." He shot to his
feet. "All right, I'm afraid."

He was. Had been, she suddenly realized, ever since
he'd said he'd go with her. "But you've been to daylight
landscapes when you've . . ." She trailed off, not feeling
enough like a tigress to talk about things Teaser did with
women, even if she did those same things with Sebastian. "And you've met Nadia."

"This is different." Teaser shifted from one foot to
the other, looking at the ground, at the trees, anywhere but at her. "What if I can't cross over to a landscape held by Sebastian's auntie? What if my crossing
with you shifts something when we reach the bridge
and we end up someplace different, someplace . . .
bad?"

"This is a stationary bridge that crosses only between
the Den and Aurora. Nadia told me so." Had made a
point of telling her before she and Sebastian left
Nadia's house.

"Even stationary bridges don't always take you
where you want to go," Teaser argued. "Not if you don't
resonate with that landscape."

"You don't have to come with me," Lynnea said
gently. "The bridge isn't that far down the path. I'll be
safe enough."

He shook his head. "You can't go alone."

She felt like she had tried to squeeze through an
opening and had gotten stuck. He wouldn't let her go
alone, and he was afraid to come with her. She'd never
crossed any bridges—at least, none that she remembered—until Ewan had left her on the side of the road
instead of taking her to the Landscapers' School. But
she knew a stationary bridge went to only a few specific
landscapes, so even if you didn't end up in the landscape
you wanted, you could usually get back to where you

started. The resonating bridges, on the other hand, held the possibility of crossing over to *anywhere,* and only the secret places in your heart knew where you would end up. And even if you turned right around and crossed the bridge again, it wasn't likely that you'd return to the landscape you'd just left.

Even though she knew the bridge in the woods crossed only to Nadia's home village from this side and to the Den from the other side, she couldn't deny that Teaser had a reason to worry.

But they couldn't just stay there.

"Why are you coming with me?" she asked.

"Because you can't go alone."

Obviously that thought was set in stone. "And?"

"Because, if we're family, I should help Sebastian."

"And?"

He sighed. "Because it's the right thing to do?"

"Yes. Because it's the right thing to do." Picking up the yarn bag, which now held a change of clothes, a few coins, and the letter to Belladonna, she held out her other hand. "I don't think Ephemera will stop us from doing the right thing."

He slung his pack over his shoulder, picked up the lantern, then took hold of her hand in a grip that made her wince. "I'm ready."

We need to find Nadia, Lynnea thought as they hurried down the path. *We need to find Glorianna. We need to save Sebastian. Nadia is the first step of the journey. We're going to Nadia's house. Travel lightly, travel lightly. We're going to Nadia's house and—*

"Daylight!" Teaser ducked his head to protect his eyes from the dappled sunlight.

"We did it!" Lynnea looked back. There had to be a marker somewhere, something solid and stable enough to hold the magic of a bridge, but she didn't see anything. Still, she couldn't deny they'd left the Den. The daylight was proof of that.

Tugging her hand free of Teaser's grip, she rubbed

feeling back into her fingers while she waited for him to blow out the candle in the lantern. Then she followed the path, moving at a brisk pace.

"I remember this," she said, slowing down after a few minutes. "We took the path that curved around this big stone to go back to the Den, so"—she pointed—"Nadia's house must be that way."

After a few more minutes that felt like forever, they reached the wooden gate in that part of the stone wall that surrounded Nadia's personal gardens. Through the gate, over the lawn, and there she was, pulling open the screen door so she could pound her fist against the closed kitchen door.

"Nadia?" she called. "Nadia! It's Lynnea! We have to talk to you!" She looked around the gardens, trying to spot something out of place, something that meant trouble had come here. Nothing looked wrong to her, so she went back to pounding on the door.

"Give her a minute," Teaser said.

"Why isn't she answering?" Lynnea cried, feeling the frustration welling up inside her. "Where could she be?"

"Maybe she's . . . occupied. You know."

Lynnea paused, fist raised, and stared at him. "You think she's not answering the door because she's having sex?" She pounded on the door with more vigor. "Nadia!"

"Not sex! I didn't say sex. Daylight, Lynnea. You're talking about Sebastian's auntie. I just meant . . . ladies take longer to answer a call of nature."

It took her a moment to work that out. Teaser was turning into a prude. Why couldn't he just say what he meant? "Well, why is she sitting on the toilet when we need her to answer the door?"

"It's not like she knew we were coming." He took a step back and looked up at the house. "Besides, I don't think she's here. With you making all that racket, she would have answered by now, no matter what she was doing."

Lynnea sagged against the door for a moment, then

stepped back to let the screen door slap shut. "You're right. She isn't here."

What was she supposed to do? She hadn't considered the possibility of not finding Nadia. Her eyes fixed on the broken part of the wall, the part she and Sebastian had stepped over when they'd come here from . . .

"We'll go to Sanctuary. People there know Lee, so they might know how to find Glorianna."

Teaser backed away. "No. I'm not going to Sanctuary. I *can't* go to Sanctuary. I'm an incubus."

"So is Sebastian," Lynnea snapped. "If he could go there, so can you."

"But—"

"Stay here then. Or go back to the Den, if that's what you want. But stop stalling!"

She pressed a hand over her mouth and stared at him, feeling as if she'd glimpsed the person she might have become if she'd stayed on the farm with Pa and Mam. Mam's tone of voice. Mam's harshness. Mam's way of cutting at a person with words, even when she didn't reinforce it with a blow. Teaser's fear was real— just as her fears, as a child, had been real. And harsh words that implied inadequacy, when it wasn't said outright, had never done anything to extinguish the fear.

"Teaser . . . I'm sorry. That wasn't kind."

For a moment his blue eyes were sharp with a predatory anger, reminding her that, no matter how he acted or how distant he was from the roots of his kind, he still came from a race of creatures that could kill you with your own emotions.

Then he looked away and was back to being the Teaser she knew.

"Doesn't matter," he mumbled.

"Yes, it does." She walked up to him and took his hand. "My . . . the woman who raised me . . . she sounded like that. She would have said things like that. I don't want to be like her. I don't want to sour the world that way."

He gave her hand a friendly squeeze and let go. "You're scared. So am I. So we're both acting like we've got half a brain between us. Time's passing. Let's do this if we're going to."

When they reached the clearing that held the bridge, she felt the difference. This was a resonating bridge. They had as much chance of reaching Sanctuary as they had of dancing on the moon.

Teaser huffed. "We're doing this for Sebastian, right?"

"Right."

"We'll be able to get to Sanctuary because we're doing a good thing, right?"

"Right."

"And if we end up in a snake-infested pit of a landscape, it was your doing because you were mean to me, right?"

She sighed and took his hand. "Right."

That said, they walked to the spot in the clearing that would let them cross over to . . .

❧

Sebastian sat on the floor, his back against the wall under the broken window. With the shutters closed, not much air came through the fist-sized hole in the glass, but he told himself the air smelled fresher in this part of the room.

He couldn't keep the voices out, couldn't do anything to block the relentless whispers.

No one will come for you. No one loves you. No one ever did. You don't deserve to be loved. Dreaming of daylight, incubus? There's no daylight for someone like you. There's no daylight in someone like you. Your heart is stone and barren earth. That's all you are. All you can ever be. That's all you deserve. A hard life. A barren life. A cold life. That's all you are, Sebastian. That's all you'll ever be. No one will come for you. No one loves you. No one ever did.

So many voices, all whispering the same thing. Some sounded cruelly gleeful, and those, by themselves, he might have been able to fight. But it was the gentle voices, the sad voices, saying the same words that wore him out and rubbed at his heart, sanding away the feelings that would have shown the words to be lies.

He *was* bleak. He *was* barren. He *was* cold.

He couldn't save himself from those relentless, whispering voices. So he put his strength into hiding the shining warmth that lived deep inside his heart.

Peace.

Lynnea breathed it in and felt her body relax. Despite the warmth of the day, there was an autumnal feel to the heat. Warm days, cooler nights. Did the leaves change and fall in Sanctuary? Did people walk through gardens that slept beneath snow? Or was it always summer here? No, not always summer. There would be a different kind of peace in seeing this landscape wearing its winter shades of gray.

"We're here," she said softly. She looked at Teaser, who had his eyes squeezed shut. "We reached Sanctuary."

His eyes opened enough to squint at the gardens that stretched out around them. Then his eyes popped open as a man strolling through the gardens noticed them and turned in their direction.

"It's all right," Lynnea said to Teaser as she moved forward to meet the man. "I met him the last time. Greetings, Yoshani," she added, raising her voice.

"Hey-a," Yoshani replied, smiling. "You have come back. And you have brought a friend." His brown eyes, so gentle and dark with wisdom, focused on Teaser.

Trying to ignore the tension building in Teaser, Lynnea shifted just enough to draw Yoshani's attention.

"We need to find Glorianna," she said. "Something bad has happened. She needs to be told."

Yoshani studied them and nodded. "Peace is cherished more after one has tasted sorrow. Come with me. Glorianna will not be hard to find."

And she wasn't. Glorianna was among a handful of men and women tidying up the flower beds in one part of the garden. Her initial smile of greeting faded as she looked into their eyes. By the time she read the message from the Wizards' Council that Lynnea gave her, her own eyes were green ice.

"Yoshani will take you to the guesthouse," Belladonna said as she folded the paper back into a packet. "I need to think."

For the first time since they'd arrived at Sanctuary, Teaser spoke. "Sebastian wouldn't want you going to Wizard City."

"I know," she replied softly. Then she walked away.

Before Lynnea could voice a protest, Yoshani laid a hand on her arm.

"She needs time to think," he said gently. "You need time to rest."

"What's going to happen?" Lynnea asked.

"What needs to happen," he replied. "If they had not closed their hearts, the other Landscapers could have learned much from Glorianna Belladonna. It is so easy, so seductive, to think that choosing the Light is always the right thing to do. But sometimes it is not. She has never chosen the easy path. She will do what needs to be done . . . no matter what it costs."

You are nothing, Sebastian. No one worth remembering, worth loving. Bleak. Barren. Empty of all Light. Cruelty birthed you. Misery suckled you. That is all there is for you. All there can ever be.

Hour after hour, they raped his heart, stripping away every memory of warmth and affection.

Helpless to stop the whispers, he curled up around the secret place inside him, keeping the shining warmth hidden, protected. He would never let them touch it. Never.

🦎

Glorianna sat on the bench near the koi pond. The heron had been by earlier that morning, and the fish were still hiding under the water plants. The message from the council was in her lap, held just firmly enough to keep the light breeze from snatching it away. It was tempting to let the air have the paper and take that taunting message somewhere else. Anywhere else.

When she heard the footsteps coming toward the bench, she didn't look away from the pond. She waited until Lee sat on the bench beside her, then handed him the message.

"Sebastian wouldn't want you to save him, not when it means bringing you within reach of the Wizards' Council," Lee said after he'd read the message.

"It's not Sebastian's choice."

"This is a trap. He's the bait. You know that."

"I know." Could she do this? Was she strong enough? What she was considering had never been done before, so the wizards would have no reason to think it was possible, let alone that it might prove dangerous to them. It also would mean putting things in motion and then leaving Sebastian's life in someone else's hands, but the strength and courage were there—if Lynnea didn't falter when the time came. And it would have to be Lynnea's choice. Every step of the journey would have to be Lynnea's choice. But it could be done, leaving her free to seek justice for other hearts—and deal with the wizards.

She looked at her brother. "Are you with me, Lee?"

He put one hand over hers. "Always."

"Then we have work to do. Talk to Teaser. Find out everything you can about where Sebastian was headed when he left with the wizard. We need to find the bridge that connects my landscapes with Wizard City. And then we need to deliver a message to the wizards."

"Glorianna . . . it's a trap. That's why they wanted Sebastian."

"It's a trap," she agreed. "But Sebastian isn't the bait."

Chapter Twenty-four

Glorianna watched Lee raise a hand in thanks as the demon cycles raced back to the Den.

"Well," he said, "that was clear thinking on Sebastian's part to ask the demon cycles to linger in this landscape to show us where the bridge was located."

She sniffed because, somehow, being miffed seemed like the right thing to do. "I'm sure he didn't tell them it was all right to chase the waterhorses."

"They didn't chase the little ones. They made a point of telling you that."

"Oh. Well. That makes it all right. What?" The last because Lee was grinning at her.

"We're squabbling."

"We are not."

"Are too."

"Are—" She stopped. She always felt as if she were ten years old when they started one of these arguments. "Maybe. So what if we are?"

"We only squabble when something has been wrong and we know it's going to be all right again. So I guess this idea of yours isn't so daft after all."

"It's not daft." Risky, certainly. And dangerous if it didn't work as well as she thought it would. But not daft. "Why did you have the demon cycles leave us here?" She waved a hand at the stand of trees.

"Because I can feel the bridge." Lee headed in a westerly direction and continued talking over his shoulder. "And I figured if we're moving at a walking pace, you'd have a better feel of the land and more warning if the Eater left any nasty surprises in this landscape."

Since she hadn't found the anchor the Eater had established in the waterhorses' landscape, and nasty surprises were a distinct possibility, she hurried to catch up to Lee and link her arm through his—both as a sign of sisterly affection and because, if there was danger, she could take them both back to her gardens in a heartbeat as long as she was touching him.

"Do you remember that time when Mother was sick for a whole week?" Glorianna asked.

"I remember." Lee smiled. "I was about nine and you were eleven."

She nodded. "Neighbors brought soups and broths for her, but we pretty much fended for ourselves—and survived my cooking."

"You went to the butcher's and the grocer's for food—"

"—with you helping to pull your sled, since it was too snowy to use anything else."

"The grocer was impressed that we were buying vegetables instead of sweets."

"And oranges, remember? They came from the south and traveled through a dozen landscapes before they got to Aurora, and each one cost more than the spending money Mother gave me for a week."

"You bought six of them," Lee said softly. "And each day you peeled one and divided the sections three ways because you said the oranges would keep us from getting sick and help Mother get well."

"We didn't squabble at all during those days," Glorianna said just as softly.

"We were afraid she was going to die. It had been a hard winter. Other people in the village had died of influenza or pneumonia. We were half-grown and so scared. She'd never been that sick before."

"So we didn't squabble. We kept the house orderly and did the lessons our teachers brought over so we wouldn't fall behind in school . . . and we didn't squabble."

"Until Mother was well again." Lee laughed. "And then we drove her halfway mad with it because we'd argue over the least little thing."

"Yes."

They walked in silence for a while. Then Glorianna said, "I love you, Lee."

"Don't." His voice got sharp. "People start saying things like that when they think they might not have another chance to say them."

"It's not that. I'm just . . . having a sentimental moment."

"Oh. In that case, I love you, too. I—" He tensed when she stopped walking. "What is it?"

"Dissonance. Up ahead. There's something there that doesn't belong in this landscape."

"The bridge is up ahead too."

They moved cautiously, Lee scanning the area around them for signs of some kind of creature, while Glorianna kept her eyes focused on the ground, looking for any telltale warnings that they were about to step into another landscape.

Small. Much smaller than the pond. She'd been able to sense the dissonance in the pond from her gardens on the Island in the Mist, but this alteration of the landscape had eluded her until she'd gotten close to it.

Lee led them to the bridge, then stopped two manlengths away. "The ground is torn up around the left side of the bridge. Looks like a struggle took place here."

Glorianna nodded. "But Ephemera stripped the grass and wildflowers around that circle of dead grass in response to whatever happened here. And that circle looks slightly higher than the rest of the ground."

"An access point to an underground den?" Lee asked.

Thinking about the creatures Sebastian had seen at the school, it came to her. "Trap spider. That's its lair. But . . . the dissonance doesn't feel strong enough. I don't think the Eater's creature is there anymore." She slowed her breathing, waited for her heartbeat to settle. She could feel the currents of Ephemera's power all around her, wanting to respond to a heart—and reluctant to respond with a piece of the Eater's landscapes so close. The currents of power were tangled up, knotted. Without direction, there was no telling what the world would manifest.

She walked a circle around the trap spider's lair, careful to stay a hand-width outside of the barren ground.

Hear me, Ephemera, she called as she circled. *Listen to my heart.* Tapping into the currents of Light and a single thread of the Dark, she altered the landscape, sending the trap spider's lair into the place of stones that she had already taken out of the world when she'd blocked the Eater's attempt to anchor the bonelovers' landscape to the Den.

The trap spider's lair and the barren ground around it disappeared, leaving a deep hole—a hole the world wanted to fill.

Listen to me. Listen to my heart.

It knew her. She was like the Old Ones who had known when to play with the Light and when a place needed currents of the Dark.

Soil, Glorianna thought, keeping her mind focused on the task, letting her heart beat with the promise of pleasure. *Rich soil to fill the hole. Soil that matches the earth here.*

Ephemera hesitated, then manifested what the heart desired. Pleasure filled the heart—and the other heart nearby. Its currents of power began to untangle. Was there more to play with?

Stone, the heart commanded. *Not the stone of anger, the stone of strength.*

It resonated with the heart, resonated with the land around it to find the stone the heart wanted and make more of it.

Stone formed around the back half of the circle, gray and strong. Not high. Not big. It stopped when the heart said "enough."

Smaller stones to shape a border. And a circle of stones where the Bad Thing had made a place for Itself.

Flowers, the heart said. *The breath of living things.* So it manifested flowers that liked to live in this part of itself.

And one more. This time the heart resonated so strongly, there was no choice but to manifest exactly what the heart wanted. But it knew this plant. This had come from the Old Ones' hearts to help the world heal. Wherever it grew, the Bad Thing could not change the world into something completely terrible, because hearts that could feel the resonance of the plant would always hold a little Light.

Glorianna sighed and stepped away from the circle. Lee came up behind her, put his hands on her shoulders.

Waist-high granite formed a half circle of stones, still with the jagged edges that time and rain would soften. Violets, wood iris, and plants with white, bell-shaped flowers sprang up from the newly made soil. In the center, where the door of the trap spider's lair had been, heart's hope bloomed.

"It's lovely," Lee said quietly.

She felt his hands tighten on her shoulders.

"But you didn't alter the landscape that time, did you?" he asked. "You didn't find stones and those flowers and shift them to this place."

"No. This is new."

He turned her to face him.

"That's what makes you different, isn't it?" he said slowly, as if fitting together the final pieces of a puzzle. "It's not just that you're stronger than other Landscapers, not just that you can alter landscapes and put together pieces from all different parts of the world. It's this—the ability to connect with Ephemera so strongly you can *create* landscapes. That's it, isn't it?"

"Yes, that's it."

He looked at her as if he'd never seen her before. "You really are like the Old Ones, the ones in the stories. The Guides of the Heart."

"A Guide, yes. But since I may be the only one left, I

guess, in a real sense, I'm Ephemera's heart." He was still looking at her as if she were a stranger.

"How long have you known?"

"Not long. Mother told me some things about our family just recently that explained why I am the way I am." She hesitated. "Does it bother you, knowing what I truly am?"

He studied her a moment longer and smiled. "No. We're still going to squabble." Then he narrowed his eyes, considering. "Have you created anything else?"

"The Island in the Mist."

His mouth fell open. "The whole island?"

"It's only a few acres."

"But . . . an island?" He thought for a moment. "The house, too?"

"No, not the house. Ephemera can create quarries of fine stone for building, but it can't build a house. Or put in plumbing."

"Or use a wrench to take apart a piece of pipe that's clogged."

"That's what brothers are for."

"How considerate of Mother to have provided you with one."

"I know. That's why I bring her flowers every year on your birthday."

He grinned. "I guess things are all right between us. We're squabbling again."

She smiled. "I guess we are—and they are."

"Then it's my turn." Releasing her, he walked over to the two wooden planks that crossed a narrow creek. "I'll break this bridge so nothing from Wizard City can reach this landscape. Then . . ." He crouched in front of the wooden planks. "I don't like the part that comes after this. I'll tell you that plainly, Glorianna."

"If you want to stir up a hornet's nest, you hit it with a big stick."

"Let's just make sure neither of us gets stung."

The student wizard hurried across the open ground, relieved his shift at the tower had finished before the sun set. Things felt ... strange ... lately in the city after the sun went down, even here at the hall.

He skidded to a halt and bit back a yelp when a woman suddenly appeared out of nowhere and walked toward him. She wore mannish clothes, the kind no respectable woman in Wizard City would wear, and her black, unbound hair flowed down her back, fanning out in the breeze that always blew at the top of the hill. For a moment he thought—hoped—she was a woman of loose morals who would be willing to do some naughty things with him in exchange for his not turning her over to the guards.

But she had the coldest green eyes he'd ever seen, and his heart trembled when she looked at him.

"The Wizards' Council has demanded Heart's Justice," she said. "Tell them the Landscaper will meet them outside the walls of the city tomorrow at sundown, and Heart's Justice will be done."

She turned and walked away.

"And who should I say gave me the message?" he asked, shaken by the brazen way she was giving orders to the council.

"They'll know."

"How are they supposed to know which Landscaper you are?"

She stopped and looked back at him. Those cold eyes went straight through him—and he felt as if she could see every secret in his heart.

"I'm the only one left." She took another step ... and disappeared.

Standing on the edge of the little island that was Lee's landscape, the piece of Ephemera he could shift at will, Glorianna watched the young wizard run toward the hall.

"Well," Lee said, "you whacked the hornets' nest."

She nodded, resisting the wind of emotion blowing through her own heart.

Lee watched her for a moment, then said quietly, "We could try to find Sebastian, get him out of here now."

So tempting to agree, because it was what *she* wanted. But . . .

Opportunities and choices. Something in Sebastian had changed—or had been changed. She could barely feel the resonance of his heart, and what she could sense was different, alien. This heart would never be at home in any of her landscapes. But deep in the core, fiercely protected, was still the cousin she knew and loved.

"No," she said with regret. "He has to make his own choices on this journey." *And if he doesn't follow the shining warmth I can still feel in his heart, we'll lose him forever.*

Lee sighed. "In that case, the bridge between this landscape and the waterhorses' is broken, and the wizards know you're coming. It's time to go back to Sanctuary and get what rest we can."

"Not yet." She thought about that shining warmth. "There's one more thing we need to do."

The voices stopped whispering. Something had stirred up the wizards, distracting them enough to stop the torment.

Sebastian opened his eyes and found himself on the floor in a fetal position, curled around the canteen with its last few swallows of water. Straightening his stiff limbs, he pushed himself up until he could sit with his back against the wall.

His head still ached, but his mind felt clear for the first time since he'd crossed the bridge. Maybe even since Koltak had stumbled into the Den.

He had the same powers as the other wizards. At least, some of their powers. Could he use them to open the door and escape? Maybe. But he didn't think he could get out of Wizard City and back across the bridge before they hunted him down, no matter what had stirred them up. And his power was raw. Not something he wanted to test against so many trained wizards.

But there *was* a power he knew how to use—a power that might help people fight against the Eater of the World. But what landscapes could he reach from here? *Who* could he reach from here?

Women. It would have to be women.

He thought of Koltak crossing bridges in the water-horses' landscape. Crossing over to places called Dunberry and Foggy Downs. Places he'd never heard of. Places that must be in another part of Ephemera—but were still connected to one of Glorianna's landscapes.

There was no hope for him, but he might be able to help the people he loved. Glorianna needed friends, needed allies, needed help in her fight against the Eater. Maybe he could give her some of those things. And by helping Glorianna, he could also save—

He wouldn't think her name. Not here.

He unfurled the power of the incubus until it filled him. Then he sent that power through the twilight of waking dreams, searching for hearts that would respond to him.

He felt them, many of them, becoming aware of his intrusion, strong-willed hearts and minds that would shut him out in another moment.

Listen to me, he said on the link that traveled through waking dreams. *Please listen. The Eater of the World has come back.*

Fear came back to him. Sharp, jagged.

Then we are lost, some of the voices whispered. *This time the Light will be devoured.*

No, he replied, putting all of his conviction into the thought. *Heart's hope lies within Belladonna. Remember that. Heart's hope lies within Belladonna.*

He felt the scratching at the edges of his mind. Some of his tormentors had returned.

He withdrew his links with those other hearts, pulling his power back into himself as fast as he could. Before the wizards were able to slip into his mind to discover what he had just done, he had the secret surrounded with all the strength he had left.

All through the torturous night, while they whispered and whispered and whispered, he held on to the secret—and the shining warmth.

Chapter Twenty-five

S tanding shoulder-to-shoulder with Lee, Glorianna watched the sun ease its way toward the western horizon of Sanctuary.

"It's almost time," Lee said.

She nodded. "You're going to be in the eye of a storm. Can you hold your island above the wizards' landscape?"

"I'll hold it. You just make sure you stay within reach of it. If the wizards keep their wits enough to unleash the lightning . . . You're not invulnerable, Glorianna."

"I know. But once things are in motion, once Heart's Justice has begun, they won't dare try anything until the power is released. By the time they realize what I've done, it will be too late for them to attack me."

"I hope you're right."

So do I.

She felt Lynnea approaching, causing ripples in Sanctuary's serenity. Fear and hope. Uncertainty and courage. The catalyst whose presence had brought change to the Den. Who had brought opportunities and choices.

Now, in the face of what was to come, she hoped Lynnea could hold on to the fledgling courage the young woman was still discovering lived inside her.

She touched Lee's arm to alert him. Then they both turned and waited for Lynnea to reach them.

"I'm going with you," Lynnea said, her voice a mixture of fear and defiance. "Sebastian needs me."

Yes, he does, Glorianna thought. *More than you realize.*

"Lynnea—" Lee began.

"She can come with us," Glorianna said, cutting off her brother's well-meant discouragement.

Teaser joined them, trailed by Yoshani. The incubus looked at Lynnea, then at her. "I'm going, too."

"No." The stricken look in Teaser's eyes surprised her, then pleased her. The young incubus she'd met in the Den fifteen years ago wouldn't have cared enough about anyone else to offer to help, let alone feel hurt when the offer was refused.

Before he could gather himself enough to argue, she added, "I need you to go back to the Den, Teaser."

"But—"

"I *need* that."

Yoshani stepped up beside Teaser. "Since Teaser is going back to the Den, would it cause a dissonance if I went with him? I have mentioned many times over the years that I would like to visit the Den."

Yoshani *had* mentioned wanting to visit, but she'd always said, "Not yet," because his presence *would* have caused a dissonance, could have shifted something before the hearts that were attuned to the Den were ready to change. But things had already changed in the Den, and Yoshani's steady heart would balance Teaser's more volatile one.

"An excellent suggestion, Honorable Yoshani," Glorianna said.

Teaser sputtered. Yoshani smiled.

Lee looked over his shoulder to gauge the sun's progress. "We'd better go."

Glorianna nodded. "I want to get there ahead of the council so that I can choose the ground."

Yoshani raised his hand. "May the Guardians of the Light watch over you."

Teaser looked at Lynnea, then Lee, and finally at Glorianna. "Travel lightly."

She turned away and followed the path that would take them to Lee's small island.

Travel lightly. She hoped she would. She hoped she could.

Everything depended on it.

Teaser watched them go, wondering how he'd gotten stuck playing keeper to a holy man instead of doing something to help Sebastian.

"I left my bag on the bench over there," Yoshani said. "I think it best if we reach the Den before the sun sets."

"Sun doesn't shine in the Den," Teaser muttered.

"Before it sets here."

Since he couldn't think of a reason to delay, he followed Yoshani to the bench, then to the bridge he and Lynnea had used to reach Sanctuary. Then he tried to argue.

"You really shouldn't be going to the Den," he said.

"Why not?" Yoshani asked mildly.

"Because you live here, and the Den is the Den of Iniquity. There's drinking and gambling." When Yoshani just smiled, he felt a reckless panic rise up inside him. "And whoring. Lots of whoring. And . . . and erotic statues. Right out in public!"

"It sounds like a fascinating place. Shall we go?"

Teaser stared at Yoshani. The man should be outraged, scandalized!

"Something has not occurred to you, my friend." Yoshani set his bag on the ground and held his hands out, holding them far apart. "You see Sanctuary and your Den as two places far from each other, too unlike to be connected in any way."

"They are," Teaser insisted.

Yoshani shook his head. "They are like this." Holding up one hand, he ran a finger down the palm, then down the back. "They are just two sides of the same heart, two facets of Glorianna Belladonna."

There was nothing Teaser could say to that, so he stared at the bridge.

Yoshani picked up his bag and rested a hand on Teaser's shoulder. "If it eases your heart, I will tell you this." He grinned. "I was not always a holy man."

"You don't have to exert yourself," Harland said. "I promise you, justice will be done."

Balanced on crutches, Koltak ignored the pain in what remained of his heavily bandaged left foot and looked the head of the Wizards' Council in the eyes. "I want to be there when justice is done. I want to see that bastard get what he deserves. And I want to see *her* destruction."

Harland studied Koltak for a moment, then smiled. "I thought that would be your answer, so I arranged a pony cart and a driver for you."

As Koltak slowly made his way to the door, Harland said, "Yes, Koltak, this day will change the world. Before it ends, we will succeed in doing what generations of wizards have worked to accomplish. We will vanquish the last enemy, and the world will be ours. All ours."

It flowed through the landscapes, a rippling shadow. The lesser enemies who had managed to escape Its attack on the school could not hurt It. Not anymore. They were caged in the landscapes they had fled to, unable to reach the other landscapes anchored in their gardens. Their power was fading in those abandoned places. Soon their resonance would be gone, leaving Ephemera without any guides to shape what was manifested. But It would be there, drifting among the landscapes, whispering to the dark side of the human heart until Ephemera changed itself to resonate with those hearts and became a dark, terrible place. But It would leave some threads of Light in those reshaped landscapes. After all, It could not crush hope if none existed. It could not devour kindness if there was no kindness left. It could not devastate love if no love could bloom. Yes, It would keep trickles of Light in Its Dark landscapes so Its prey would remain a delicious feast. But the Places of Light, those beacons of power . . . *They* had to be destroyed.

The Dark Guides' leader, trembling with delicious fear, had reached through the twilight of waking dreams to tell It they had found a way to lure the True Enemy into their grasp. They would destroy her to prove they were friends. And when *she* was eliminated, the Places of Light she had hidden would be revealed once more— and It would devour them.

Something shivered through It. Anticipation. Excitement. It wanted to be there when the Dark Guides destroyed *her*.

Moving swiftly, It headed for the closest access point that would take It back to the Landscapers' School, where It could be sure of finding a way to reach the city in time to feel the True Enemy die.

✖

Standing at the edge of Lee's island, Glorianna studied the land in front of her. On her left was a road leading out of Wizard City. Ahead of her was the eastern side of the city. East of that . . .

Revulsion clogged her throat, her lungs. Made her heart heavy. She was still standing on the island, still, in a way, standing in Sanctuary. She shouldn't have felt the Dark emanation coming from that field, not until she'd actually stepped into the wizards' landscape.

The wizards would want to use that field for Heart's Justice, would want her standing on that ground when she became the channel that would direct Ephemera for a specific purpose—to send someone to the landscape that resonated with that person's heart.

Raising a hand, she waggled a finger. Lee immediately stepped up beside her.

"This will do," Glorianna said softly. "But I need to go out there for a few minutes and connect with Ephemera in this landscape."

"You'll be seen," Lee protested. "There's a wagon and riders coming through the gate right now."

"But they aren't turning away from the road. They aren't the wizards, just ordinary folk. I have to know what I can work with."

"You've got all of Ephemera to work with," he growled.

Do I? She shifted her feet, started to take the step that would bring her into the wizards' landscape. Then she hesitated and turned to look at her brother. "Lee, there's something you have to do once this starts. It will be hard, but you have to do it."

"What?" he asked warily.

She looked toward the center of the island. She couldn't see the other woman, who was sitting in the enclosure, but she could feel the resonance of that heart. "Don't interfere with Lynnea's journey."

Startled, he, too, looked toward the center of the island. "What about Sebastian? Once you begin Heart's Justice—"

"Don't interfere with Lynnea's journey."

Lee stared at her, understanding better than anyone else could—because he understood her. "Have you told her Sebastian's life is in her hands?"

"No. It has to be her choice. And it has to be his."

Lee closed his eyes. "We could lose him."

"I know."

He opened his eyes and nodded.

"We're about to start a war," she whispered.

"Just make sure you win the first battle."

Turning away, she stepped off the edge of Lee's island—and almost cried out in dismay.

Thick currents of Dark power crisscrossed this entire landscape, but the Light . . . thin threads. Nothing more. Just enough to indicate the Light was sustaining—and was sustained by—some good hearts, just enough to keep the whole place from turning malignant. But not enough to provide any chance of change, of truly making the city a good place for people to live.

The Dark Guides and the Eater of the World abhorred the Light. So why hadn't they snuffed out those currents of power completely?

The obvious answer: because they needed those currents of Light. Why?

That was something she would have to consider later. Now she had to travel lightly, be the channel for Heart's Justice.

Ephemera, hear me. Listen to my heart.

As she began to resonate, opening herself to the hearts around her, she felt a flickering response nearby. Turning her head, she stared at the wagon and riders still coming down the road. Hearts yearning for the Light—and hearts yearning for a different kind of darkness.

Then she saw the carriages coming out of the gate and knew she had only a few minutes left to prepare.

"Lee," she called softly. "Get Lynnea. It's time."

Ephemera, hear me. Listen to my heart. Today we give Heart's Justice.

Feeling the world's resistance, she resonated more strongly, attuning herself to the Light. Some hearts behind the city walls resonated in response to hers.

Those hearts don't belong in this place.

She felt Ephemera slowly respond, becoming fluid to match her resonance, ready to manifest what she commanded. She felt the currents of Light grow stronger around her. As the Light filled her, she added her Dark resonance.

And felt some of the Dark currents of power already in this landscape break as the resonance of her heart began to take over this place.

That was something else to think about. But not here, not now.

While she watched the carriages that held the Wizards' Council turn off the road and bump along the open land to the place where she waited, she thought of nothing but the terrifying power that was called Heart's Justice.

A power she was about to unleash.

Dalton stared at the woman who came out of nowhere. His heart thundered in his chest. Was that Belladonna?

When she turned her head and looked in his direction, he felt as if his heart had just been stripped naked. Even when she looked away, he felt breathless . . . and shaken.

"Dalton?" his wife, Aldys, asked nervously. "Why did we stop?"

"Best be moving on, Cap'n," Addison said. "Heart's Justice. Not something you want the youngsters to see."

"Why?" Aldys asked. "We've always been told it was a humane punishment. That no one got what wasn't deserved."

If there truly is any justice, the man Koltak tricked into coming here will be sent back to wherever he calls home, Dalton thought.

As he gathered up the reins, he saw two more people suddenly appear behind the woman.

Was the man a Bridge? Had they just crossed over from a different landscape? Was there time for him to ride out to where they waited and ask where the bridge crossed over?

"Cap'n." A warning.

Dalton looked back and saw the carriages moving across the open land. *Too late,* he thought with regret, not sure if he was thinking about himself or the man who was riding in the closed prison wagon. *Too late.*

Something shimmered around his heart, as if considering the flavor of his feelings.

"Best be moving on, Cap'n," Addison said.

But he couldn't look away. He watched the carriages come to a halt, watched the Wizards' Council descend to form a line facing the Landscaper, watched . . . Was that Koltak being helped out of that pony cart? It figured. The bastard would have shown up for this if he'd had to crawl all the way down from the Wizards' Hall to get there.

The prison wagon moved farther on before it halted. One of the guards unlocked and opened the door. The man he'd helped Koltak capture stepped out of the wagon and moved away from the guards and wizards.

There was no escaping Heart's Justice. Everyone knew that. You couldn't run fast enough to escape the reach of a Landscaper focused on Heart's Justice.

Still, he admired the man for standing tall and looking the Landscaper in the eyes.

And he wished, once again, that he'd made a different choice.

Lynnea twisted her fingers until they hurt. Something was wrong with Sebastian. Terribly wrong. His face seemed carved out of wood, and there was such emptiness in those beautiful green eyes. What had those wicked men done to him?

He didn't seem to notice—or care—that she had come here to help him.

Maybe he didn't care. Maybe he had never loved her. Maybe coming here had been the wrong thing to do.

Her courage faltered. She wobbled suddenly, as if the ground had shifted under her feet. Lee grabbed her arm to steady her.

Sebastian, she thought, feeling her heart ache. *Sebastian.*

What had they done to Sebastian to turn his heart into a desert in so little time? Glorianna wondered as she stared into his empty eyes.

Then she felt a blast of heat that shot straight from

his heart into hers. A heart wish so intense the ground around her trembled with the strength of it.

She turned her back on Sebastian and the wizards, focusing on Lynnea.

"His heart is bleak, barren, cold," she said, stripping her voice of all emotion. "When Heart's Justice takes him, he'll end up in a landscape that is bleak, barren, and cold."

"It's not right," Lynnea whispered. "He's not like that. He deserves more than that."

"Ephemera will send him to the place that resonates with his heart. I can't change that." Glorianna waited, hoping for some sign of defiance, but Lynnea's courage was withering. "But his last heart wish was for you. That you find a landscape that truly feels like home. That you have what your heart most desires. I will honor that wish, Lynnea. I, and Ephemera, will give you what you most desire."

"How am I supposed to choose?" Lynnea cried.

"Follow your heart."

Before Lynnea looked away, fixing her eyes on the ground, Glorianna saw a flash of strength.

Turning away from Lynnea and Lee, Glorianna walked a few paces away, ignoring Lee's low protest.

Hear me, Ephemera. Feel this heart. She focused on Lynnea, on the resonance growing stronger and more determined moment by moment. *Give this heart what it most desires. And this one.* Now she focused on the resonance that was Sebastian. *Let him follow his heart. Listen to nothing in him but the core of his heart.*

The currents of Light and Dark power that resonated with her grew stronger, almost too strong to contain.

She stared at the Wizards' Council. They stared back at her, not quite able to hide their malevolent glee at finally getting her within reach.

What they hadn't considered was that they, too, were within reach. Because no Landscaper had ever tried to give Heart's Justice to more than one person at a time.

Listen to every heart in this landscape, she commanded. *Find the landscape that resonates with each of those hearts and send them on to that place. Send every heart to the Light or the Dark that it deserves. Strip every heart of the masks used to hide its true resonance. Now, Ephemera.* Now!

Throwing back her head, she raised her arms—and let the world channel Heart's Justice through her.

"Guardians and Guides," Dalton whispered, as something powerful swept through him, resonating, seeking. "She's unleashed Heart's Justice on all of us!"

He set the brake and tied off the reins to keep the horses from bolting, then turned to grip his wife's arm, forming a barrier in front of their children. "Henley! Addison! Tie up your horses and get in the wagon."

Henley and Addison dismounted. But they moved away from the wagon.

"You're a good man, Cap'n," Addison said. "But I'm not a good man. Not that way. I like drinking and gambling and the company of women who aren't ladies. Same with Henley."

"But—"

"You hold tight to your family," Addison said. "Henley and me, we'll make our own way. Good-bye, Cap'n. Travel lightly."

The two guards were fading, as if they weren't quite there anymore.

As he held on to his family, waiting to be swept away by the storm of power, one thought echoed through Dalton's mind: *Heart's hope lies within Belladonna.*

He hoped, for all their sakes, the man Koltak had brought to Wizard City was right.

Follow your heart. I, and Ephemera, will give you what you most desire.

Lynnea looked up, startled. The ground felt so strange, so . . . fluid. And everything around her looked . . . wispy.

It was happening. Heart's Justice.

I, and Ephemera, will give you what you most desire.

"Sebastian," she whispered, pulling away from Lee and taking a step toward the man who had shown her laughter and love. Who had given her a chance to discover she was more than Mam and Pa and Ewan told her she could be. She was a tigress, and she could do anything she wanted with her life. *Anything.*

Follow your heart.

She took another step, feeling as if she were being buffeted by fierce winds even though no wind tugged at her clothes or blew on her skin.

The winds of change. And she could have anything she wanted.

"Sebastian," she whispered again, taking another step.

He didn't deserve a place that was bleak, barren, and cold. He deserved to live in the Den, where the people needed him to be their Justice Maker. And he deserved to live in his cottage, where he could just be a man. And he deserved sunlight and warmth and friends and family and . . . love.

She took another step. And another.

Those wicked men had done something to him, had made him believe he didn't deserve those things, just like Mam had made her believe *she* didn't deserve anything. No. Mam hadn't made her believe anything. She just hadn't been strong enough to believe anything else.

She was strong enough now. She was a tigress.

He needs me.

If he wasn't able to believe for himself, *she* would believe for him.

Follow your heart.

Sebastian. Sebastian. Sebastian.

She ran while the ground seemed to fall away beneath her. She ran, keeping her eyes on Sebastian.

He was her heart's desire. They deserved laughter and friends and love. They deserved to live in the cottage, in sunlight. And they deserved the Den, that strange carnal carnival. And they deserved to be together.

Sebastian. Sebastian. Sebastian.

She felt the world shifting, trying to reach for her heart to take her away.

Not yet. Not yet.

She bore down, striving with everything in her to reach him before the world swept them away.

Closer. Closer.

His eyes were closed. That was why he didn't see her, why he wasn't reacting. But she had no breath to call out to him. So she let her heart call for her.

Sebastian!

His eyes snapped open. His beautiful green eyes weren't empty anymore. They were filled with shock, disbelief, and a frightened yearning.

Ephemera pulled at her. In another moment it would be too late.

With all the strength she had, she leaped.

The last thing she saw was Sebastian reaching up to catch her. The last thing she felt was his arms wrapping around her.

Then the world swept them away . . . and there was only darkness.

Glorianna staggered, barely able to stay on her feet. She felt hollowed out, scoured clean.

Insanity. That was what it must have been to think she could give Heart's Justice to an entire landscape. But . . .

The city was filled with Dark currents that didn't

match her Dark resonance. And the hearts in the city that had yearned for the Light . . .

Gone. All gone. Free of this place.

She looked around. Sebastian and Lynnea were gone, and she hoped with all her heart that she'd done the right thing for both of them.

Everyone had disappeared . . . except a wizard with a bandaged foot. He was on the ground, moaning.

She looked up at the city, then at the man. Not one of them, but too much like them. Had there been a moment when his heart could have made a choice? Was that why he was still outside the city?

Pity stirred in her, and she wondered if there was something—anything—she could do rather than leave him in this place.

Then the wizard saw her and struggled to sit up.

"Glorianna," Lee said in a low voice. "Just back up. I'm right behind you, on the island. Get out of there before that bastard has a chance to do anything."

She took two steps back, then stopped. "I have to finish this. If I don't, all the risks we took will be for nothing."

"Glorianna."

She reached inside herself for all the power she had left—and altered the landscape, taking the piece of Ephemera that held Wizard City out of the world.

So exhausted she could barely stand, Glorianna backed up another step closer to Lee and the island. Almost there. Almost.

"You bitch!" the wizard screamed. "What did you do to the council?"

"I gave them Heart's Justice," she replied, although her voice was so weak, she doubted he could hear her.

Fury twisted his face. He raised his hand.

She stared at him, knowing what was about to happen but too drained to move.

Then Lee grabbed her and hauled her onto the island just as the wizard's lightning struck the ground where she'd stood a moment before.

"That was too close," he said, sounding scared and furious.

"I know." Her voice sounded funny, far away. "Lee?" Then everything faded away.

There are weeds in every garden.
—*The Book of Lessons*

What is considered a weed in one garden
is a vital plant in another.
—*Belladonna*

Chapter Twenty-six

Still scared and furious.

That was Glorianna's first thought when she opened her eyes and found herself staring into Lee's face. "What happened?"

"You fainted. Don't ever do that again."

"I didn't like it much either," she grumbled. He looked mad enough to punch her, but the moment she tried to sit up, he was there, helping her. Then she found herself pressed against his chest, his arms around her while he rocked them both.

He's shaking. "Lee," she said, wrapping her arms around him.

"Scared me, Glorianna. When I saw that bastard wizard raise his hand, I wasn't sure I could reach you before . . ." He swallowed hard. "It scared me."

"Me too." But listening to his heart slowing to its normal, steady beat combined with the sound of water trickling in the fountain began to pull her under. "Lee?"

"Hmm?"

"So tired. Can we yell at each other later?"

He didn't answer for so long, she started to drift off. Then, "Okay. We'll yell later. Just sit here while I shift the island back to Sanctuary. I was feeling a bit too unnerved to do it before."

He got up and left the sheltered center of the island.

She knew the moment he made the shift—not because anything about the island changed, but because of the resonance of the land around it.

Strong currents of Light flowed through the landscape, along with thin threads of the Dark.

Glorianna struggled to keep her eyes open, struggled to keep her mind working. The currents of power in Sanctuary and Wizard City were exact opposites. One current dominated the landscape, but threads of the other still existed, were still necessary. She knew why she nurtured those threads in Sanctuary. What did the wizards gain by nurturing those threads of Light?

Once she understood that, she might be able to figure out how to face the Eater of the World . . . and survive. But for now . . .

She felt herself being tugged, shifted. Then Lee kissed her forehead, and said, "Just rest now, Glorianna. Get some sleep."

❧

Panting and sweating—and hoping that Sebastian had ended up in the foulest landscape that existed in this world—Koltak hobbled up the stairs closest to Harland's chambers. Harland had to be here. Harland had to be all right, despite that bitch's attempt to use Heart's Justice as an attack on the council.

It had been agony to get himself into the pony cart and drive back into the city. What had happened to the guards and drivers who had come out with the council? And where was the council?

Reaching the top of the stairs, Koltak stopped to rest.

Order had to be restored—and quickly. He'd driven through streets swarming with angry, confused people who realized *something* had happened to them, but not *what* had happened to them. At least in the upper levels of the city, there was a more orderly confusion, mainly butlers and housekeepers standing outside shouting the names of missing servants. Not that any of those servants would respond.

Heart's Justice.

Koltak shuddered. Who would have thought, even in the wildest moment, that a Landscaper could be powerful enough to send Heart's Justice sweeping through an entire city?

Powerful. But not invincible. He'd been able to fight back, had been able to hold on to where he was instead of being swept away to another landscape. If *he* could resist her, then surely Harland and the rest of the council had been able to do the same.

Koltak resettled the crutches, but he didn't move as a thought filled him. Of course most of the council had withstood Belladonna's attack, but maybe there would now be a vacancy that needed to be filled by a wizard who had stood against Belladonna and fought back?

Excitement had him moving down the corridor with as much speed as he could manage. When he reached Harland's door, he flung it open and went inside, relieved to see the tall wizard standing at the window, wearing rumpled, grass-stained robes.

"Harland! I—"

What turned away from the window was—and wasn't—Harland. Human shaped . . . but not human. Terrifying and yet compelling.

Koltak's heart thudded in his chest. He knew what he was looking at. He just couldn't believe it.

Fury blazed from Harland's eyes. "It wasn't time yet to show our true faces. *It wasn't time!*"

"Dark Guide," Koltak whispered, knowing the moment he said it that even that much recognition had been a mistake.

Harland moved toward him, smiling. "We hid well, did we not? Justice Makers. Champions of the Light. The ones willing to shoulder the burden of deciding who was unworthy of living in the daylight landscapes. By stripping a heart of all hope, by twisting happy memories into something painful, by preparing that heart before calling on a Landscaper to perform Heart's Justice . . . We couldn't reach the Eater of the World, but with the Landscapers' unwitting help, we were able to use It to rid ourselves of people who would have gotten in our way." His smile widened, turned savage. "Why do you look so shocked, Koltak? You always wanted to know the inner secrets of the council. Now I'm telling you."

Koltak couldn't move. This was wrong. All wrong.

"We hid well," Harland said. "So well that when we finally brought ourselves to their notice, the Landscapers and Bridges accepted us as allies. Over time we poisoned their minds, blinded them so they couldn't recognize the truth about the ones whose power was different from theirs. Generation after generation, they helped us eliminate the true Guides of the Heart, preparing Ephemera for the day when *we* could take control of the world." His mouth twisted into a snarl. "*We failed only once.* And thanks to your brother, *that* one is more powerful than all the others before her."

"Peter?" Koltak stammered. "What does Peter have to do with this?"

"By mating Dark power with Light, he helped create a child who has both! No one else could have revealed us for what we are! No one else could be a real threat to the Eater of the World."

I have to get out of here, Koltak thought. *I have to get away from this city. I have to warn . . . someone.*

Harland looked past Koltak. "I think it's time Wizard Koltak was initiated into the council."

"No," Koltak said. "No, I—"

Feet kicked the crutches out from under him. Hands grabbed his arms before he fell.

He could call the lightning. He could fight, get away. He could—

Kill your ambition, Koltak? voices whispered in his mind. *If you fight us now, you will never have what you most desire. Isn't that why you struggled to stay in this landscape? Because here is the only place where your ambitions could bloom?*

He didn't fight, didn't struggle. He tried to keep his injured foot off the floor as members of the council—barely recognizable as the men they'd once pretended to be—opened a panel in the wall and dragged him down flights of stairs and through secret corridors.

Finally they stopped in front of a heavy wooden door.

Harland pulled back the bolts and opened the door, closing it behind them once the Dark Guides dragged Koltak to the edge of a barred gallery that looked down into a dimly lit pit.

Holding on to the bars to stay upright, Koltak stared into the pit. Was there something moving down there? Yes. Something moving out of the shadows.

The female—since the creature was naked, there was no doubt it was female—stared up at them. Then she screamed—a sound that lifted the hairs on the back of Koltak's neck.

"That is the reason you will never be part of the council, Koltak," Harland said.

"I . . . I don't understand."

Harland smiled as he watched the female, who was now stroking her breasts and moaning. "These are our breeders. They were never able to alter their appearance to pass as humans, so they had to be hidden, protected. They have a feral intelligence, and they're quite vicious. When they come into season and are desperate to be mounted and mated, they have to be restrained to keep them from savaging the males." He turned his head and looked at Koltak. "The council is made up of purebloods. Has always been made up of the purebloods. Your ambition made you a useful tool, but you're too human to be one of us."

"Why . . . why are you telling me this?"

"So that you understand."

"But . . ." Koltak's head was reeling as all the things he'd believed shifted into a different pattern. "But if this is what you are, why were you so opposed to Sebastian?"

"We weren't," Harland replied. "There was no way of

knowing the boy's potential, but by our exploiting your shame in having sired a child with a succubus, you became a useful tool. And the boy ..." He sighed. "The incubi and succubi are two branches that came from the same root as the Dark Guides. Like us, they have the power to slip into other minds through the twilight of waking dreams. As one of us, Sebastian would have been a more powerful wizard than you could dream of being. But as an enemy and Belladonna's ally ..." He smiled. "But once again, you proved yourself useful by helping us eliminate him."

Sebastian. Tears stung Koltak's eyes. All of these years, he could have had a son, could have taught the boy to use the power that lived inside him. They might have worked together ... as Justice Makers.

Harland studied the females gathering to stare at the males who were out of reach. "They cannot go out among the humans, so they need toys to play with. It makes them easier to handle when it's time for us to mate with them."

"Toys?" Koltak stammered, pulled back to the danger present all around him. What kind of toys ... It suddenly clicked. "The people who disappear, who are thought to have gotten lost in another landscape."

Harland nodded. "It's convenient that some people *do* cross over to another landscape and aren't able to return. So no one suspects that anything else might have happened to them." He paused. "Except Peter. A true Justice Maker, he wandered where he shouldn't have while helping a shepherd boy round up some sheep. He discovered one of the barred openings that let light and air into this chamber. When we realized he had seen our secret, he had to disappear."

Koltak just clung to the bars and stared at Harland.

"Your brother was a strong man," Harland said. "He lasted for weeks before the females broke him, body and spirit. I wonder if you'll last even half as long." He lashed out, kicking Koltak's injured foot.

Koltak screamed as the pain tore through him. He

couldn't fight, could barely struggle as two members of the council dragged him down the stairs and through a tunnel carved out of the pit's stone walls. Then they opened a door and shoved him into the pit, swiftly locking the door behind them.

Gasping from the pain and unable to stand, he cowered by the door, watching the females as they moved toward him.

"Harland!" he shouted. "Harland! I can still help you!"

But Harland and the other males were gone.

As he felt something brush against the edges of his mind, as he realized he was going to die in this pit and the violation these creatures did to his heart would eclipse anything they did to his body, he accepted a painful truth.

Sebastian had been right. Belladonna was Ephemera's only hope.

🙙

Swallowing down the sick churning in his stomach, Dalton raised his head and opened his eyes.

Dark.

Guardians of the Light and Guides of the Heart, where were they?

He was still in the wagon, still holding his wife's arm. "Aldys?"

"D-Dalton?"

"Lally? Dale?" He touched his children. "Anyone hurt?"

"Hey-a!" a voice called.

A lantern, bobbing to the rhythm of a fast walk, came down the road toward them.

Releasing his family, Dalton's left hand closed around the sheath of his sword. His right hand curled around the hilt.

"You folks all right?" the man asked.

"We're fine," Dalton replied warily. He relaxed a little when the man got closer and raised the lantern high enough so they could see his face. A good face. Older. Strong body and arms that came from solid work.

"Where did you folks come from?"

"Wizard City." Seeing the man's friendly expression fade, he added, "Heart's Justice sent us here." Wherever "here" was. "Is this one of Belladonna's landscapes?"

"Do you want it to be?"

"Yes."

The man relaxed. "Well, Glorianna is never wrong about a heart."

"So this *is* one of Belladonna's landscapes?"

"Well, it is and it isn't. Glorianna's mother, Nadia, looks after this landscape. Village of Aurora is just down the road a ways, but the house is closer." The man looked up at the sky. "It'll be dawn in another hour or so. Easier to find your way to the village once the sun comes up. You follow me up to the house. I reckon the youngsters could use some warm milk, and you folks could use a bite to eat."

"We don't want to intrude," Aldys said nervously.

"Never you mind that," the man said with a smile. "Things are plenty stirred up tonight, so Nadia's already in the kitchen." He started to turn away, then turned back. "I'm Jeb, by the way."

Relief that they had found a safe place made Dalton light-headed, but as he untied the reins and released the brake, something occurred to him.

"Jeb? Why are you out on the road this time of night?"

"Was keeping watch for someone we're expecting. They haven't shown up yet, but they will. They will."

A good man, Dalton thought as they followed Jeb back to the Landscaper's house. Caring people.

He hoped whoever they were watching for made it back to them.

❧

The Eater of the World screamed in rage and fear. The True Enemy had taken the Dark Guides and their city out of the world, so far out of reach It couldn't feel *any* resonance. Even when It had been caged, It had been able to feel the resonance of the Dark Guides. How could *she* control a place that held so much of their Dark power? *How?*

And how could she defeat the Dark Guides? There were so many of them in that city! If she was powerful enough to cage all of *them* . . .

It had to hide. It had to find a place far from these landscapes, a place where she wouldn't look for It.

As It fled back to the school, It considered all the landscapes It could reach through the gardens. But she would know about those places.

The sea. It could hide in the sea. Hunt in the sea. Until It figured out a way to destroy the True Enemy.

It moved through the gardens, flowing beneath the paths that were now cracked and growing noxious weeds until It came to the garden where it had left the stones it had taken from a stream that was, and wasn't, in the four-footed demons' landscape.

It had recognized the resonance of a wizard, and the dark feelings in that heart had left the land around a bridge vulnerable to Its influence. So It had taken the stones to make an access point.

Now It flowed over those stones, into those stones . . . and out into the stream. For a moment It lay at the bottom of the stream, blacker than the darkest shadow. Then It flowed up the bank and under the land, sensing the currents of Light and Dark—and a power, a strength of will and heart that resonated with those currents. But it wasn't *her.*

Rising to the surface, It changed shape.

A well-dressed, middle-aged man walked down the road toward the village of Dunberry.

"Daylight," Teaser said, pushing back his chair.

"What is it?" Yoshani asked, looking around.

"Visitors. And not the kind we welcome around here."

"Teaser—"

But he was already out of Philo's courtyard and stepping into the street to block the two men riding toward him.

"Evening," the older man said, reining in before his horse reached Teaser.

Teaser studied the two men. No badges, but he knew a guard's jacket when he saw one. "Go back to where you came from."

"Can't. And wouldn't want to if we could." He looked around and gave Teaser a smile that was sad and hopeful. "Looks like a nice place."

"This is the Den of Iniquity."

"The . . ." Both men looked startled. The older one whistled softly. "One of Belladonna's landscapes."

Teaser bristled. The last thing anyone here needed was guards who were interested in Belladonna. "You're not wel—"

A strong hand on his shoulder stopped him. He looked at Yoshani, who was studying the guards.

"Heart's Justice?" Yoshani asked softly.

The older man nodded. "I'm Addison. This is Henley."

"Teaser," Yoshani said, "if this is where they ended up, this is where they belong. At least at this stage of their journey."

"They could be lying."

"No heart can lie to Glorianna Belladonna."

He felt stubborn. He felt scared. The hours since he'd brought Yoshani to the Den had been endless.

"All right," he said. "We'll find a place for you to stay until the Justice Maker gets back. When he does, he'll decide if you stay or go."

The guards looked uneasy. "You have a wizard here?"

"A *Justice Maker.*"

"Gentlemen," Yoshani said. "Why don't you take a seat in the courtyard and have something to eat?"

While the guards tied up their horses and found seats in the courtyard, Teaser stared at the street, at the people going in and out of the taverns and gambling houses.

"He'll come back," he said, softly but fiercely. "Sebastian will come back."

"And that, my friend, is why Belladonna wanted you here. Needed you here," Yoshani said gently. "Because you believe he'll come back. You believe it with all your heart."

Teaser felt the truth of those words settle inside him. "Yeah. I guess I do."

Glorianna woke up groaning. "I'm too old to sleep on the ground."

"You're not ancient; you're thirty," Lee replied. "And you're not on the ground; you're on a blanket."

"Doesn't make the ground any softer." She pushed herself up. Her eyes felt gritty, her mouth tasted foul, and she was pretty sure she was the smell that made her nose wrinkle. But the other smell . . . Her eyes opened all the way. "Koffee?"

"And some food." Lee tipped one hand toward the basket beside him. The other hand held a mug of koffee.

"Why didn't you wake me so we could sleep in the guesthouse?" she grumbled, pushing her tangled hair off her face.

"I banged a stone against an empty pot long enough and loud enough to wake up everyone *in* the guesthouse. You didn't even twitch. Had to roll you onto the blanket." He set down his mug, got another from the basket, and filled it with koffee from a jug. "So stop whining."

"I'm not whining."

"Are too."

"Am . . . not." She stared at him. "Are you going to give me that koffee?"

"Are you going to keep whining?"

"I'm— Just give me that."

Grinning, he handed her the mug, took a sip of his own, then dug into the basket and put out a plate of bread, cheese, and grapes.

They ate in companionable silence, listening to birdsong and the trickle of the fountain.

"So," Lee said, dividing the rest of the koffee equally between them. "The Dark Guides are locked out of reach of the world."

"There are others who weren't in the city," Glorianna said.

"But their true faces are revealed. They can no longer pretend to be humans with magic."

"No, they can't. But there are also wizards who have enough human blood that their appearance won't change."

"Then they have a choice, don't they? With the others exposed as Dark Guides, they can choose to continue following the Dark currents nurtured by the Wizards' Council or they can become Justice Makers in the true sense."

She nodded. "The Landscapers who survived the attack on the school, if there are any, will have to make choices, too. I can help them, if they'll let me. I'm not sure they will."

"Can they help you?"

She shook her head. That's something she already knew with certainty. "They don't have inside them what is needed to fight the Eater of the World."

"You can't fight It alone, Glorianna."

I don't think that's going to be a choice. "We'll see."

He hesitated, then asked softly, "What about Sebastian?"

"I know where to find Sebastian." Then she added just as softly, "If he followed his heart."

Chapter Twenty-seven

The sound of waves rolling into shore. A steady sound. Familiar. Comforting.

Sebastian rolled onto his back and opened his eyes. Dark. He hadn't expected anything else. Not really. And yet, some small part of him, right before Heart's Justice had swept him away, had hoped—

Lynnea!

His body jolted into a sitting position. He twisted to his left when he heard a soft groan. Patting the ground, he found her hand, her arm.

Shifting to his knees, he gently explored, his hands roaming over her body. No jagged pieces of bone. No wet spots that would indicate she was bleeding.

She groaned again, then said hesitantly, "Sebastian?"

"Lie still, sweetheart." His hands went to her shoulders to hold her down. "Are you hurt? Is there any pain?" Her neck. What if she hurt her neck? "Can you move?"

"I could if you weren't holding me down. Let me up. There's a stone digging into my butt."

He helped her sit up, then pulled her into his arms and hung on, choking on the sobs that were going to explode out of him at any moment.

"You foolish woman," he said, his voice breaking. "Why did you do that? I asked Glorianna to let you have your heart's desire. I *asked* her, heart-to-heart. And she would have given it to you, because I asked. Heart's Justice or not, she *would* have done it."

"And she did," Lynnea said, reaching up to rest a hand against his face. "She did give me my heart's desire. I wanted to be with you."

He cried. He couldn't stop it, couldn't hold the tears back. "I love you, Lynnea. I love you."

"And I love you, Sebastian. With all my heart."

He sniffed, brushed away the tears. Tried to regain some control. "We'll make a good life. Somehow we'll make a good life."

"Yes, we will. Together. But . . ."

He felt her head move as she looked around. No, he *saw* her head move.

It wasn't quite as dark as it had been a few minutes ago.

"Where are we?" Lynnea asked.

He looked around—and felt a jolt deep in his gut. It couldn't be. Could it?

The lake. The line of tall bushes that had been planted as a windbreak. The trees. And there. The long break in the trees that gave him a clear view of the lake . . . and the moonlight.

"I think I know where we are," he said, pulling Lynnea to her feet. "Come on." Taking her hand, he led her through the trees until they reached a dirt lane.

"It's your cottage," Lynnea whispered.

"Our cottage."

He approached it slowly, studying it in the strange gray light. It was definitely his cottage, but it wasn't the same landscape. There was something very odd about this moonlight.

He frowned at the cottage. The shutters needed painting.

"Sebastian?"

The moonlight had never made that apparent before. *"Sebastian."*

He turned, felt a fizz of panic when he realized Lynnea had wandered a little way away and was staring at the break in the trees. When she started heading toward the cliff and the lake, he hurried after her.

"Lynnea, wait. We don't know anything about this landscape. We don't—" He stopped. Stared.

"Oh," Lynnea said, laughing and crying. "Oh, Sebastian." She flung her arms around him. "Isn't it beautiful?"

He couldn't speak. He just stared, blinking back tears. He hadn't seen one in fifteen years. He wanted to see every moment of this one.

With his arms wrapped around Lynnea, he watched the sun rise.

Thank you, Glorianna Belladonna.

In sunlight, they walked back to the cottage and heard someone calling, "Hey-a, the house!"

Hurrying around the cottage, they saw Jeb standing near the trees, holding a basket. Relief swept over the other man's face when he saw them.

"How . . . ?" Sebastian said.

"Glorianna came by yesterday and told us about your being taken to Wizard City. She said if you followed your heart, this is where we'd find you come morning." Jeb grinned at Lynnea. "And here you are." Then he sobered. Looking at Sebastian, he added, "I think she's been waiting these past few years for you to be ready to walk in the Light again. Guess you finally found a reason to try."

"Guess I have," Sebastian said, his voice thick with too many feelings. The heart had no secrets from Glorianna Belladonna.

"But . . . where are we?"

Jeb scratched the back of his neck. "Well, I'm not a Landscaper, so I can't tell you for certain, but from what I gathered, the Den is still down the lane that way. And if you follow the lane the other way, you'll come to the main road that leads into Aurora."

"Then the cottage must belong to somebody." Sebastian felt a pang of regret. While the cottage had been lost in a dark landscape, whoever owned it wouldn't want it, even if the person could have found it. Now . . .

"Your auntie owns the cottage and the land around it. She and Glorianna . . . Well, you'll have to ask them how they worked things out between them." Jeb studied the back of the cottage. "Shutters could use a coat of paint. I can give you a hand with that, if you like."

"Thank you."

"It's a kindness. Oh. Your auntie sent this basket." Jeb put the basket down beside Lynnea. "Figured you wouldn't have anything to eat here. She said you're welcome to come by for dinner tonight."

"I need to check on the Den tonight. I want to make sure everyone is all right."

"Well, tomorrow then. Glorianna and Lee will be coming for dinner. Reckon you'll need to talk to Lee about what bridges might be needed now that the landscape has altered."

"Oh!" Lynnea said. "Is the bridge to Nadia's house still in the woods?"

Jeb chuckled. "No need for a bridge anymore. You're in the same landscape. Just follow the path. That's where it's always led." He shifted his feet. Studied the cottage's roof.

"Was there something else?" Sebastian asked.

"Coupla things, actually. First . . . " Jeb dug into his pocket. "Your auntie wasn't sure either of you would have a key on you, so she sent this one along. Second . . . " Now he looked uncomfortable. "I know folks in the Den might see things differently than in other landscapes, and I know you're both straddling a line here, but you're going to be spending time in Aurora, too, shopping and whatnot. The thing is, if you don't want some folks saying things they've got no business saying, you should marry the girl."

Sebastian tipped his head. "I could say the same to you."

Jeb looked sheepish. "I did ask her."

"And?" He drawled the word.

Jeb squared his shoulders. "Your auntie said she'd marry me a week to the day after you become a husband."

Sebastian gave Jeb a wolfish smile. "Tell Aunt Nadia her wedding is two weeks from today." Then he realized he'd missed a step when Lynnea just cocked her head and looked at him. "If you wouldn't mind getting married a week from today. And . . . if you're willing to marry me."

"Is that a proposal?" Lynnea asked, sounding puzzled enough to make him sweat.

"A fumbled one," Jeb said sourly, "but it sounded like a proposal to me."

Lynnea threw her arms around Sebastian's neck. "No, I don't mind, and yes, I'll marry you!"

Wrapping his arms around her, he swung her in a circle. When he set her down, he lowered his head to give her a kiss that would make the air sizzle. Before his lips touched hers, Jeb cleared his throat.

Sebastian rested his forehead against Lynnea's. "Are you still here?"

"One other thing your auntie wanted me to mention."

His auntie was a bundle of messages.

"A mated pair of keets hatched three babies a few weeks ago. Nadia thought maybe you'd—"

"A baby Sparky?" Lynnea's eyes shone with excitement.

Seeing that look in her eyes, Sebastian stifled a groan. He could learn to live with a little featherhead.

"You can take a look at them when you come to dinner." Lifting two fingers in a salute, Jeb finally turned and walked back into the woods.

"This is what I wanted," Lynnea said, looking at the sunlit grass behind the cottage. "For you. For me. For us."

And you're everything I wanted, even during the years when I didn't know what I was looking for, waiting for.

Sebastian brushed his lips over hers. Then he unlocked the door and pushed it open. "Welcome home, Lynnea."

She smiled. "Welcome home, Sebastian."

Picking up the basket, he followed her into the cottage.

Read on for an exciting excerpt from

Belladonna
by Anne Bishop

Available from Roc

Glorianna fastened the gold bar pin to the plain white blouse, then stepped back to get a full view of herself in the mirror. The dark green skirt and the matching jacket that had flowers embroidered around the neckline and cuffs were probably too formal for this meeting. With her hair pinned up, she looked like she was attending some afternoon society function instead of meeting colleagues to discuss the danger to their world.

But we aren't colleagues, Glorianna thought as she dabbed a little scent on her pulse points. *I was never one of them.*

But she had to see the Landscapers who had found their way to Sanctuary, had to talk to them and hope they would be willing to work with her to protect Ephemera from the Eater of the World.

Guardians of the Light, please help them accept me, listen to me. If they can't, if they won't, Ephemera will end up more shattered than it is now.

The woman who looked back at her from the mirror had eyes filled with nerves instead of much-needed confidence. The woman in the mirror was tired of being an outsider who couldn't count on her own kind to stand with her in the battle that was coming. Even though she still believed in her heart that she would have to face the Eater alone, it would be a relief to know her family didn't have to shoulder the weight of being the only ones supporting her.

Which was why she had chosen these clothes for this meeting—as a reminder that her family *did* support her. Her mother had given her the blouse as a gift for her thirty-first birthday; Lee had purchased the fine green material, and Lynnea had made the skirt and jacket. Jeb, still a little uncertain of his place in the family beyond being Nadia's new husband, had given her the bar pin, which had belonged to his mother. Yes, the outfit was lovely, but it was the love and acceptance it represented that she had donned with each piece of clothing, like a shield that would protect her heart from whatever was to come.

As she turned away from the mirror, she was drawn to the watercolor that hung on the wall next to her bed. Titled *Moonlight Lover,* the view was of the break in the trees near Sebastian's cottage, where a person could stand and see the moon shining over the lake. The dark-haired woman in the painting wore a gown that was as romantic as it was impractical and looked as substantial as moonbeams. Standing behind her, with his arms wrapped protectively around her, was the lover. His face was shadowed, teasing the imagination to provide the details, but the body suggested a virile man in his prime.

There was something about the way he stood, with the woman leaning against his chest as they watched the moon and water, that made her think he was a man who had journeyed far and now held the treasure he had been searching for.

Sebastian, the romantic among them, had painted it for her. He had captured the yearning for romance that she thought she kept well hidden. But in the same way that the secrets of the heart couldn't be hidden from a Landscaper, could romantic yearnings be hidden from an incubus?

It worried her sometimes when, in the dark of a lonely night, she conjured the image of a fantasy lover. But when that shadowy lover began to feel almost real enough to touch, was she still alone in her fantasy or had an incubus joined her by reaching through the twilight of waking dreams? Or was something else trying to reach her through that yearning? Sometimes it almost felt as if she could extend her hand across countless landscapes, and touch—

Bang, bang, bang. "Glorianna?"

Muffling a shriek that would announce her abrupt return to the present—and give Lee the satisfaction of knowing he'd startled her—Glorianna pressed her hand against her chest to push her jumping heart back into place. There was nothing quite like a brother when it came to shattering a sensual fantasy. She hoped to return the favor some day.

Annoyed with herself for procrastinating and annoyed with him for interrupting, she hurried across the room and opened the door; she realized he wouldn't have been banging on her bedroom door if they weren't already late, and that meant he *knew* she was procrastinating,

All her annoyance disappeared, because all she could do was stare.

He was wearing his best black trousers and jacket, with a white shirt, a patterned green silk vest, and a black necktie. He'd worn those clothes for the weddings—Sebastian and Lynnea, and then, a week later, their mother and Jeb. Except for those two occasions, she couldn't remember the last time he had dressed so well.

"My handsome brother," she said, intending a light compliment. But seeing him standing there, polished up because he was as nervous about this meeting as she, was a sharp reminder that his life would have been so much easier if she hadn't been his sister.

Or if he had refused to acknowledge her after she had been declared rogue.

So she couldn't keep her voice light, couldn't wave aside how much his loyalty had meant to her over the past sixteen years.

"Don't get maudlin," Lee said, grabbing her arm and pulling her out of the room.

"I am *not* getting maudlin," she snapped, insulted because she was so close to feeling that way. "I was just trying to be pleasant."

"Uh-huh." He kept pulling her along, slowing down when they reached the stairs to give her a chance to lift her skirt so she wouldn't trip and send both of them tumbling.

"Will you stop pulling at me?" Glorianna snapped when they reached the bottom of the stairs.

"No." He pulled her out of the house and around to the side. "We'll use my island to reach the rest of Sanctuary. It will take too long to use a boat. You spent so much time primping, we're late as it is." He gave her a calculating look. "Or did you get distracted by something else?"

Heat flooded her face, and Lee, being an odious sibling, laughed.

"Sebastian will be pleased that you like his gift," he said.

"I wasn't mooning over a painting," she replied, clenching her teeth.

"Did I say mooning? I *never* said mooning." He stopped at the edge of where his island rested over hers, visible since there was no reason to hide it.

Lee's little island was anchored in Sanctuary. She had originally created it as a private place for herself, but it had resonated with Lee from the moment he'd set foot on it, and the connection was so strong, he could impose the island over any other landscape. Unseen unless he chose otherwise, the island provided safe ground if he found himself in a dangerous landscape.

"So," he continued, "do you want to sit around with the other Landscapers indulging in sterile, suffocatingly polite talk, or just ask Ephemera to conjure up a big mud wallow?"

"What?" She stared at him. "Did you knot that necktie too tight? I don't think there's any blood getting to your brain."

"There's a custom in one of the landscapes—not one of yours but one I visited with another Bridge a couple of years ago. When two people—usually women since men tend to deal with things in other ways—start hurling insults at each other and the disturbance starts dragging other people in to take sides, the village leaders have the two women—people—escorted to a wallow at the edge of town that was created just for that purpose. The two . . . contestants, let's call them . . . are assisted into the wallow—"

"Shoved, you mean."

Lee shrugged. "And they go at it. Every insult is accompanied by a handful of mud that is slung at the other contestant."

"Mud-slinging in the literal sense."

He nodded. "So they scream and rant and rave and sling mud at each other until they're too tired to continue."

"Must be humiliating, to publicize things meant to be kept private."

"But they don't keep it private. They've been saying the same things to people behind the other person's back. This gets it all out in the open, and beyond showing everyone else how petty the argument truly is, it's also highly entertaining."

"Does it do any good?"

"Sometimes I think it really does clear things up between people who care about each other but stumbled somewhere along the way."

Glorianna cocked her head. "Like siblings?"

Lee grinned. "From what I gathered, some of them start a ruckus just to go play in the mud."

She laughed. "Too bad you didn't know about this custom when we were younger."

He laughed with her; then he turned serious. "You're not like other Landscapers, Glorianna Belladonna. You never were. You're a heart-walker as well as a Landscaper. Never forget that."

Tears stung her eyes, and she didn't resist when he put his arms around her in a comforting hug.

"Do you ever wish that I had been like them?" she asked, resting her head on his shoulder.

"Sometimes," he replied quietly. "But only because of what it cost you to be different." He hesitated, then added, "I wouldn't change anything, Belladonna. I've worked with other Landscapers. Had to. And I'll tell you this, and not as your brother but as a Bridge. There is no one else I would want leading this fight against the Eater of the World. There is no one else I would trust enough to follow."

She lifted her head and looked into his eyes. Not that she needed to see the truth; she could feel his heart.

"Let's go meet with the others."

With their hands linked, they stepped on to the island. Within moments, Lee had shifted them back to the part of Sanctuary where the island physically existed. A few minutes later, they entered the guest house and found the room Yoshani had reserved for this meeting.

The Landscapers and Bridges in the room didn't look bedraggled, exactly, but there was a dazed expression in all their eyes. They had seen the end of their world as they knew it, and none of them were sure how to take the next step toward healing what had been savaged by the Eater of the World's attack on the Landscapers' and Bridges' schools.

Had the Guides of the Heart looked the same way? Glorianna wondered. *When the battle was over and they*

*looked around at their shattered world, had they, too, felt
lost and uncertain?*

Yoshani smiled when he saw them, but she felt the
sadness resonating from his heart, felt the Dark currents of power that flowed through the room, fed by the
five Landscapers and three Bridges who sat waiting.

"Hey-a," Yoshani said softly.

One of the Bridges looked over and saw them. For a
moment, his eyes remained blank. Then anger filled him
as he leaped to his feet and pointed. "What are *they*
doing here?"

"They are the ones you have come to see," Yoshani
said.

"Not them," the oldest Landscaper said. "Not *her.*"

"There are things you need to know," Glorianna said,
moving further into the room. "Things you can do to
protect your Landscapes if you just—"

"You did this!" the Third Level Landscaper
screamed. "The wizards should have destroyed you
when they had the chance!"

"Glorianna didn't release the Eater of the World,
and she didn't destroy the school!" Lee shouted. "She's
never done anything to any of you! The Dark Guides
poisoned your minds and hearts against her, but she's
the only one who can help you now."

"We don't need *her* help," the oldest Landscaper
said, her whole body shaking with anger as she got to
her feet. "She was declared rogue for a reason, and
we've finally seen Belladonna's true face."

"Do you really see it?" Glorianna asked. "Can you
calm your own hearts for just a moment to really see me
for who and what I am?" She held out a hand and focused on the oldest Landscaper. "You don't need the
garden at the school to connect with your landscapes.
They resonate within you. You *can* reach them. If the
landscapes you came from are secure, you can build another garden to help you protect the places in your
keeping. And the Bridges can connect the landscapes

the five of you hold. I need your help in fighting the Eater of the World."

"Our help?" the oldest Landscaper said. She laughed bitterly. "If anyone unleashed these horrors on the landscapes, it is *you*. You dare to come here to Sanctuary? This is sacred ground, a Place of Light. You sully it with the mere presence of your filthy heart!"

"Enough!" Yoshani shouted.

No, Glorianna thought. *It is not enough.*

The Dark currents inside her swelled with an anger that was black and undiluted. She stepped away from Lee. But before she said the words that were straining to break free, she sent out a command.

Ephemera, hear me. The anger in this room is nothing more than wind, a storm that cleanses and is gone. This anger manifests nothing, changes nothing.

But it would change everything.

"I am not like you," Glorianna said, the fierce anger that flowed through her making her voice rough. "I have *never* been like you, because I am a direct descendant of the Guides of the Heart who walked this world long ago. I am like *them*, and I am connected to the world in ways you cannot imagine. But I also have the bloodlines of the Dark Guides flowing through my veins, so I command the Light *and* the Dark. I am not human. Not like you. I am Belladonna. You have never wanted any part of me. Now I want no part of you." She raised a hand and pointed at the Landscapers and Bridges. "Ephemera, hear me! Know these hearts. Any place that resonates with me is closed to them for all time. They may leave this landscape of their own choosing, but if they do not leave, send them to the landscape that resonates with their hearts. This I command."

She turned and walked to the door. Then she paused and looked back at them. "The Eater of the World is free among the landscapes. If you don't hold on to your pieces of the world with all the Light in your hearts, It will destroy you and everything in your care."

She walked out of the room, walked out of the guest

house. Then she ran from the pain that threatened to cripple her.

But even as she ran, she knew no one, not even Glorianna Belladonna, could run fast enough or far enough to escape the pain that lived in her own heart.

Yoshani stepped in front of Lee. "It is done," he said, keeping his voice low so that only Lee would hear. "There is no need to say more. Go away for a few hours. Go see your cousin."

Lee's green eyes were filled with icy anger. "My sister needs me."

"There is too much anger in your heart, my friend. You cannot help her. Let your feelings spill on someone who can drink them in and not be hurt by them. Sometimes anger needs an echo before it can be washed away. Go. I will look after Glorianna."

Lee glared at the Landscapers and Bridges, but he left the room.

Yoshani closed his eyes and tried to calm the turmoil in his own heart.

Opportunities and choices. It was a saying Glorianna often used to explain how the world worked to fulfill true wishes of the heart. He had seen the Light side of that saying, but until today, he had never seen the tragic side of it when the choices might cost so much.

He turned to face the eight people in the room.

"I am sorry," he said, "but you can no longer stay in Sanctuary."

He gave them a few moments to deny and protest his words, then he raised a hand to command silence. "You cannot stay."

"But we came here looking for help, looking for answers to what was happening in the landscapes—and what happened at the school," one of the Bridges protested. "You said we might find the answer here."

"The answer stood before you, and you would not

see. You chose to turn away from her, and now she has chosen to turn away from you."

The oldest Landscaper stared at him in disbelief. "Belladonna? *She* was the answer? She's a rogue!"

"And that is all you see," Yoshani said sadly. "For you, she is nothing more than a word that evil used to shroud your hearts. So now you do not resonate with the currents of power that flow through Sanctuary, and you cannot stay here."

"But *she* can?" one of the Bridges shouted.

"Sanctuary is one of Belladonna's landscapes," Yoshani replied quietly. "She altered Ephemera in order to bring the Places of Light together so that we might learn from each other, draw strength from each other."

They just looked at him, too stunned to speak.

BELLADONNA

Anne Bishop

The thrilling follow-up to *Sebastian*

The Eater of the World continues to
spread its dark influence across the
realm of Ephemera, corrupting
people's souls with doubts and fears.
Only Glorianna Belladonna possesses
the ability to thwart the Eater's plans.
But she has been branded a rogue,
and stands alone against
the encroaching enity.

THE TIR ALAINN TRILOGY

by

Anne Bishop

***The Pillars of the World*, Book I:**
"Bishop only adds luster to her reputation for
fine fantasy." —*Booklist*

***Shadows and Light*, Book II:**
"Plenty of thrills, faerie magic, human nastiness, and
romance." —*Locus*

***The House of Gaian*, Book III:**
"A vivid fantasy world....Beautiful." —*BookBrowser*

Available wherever books are sold or at
penguin.com

The *New York Times*
bestselling
Black Jewels Series

by Anne Bishop

"Darkly mesmerizing...fascinatingly different."
—*Locus*

This is the story of the heir to a dark throne, a magic
more powerful than that of the High Lord of Hell,
and an ancient prophecy. These books tell of a
ruthless game of politics and intrigue, magic and
betrayal, love and sacrifice, destiny and fulfillment.

Daughter of the Blood
Heir to the Shadows
Queen of the Darkness
The Invisible Ring
Dreams Made Flesh
Tangled Webs
The Shadow Queen
Shalador's Lady
Twilight's Dawn